I0677917

WINTER

The Beartooth Chronicles

RESURGENCE

Book 5

Kim McMahill

WINTER RESURGENCE
Copyright © 2025 by Kim McMahill

ISBN: 979-8-88653-459-7

Fire & Ice Young Adult Books
An Imprint of Melange Books, LLC
White Bear Lake, MN 55110
www.fireandiceya.com

Names, characters, and incidents depicted in this book are products of the author's imagination or are used fictitiously. Any resemblance to actual events, locales, organizations, or persons, living or dead, is entirely coincidental and beyond the intent of the author or the publisher. No part of this book may be reproduced or transmitted in any form or by any means, electronic or mechanical, including photocopying, recording, or by any information storage and retrieval system, without permission in writing from the publisher except for the use of brief quotations in a book review or scholarly journal.

Published in the United States of America.

Cover Design by Ashley Redbird Designs

For my husband, Jim.
His faith in my work has never wavered.

ONE

AN ORANGE GLOW LIT up the sky to the southwest of the small, isolated mountaintop community of Beartooth, Wyoming. After the volcano erupted, the heavens turned the color of worn asphalt, and volcanic ash drifted to the ground like dirty snow from a storm that had stalled overhead. A month later, the sky wasn't as dark, but ash continued to fall toward Earth.

The massive eruption a month ago, coupled with the government's release of sulfur particles into the stratosphere just days before the event, had brought winter conditions to Beartooth like no resident had seen before. It hadn't snowed, but the cold temperatures and biting wind were miserable.

Nearly a month after the eruption began, the volcano was still sending fire and particles high into the sky. The community watched helplessly as the depth of fallout grew to six inches or more in some areas, smothering out much of the fragile winter vegetation they depended on to sustain their livestock and the nearby wild game herds over the colder months.

A faint roar resembling a distant jet engine had become part of the natural soundscape. The land no longer shook as much as it had before the eruption, but the residents still felt the occasional tremor as the earth adjusted to the ongoing volcanic activity.

The air smelled like a wildfire burning out of control, which was likely the case, with a hint of sulfur. Combined with the particulates, the air outside was unhealthy. Everyone stayed in their cabins as much as possible, but many residents had to venture out for food and to tend to the livestock.

Ashley Solomon held her fourteen-month-old baby, Sara Olivia, as she stared out the cabin window.

"What are you looking at?" Caleb asked as he walked up behind her, wrapped his arms around her waist, and placed a kiss on her cheek.

"Just watching for your siblings and their significant others. Sara and I have been spending so much time inside since the volcano erupted that I'm really looking forward to game night."

"I know it's been difficult, but I think we're wise to keep Sara inside until the air quality improves. Let's check with Mom and Miranda. I'm sure one of them would come over and watch Sara for a few hours. I'd love to have your help, and I'm sure Graham wouldn't complain either."

Caleb's younger sister, Miranda, took over most of the community nurse's duties once she graduated from high school less than a year ago. Graham had come to Beartooth with two other geologists, Melora and Fiona, several years back to seek refuge as the rest of the United States descended into chaos.

"I don't want to ask your mom to come outside until things clear up a bit, but if Miranda is making rounds anyway, maybe she wouldn't mind spending a little time with her niece."

"I'm sure she'd love it. And speak of the devil."

Miranda and her fiancé, Ryan Ferguson, entered the cabin and hung their coats in the mudroom.

"Are Dillon and Evelyn here yet?" Miranda asked as she reached for Sara.

"Nope, you're first," Caleb replied.

"Good, that gives me more time with my niece before her aunt Evelyn arrives."

Caleb's younger brother, Dillon, married Evelyn Adler last summer, and Miranda and Evelyn had a friendly competition going for the title of Sara's favorite aunt.

"Is it true that you're making house calls rather than having people come into the clinic?" Ash asked.

"Most of our patients are dealing with respiratory issues right now, so it seemed to make sense. I'm handling all but the worst cases myself since I don't want Emily out any more than necessary. She's really never engaged full-time since recovering from her ankle injury anyway. I think she's in semi-retirement as the community's nurse."

"Would you mind watching Sara for a few hours after your rounds?" Ash asked.

"I'd love to. I think you're wise to keep Sara inside until the air quality improves. Most of the respiratory issues have been in the babies, toddlers, and older residents. I start my rounds at nine each morning, so I could be here by about ten, unless someone has taken a turn for the worse."

"I'd really appreciate it."

"My pleasure. Just don't tell Evelyn."

"Tell me what?" Evelyn asked as she and Dillon walked in.

"Miranda is going to watch Sara for a few hours after

her rounds so I can get out of here. I'm about to lose my mind being couped up for so long."

Evelyn chuckled. "In that case hand my niece over so I can have a little time with her before Aunt Miranda bogarts more of her attention."

Miranda handed the toddler to Evelyn. Ash smiled as she watched her sister-in-law cuddle Sara. Evelyn taught the four to eight-year-olds when school was in session, so Evelyn's mom, Gretchen, could focus on the older kids.

Evelyn clearly loved children. Ash wondered if the world weren't so out of whack, would Evelyn and Dillon try to have a baby of their own? She couldn't imagine how frighting it would be. Evelyn was nearly blind. She had adapted well, but it would make caring for a baby much more difficult, especially when he or she started to crawl and then walk.

"I've already fed Sara, but you can help me put her down for the night while the others set up the game," Ash said to Evelyn.

Evelyn followed Ash into Sara's room. By the time Sara fell asleep and they joined the rest of the group, everyone was standing around the kitchen table.

"Pick a button," Caleb said, holding out a cup for Evelyn.

The cup held six buttons, two of each were identical in size and color. After everyone drew, they held up their buttons.

Ash smiled when she saw that she and Caleb had identical buttons. She walked over to him, wrapped her arms around his neck, and kissed him. "Looks like we're partners."

"Tonight, and always," he said as he kissed her again and smiled.

"Well, this isn't fair," Ryan stated as he held up the same button as Evelyn.

"I can't see very well, but I'm not stupid. All you have to do is guess the word on the card that I draw out of the bowl with fewer clues than anyone else."

Ryan stammered. "I, I didn't mean you were stupid, it's just Caleb and Ash practically share a brain, and Dillon and Miranda are about as close as siblings can get. They probably have their own made-up language so we wouldn't even know if they're cheating."

"We'll just have to work twice as hard so when we beat them, our victory will be all the sweeter," Evelyn replied.

Dillon put his arm around Evelyn and pulled her close. "Just one of the many reasons why I love her so much. There's no challenge she won't tackle head-on, and she plays to win. Don't let her small size and adorable blonde curls fool you, she's a beast when it comes to winning."

They all took seats around the table across from their partner. A bowl filled with worn-out cardboard cards pilfered from other games was placed in the center of the table.

"We'll go first since apparently my partner thinks we need all the help we can get," Evelyn said as she grabbed a card from the bowl and held it in front of her face nearly touching her nose in order to see the word.

Evelyn looked up with an unreadable expression on her face. She set the card on the table and stood up.

"What is it?" Dillon asked, concern lacing his voice.

"I don't hear anything," she replied.

"So?" Ryan asked.

"I don't hear anything. The rumble from the volcano has stopped."

TWO

ASH LOOKED IN ON SARA. The toddler slept soundly, so she backed out of the room, quietly closing the door behind her. By the time she reached the mudroom, everyone had their coats on.

The moment they stepped outside, Ash knew Evelyn was correct. There was no orange glow in the night sky. Silence embraced them.

They made their way to the center of the community and climbed on top of the flatbed trailer that served as a platform for community events. The higher vantage point allowed them to get a better view, less obstructed by the trees surrounding the community. Staring toward the southwest, they still heard and saw nothing.

Before long, other residents began arriving. Dan Phillips, a member of one of the three founding families of Beartooth and the current chair of the Community Leadership Board known as the CLB, jumped up onto the trailer and joined in the silent vigil.

After nearly ten minutes of staring in the direction that had been aglow for weeks, Dan turned to the group assembled around the flatbed. "It might just be a pause, so don't get too excited yet."

"If the eruption is over, how long will this continue to drift down on us?" Emily Craig, another member of a founding family and the community's nurse since its inception, asked while holding her palms skyward.

"Depending on how much particulate is suspended in the atmosphere, we'll continue to get a fine dusting for at least a few days. Go home, get some sleep, and pray it's really over."

"I don't see Mom and Dad. Ryan can walk me home. I'll see you tomorrow," Miranda said as she and Ryan left.

Dillon and Evelyn also went home. Most of the other residents wandered off, leaving Ash and Caleb with Dan. As they climbed down from the trailer, Melora and her husband, Tyler Hewitt, a civil engineer in his life before Beartooth, joined them.

"If it hasn't started back up by morning, we'll fly the drone and see if we can locate the deer and elk herds or any of the predators that follow them," Melora said.

"Let's keep our fingers crossed that you find the herds. Eggs, mutton, and pork from Bob and Maggie's ranch and goat cheese from the Fergusons is running low. I guess we didn't appreciate how much we relied on Caleb's hunting to supplement the meat in our diet until we've had to go without any for well over a month," Dan added.

Ash hated to leave Sara alone for long even though the toddler generally slept soundly once she was down for the night, so she and Caleb headed back to their cabin. After hanging up their coats, they went into Sara's room. Their little girl was still fast asleep.

"She looks like such an angel when she sleeps," Ash whispered, while smiling down at their daughter.

"Just like her mama," Caleb replied as he placed his arm around her waist and led her out of the room.

Ash left Caleb in the living room trying to find a station on the radio that might provide more information on the status of the volcano and the country, while she went to get ready for bed. He didn't hear her when she returned, so she stood for a moment in the doorway between rooms and watched him.

The Solomons moved to Beartooth not long before Ash and her mom. Caleb was five and Ash was three at the time. They had known each other nearly their entire lives. He had been her best friend growing up, and now he was her husband and partner in life.

They got married just over three years ago, and so much had changed in that time. Shortly after the wedding, Ash's mom died. She couldn't have endured the sorrow without Caleb and the rest of the Solomon family.

With the passing of her mom, she was suddenly responsible for the community's apiary. The bees provided honey for the residents and pollinators for the gardens and crops. The bees were important, and she knew everyone was depending on her.

Ash was afraid of entering adulthood without her mom, but together, she and Caleb had dealt with tragedy and grief. They were still learning about love and each other, while working to protect their community and find solutions to a rapidly changing environment and deteriorating world. They had encountered deadly predators and ruthless neighbors and experienced epic adventures. But the greatest change in their lives was the arrival of their beautiful baby girl.

As she continued to watch Caleb, Ash realized just how much he had matured, physically and emotionally, since they married. He now had a lot of responsibilities.

He played a key role in feeding the community and protecting it from animal and human predators, and he was a great father.

She was eighteen and he had just turned twenty when they married. He was strong, lean, and handsome, but held the naïve look of youth and a physique not quite filled out. He had grown into an incredible man. He was stronger, even more handsome, and all traces of youth were gone.

Caleb turned the radio off, having no luck finding any sort of broadcast. He turned and saw Ash watching him. "Everything okay?"

She smiled and walked over to him. She wrapped her arms around his neck and kissed him deeply. He returned her passion and held her tight. He kissed her until she was breathless.

Ash stepped back and looked up into his warm, hazel eyes. "I was just thinking about how much my life has changed since we moved from best friends to husband and wife. We've faced a lot of challenges, and you've scared me to death several times, but I just can't imagine my life any other way or with anyone else. I love you so much."

"You've scared me a few times too, and I agree. You and Sara have blessed my life. I pray every day that we can survive all the obstacles that keep getting thrown at us so we can give Sara a brother or sister or two and grow old together."

Ash desperately hoped that would be possible. She was an only child of a widowed mother. Despite being close to her mom, she had been lonely growing up. She wanted a large family, siblings for Sara, and a lifetime with Caleb. He was her soulmate.

Caleb pulled her closer. She lay her head on his chest

and listened to the steady beat of his heart, feeling content and safe in his strong embrace.

"I love you, Ash," he whispered into her ear as he continued to hold her.

After several minutes, she took a step back. She could feel him watching her as she slowly worked each button on his shirt free. She ran her hands up his warm, muscular chest and slid the shirt off his shoulders. When she looked up, Ash saw so much love and desire in his eyes that it made her heart beat just a little faster.

"Come, you'll get chilled standing around like that," Ash said as she smiled, took his hand, and led him to the bedroom.

THREE

WHEN ASH EMERGED from the bedroom the next morning, she found Caleb holding Sara in one arm and trying to tune the radio with the other. She walked over to him, kissed him, and took Sara.

"You'll have better luck finding a station without this beautiful, little distraction," Ash said as she nuzzled her baby girl.

Ash put Sara in her highchair and handed her the fuzzy, stuffed bee that Caleb's mom, Olivia, made for her a few months ago. It was still her favorite toy and kept her entertained while Ash made breakfast.

By the time the oatmeal was on the table, Caleb had given up. He sat down next to Sara and alternated feeding Sara a spoonful of cereal and then himself. Sitting across from him, Ash dug into her oatmeal, drizzled with a small amount of honey.

Her mom brought bee hives to Beartooth when they moved here. Ash grew up helping her mom in the apiary to provide pollinators, honey, and wax for the community.

Now that the responsibility for the bees fell solely on her, she sometimes felt overwhelmed.

Prior to the government's stratospheric aerosol injection (SAI) program, they could grow food and harvest honey nearly year-round. Now, they had to ration to make it through the colder months. The government's plan to introduce aerosols into the stratosphere to cool the planet worked in the short-term, but it had also severely impacted many parts of the world, pushing millions closer to starvation. At nearly 9,000 feet in elevation, Beartooth was especially vulnerable.

"If the volcano has truly stopped, do you think the fallout will be too deep for us to plant crops and gardens in a few months?" Ash asked.

"Dillon, Dad, and I plan to check the fields as soon as we can get out there. The plots are scattered in locations with different elevations, aspects, and slopes, so depending on where they are in conjunction with prevailing winds, maybe some fields will have shallow enough deposits to plow under once it warms up."

"If you can work the fallout into the soil, it'll make the fields more fertile. Our thin soil here is on the acidic side, so the volcanic deposits should help neutralize the PH and add nutrients."

"According to your mom's horticulture books, we can take advantage of the volcanic fallout by changing what we plant, like maybe more corn and beans. The books also mention that mountain wildflowers like volcanic soil."

"I hope so. The bees are good for now, but if we don't have any nectar and pollen, we'll lose the bees along with much of next winter's food supply," Ash replied.

"Let's not worry too much until we learn more."

Ash nodded. She tried to push the fears from her mind and focus on the positive—the volcano had gone silent, at least for the time being. Unfortunately, the massive eruption not far from their community was just one of many factors threatening Beartooth's survival.

Five days prior to the eruption, the government commenced with its fourth round of stratospheric aerosol injections. Shortly after the process began, the U.S. capital in Denver and other large cities were destroyed by a massive bombing campaign conducted by a multinational military force amassed south of the U.S.-Mexico border.

Several years ago, they discovered dangerous predators living to their north and south. Their closest neighbor, Pryor, Wyoming, a resettlement city riddled with hate and violence, was controlled by a brutal faction calling themselves the Freedom and Morality Alliance or simply, FAMA. Pryor was made up of citizens relocated from the coasts when the rising sea levels forced cities to evacuate. It was sprawled out below the mountain on which Beartooth was located, less than a two-day ride on horseback. They had only encountered FAMA militia once, and it had taken the life of one of Beartooth's residents and founders, Neal Yandell.

Beartooth's only connection to the outside world came from listening to a radio station located in the nation's capital. When the capital was attacked, the operators of the station evacuated and have been broadcasting sporadically ever since. Ash, Caleb, and nearly everyone in the community who possessed a radio, continued to monitor the frequencies, hoping for news.

All that the residents knew for sure was that the capital had been destroyed, and the SAI program had been terminated, but not until multiple releases over North America were completed, including a release near Beartooth.

The last they heard, no one was able to verify if the

President had been evacuated before the capital was razed. And, the security personnel who were manning the food distribution warehouses across the country before the attack, took over control, no longer reporting to the government. Each warehouse was now a mini-war zone.

Unless they could get word from the radio, there was no way to know how far and deep the volcanic deposits fell across the country. Some areas likely fared far worse than Beartooth, but Graham believed the new east coast, Mexico, South America, and much of Canada probably received only a dusting from the volcano.

Despite all of the hurdles stacked against them, Ash remained optimistic. They were survivors, and the community always pulled together to overcome the challenges thrown at them.

"Hopefully, Melora and Tyler will find the herds nearby. As long as we have meat and the greenhouse, we can limp along for quite a while," Ash said, breaking the silence.

"I'm anxious to hear what they discover. Spring hunting has always been important for the community. With most of the mature ewes and sows set to give birth in the next month, that leaves only excess rams and boars not needed for breeding. Having to rely exclusively on those since the eruption to feed the community has left the livestock herds a lot smaller than normal for this time of year," Caleb replied.

There was a knock on the door. Before they could get up to answer it, Miranda walked in.

"Hope I'm not too early. My rounds didn't take long this morning. I think the mere thought of the eruption being over has had a miraculous effect on most of my patients. Diane Garland was hit pretty hard, but the rest seem to be over the hump."

"Can I get you some tea?" Ash asked.

"That sounds great, especially if you can spare a few drops of honey."

"Sure, we've still got several jars but keep that to yourself. I imagine most people are running low."

"We've got a few jars too, but Mom rations like crazy. Honey in tea is a luxury at home since she needs it for her stress-baking."

While Miranda entertained Sara, and Caleb washed the dishes, Ash brewed another pot of tea made from herbs found around the community and dried. If the deposits were too deep, even that basic staple could be in jeopardy.

"I haven't mentioned Ryan and I getting married to Dad for over a month. Everyone has been so stressed with the volcano erupting that I haven't wanted to add to it. How much longer should I wait?" Miranda asked her brother.

"I'd give it another week. The volcano could come back to life at any moment, but a week will give us time to assess the damage. If it looks like we might have a growing season, Dad will loosen up."

"At this point, I'll probably be nineteen by the time Ryan and I get married like Dad wanted all along, so it looks like I've been harping on him for the past year for nothing."

Ash chuckled. "Who could have predicted that a volcano would erupt just as you were wearing him down?"

"I also fear we'll need to do like Dillon and Evelyn and invite the entire community, so we'll need to wait until the air clears and the temperatures warm a little. I'd like to do what you two did and just have our families, but now that includes the Adlers since Dillon married Evelyn and the

Gallegos family since Ryan's brother is married to Serena. Serena's brother and sister are married. I just can't figure out where to cut it off to avoid insulting anyone, so I guess it'll be everyone."

"I'll do what I can to help. I owe you big for all the babysitting you do," Ash said.

"You don't owe me anything. I love spending time with my niece."

"In that case, Ash and I will get out of here," Caleb said as he kissed Sara goodbye.

"Should I be sad that my little girl hardly notices when I leave?" Ash said as she and Caleb walked toward the Solomon farm.

"No, it means she's comfortable with Miranda and trusts us to return."

When they reached the Solomon cabin and went inside, Dillon was already there.

"Ash, wonderful to see you again. I've barely left the cabin in the past month, and I know you haven't either. I hate that I haven't seen my beautiful granddaughter in so long. Miranda said she is growing like a weed," Olivia said as she hugged Ash and then Caleb.

"I've missed you too, and so does Sara. I just hope the volcano is done and the air clears soon. I've been going absolutely stir-crazy being couped up."

They all sat around the kitchen table, and Olivia brought out warm scones and tea.

"So, boys, do we venture out to the fields today?" Owen asked.

"No sense in waiting," Caleb replied.

"Are you going with the guys or can you stay and visit for a while?" Olivia asked Ash.

"I'd love to catch up, and then I'll head over to the greenhouse and check in with Graham."

"That would be lovely. I've been working on some new outfits for Sara. I hope they won't be too small already."

Ash loved her mother-in-law. Olivia helped fill the painful void left by her mother's death. She leaned heavily on Olivia the first year of Sara's life for advice, babysitting, and moral support. No matter how hard Caleb tried, there were just some things only another woman could provide, especially when Ash felt like an inadequate mother.

"Should we just meet back home?" Caleb asked.

"Sure, I'll relieve Miranda in a couple of hours, so if you need to be out longer that's fine."

Ash kissed him goodbye and watched him walk out the door with his dad and brother. She turned around and saw Olivia watching her.

"I'm so happy that you love my son so much," Olivia said as she hugged Ash.

"I can't help it. He's so kind, smart, handsome, and he's such a great dad."

"I doubt his siblings would agree with the first three, but no one will argue with the last," Olivia said as she led Ash into the kitchen and poured tea.

FOUR

ASH WASN'T SURPRISED to find Graham in the greenhouse when she entered. "Good morning. I thought maybe you could use some help since I abandoned you once the eruption started."

"I'd love help and some company. Don't worry about the absence. It was wise to stay inside as much as possible."

"Hopefully, the eruption is really over and not just paused as Dan suggested might be a possibility."

"Without any current data, only time will tell if we're done or in a lull, but I'm happy to see it stop, no matter how long it lasts. Even though I'm keeping busy, I know others are suffering from cabin fever."

"Have I told you lately how fortunate this community is to have you, Melora, and Fiona? When you three showed up on horseback, leading six llamas packed with so many essentials, it was truly a blessing. You all are wonderful additions to our community, and this greenhouse kit you brought may just save Beartooth."

Beartooth's young history flashed through Ash's mind.

The community was established roughly twenty-eight years ago when three families, the Yandells, Phillips, and Craigs, purchased a mountain resort to build a sustainable community. They wanted to live a simple life and escape the division, corruption, violence, political unrest, and hatred plaguing the country. For the first ten years, settlers came and went until most of the roads and all of the bridges were damaged or destroyed by earthquakes, floods, and tectonic shifting, cutting the community off from the outside world.

After Beartooth became isolated, there were no new arrivals until Graham, Fiona, and Melora rode up a couple of winters ago seeking refuge. The community had been nervous about the possibility of introducing pathogens none of the residents had been exposed to but the transition had gone smoothly, and the new arrivals quickly became part of the community.

"We think it was you all who saved us. I have no doubt Melora would have been pulled back into the military immediately when things started getting out of control in the rest of the country, and who knows what would have happened to Fi and me."

After Ash and Graham finished watering the plants and sowing seeds in every vacant speck of soil, they harvested the ripe produce. Prior to erecting the greenhouse, the community had limped along over the winter with just salad greens for fresh vegetables. They now were able to grow tomatoes, squash, beans, peas, green onions, and cucumbers year-round.

"I'll help you carry all of this to the storehouse, and then I'd better head home. I don't want to take advantage of Miranda's generosity," Ash said as they headed toward the storehouse, laden with produce.

The storehouse had originally been a restaurant, gift

shop, convenience store, and back-of-the house support for lodging operations. The restaurant kitchen's commercial ovens were still functional and used primarily for baking large quantities of bread for the community. The refrigerated cooler in the back was used to hang meat to be processed. Opposite the kitchen was a large room that had been the laundry and lodging support area. They kept the commercial washers and dryers, though they seldom used them, and installed a mill to turn the grains grown on the Solomon farm into flour. In the front of the building, the dining room, gift shop, and convenience store, complete with refrigerated coolers, were now used to store and distribute goods to the residents.

When they entered the storehouse, they were hit by the aroma of bread, fresh out of the oven.

"It smells like Serena has been up to something wonderful," Ash said.

"My daughter has become quite the accomplished baker if I do say so myself," Tony Gallegos replied as he grabbed a heavy canvas bag full of produce from one of Ash's hands and set it on the counter.

"You may, since everyone agrees," Ash added.

"We were getting a little low on veggies. I harvested greens and herbs out of the cold frames alongside the storehouse yesterday to help tide us over, but this will be a welcome sight," Tony said as he began unloading the bags.

Ash looked around. The shelves were emptier than usual for this time of year. The storehouse was getting low on a lot of items, but the biggest concern was the lack of meat. If Melora couldn't locate the deer and elk herds with the drone, things were going to be tight.

"Glad I caught you two," Dan said as he walked in the door. "Let's have a CLB meeting in five days. That should give everyone time to assess the situation out there. Graham, I'd like you to come too since you know more about the volcano than I do, and you can give us an update on how the greenhouse is holding up."

"I'd be happy to come to the meeting even though I probably won't have much to add as far as the volcano. As you know, without access to any of the data from the monitoring equipment we had in place, we're kind of just guessing on what will happen next."

"True, but your guess is better than most. We'll meet at 4:00 p.m." Dan said.

"Caleb is in the fields with his dad and brother as we speak, so he'll have an update on their condition for the group," Ash added.

"I hope the news is promising," Dan said.

Ash said goodbye to Dan, Graham, and Tony and quickly made her way home. It felt good to get outside and visit with other adults besides Caleb, but she already missed her little girl.

After Miranda left, Ash fed Sara and put her down for a nap. She pulled a chair up to the radio and tried to find a broadcast. She was about to give up when a scratchy voice came over the air. She recognized the newsreader's voice as the one who usually did the broadcasts from the nation's capital before the bombing.

"Found some new digs not far from...old capital. Hopefully we'll be on air more regularly...try to increase signal...not piss anyone off to avoid being shut down."

Despite the words cutting out, Ash understood the gist of it. She was trying to tweak the frequency a little more to get a clearer reception when Caleb walked in the door. Before he could speak, she placed a finger to her lips and pointed to the radio.

Caleb kissed her cheek and then pulled up a chair. He

sat quietly next to her as the newsreader began the next story.

"So far...unable to contact...verify if the volcano... erupting. Communications severely damaged...bombing...south of the border. Confirmed President did not survive... Vice President, Vivian Steele...assumed...and appointed army general, Nathan Nevins, as Vice... According to...priority is to stop fighting...for food. Reports from Pryor and... closest to the eruption, indicate...foot of ash...smothered out... Other news out of Pryor suggests..."

Ash stood and frantically tried to get the broadcast back, but it was gone. "Darn. I wish we could have heard what the other news out of Pryor is."

"Me too. Hopefully, they're focused on digging out from a month's worth of fallout and not terrorizing its citizens or neighbors. Anything worthwhile before I walked in?"

"I believe the radio station is set up somewhere close to the old capital. They hope to broadcast more regularly, strengthen their signal, and will try not to anger those in charge to avoid being shut down."

"That might be difficult if they actually report the news. Those in charge never like to hear the truth."

"Well, some news is better than no news." Ash stood, placed a light kiss on Caleb's lips, and then turned to check on Sara.

He grabbed her arm and pulled her into his lap before she was out of reach, wrapping her in his embrace. "I need a little more than a peck," he said as he captured her lips in a deep kiss.

When he finally let her go, Ash was breathless. She stood up and smiled down at him. "But often when you kiss me like that, we end up missing lunch, and I'm starved."

"Can't blame a guy for trying. I would happily forgo lunch for a repeat of last night," Caleb replied with a sly smile.

"As tempting as that sounds, I'm anxious to hear what you found while inspecting the fields this morning. Get washed up. I'll check on Sara and then whip up some lunch."

While Caleb cleaned up, Ash assembled salads with fresh herbs, cucumbers, and tomatoes, and dressed it with a honey-vinaigrette dressing. She made grilled goat cheese sandwiches with sourdough bread.

"Wow, no wonder you opted for lunch." Caleb picked up the sandwich and took a bite.

"Serena had just pulled the bread out of the oven when Graham and I walked in with a load of produce, and the Fergusons had brought in a small supply of goat cheese earlier."

"Our window boxes provide regular greens, but it's nice to have some variety. How is Graham holding up without you?"

"He has everything under control."

"Good to hear. Did you run into anyone else? I didn't talk to anyone other than Dad and Dillon."

"Dan came into the storehouse while we were there. He's scheduled a CLB meeting in five days."

"That should give us time to assess all of the fields. We made it to those on the windward-facing slopes. Depending on the terrain, the ash was only about four to six inches deep, but we suspect the leeward fields will be deeper since the deposits might have been protected from the wind and settled in place. We think we can plow the ash into the soil on the windward fields and plant if the temperatures warm up enough. Unfortunately, the irrigation ditches are nearly full of deposits which might be the biggest problem if we don't get enough rain and need to irrigate."

"The news could be worse. How many of the fields are windward?"

"About half."

Even though the initial assessment could have been worse, it still wasn't great. If it got warm enough to have a growing season, the Solomon's arable land could be half of what it was the previous year.

"I suppose we shouldn't panic until you get eyes on the other fields, and we see if the temperatures warm up enough to grow anything," Ash said while finishing her salad.

"That's what we thought. Did you get enough time outside for the day?"

"Yes, I had a great visit with your mom. She's almost done with a few new outfits for Sara, and just in time. Her current wardrobe is getting a little snug."

Caleb reached over and took Ash's hand and smiled. "Sometimes when I look at you and our baby girl, I think I must be dreaming. You're both perfect."

Ash still had a hard time knowing how to respond when he said such things, but she agreed with his opinion of Sara.

"She is a miracle and a blessing, and she is currently fast asleep. Do you need help with anything?"

"Well, since you shot down my earlier idea, I guess I could use a little help fletching the arrows I have shafts for. If Melora and Tyler find the deer and elk herds with the drone, we'll need to go hunting as soon as possible."

Ash enjoyed building arrows with Caleb. He taught her to shoot and make arrows before they got married.

Both were activities they'd shared ever since. She hadn't hunted since she realized she was pregnant with Sara and she missed it, but it was a small price to pay for her little girl.

She relished spending time with Caleb out in the woods and hated to stay behind. She had been unable to shake the fear she felt every time he went without her. She had nearly lost him in the wild. Somehow, they survived the ordeal, but the thought of him leaving and not coming home always haunted her, no matter how hard she tried to push the thoughts from her mind.

Caleb stood and walked around the table. He reached for her hand and eased her out of her chair. "You've suddenly gotten mighty quiet."

"I understand the community needs wild game to supplement the meat from our small livestock herds, but I hate you going away without me. Maybe someday Ryan or someone else can lead a hunting party, but for now, I know it has to be you."

Caleb wrapped his arms around her and held her tight. "I know you don't like being left behind, but I can focus more on any danger we encounter knowing you and Sara are safe. And, there is no one I have more confidence in than you when it comes to protecting yourself and Sara in my absence. You're my life, Ash, I can't bear the thought of ever losing you or our little girl."

Ash just nodded as a tear slipped down her cheek. She never knew her own father. He died when she was a baby. She wanted Sara to know hers. Whenever Caleb left, Ash couldn't keep her fear at bay, especially when he was far from home and at the mercy of the wild and all the predators that called it home.

FIVE

IN THE DAYS leading up to the CLB meeting, Miranda stopped by every morning to watch Sara so Ash could get out of the cabin. Despite the cold weather, gloomy skies, and the ground being covered with a gray layer of gritty fallout, it still felt good to be outside again.

Ash enjoyed catching up with Emily, Fiona, and Melora. She also made several trips to Bob and Maggie's ranch to visit Luna. She had ridden Luna into the wild, and the little mare had performed admirably in several terrifying instances. Ash had been a novice rider then, but Luna took good care of her. They formed a special bond, and she loved the gentle horse.

Everyone was relieved when they received a small amount of rain each afternoon. It didn't fill their rain barrels, but it was enough to wash off the roofs and other surfaces that had collected volcanic fallout over the past month.

Even though it was still far too cold to plant anything, Caleb, Owen, and Dillon hitched Thor, the older of the two studs at the ranch, to the plow and made a few passes across one of the fields. The dirt and volcanic deposits created a rich mixture. They were confident that if the temperatures warmed enough, the crops would thrive in the enhanced soil.

Ash was anxious to check on the bees. The hives were located a short walk from her cabin in a storage shed they built last fall in the Ferguson's orchard to protect the bees from predators and cold temperatures. Prior to last fall, the hives were spread out in three clusters between the Solomon farm and the Ferguson orchard and vineyard, but that no longer seemed feasible.

Caleb stowed his 9mm semiautomatic in its holster at his hip, and Ash retrieved her bear spray. She thought he was being overly cautious with the gun but understood his concern after her run-in with an aggressive grizzly while he was away over a year ago.

"I don't want to keep you from your work if you're needed at the farm," Ash said.

"I'd rather you not check on the bees alone, at least until we scope out the area better."

"I suppose the latest SAI coupled with the eruption may make the wildlife behave even more unusual than they have in the past, but so far, we haven't seen any."

"Better safe than sorry." He smiled, kissed her, and strode out the door.

Ash followed him outside. The air quality had cleared considerably over the past few days, but the sky was still a grayish-white due to the effects of the stratospheric aerosol injection. She missed the blue skies that once dominated overhead and hoped they would return soon.

While most of the world was overheating, Beartooth had never been unbearably warm. The aerosol injections were not needed or welcome here. So far, all the proce-dures had done was shorten their growing season and threatened their survival by bringing a slow resurgence of winter.

When they reached the shed, nothing looked disturbed. They unlatched the door and stepped inside. It was reasonably warm since most of the normally empty space was filled with wheat stems that could be used to feed livestock if they ran out of better-quality feed before the grasses returned.

Ash listened closely. Before long, she heard a faint hum coming from all of the hives. She let out a sigh of relief.

They removed the thin board they had installed over the gap near the roof line when the volcano erupted to keep out the falling ash. If, and when, the bees decided to venture out of their hives, they would be able to leave the shed.

"Feel better?" Caleb asked as he took her hand and brought it to his lips.

"Much. Even if wildflowers and weeds can't poke through the volcanic deposits, if the temperatures warm enough, the fruit trees will blossom, providing the bees with a source of nectar and pollen. I'm more optimistic about our growing season now that I've heard life inside the hives."

They continued walking further from the community toward where the hives had been located prior to last fall.

"The volcanic deposits are deep here. Maybe we should wait and see what blooms before we move the hives. No sense bringing them back to their old locations if there are no pollen sources," Ash said.

Caleb agreed. They hiked until they reached the original location of hives one and two. They walked over to where the grizzly that attacked Ash was buried. The deposits on the ground camouflaged the predator's final resting place. It was the only positive Ash could see here.

"It kind of looks like a bomb went off and destroyed everything. Yet, given time and the right conditions, the vegetation should come back, maybe even better than before," Caleb said as if reading her thoughts.

Ash nodded. Caleb was right, but it still didn't change the fact that she barely recognized the place where she had spent so much of her life tending bees with her mom. The sky was gray, and the ground was a darker shade of gray with no signs of life poking through. Many of the needles on the pines had turned an orangish-brown, and the deciduous trees had lost their leaves. She didn't spot a rabbit, which was once very common in the area, or even a track from a small mammal. She used to tease Caleb about bringing home what she called 'creative cuisine,' but she now wished for a rabbit to jump out and prove that life would return.

"Have you heard how Melora and Tyler's drone flights are going?" Ash asked as they headed back towards the community.

"Last time I talked to Melora, it didn't look promising. They plan to fly near the lake and further north and east."

"Hopefully, they'll have the flying done by the CLB meeting tomorrow. I'm also anxious to see what things look like around the lake. If the herds have moved off, maybe we can at least start fishing again."

"I'm curious to hear what our biologist and geologists have to say about water quality in the lakes and streams, and if the fisheries will be impacted."

"Let's keep our fingers crossed that the water hasn't been polluted," Ash said.

"If the water hasn't been impacted and there aren't any predators hanging close by, let's see if Mom can watch Sara for a few hours and try our luck at fishing soon."

"Nothing would make me happier. If we could go fishing, that would be one thing that would make life feel normal."

Caleb chuckled. "After everything we've been through in our first three plus years of marriage, I don't even know what normal is anymore."

"True, but you have to admit our life hasn't been boring."

Caleb put his arm around her shoulders and pulled her close as they continued the walk. "No, it definitely hasn't been boring."

SIX

IT WAS the first time Ash took Sara outside since the eruption began. The volcano had been silent for nearly a week. Very few particles continued to fall from the sky, but she was still nervous about exposing Sara to potentially unhealthy air.

Ash put Sara's hat on with its protective brim and handed her to Caleb. With Caleb holding Sara tight to his chest, shielding her from the elements, they left the cabin and made the short walk to the Solomon farm.

The moment they started up the front porch steps, Olivia opened the door and raced out to greet them. She snatched Sara from Caleb's arms.

"I've missed my precious granddaughter so much." Tears slid down Olivia's cheeks as she cuddled and kissed the toddler.

Sara looked at her grandma with wide eyes, not sure what to make of the emotional outburst. She reached up with a chubby finger and wiped away one of Olivia's tears, which made the woman cry even more.

After several minutes, Owen walked over and plucked

her out of Olivia's arms and held her up in front of him. Sara seemed a little confused over Olivia's reaction but smiled at Owen.

"Boy, have you grown in the past month," he said as he set her down on her feet.

"Grampa, up," Sara cried, reaching for Owen.

He picked her up, and the family went inside the cabin and sat down in the living room. As Owen bounced his granddaughter on his knee, the door opened and Dillon and Evelyn walked in.

"Eflin," Sara exclaimed.

Owen set her down, and she toddled over to Evelyn, who scooped her up.

It filled Ash's heart with joy to see how much the excited greeting meant to her sister-in-law. It was obvious that Sara was just as happy as everyone else to be out and around others again.

"What about me?" Dillon asked as he placed noisy kisses on her cheeks.

She giggled and burrowed in tighter to Evelyn's chest.

"I can take a hint. I'm not the flavor of the day. So, what's the plan?"

"Caleb and Ash are heading to the CLB meeting. Even though we don't know if it will warm up enough in a month or two to plant, we might as well keep plowing any field that looks promising. Turning soil with a horse-drawn plow is time-consuming, so it wouldn't hurt to keep at it so we're ready if we get the conditions we need," Owen explained.

"After the meeting, I'll come and help," Caleb added as he and Ash stood to leave.

"I'll walk to the schoolhouse with you so Dillon can get to work," Evelyn said, joining them.

"How soon do you and Gretchen plan to resume classes?" Ash asked as they headed toward the schoolhouse.

"Dad is going to bring it up at the meeting, but if everyone thinks it's safe for the kids to venture out again, we'd like to start back up the day after tomorrow. Mom, Dad, Lauren, and I have already cleaned the classrooms and have everything ready to go. I miss my students. I hope it won't take long to get them back in the rhythm of learning after over a month off."

"I'm sure they miss you too and will get back into the groove quickly," Ash replied.

Ash was happy to see the sky was less gray. With the little bit of rain that had fallen and efforts with targeted clean-up, the area around the community was starting to look less desolate.

They walked Evelyn to her cabin and then backtracked the short distance to the schoolhouse for the meeting. Ash and Caleb were the last to arrive. Glancing around, they spotted two vacant seats between Ryan and Melora. Dan sat at the head of the table with Graham next to him. The remaining members consisted of Tyler, Bob, Heath Garland, Henry Adler, and Maria Gallegos.

"We haven't heard a peep out of the volcano since it stopped. It doesn't mean we're out of the woods, but it looks promising," Dan said to open the meeting.

"I wouldn't have offered to move into one of the small, one-bedroom cabins last year if I'd known I would be confined indoors for a month," Maria joked. "Tony was thankful he needed to go to the storehouse each day to manage food distribution, but I didn't have any excuse to go traipsing around outside."

"And we appreciate everyone's good sense. Miranda and Emily had their hands full with respiratory issues as it was. It sounds like most are pretty much recovered. Heath, how's Diane doing?" Dan asked.

"She is recovering but slowly. Miranda and Emily have been watching her closely, but with no antibiotics, there is only so much they can do. Lexie and Joy have taken good care of their mom."

"If there is anything we can do to help, just say the word," Dan replied.

Heath nodded.

"I've asked Graham to join us since he, Fiona, and Melora are the most knowledgeable about the volcano. I wasn't working in the field like they were when we were all employed with the U.S. Geological Service, so what they know is nearly thirty years more current than what I know," Dan said.

"Based on the data we had before moving here, I'll give you my best guess, but without current information, that's all I can do. Melora, feel free to jump in anytime."

Melora nodded, and Graham continued.

"The caldera has been monitored for hundreds of years. Historical data about past eruptions combined with mathematical models of volcanic ash dispersion have given us a decent idea on where and how much ashfall could occur. During the three caldera-forming eruptions that occurred between about 2.1 million and 650,000 years ago, volcanic ash covered much of the western half of North America and was likely over a foot deep up to a hundred miles away from the eruption zone. Wind carried sulfur aerosols and tiny ash particles around the planet and likely caused a notable decrease in temperatures around the world. Fortunately, this latest eruption was not a caldera-forming super eruption. However, it was big, it lasted quite a while, and only time will tell what the impacts will be on our growing season."

"If it was a super eruption, we wouldn't be sitting here having this conversation right now," Melora added.

"So, what does that mean and where does that leave us?" Henry asked.

Graham rubbed the stubble on his chin. "Fi, Mel, Dan, and I have discussed this at length. Based on historical eruptions, we believe the pressure has been released and the eruption is over, not just paused. But we honestly don't know if the eruption coupled with SAI will create conditions that might threaten our survival at this elevation."

"With what we've seen since the eruption stopped, I think we can weather the fallout, but coupled with the latest SAI release…Heath, do you have any thoughts?" Dan asked.

"Like Graham and the other geologists, climatologists can only predict so much without current scientific data, but I'll give you my two cents. I believe we're near a SAI release zone by the way things played out after the previous releases. Even though the U.S. wasn't able to distribute all of the sulfur aerosols worldwide, we have to assume they started in North America, and we will be impacted."

"Give us the best-case and worst-case scenarios," Maria said.

"It's likely that tiny particles from the eruption reached the troposphere and may have even reached the stratosphere, which would shade and ultimately cool the areas below the eruption and around the western U.S. Most particles would fall out of the atmosphere within rain in a few hours or days after an eruption, which is the best-case scenario. Worst-case-scenario is a year without a summer. Volcanic eruptions emit gases like sulfur dioxide, which can cause global cooling while volcanic carbon dioxide has the potential to promote global warming. Only time will tell if the eruption warms or cools areas around here, but I don't think the eruption was big enough to impact global climate."

"So, in a nutshell, you have no idea," Henry said.

"Exactly," Heath replied with a shrug and a grin.

"That doesn't sound too dire, so let's move on. We'll just go around the table and everyone can update the group on their respective bailiwicks, and then we'll talk about anything that might need to be done," Dan instructed.

"Melora brought back a water sample from the lake when they were out flying the drone. I tested it along with samples from a couple of nearby creeks. I haven't detected any noticeable change in PH. I think we're good as far as water quality goes, and the turbidity isn't bad either. Other than that, if we all think it's safe enough, Gretchen and Evelyn would like to reconvene school the day after tomorrow," Henry said.

They took a quick vote and unanimously agreed to send the kids back to the classroom.

"Tony says the produce is holding out well, but as everyone is probably aware, with the lapse in hunting, we're going through the livestock much quicker than usual, and he hasn't seen much goat cheese come in lately. Serena has upped the frequency of baking bread to supplement the shortfall since we have plenty of wheat flour and other grains," Maria said.

"Our goats aren't producing much milk right now. We think it's a combination of stress and not being on fresh grass," Ryan replied. "Mom and Dad also said to let you all know that there are no male goats or llamas to spare for meat. All we have are pregnant females, last season's lambs and cria, and a few males for breeding."

"We're in a similar boat at the ranch. I can spare six more pigs and seven sheep for butchering at the moment. The rest are either pregnant, need to be fattened up, or are needed for breeding. As far as feed, that's holding out well, but hopefully, Heath is right, and we don't have a year without a summer. We will need some grazing in a couple months," Bob added.

"It's been a challenge keeping the dam and turbine from silting up with abrasive volcanic deposits. Nonetheless, we've kept electricity flowing," Tyler stated.

Ash thought the news so far wasn't too bad. Everyone had challenges, but nothing sounded insurmountable. As she watched Melora set up the portable projector, she feared the encouraging news was about to come to an end.

"We've been flying the drone nearly every day since the eruption stopped. There has been no sign of wildlife within five miles of the community center. We then decided to focus on the north since that's where we spotted deer, elk, and wolves prior to the eruption. We hiked to the lake and flew. Still nothing. We then hiked about three miles northeast of the lake and flew as far as we could and caught sight of a few deer and a small elk herd," Melora reported as she showed footage of a rocky area with deep volcanic deposits on the ground.

"So, a mile to the lake, you hiked three more, and flew about five more miles?" Caleb asked.

"Yep, the closest game sighting was nearly nine miles away. They were on the move, which is no surprise. As you can see, there isn't much grass poking through," Tyler replied.

Ash looked over at Caleb, and he nodded for her to go next.

"I helped Graham in the greenhouse. Vegetables are ripening at great intervals. Tony has been doing an awesome job harvesting the greens in the cold frames so they keep growing without replanting. Caleb and I checked the bees. I was relieved to hear humming inside the hives. We removed the board sealing off the small gap along the roofline, so when they're ready to venture out, they can."

"Anything else before we have Caleb close things out?" Dan asked.

"We caught a few minutes of a broadcast. It was the same station we all used to listen to, and close to the same frequency. We learned the President did not survive the bombing and Vice President Steele has assumed his position and appointed a general for her new Vice. The newsreader said her priority is to stop the fighting in the streets. It sounds like some areas close to the eruption site got about a foot of ash. They also started to say something about Pryor before we lost the station," Ash said.

"What time of day did you catch it?" Heath asked.

"It was a little before lunchtime. I try a few times a day and haven't caught anything since, but I thought I'd let you know that we might start getting a little news again."

"Let's all start putting more effort into monitoring the radio and let me know if you hear anything. Last, but not least, Caleb, what are your thoughts on things?" Dan asked.

"Dad, Dillon, and I have inspected all of the fields. Most of the windward plots don't look too bad since the wind blew much of the volcanic deposits away, but some of the leeward fields have around ten inches. We hitched Thor up and were able to plow the fallout under in about two-thirds of the fields. Most of the irrigation ditches are full of deposits, so those will need cleaned out if it gets warm enough to plant, and we need to irrigate."

"Heath, what's your crystal ball say on upcoming temperatures and rainfall?" Dan asked.

"I wish I had a crystal ball. As far as moisture, I'd expect the erratic rainfall pattern we've seen over the past few years to continue. We'll probably alternate between extended periods of dry conditions, but when it rains, we'll get more than we can handle. Based on the trend we've experienced after the last three SAI releases and factoring in an even more extreme response due to the volcanic eruption, I suspect we'll be two to four weeks behind last year as far as planting goes, and the growing season could be shortened by that much on the other end."

Dan winced. "If we're looking at planting mid- to late-June and have to start harvesting in September we could be in trouble."

"That'll be cutting it close on getting harvestable spring wheat, so we're planning to go heavier on oats which only need about ninety days. It's also possible the winter wheat could push through the fallout in the fields we haven't been able to plow," Caleb replied.

"After listening to everyone's updates, it sounds like you're on top of everything you can be, but what should we do about our meat supply?" Dan asked.

"I think we have no other option except to try and track the deer and elk down that Melora and Tyler spotted with the drone," Caleb said.

"We've never hunted further than three miles from the community, so this will be new territory. What do you suggest?" Dan asked.

"We'll want to make the most of the trip. We'll need to take horses so we can pack any meat we harvest back to the community. Bob, how many horses would you feel comfortable with us taking?" Caleb asked.

"You could take the three geldings, but only one of the studs. I'd suggest Felix since you've packed him before. I don't plan to breed Luna anymore, she's done her duty, and of course, June. Depending on how many you think you need, you could take Bella and Sierra too."

"I'd like archers capable of taking down a deer and maybe we can try to harvest elk if we catch up to them. I wish Ash could go, but I know she won't leave Sara, so as far as archers who have successfully harvested deer, that leaves Ryan, Archie, Dillon, and Gavin Winters. Dillon is good and Gavin has shot a few, but neither are horsemen. That might be as important as a shooter. If Melora is willing to come and bring the drone, it could help in locating the herds. I've never packed game on a horse, so Fiona would be a real asset."

"I'm in. Fiona has packed meat out of a hunt camp on her three geldings before, so I agree, it would be essential to have her along. I'll talk to her, but I'm sure she'll be in," Melora said.

"If your sister doesn't kill me, I'm in too," Ryan added.

"Archie would be great to have along. He's a competent horseman and a good shot with a bow. He has a sixty-five-pound recurve like mine, and I wouldn't shoot at an elk with anything less. Archie's skill with meat processing would enable us to field dress and bone anything we get more efficiently for transport back to the community, which is a bonus," Caleb replied.

"I'll check with Archie, but my daughter won't be happy. If he's on board, how soon do you want to leave?"

"I don't see any point in delaying, especially if the herds are on the move. I think we should head out just as soon as we can get everything together."

Ash hoped she didn't look as sick as she felt. The thought of Caleb taking off in search of the herds, which were most likely being followed by predators, was terrifying. But she knew he had to go. The community needed meat.

The greenhouse had been a game-changer, but it couldn't be the sole food source for the community indefinitely. If Beartooth hoped to survive this latest challenge, she had to be strong and let Caleb do what he needed to do without worry or guilt. She didn't want him to go, but she would not ask him to stay.

SEVEN

IN THE DAYS leading up to the hunt, Caleb, Ryan, Fiona, and Archie gathered up the gear and supplies they'd need. Melora and Tyler continued to fly the drone, hoping a few deer or elk would wander close by, making the expedition unnecessary. They found nothing.

Since Caleb was the most experienced rider, he would ride Felix. The stud was big, strong, and high-spirited, making him a bit of a challenge. The rest of the group would ride the three geldings and Sierra and lead June, Bella, and Luna.

"How long do you think you'll be gone?" Ash asked as she helped Caleb carry his gear to Bob's ranch to pack in June's panniers in the morning.

"If we can catch up to the herds quickly and none of us have gotten too rusty, we might only be gone a night or two, but probably more," he replied.

"Normally, I don't worry too much about sending you enough food, but you won't be able to rely on shooting rabbits or other small animals if you run out. We haven't seen any wildlife in the area except for a few birds since the eruption."

"I'm taking some fishing gear just in case, but if you can round up enough food to sustain me for at least three days, that should be enough."

Ash didn't like all the unknowns. But this wasn't the first time Caleb left on a potentially dangerous venture without her, and it probably wouldn't be the last.

After leaving Bob's ranch, they stopped by Tyler and Melora's cabin. They found Melora stowing the drone in its protective case for transport, and Tyler putting the batteries they'd used earlier into the chargers.

"Find anything new?" Caleb asked.

Melora just shook her head, snapped the case shut, and looked up with an apologetic grin.

"Worth a shot. Anyway, I was thinking we should take the radios," Caleb said.

When the three geologists arrived in Beartooth seeking sanctuary, they packed in a treasure trove of goodies on a pack-string of llamas. They brought a kit to construct a greenhouse, a drone, three handheld radios, medical supplies, ammunition, and many other essential items.

"I hadn't thought about it, but it's a good idea. What about weapons?" Melora asked.

"We should probably take all the firearms and ammunition we can without stripping the community completely," Caleb replied.

"That doesn't make me feel any better about Melora taking off into the unknown without me," Tyler added.

"Just precautionary. We don't know what we'll find out there, so it's good to be prepared," Caleb said.

Ash felt sick to her stomach but said nothing. They didn't stay long since they were on their way to retrieve Sara from Olivia. When they reached the Solomon farm, they found Owen, Olivia, and Dillon on the front porch. It made Ash smile to see Dillon holding his niece, but one glance at Caleb and she knew he didn't share the feeling.

"Be careful, son, and hurry back. Ash isn't the only woman who worries about you when you're gone," Olivia said as she hugged Caleb.

"Don't take any unnecessary risks. We can get by a while longer here. Bob isn't totally out of animals that could be butchered," Owen added.

"True, but if we don't slow the pace, the livestock won't last long. Don't worry, I plan to make this a quick, uneventful trip."

Ash couldn't help but chuckle.

"What?" Caleb asked.

"Past history is not in your favor. Just remember we need you. Come back in one piece," Ash said.

"And I need you," he replied as he pulled her into his arms and kissed her on the lips.

"I don't know if I should be glad or insulted that you didn't ask me to come along," Dillon said, interrupting the moment.

Caleb released Ash and turned to his brother. He took his daughter from Dillon and handed her to Ash. "You're needed on the farm. Trying to grow crops this year will be a huge challenge, and our success in that area is probably more important than a successful hunt. Besides, you're a crappy horseman, Evelyn needs you, and I'm holding you to your promise to protect my family with your life."

Dillon pulled Caleb into a firm hug. "You know I'll protect your family. In fact, I'll never take my eyes off Ash," Dillon said with a crooked grin and a wink.

Caleb stepped back and slugged Dillon on the arm. "That's what I've always been afraid of, but I hoped that had changed once you got married."

"A guy can always look," Dillon explained.

Owen and Olivia rolled their eyes, and Ash shook her head. The brothers tormented each other, but the love they shared always came through. The last time Caleb left, they had come to blows over her, but she had no doubt that was in the past, and Dillon was just trying to needle his older brother.

After they returned to their cabin, Caleb sharpened his broadhead arrow tips while Ash mixed up a large batch of fry bread. Once that was done, she assembled as much food as she could that didn't need refrigeration and would hold up in Caleb's saddlebags.

"That should be enough to tide me over." Caleb walked up to Ash, pulled her into his arms and kissed her. When the kiss ended, he kept his arms around her. "God, you're beautiful," he whispered as his lips descended on hers again.

He finally let her go, and she stepped back. "If I knew I'd get that reaction from fry bread, old deer jerky, dried apples, oatmeal, honey, and the last two freeze-dried meals we found in the dead hiker's pack, I'd have pulled it all out a long time ago," she replied.

Caleb laughed. "You know your uncanny ability to make something out of nothing has no bearing on how much I love you. Even though we grew up together, you still surprise me all the time. You're strong, independent, smart, funny, and the best wife a man could hope for, not to mention an incredible mom to our beautiful baby girl."

Ash wanted to be all of those things, but every time Caleb left, she couldn't help but feel insecure and needy. "And you are the best partner a woman could hope for and an amazing dad."

Sara cried out. Ash turned to leave, but Caleb grabbed her arm before she was out of reach.

"Never forget that it is you, and it has always been you. You are my world Ash, and I love you like crazy."

She knew he hated to leave them once again. She didn't want to make it any harder on him than it already was. "I hope you know the feeling is mutual. When I look at you, my heart nearly skips a beat, but right now your daughter calls, so any demonstration of my affection for you will have to wait until later."

"I'm holding you to it," Caleb called after her as she left the room.

EIGHT

IT WAS STILL DARK out when Ash woke up. She could hear Caleb in the shower, so she slipped out of bed, went into the kitchen, and made breakfast. She grated and fried potatoes, scrambled eggs, and toasted the rest of the sourdough bread.

"This is the second-best part about leaving," Caleb said as he walked up to her and placed a kiss on her cheek.

"What's the first?"

"Last night," he replied as he retrieved two cups and poured the tea.

Ash turned away so he wouldn't see her blush. She filled their plates and then carried them to the table.

"When are you taking off?" she asked.

"First light, which will give me just enough time to enjoy this amazing breakfast."

Ash was relieved when Sara called out for her. She didn't want Caleb to see her fear. She dressed Sara in warm clothes, attached a can of bear spray to her belt, and waited while Caleb grabbed the rest of his gear.

"Are you sure you don't want me to leave the gun?" he asked as he slid it into its holster.

"I'm sure. I won't be checking the bees, so I'll stay close to the community. If I do need to venture away from the buildings, I'll carry bear spray. I doubt there are any predators nearby since the herds moved out."

"True, but if they've caught wind of the livestock, they may be waiting around for an opportunity at an easy meal."

"Thanks for that lovely image."

Ash followed Caleb out the door. The last time Caleb left her, he, Ryan, Melora, and Tyler rode off the mountain to sneak into the dangerous resettlement city of Pryor and disable FAMA's only helicopter to prevent them from ever returning to Beartooth. While he was away, she had a terrifying encounter with a grizzly bear. Since then, she seldom left the cabin without bear spray.

When they reached the ranch, Fiona, Bob, and his oldest son, Jacob, had already haltered and brushed the horses. They were saddling the five that would be ridden. Caleb jumped in to help while Ash walked over to Luna. She held Sara out toward the horse. The toddler tried to hug the horse's neck and seemed to be having a serious conversation with the small mare. It pleased Ash to see that Sara and Luna shared the same bond as she did with the horse.

"I think your little girl is already taking after her daddy," Maggie said as she walked into the barn with Miranda alongside.

"I'm not sure how happy I am about that, especially if she runs off on terrifying adventures when she gets older," Ash replied as she smiled at Caleb, who was watching them.

Quicker than Ash hoped, they were ready to ride. Five

of the eight horses were saddled, and three were packed. Ash ran her hand down Luna's neck. "Keep an eye on him for me," she whispered in her ear.

Luna tossed her head up and down as if she understood and was accepting the assignment. Ash chuckled and stepped back as Jacob took the mare's lead rope and led her over to Fiona.

Outside the barn, Caleb checked Felix's cinch one last time. He turned to Ash and wrapped his free arm around her waist and pulled her close. He kissed her deeply, and then placed noisy kisses all over Sara's cheeks, making her giggle.

"I love you two. Don't do anything scary this time. Sara, be good for your mama," Caleb said as he put his toe in the stirrup, swung his leg over the saddle, and settled atop the sorrel stud.

Sara reached for him and called out. When he didn't get off the horse, she started to cry. Ash tried to soothe her, but Sara expressed openly what Ash was feeling.

Ash was proud of Miranda for not making a scene. She had matured considerably since the last time Ryan left. She also caught a glimpse of Jacob hugging Fiona. Beth kissed Archie goodbye and then stood near Ash, Miranda, Bob, Maggie, and Jacob.

"Geez, I'm feeling a little unloved here. Tyler barely got out of bed long enough to say goodbye," Melora added as the group headed out.

Ash watched as Caleb led the group away from the community until they disappeared from view. She fought to keep the tears at bay so that Sara would believe that everything was fine.

"Doesn't get any easier, does it?" Maggie asked as she put her arm around her.

Ash just shook her head, not trusting her voice.

"Come home with me," Miranda said. "I doubt it will make you feel any better, but it will cheer up Sara, and Mom and Dad will be happy to see their grandbaby."

When they reached the Solomon cabin, Sara brightened at the sight of her grandparents. Ash could see that Miranda was now stewing, and it was easy to guess why.

"I'm tired of waiting. Ryan and I are getting married," Miranda blurted out.

"Okay," Owen replied.

"He is a very nice young man," Olivia added.

"First, you said I had to wait until I was nineteen. Finally, you agreed to let us get married sooner but have been stalling. Don't think I haven't noticed. Now, I get 'okay' and 'he's a very nice young man'."

"What would you like us to say, dear?" Olivia asked.

"I...I...I don't know. I guess, that," Miranda fumed.

"Then why are you so mad?" Owen asked.

"Errr," Miranda ground out through clenched teeth. "I'm going to the clinic."

After Miranda slammed the door shut behind her, Ash, Olivia, and Owen burst out laughing.

"We like to keep her guessing. Besides, her nineteenth birthday is just over a month away," Olivia said.

"By the time Ryan gets back, Emily and Fiona move to the duplex, we plan a wedding, and it happens, she'll be nineteen," Owen added.

"Well, even if you were messing with her, I'm glad you said what you did. If she's as worried about Ryan as I am about Caleb, it's good you gave her something positive to focus on."

Olivia handed the toddler to Owen and went to Ash. When Olivia wrapped her arms around her, Ash couldn't hold it in any longer. She cried.

After a few moments, Ash stepped back. "I'm sorry, I know you worry about him too."

"I do, but you can't let the fear consume you,"

Ash nodded. She loved these people. They had been there for her through so many tragedies, starting with her mom's passing.

"So, what's going on? Did my jerk of a big brother make you cry again? I may have married Evelyn, but I'm still willing to beat the tar out of him for you," Dillon said as he strode into the cabin.

"I already miss him. I'll worry until he returns, but these are tears of joy. I just love this family so much, even you," Ash said as she gave Dillon a hug.

"Well, maybe I'll punch him anyway because I'm sure he'll screw up sooner or later," Dillon replied as he headed into the kitchen.

NINE

THEY'D BEEN RIDING for hours and had seen no sign of wildlife except for one nervous squirrel scampering up a tree. Caleb had never been fond of squirrel meat, but if it hadn't been moving so fast, he might have grabbed his bow and taken a shot. With the shortage of game to harvest and livestock to butcher, he would never take meat for granted again.

Each person kept their horse to a slow, smooth pace and a good distance behind the one in front of it to avoid breathing in dust kicked up by the rider ahead. At times, they navigated through the course, abrasive fallout hidden under a fine layer of ash nearly a foot deep. They worried that the gritty particles might irritate the horses' unshod hooves, and the volcanic dust could cause respiratory issues in humans and animals.

"Let's take a lunch break by that rock outcrop up ahead. I'll get the drone out and do a quick recon while we eat and rest the horses," Melora said.

The group dismounted, secured the horses, and

retrieved food from their saddlebags. Fiona and Melora took the drone and climbed on top of the tallest boulder.

Caleb, Ryan, and Archie sat down on a flat rock below and ate. They looked up when they heard the hum of the drone.

"I sure hope they find something nearby. Beth would be thrilled if we were back tonight. She really didn't like me leaving her and the kids," Archie said.

"Dan will keep an eye on them," Caleb replied.

"He'll try, but she's blaming her dad for even suggesting I come along on this hunt."

"It's getting harder all the time to leave Ash and Sara. Ash doesn't say much, but I can tell she doesn't like it."

"Can you blame her. The time she went with you into the wild, you almost got yourself killed, if I understand the story correctly," Ryan said.

"You do, she saved my life. Now, every time she looks at my scars, I can see fear in her eyes. I wish the marks would fade away, but as deep as those gashes were, Emily said that isn't likely to happen," Caleb replied.

Melora and Fiona returned, ending the conversation.

"Sorry guys, didn't see so much as a rabbit track," Melora reported.

Fiona and Melora ate their lunch, packed the drone, and then the group got back on the trail. They kept to a northeast trajectory as much as possible. The terrain was rough. They rode into steep, rocky gorges, crossed deep rivers and fast-moving creeks, and climbed mountain slopes. But by mid-afternoon, they still hadn't seen any sign of the herds.

When they crested a windswept ridge, Caleb pulled Felix to a stop and waited for the group to catch up. "Should we take a break and fly again or keep riding?" he asked.

"I think the horses could use a rest after that last climb, and it couldn't hurt to get the drone back up. It would really suck if we're passing by elk or deer just to the north or south of us and don't even know it," Fiona replied.

Melora and Fiona launched the drone while the guys tended to the horses.

"Is it my imagination or are the depths of the deposits thinning the further we ride?" Ryan asked.

"It's not your imagination, and it makes sense. As we ride east, we're getting further from the eruption site. Graham said they probably only got a dusting on the new east coast," Caleb explained.

"And I've spotted a little more grass poking through. It's all brown, but that could just be the cold temperatures," Archie said as he pulled his jacket tighter around his neck.

"It isn't warming up much. I'm not looking forward to a night out at this elevation," Caleb added.

"Hey, guys, take a look at this," Fiona said as she and Melora approached.

The group crowded around Fiona as she played back the footage they just captured. The small screen showed three small buck deer. Their coats were shaggy, and they didn't look very fat, but it was the first wildlife they'd seen.

"How far away is this?" Caleb asked.

"Probably three miles and more north than east. If we want to catch up to them, we'll need to adjust our course a bit," Melora replied.

"Seems like the best option. If they're finding enough grass to survive, maybe other deer or elk are also in the vicinity," Caleb said.

They mounted up and rode out, adjusting their route

in hopes of intercepting the deer. It was nearing dusk when they finally spotted tracks.

"We don't have much daylight left. There's a creek nearby, grass for the horses, and the volcanic deposits are relatively thin here. Let's make camp, fly the drone once more before nightfall, and try to pick up their trail in the morning," Caleb suggested.

Everyone agreed with the plan. They had been riding for over ten hours and, according to the coordinates on the drone, had covered nearly twenty miles as the crow flies. They all felt tired and discouraged.

While the guys unsaddled and picketed the horses, Fiona and Melora launched the drone. To save space, they had skipped bringing tents. Instead, they brought a couple of tarps, one to put on the ground to sleep on and one to drape over a pole hung between trees to offer a little protection if it rained or if the wind kicked up.

Once Caleb, Ryan, and Archie finished setting up camp, they joined Melora and Fiona.

"Have you found anything yet?" Caleb asked.

"We caught a quick glimpse of the same three deer, probably two miles due north. Something spooked them, and we lost them," Melora replied.

"That doesn't sound good. I hoped the lack of prey would mean a lack of predators," Caleb stated.

"Maybe the wind snapped a branch, and it startled them," Ryan added, hopefully.

Fiona and Melora put the drone away while Caleb and Ryan checked on the horses, and Archie built a fire. They sat around the flames, eating jerky, fry bread, and dried apples.

"I'm not sure what it is, but this place feels so different at night than Beartooth or any of the areas south of here that we've ridden," Caleb said.

"Even though the volcanic deposits have thinned to a dusting, the ground is still gray, none of the deciduous trees have leaves, and many of the coniferous trees have brown needles or none at all. I hope they can recover, or this place won't just look dead, it will be dead," Fiona added.

"The terrain is even steeper and rougher here than what we experienced riding to Pryor," Ryan said.

"But at least the slopes have been more stable. We haven't had to ride around any landslides," Melora added.

They continued to sit around the fire, all deep in thought. Caleb was just about to speak when an unfamiliar sound pierced through the silence. He looked around at his companions. They were all as startled and baffled as he was by the deep guttural roar. They froze and listened as the terrifying sounds resonated through the night a half dozen more times, seemingly from multiple animals.

"What in the heck was that?" Archie asked.

"After what Ash and I experienced in the wild, I consider myself a bit of an expert on mountain lions or cougars, and that didn't sound like any we encountered," Caleb replied.

"And, it didn't sound all that far away," Melora added.

"I suggest we sleep in shifts. Melora has a shotgun and Archie has a rifle, so they should take opposite turns keeping watch," Fiona said.

"How about you, Melora, and Ryan take the first shift. Wake us up in four hours, and Archie and I can take the second," Caleb offered.

They all agreed. Once they finished eating, they stowed their food high up in a tree away from camp, gathered more firewood, and brought the horses closer to camp. Melora, Fiona, and Ryan spread out with their backs to the fire. Caleb and Archie crawled under the tarp and tried to sleep.

Caleb hoped he could get some rest, but he couldn't push the disturbing calls from his mind. The roar sounded distinctly different from any cougar he'd ever heard, but still feline. Maybe the rougher geology altered how sound carried, or maybe the big cats to the north had adopted a different call. He prayed that was the case, because the only other option was a species he'd never encountered.

TEN

LIKE THE LAST time Caleb left her and Sara alone, Ash found it impossible to sleep in her own bed. After several hours of tossing and turning, she gave up and spent the night in the single bed that had been hers before marrying Caleb and was now in Sara's room near her crib.

When the morning light filtered through the curtains, Ash slipped out of bed and got ready for the day. Once dressed, she heated water for tea and then started oatmeal for breakfast.

Sara was still asleep when the tea and oatmeal were ready. Ash set the pan of oats aside, poured her tea, and walked outside, cradling the steaming cup in her hands. She strolled behind the cabin and looked at the thermometer. The temperature had dipped below freezing overnight. Until that changed there wasn't much point in even thinking about the garden.

Back inside the cabin, she tried to find news on the radio but gave up when she heard Sara fussing. After breakfast, she dressed Sara in multiple layers of warm clothing, and they made their way to the greenhouse.

Graham was absent, but Ash had tended plants all her life, so she knew what needed to be done. She enjoyed working in the greenhouse when it was cold outside since it felt like a balmy early-summer day inside.

Sara toddled down the length of the greenhouse and back. She looked at all the different shapes and colors of vegetables and smelled blossoms, but fortunately, she refrained from picking anything. She was on her second pass when Graham walked in.

"What a pleasant surprise," he said as he scooped up Sara. "It's kind of amazing that she loves the colors and shapes of the blossoms but never picks them. She may just be the next community horticulturist."

"But she also loves horses and her stuffed bee, so it could go a number of ways," Ash joked.

"I guess we'll just have to wait and see if she has an affinity for archery too."

"I hope you don't mind that I'm in here working. With the bees holed up, the temperatures too cold for gardens, no reception on the radio, and Caleb gone, I didn't have a lot going on this morning. Now that Sara is so active, she doesn't like being couped up in the cabin."

"Not at all. In fact, if you can carry Sara with one arm, we can load up three canvas bags of fresh produce and you can help me haul it to Tony," Graham replied.

Ash and Graham loaded the bags with vegetables. By the time they reached the storehouse, they were joined by several residents who spotted the bags.

"I see you brought more produce and plenty of eager recipients for the bounty," Tony chuckled as he took the bag from Ash's hand.

Ash set Sara down and turned to face the group that followed them in.

"How's your mom doing?" Ash asked Joy and Lexie Garland.

"She's still fighting the rattle in her chest and a nasty cough. She's getting a little stronger every day, so we think she's over the hump," Joy responded.

"If there is anything I can do, don't hesitate to ask," Ash replied.

"Uncle Dillon," Sara cried out as she toddled toward the door with outstretched arms.

Dillon scooped up his niece and placed noisy kisses on her cheeks as he always did, making her laugh and nuzzle into his chest.

"When I didn't find you home or at the greenhouse, I hoped you were here. I was starting to worry that my brother's wife was getting into some kind of trouble again."

"Very funny. You've found me, so what's up?"

"Evelyn said some of the kids want to shoot and thought maybe you could set up an archery clinic in Caleb's absence. I ran into Gavin. He, Miranda, and I would come out and practice and give you a hand if you're willing."

"Sure, it would be a great activity for the community. I imagine everyone is still suffering from cabin fever after a month mostly inside. Let's meet up Saturday afternoon, about 2:00 p.m."

"Perfect, I'll have Evelyn make sure all the kids know."

"I'll let Dennis know, too. We're helping Beth with the kids while Archie's gone. Their oldest is bored and a bit of a handful for Beth," Ginger Craig added.

"Dillon, let's grab a few veggies for your mom and Evelyn while you're here. I have a feeling everything will be snatched up pretty fast. With serious rationing on meat, we're going through a lot more vegetables as a community than usual," Ash said.

Ash selected some produce for her and Sara and helped Dillon decide what he should take for his mom and his wife.

"I'll swing by the farm on my way home and see if your mom can watch Sara on Saturday afternoon while we shoot. I can take the produce if you're busy," Ash offered.

"I'm heading that way. Let's drop this stuff off at my cabin, and then I will walk with you to the farm. The last time Caleb left, you scared the heck out of us and forced me to beat some sense into my clueless brother. I'm trying to keep a better eye on things this go around."

"The violence was totally unnecessary, but if you insist on walking with me, I'll let you carry Sara, she's a lot heavier than a few bags of vegetables," Ash chuckled.

"She's light as a feather," Dillon replied as he lifted her over his head, tossing her up slightly, and catching her, making her giggle and ask for more.

They made a quick stop at Dillon and Evelyn's cabin to drop off the produce and then headed toward the Solomon farm. Once they reached the cabin, Dillon handed Sara off to his mom and left to find his dad.

"I'm so glad you stopped by. I just finished a new jacket for Sara," Olivia said as she set Sara down and retrieved a puffy coat from another room.

"It's adorable, and it looks a lot warmer than what she's been wearing. She's about outgrown this sweater," Ash replied as she admired the coat.

"I filled it with lamb's wool I got from Maggie, so it should be very warm."

Ash took Sara's sweater off and put the coat on.

"Absolutely perfect." Ash hugged Olivia while Sara made a lap around the living room wearing her new coat.

They visited until Sara started fussing. As Ash got up to leave, Miranda walked in.

"You were going to leave before I got to hug my niece?" Miranda scolded.

"I didn't know when you'd get home," Ash explained.

Miranda picked up the toddler and hugged her tight. "I'll walk home with you so I can enjoy a few minutes with this little angel. Besides, the last time Caleb was gone, you got yourself into a heap of trouble."

Ash rolled her eyes. "You aren't the first to point that out today, and it wasn't like I went looking for it."

"No, you didn't, but I still have nightmares and have no desire for a repeat."

"Me neither. Even though Melora found no sign of animal tracks when she flew the drone after the eruption stopped, I still don't leave the cabin without this." Ash patted her canister of bear spray secured to her hip.

"You don't need to explain to me. I was there, remember?"

"Like it was yesterday," Ash said as she followed Miranda out the door.

ELEVEN

CALEB WOKE MELORA, Fiona, and Ryan while Archie gathered more wood for the fire.

"It may be dipping below freezing in Beartooth, but it's a lot colder up here overnight. I think this is the first time I've actually seen frost and ice," Archie said as he dropped a load of wood next to the fire and blew warm air into his cupped hands.

"Did you hear or see anything overnight?" Melora asked as she approached, rubbing her arms for warmth.

"Nothing. Hopefully, whatever we heard shortly after it got dark last night moved on," Caleb replied.

While Archie got a pot of oatmeal going over the flames, the rest of the group packed up camp and stowed the gear behind their saddles or in June's panniers. By the time they secured their gear, the oats were done.

"Sorry, no tea. We only brought one pot for cooking," Archie said as he scooped oatmeal into each bowl.

After they finished eating, Melora and Fiona took the drone out while the guys saddled the horses. When the women returned, they were ready to ride.

"We spotted four small bucks about three miles north-east of camp. Even though I only saw three yesterday, I think it's the same group judging by the antlers and shaggy coats," Melora reported as they loaded the drone and mounted up.

After an hour of riding, they spotted the deer. Caleb pulled up, got off Felix, and tied his rein to a tree.

"There's no way we'll get close enough to shoot with eight horses. Ryan, Archie, and I will take our bows and try to sneak up on them. The bucks seem nervous, which makes me a little nervous, but we have to try."

"No sense getting this close and turning back without even a shot. We'll get comfy here. Take a radio and call if you get something, and we'll bring the horses," Melora replied.

Caleb checked the load on the 9mm, slung his quiver of arrows over his shoulder, and strung his sixty-five-pound-recurve bow. Archie carried an identical bow along with his hunting rifle slung over one shoulder.

"I feel a little under-armed for this party," Ryan said as he secured his quiver and held his long bow.

"You can take the radio and my sidearm. I've got my shotgun if anything shows up. I may be a serious badass, but I can only shoot one gun at a time," Melora replied with a grin.

"And I have my 9mm in the unlikely event she needs back up," Fiona added with a roll of her eyes.

As soon as Ryan secured the radio to his belt and stowed the gun, the three men left. They caught sight of the deer a quarter of a mile away. The bucks grazed on dry, stunted grasses at the edge of a small meadow surrounded by forest, looking up often with ears and noses twitching, scanning the trees nervously.

They wove their way through the trees downwind of

the deer so the animals wouldn't catch their scent. They made it to within twenty-five yards of the closest buck when Caleb decided they couldn't risk getting any closer without spooking the animals. He and Archie were shooting more powerful bows than Ryan, so he motioned for Ryan to focus on the closest buck and Archie to shoot at the one to the right nearly forty yards away.

As soon as Archie silently propped his rifle against a tree and retrieved an arrow from his quiver, Caleb lifted his bow, nocked an arrow, and pulled the string back. He glanced over to his companions and saw they were ready. He nodded and all three arrows flew in unison. Caleb didn't wait to see the results before pulling another arrow and getting off a quick shot. The deer bolted. The hunters quietly moved toward each other, staying hidden in the trees.

"I know I hit my first deer but was busy trying to get a second shot off before they bolted, so I didn't see where the arrow lodged. I hit the second buck right in the shoulder-crease, so he should go down pretty quick," Caleb said.

"My arrow struck about four inches behind its front shoulder," Archie added.

"Mine might be a little further behind the shoulder blade, but it should be a fatal shot," Ryan stated.

Caleb called Melora on the radio and said they were successful, but to hold tight and they'd come back and help with the horses.

"I think we got all four, but they ran, so we need to give them some time to drop," Caleb said when they reached Melora and Fiona.

"The last time I shot a deer, it just looked up and went back to grazing. When the herd moved on fifteen minutes later, it took two steps, and crumpled to the ground," Ryan said.

"These deer were nervous, which isn't a super comforting thought. We need to give them time, but not too much or we might find a scavenger or predator on the meat," Caleb replied.

"Do we call it good with four deer, or do we keep hunting as long as we have pack horses? I'd kind of hate to go back with less than we have the capacity to carry," Melora asked.

Caleb thought for a minute. They heard an unusual feline call the night before, and the deer were clearly on edge, but the bucks weren't huge. The small deer wouldn't take pressure off butchering livestock for long.

"Once we find the deer, maybe you can fly the drone while the rest of us prep the game. If you can't find any sign of other deer or elk within the drone's range, I say we head back to Beartooth. If we can confirm there is something out there worth going after, we might as well try to harvest as much as we can," Caleb said.

With everyone in agreement, they mounted up and rode to where they shot the deer. After securing the horses, they began searching the area for signs.

"There's quite a bit of blood, so they should be easy to track," Caleb said as he studied the ground.

Melora and Fiona launched the drone and flew from the meadow while Caleb, Ryan, and Archie followed the blood trail. They had only tracked the animals for fifty yards when they spotted the first downed deer. Caleb could tell by the fletching on the arrow that it was his.

"Should I get started?" Archie asked.

"Normally, I'd say yes, but let's stay together," Caleb replied.

They kept walking and within a quarter of a mile, they

located the rest of the deer. They each took a deer by the hind legs and dragged it back to where they left the first.

"We've located all the bucks. We're only about fifty yards from where we left you, just below the little rock outcrop. As soon as you're done flying, bring the horses, and we should be ready to start loading up," Caleb said into the radio.

"Copy. I think we might have found a small herd of elk, but I'll take another pass to confirm. We'll be there in about twenty minutes," Melora replied.

By the time Melora and Fiona arrived with the horses, all the deer were gutted, skinned, and Archie had just started boning out the second deer. Caleb and Ryan watched him closely and mimicked his technique on the rest.

"We spotted about a dozen elk moving just inside the trees along a decent-size meadow with some marginal forage. They were probably less than four miles northeast of here. I don't know if we can catch up to them if they don't slow down or stop to graze, but it might be worth a try. They seemed pretty agitated and weren't staying in one spot for long," Melora said.

"It's not even 10:00 a.m. yet. I vote for giving chase until lunch, if we aren't gaining on them by then, turn around and head home. That would still give us a lot of daylight to travel in," Fiona offered.

"I agree, if we can't narrow the gap by noon, we probably won't catch up to them. They've got a good head start on us," Caleb added.

"Let's pack two of the geldings first since I've packed wild game on them before, so I know they won't go nuts. The boned-out meat from each of these deer can't weigh too much, so we can pack two deer per horse," Fiona said.

They unsaddled two of the geldings, moved the pack

saddles from Bella and Luna to the geldings, and put the riding saddles on the smaller mares. By the time the horses were ready, Archie and Caleb had the meat ready to pack. Following Fiona's instruction, they quickly stowed the meat in gamebags and loaded the panniers on the two geldings.

Melora took out a compass and oriented them the best she could on which direction the elk were moving. They set out as fast as possible while leading pack horses. Caleb was happy they wouldn't be going home empty-handed, but the lure of the large elk was strong, so they rode on.

TWELVE

THEY RODE about four miles and were just about ready to stop for lunch and fly the drone again when they heard crashing in the trees. Caleb motioned for the group to turn around and backtrack.

"How did we get on them without us realizing we were so close?" Caleb asked.

"We're downwind, so the elk must have heard the horses," Fiona whispered.

They continued to ride away from the herd until it sounded like the animals had quit running.

"We need to go on foot from here. I doubt Ryan's bow can take down an elk, so if Archie is willing, I think he and I should go after the elk with our bows and his rifle. The rest of you stay here and monitor the radio and keep an eye on the horses and the deer meat," Caleb said as he looked over at Archie.

"Not in love with the idea, but it makes the most sense. The elk are probably at least a half mile away already, so let's get moving," Archie replied.

Caleb and Archie left the others and took off on foot.

Thirty minutes later, they caught their first sight of the herd. They were still out of range, but at least they knew they were on the right track.

It was difficult getting close. The short grasses, leafless shrubs, and thin lodgepole pines provided scant cover. But after another twenty minutes, they were within range of two bull elk grazing a short distance from the main herd. The rest of the herd consisted of mostly cow elk, a few spike bulls, and one massive bull.

Caleb nodded to Archie and Archie nodded back. Both men raised their bows, pulled back and shot. The two wounded bulls bolted from the area, and the rest of the elk followed.

"I hope I got a good enough hit. I've never shot an elk before," Archie whispered, excitement lacing his voice.

"Me neither. My shot hit just where I wanted it, but these guys are more than twice the size of any deer I've ever harvested."

"I think we'll easily get over two-hundred pounds of meat from each bull, maybe more. Felix and the biggest gelding can handle an elk a piece, but as rough as the terrain is and with the weight of our saddles, maybe we should put around eighty pounds on Sierra and the hides and horns on Luna. The elk hides look much nicer than the deer we got earlier, so I'd like to take them back. I bet it would be nice leather, and the antlers would be good for something too."

"First things first, let's hope they didn't go far," Caleb said, still grinning.

Caleb called Melora on the radio and reported that they probably had two elk down. He gave her directions and said they'd stay put until they arrived with the horses. It took he and Archie nearly an hour to reach this spot, but they were moving slowly as they stalked the elk on foot. On horseback, Caleb figured the rest of the group would find them in half the time.

When Fiona, Melora, and Ryan arrived, Caleb and Archie took the reins of their horses and walked to the spot where the elk were grazing when they shot. There was enough blood that the trail was again easy to follow and verified they made solid shots.

Caleb and Archie continued to walk and lead their horses so they could follow the tracks and trail of blood on the ground, while the rest of the group rode slowly behind them. Caleb abruptly stopped and knelt down. He looked up at Archie, and his friend knelt down beside him.

"Are they supposed to be this big?" Archie asked.

"What's big?" Ryan demanded with fear in his voice.

Fiona and Melora jumped off their horses, handed the reins to Ryan, and crowded around Caleb and Archie.

"Holy moly!" Melora exclaimed as she stepped back and ran her fingers through her short black hair.

"There are clearly a number of animals, but it's hard to say how many," Fiona added.

"What animals?" Ryan asked, clearly frustrated that he couldn't join them while riding one horse and holding the reins or lead ropes for the rest.

Caleb stood up. "Some kind of cat tracks. The smaller ones look like the cougar tracks Ash and I saw in the wild, which at the time, we thought were huge. The bigger ones, whew, look feline but are twice the size and a little different in shape than the others."

"The small ones have four toes, and the big ones have five," Fiona noted.

"They look fresh, too. No wonder the herd was so skittish," Archie added.

While the group stood staring at the tracks in the dirt,

Fiona pulled out her cell phone and snapped some photos.

"Do the tracks lead the same way as the elk?" Ryan asked.

"No, they veer off to the left," Caleb answered.

"If the cat tracks head left, I say we stay straight and try to find the elk as quickly as possible. Then, we get out of here," Melora added.

Fiona and Melora relieved Ryan of the reins and lead ropes he was holding and mounted up. They followed Caleb and Archie as they continued to track the injured bulls.

It took them nearly two hours to locate both elk. Fortunately, they fell within sight of each other. While Caleb and Archie field dressed the elk, the rest of the group unloaded all the supplies from June's panniers that they'd need to pack the meat on the horses.

"By the time we pack the horses and head out of here on foot, we'll have less than two hours of daylight left. Then we'll have to unpack everything again and hang the meat for the night. Is it worth the effort or should we make camp here, and head out in the morning?" Archie asked.

Caleb looked around at the landscape and then at the group. They were all exhausted. "Archie has a point. I can hear water not far from here. We could hang the meat from those trees over there and set up camp in that little grove of aspen not far from water."

"On foot and leading horses, we won't get far tonight anyway. I don't love the idea that something big is out there by the size of the tracks we just saw and the sounds we heard last night, but we have no idea if whatever it was kept moving or is still in the area," Melora added.

After hashing over the pros and cons, they decided to

make camp. They hung the meat and any tack that had blood on it high up in the trees and then led the horses toward the sound of running water until they found a robust creek. After letting the horses drink and washing up to remove the scent of blood from their hands and clothes, Archie rinsed off one of the elk's livers, and they returned to the aspen stand in the meadow.

Working together, it took only minutes to set up their simple camp. They laid one tarp on the ground, hung the other over a pole to create shelter, and rolled the sleeping bags out under the tarp. They picketed the horses nearby on the side of the tree grove closest to the creek, where there was some decent grass for grazing.

Caleb, Melora, and Ryan took the small pot and returned to the river for water while Archie built a blazing fire and Fiona watched his back. On the return to camp, they gathered up as much firewood as they could carry.

"Here's some water for tea." Melora handed Archie the pot.

"Let's gather another load of wood before it gets too dark. I think we better keep the fire blazing all night," Caleb said.

By the time they got back with more wood, Archie had cubed the elk liver and skewered it on thin green willows he'd sharpened with his knife. He placed the skewers between rocks at the edge of the fire where the flames were smallest, and five potatoes rested in the coals.

"Normally, I'd wrinkle my nose at liver, but with the shortage of meat, it's not sounding half bad. Besides, I'm starving," Fiona said as they stood around the fire watching the meat cook and enjoying the heat from the flames.

"I thought we might as well cook it since it won't hold

as long as the rest of the meat. No sense wasting anything," Archie added.

"Compared to last night's dinner and today's lunch, I'm not complaining," Caleb said.

Each person retrieved their cup, bowl, and fork from their saddlebags. When the herbs were done steeping, they poured the tea and enjoyed the hot beverage while continuing to watch the meat cook.

"This really hits the spot after drinking tepid water all day," Ryan said.

"Agreed, in this frigid weather, hot beverages are most welcome," Melora added, cradling her warm cup between her hands.

By the time they finished eating, it was dark.

"Same as last night? Me, Fi, and Ryan take the first watch and Caleb and Archie take the second?" Melora asked.

"Sounds good. The trees in this little grove of aspen are too thin for anything to sneak up on us. We've got the horses nearby, so they'll notify us if they sense any danger. Hopefully, it will be an uneventful night, and we can get some sleep," Caleb said as he headed for his sleeping bag.

"Don't take this wrong, but I'm going to cozy my bag up to yours," Archie said has he moved his sleeping bag next to Caleb's.

"No argument here. I really didn't expect it to get this cold when the sun went down, and I thought all five of us would be under the tarp which would trap body heat. Just keep your hands to yourself," Caleb joked as he took off his boots and slid into his sleeping bag.

Archie chuckled. "No offense, but you're really not my type."

"None taken, Beth is way prettier than me."

Archie fell silent for a few moments before he spoke. "I

wish we could go back to before the government started the SAI program. We had everything we needed in Beartooth, and I felt my family was safe. Now, I worry about Beth and the kids all the time. Like you and Ash, we've known each other nearly our entire lives. She's my wife, my partner, the mother of our children, and the one thing that has always been constant in my life. When dad died, I couldn't lean on mom, she needed us too much. I leaned on Beth, and she got me through it. Every time you and I leave, I fear we won't make it back. The thought of leaving her and the kids alone terrifies me more than anything we've ever encountered."

"Unfortunately, I fear that we've never encountered anything like whatever beast owns the tracks we saw and the sounds we heard," Caleb whispered.

Archie didn't answer, and soon they both fell asleep.

THIRTEEN

CALEB WASN'T sure how long he'd been asleep when he was startled out of a nightmare about a helicopter filled with FAMA militia from Pryor touching down in Beartooth, by a booming, scream-like sound. He sat upright and glanced over at Archie, who was wide-eyed and alert.

They scrambled out of their bags, pulled on their boots, grabbed their weapons, and hurried to the fire. Melora, Fiona, and Ryan were spread out with their backs to the flames. Ryan had an arrow nocked, Fiona pulled her 9mm out of its holster, and Melora gripped her double-barreled shotgun in front of her chest with both hands.

A chorus of loud, wailing screams and unfamiliar roars pierced the night. The sounds were clearly coming from multiple animals in the throes of battle. The desperate pain-induced shrieks sent chills up Caleb's spine.

"Some of that doesn't sound like what we heard last night," Caleb whispered just as a deep, rumbling roar overpowered the screaming.

"But that does," Archie added.

They listened to the screams, screeches, roars, and growls for nearly half an hour before all noises stopped. No birds of prey or insects uttered a sound. The only noise that cut through the night was the crackling of the fire and the horses stomping, pawing, and snorting nearby.

Caleb was relieved that at least none of the horses neighed. The predators had probably been lured in by the smell of blood from the meat hanging in the trees, but he prayed they wouldn't hear the sound of live prey.

"What's the chance they've moved on?" Fiona asked.

"Hard to say, but I won't be going back to sleep, so if anyone wants to take my place, have at it," Caleb said.

"Me neither," Archie added.

No one took them up on the offer. Caleb and Archie had only gotten two hours of sleep, but the rest of the group had gotten none.

"In that case, let's bring the horses in as close to the fire as we can without frightening them further. We'll keep the fire blazing and spread out in as tight of a circle as we can to keep anything from sneaking up on us or the horses. Ryan, you still got Melora's sidearm?"

Ryan nodded and Caleb could see the fear in his eyes. He liked Ryan and felt the need to protect him. If he didn't come home with the love of his sister's life, she'd never forgive him.

"Good, we all have a firearm of some sort, though I'm more accurate with my bow," Caleb said as he kept his gun holstered and clutched his recurve.

Melora and Ryan stayed by the fire to keep watch while the rest of the group brought the horses in close and secured them. The horses were still agitated, but calmer now that they were closer to their people and the fire, and the disturbing noises had ceased.

Archie fed large logs into the fire, sending flames and

sparks high into the sky. They spread out in a circle around camp and settled in for a long night.

Caleb paced, unable to relax. The rest of the group remained equally on edge. They didn't speak. Everyone was too focused on the darkness between the trees.

After hearing no more disturbing noises for the next several hours, they decided that Ryan, Melora, and Fiona should try to get a couple hours of sleep, one at a time. Ryan left first. After two hours, Fiona woke him up. He returned to the fire while she slept. When Melora woke Fiona, she handed Fiona the shotgun.

"We're probably only a couple hours from sunrise. Hopefully, Melora can get a few hours rest. We'll break camp at daybreak and get out of here as fast as we can while traveling on foot and leading horses," Caleb said.

"Maybe we should leave the meat behind or take only what we can get on three pack horses so we can ride instead of walk and make better time," Ryan offered.

Caleb had the same thought, but he hated to waste meat. He decided not to try to sway the group. Whatever they decided, it needed to be a group decision. "When Melora wakes up, we'll take a vote."

As the sun slowly began its ascent, Melora joined the group at the fire.

"Did you get any sleep?" Fiona asked.

"Surprisingly, yes. Two hours isn't much, but often on military operations we'd go days without sleep," Melora replied.

"Ryan suggested we leave most of the meat behind so we can ride rather than walk and put some distance between us and this place a lot faster. It would probably be the safest and smartest thing to do, but I'd sure hate to go home with less than we harvested after traveling so far. Any thoughts?" Caleb asked.

After a few moments of silence, Melora spoke. "The tracks we saw yesterday were definitely concerning and what we heard last night made the hair stand up on the back of my neck and will probably give me nightmares for years, but so far, we've had no encounters. Maybe whatever it was is cautious of humans and will stay away."

"We probably have over eight hundred pounds of meat hanging in the trees. With the cold daytime temperatures and the overnights dipping below freezing, if we can get it back to Beartooth, we can hang what won't fit in the walk-in cooler in one of the horse trailers down at the boneyard. It would keep well and be protected. I can't see wasting that much meat." Archie added.

"I can't help but think that what we're hearing is even worse than what Ash and I encountered in the wild, but we have a lot more people and firepower. Ash and I had one sidearm that neither one of us had shot at the time, and my bow. The five of us have three sidearms, three bows, a large-caliber hunting rifle, and a double-barreled shotgun. Whatever's out there, I like the odds a lot better this time."

"I say we stick to the plan. Let's eat something, load up, and get out of here as quickly as possible. We can always ditch the meat later if things get worse," Fiona said.

"Based on my GPS, maps, and drone flights, I'm estimating we're nearly thirty miles from Beartooth as the crow flies. On flat terrain without leading horses, we might be able to cover that in a long day. Considering the terrain and being on foot, I'd say we have at least two hard days of walking between here and Beartooth," Melora added.

Caleb looked around the group and everyone, including Ryan, nodded that they agreed with Fiona.

Archie cooked breakfast while the others tore down camp and started saddling and packing the horses.

After a quick breakfast, they put out the fire and headed toward the trees where the meat was hanging high above the ground. They lowered the elk and deer meat to the ground. Felix had been packed before but not with a dead animal. He shied and reared up, trying to pull away when he got close to the game.

"Let's try blindfolding him," Fiona suggested.

She tied a bandana over Felix's eyes and then positioned herself close to the stud's head and spoke reassuringly in his ear.

"Ryan, stand on the other side of Felix and get a good hold on his halter," Fiona said.

Once Fiona and Ryan had a firm hold on the horse, Caleb, Archie, and Melora tried to secure a hind quarter. Felix reared back, throwing his head up, catching Ryan in the face.

Ryan reeled off a string of profanity as he let go of the halter and stepped back out of Felix's reach.

"You, okay?" Caleb asked.

"Do I look okay," Ryan replied as blood from his nose gushed between his fingers. "I think he broke my nose."

"Let me take a look," Melora said as she pulled Ryan to the side. "Yep, it's broken. Move your hand."

Ryan dropped his hand and before he could ask why, Melora reached up and straightened his nose. He yelled, cursed, and shot Melora an angry look.

"What did you do that for? That hurt like hell."

"It needed to be straightened, and there was no point in waiting for the pain to ebb and the blood to stop, just to hurt you and make you bleed again. Lean your head back, and put some pressure on it," Melora said as she returned to where Fiona had just calmed the horse back down.

Melora took Ryan's place, and they tried again to pack Felix. The stud fought, but Melora and Fiona held on and Caleb and Archie finally managed to secure the game. The geldings were much more agreeable and after watching the first four horses, the mares only put up a token fight.

"I've led the geldings in a pack-string before. They seemed good with it, so we'll use these ropes to string them together. That way I can lead three horses with one rope," Fiona said.

"That would work with Bella and June. June would practically follow Bella even without being secured together," Caleb added.

It took much longer than Caleb had hoped to pack all the meat on the horses and get the animals ready to move out.

"How's the nose?" Caleb asked.

"I think it's done bleeding, but it hurts bad," Ryan replied as he took Bella's lead rope.

"Glad you're done bleeding, but I wish we had something cold for the swelling and that black eye," Caleb said.

"Black eye? Man, Miranda is going to be really upset," Ryan groaned.

Felix had finally started to calm down as Caleb led him away from the trees. Ryan followed with Bella and June, and Melora fell in behind him, leading Luna, who was packed with the elk antlers and hides. Archie lined up next, leading Sierra, and Fiona was last in line with the three geldings.

"Hold up for a second. I need to make a quick trip to the trees before we get too far down the trail," Fiona said as she handed her lead rope to Archie and darted off.

As Caleb turned to give each strap on Felix another check, Fiona screamed. Melora dropped her lead rope, grabbed her shotgun, and took off at a run. Ryan quickly picked up Luna's lead rope before the mare noticed she was loose.

"Stay with the horses," Caleb shouted at Ryan and Archie as he tossed Felix's lead rope to Ryan and darted off after Melora, pulling an arrow from his quiver as he ran.

Caleb skidded to a halt next to Melora. Fiona held her hand over her mouth as if trying to stifle another scream or avoid vomiting.

"What could do this?" Melora mumbled in shocked disbelief.

"Nothing I've ever seen or heard of," Caleb replied, eyes glued to the scene in front of him.

"Got your phone on you?" Melora asked Fiona.

Fiona pulled it out of her pocket and took dozens of pictures.

"The battle we heard was much closer to our camp than we thought," Caleb said.

"That's enough, let's get out of here before whatever did this returns to the scene of the crime," Melora added.

They quickly made their way back to Ryan and Archie.

"Let's move out. Everyone, stay sharp and keep your weapons ready," Caleb said as he took Felix's lead rope in one hand and kept his bow in the other.

"What was it?" Archie asked.

"Five mutilated cougars. Their throats were ripped out. Their guts were strung across the ground, but not much was eaten. It looked more like killing for sport or territory than predation. What we heard last night must have been one heck of a fight," Caleb replied.

"What could have done that?" Ryan asked.

"I don't know, and I sure as heck don't want to find out. Let's get out of here."

FOURTEEN

CALEB HAD BEEN GONE for just three days and two nights. Ash doubted there was any reason to worry yet, but she couldn't help it. In front of Miranda, she tried to act nonchalant about the trip because she knew her sister-in-law was worried sick about her brother and her boyfriend.

While Sara slept, Ash went into Caleb's archery room and gathered up all of the equipment he always provided whenever he organized an archery clinic. Ash suspected that most of the participants would bring their own gear, but she would take what they had in case there were any new archers.

Once Sara was awake, fed, and dressed, Ash left the cabin. She stopped by the greenhouse and found Graham inside tending the plants.

"Good morning," Ash said as she went inside and set Sara down.

"Good morning to you, too. How are you holding up?"

Ash knew what he was talking about without further

explanation. "I miss Caleb like crazy, and I'd be lying if I claimed I wasn't worried sick."

"Me too. Mel and Fi are like daughters to me. Fear for Melora being called back up into active duty as everything started coming apart in the country and Fiona getting pulled into the mess, is what made me take a risk on you all letting us in and riding for Beartooth."

"I'm sorry I haven't offered you any support. I've been trying to be strong in front of Miranda and Beth, but I know everyone has to be worried, especially you and Emily, probably even Jacob."

Graham chuckled. "Fiona's pretty tight-lipped about Jacob. I hope there is something going on there, but I try not to pry."

"I think he's interested, but she has expressed hesitancy when we've talked. He's not overly ambitious, not super into horses, and still lives with his folks, but he's a nice guy. I think he'd treat her well. They went fishing with Caleb and I once. We had a great time. Jacob is learning to shoot a bow, and Caleb said he's been helping more with the horses."

"Sounds like he's trying. I just want her to be happy like Melora and Tyler. Speaking of Tyler, once we're done, I wonder if we should go check on him and see how he's doing with Melora gone. I haven't seen him around at all."

"Caleb and Tyler have buried the hatchet for the most part, but I doubt Caleb would like me going over there."

"I thought Dan was joking when he asked if Melora or Fiona might be interested in an engineer when I approached you all about moving here. Apparently, he wasn't. I'm glad we could help, for everyone's sake. If you ever want to tell me the story, I'm curious to hear it. In the meantime, I sure would love the company. Afterwards, we can swing by the storehouse and see how the produce is holding out," Graham said.

"I guess it won't hurt anything." Ash bundled Sara back up and followed Graham out of the greenhouse.

They walked over to Tyler's cabin. Ash hung back as Graham knocked on the door. They waited several minutes before he answered. Ash was taken aback. It didn't look like he'd showered, shaved, or changed his clothes since Melora left. She couldn't help but stare.

"Uh, you wanna come in?"

Ash followed Graham inside and was shocked by all the mess. They sat down at the kitchen table after Tyler cleared off a couple chairs. She wasn't sure what she was smelling, but she kept Sara on her lap, afraid the curious toddler might find out.

"I could heat up some water for tea," Tyler mumbled.

"No thanks, we just came by to see how you're doing without Melora. To be perfectly honest, I expected you to be doing better since you were a bachelor for so long before she arrived," Ash said.

"Yeah, man, you look rough. Are you okay?" Graham asked.

"I didn't think I'd miss her so much, but I do. I can't sleep, I have no appetite, I'm worried sick, and I just can't find the motivation to do anything."

Ash could relate. "I get it, but you've got to pull it together."

"How do you do it, Ash?"

Ash nuzzled Sara close to her chest and wrapped her arms around her to hopefully keep her from hearing her response. She wasn't sure if the toddler would understand but didn't want her to be frightened.

"I'm worried to the point that I can't sleep either, but with her, I have to cook and pretend everything is normal.

The thought of something happening to Caleb, leaving me a very young widow and her without a father is nearly paralyzing, but I can't let the fear overcome me. I have to believe he's coming home."

"Once all the roads and bridges accessing Beartooth were wiped out, I thought I'd spend my life alone. I had all but given up on ever finding someone to share my life with after you rejected me. What's the chance a beautiful, strong, kind, single, and more age-appropriate woman would just happen to ride into our community one day? Even more unbelievable, she loves me just the way I am. No one has ever done that before. I don't know what I'd do without her."

Ash didn't know what to say. She had no idea that Tyler had such a sensitive side. Until Melora, she thought he was arrogant and socially awkward, and that was before he assaulted her and tried to stop her from marrying Caleb.

"When's the last time you checked on our electrical system?" Graham asked, breaking the uncomfortable silence.

"I don't know, I guess the day before Melora left."

"We're going to leave now. Since I think of Melora as a daughter, think of me as your father-in-law and take my advice. I want you to clean up this place, take a shower, shave, and I'll be back this afternoon. I know you usually check the hydropower system every day, so we'll go have a look and check the rest of our energy grid while we're at it."

Tyler nodded. Ash and Graham got up and left.

"That was some mighty tough talk, but I think it's just what he needed," Ash said as they headed toward the storehouse.

"Rejected him, huh? I think I'm starting to piece it all together."

"It turned into a real mess. He tried to stop my wedding, and it got a bit physical. I hit him in the head with a big stick, trying to get away, and Caleb broke his nose when he found out. Needless to say, things have been a little tense between us ever since. It made matters worse when I told Melora before she married him, but I thought she deserved to know."

"If Melora wasn't the toughest woman I know, I might be a little concerned. I'm assuming there's nothing to worry about."

"No. He knows he screwed up. I'm confident he learned his lesson. We've kept the incident to a very small group. We saw no benefit in adding insult to injury."

"Understood," Graham replied.

When they reached the storehouse, they found Tony outside picking greens and herbs out of the cold frames.

"Just the man we're looking for. We thought we'd stop by and see how the produce is holding out," Graham said.

"It's getting low, which is why I decided to pick some greens today."

"I've got some ripe stuff, but nothing is over-ripe, so I'd like to let it mature a bit longer unless the shelves are bare."

"Darn close to it, so you might bring over what you can," Tony replied.

Ash and Graham left and returned to the greenhouse. They picked a couple bags of barely-ripe tomatoes and small cucumbers. He didn't need help carrying it back to the storehouse, so Ash left and headed for the farm.

As strong as she tried to sound in front of everyone, she was a mess. Caleb's family always assured her that no matter what, she would never be alone. At the moment, she desperately needed that reminder.

FIFTEEN

THE HORSES WERE ON EDGE, and the sensation of being watched just wouldn't go away. Caleb had no doubt everyone heard the noises in the trees, but no one spoke as they kept walking at a strong pace. After several hours without a break, Caleb stopped.

"I'm sure we can all use a breather," he said as he tied Felix to a tree.

They secured the horses, retrieved their water bottles and snacks, and found a mound of rocks clear of volcanic fallout. They sat down, keeping their guns and bows within arm's reach.

"Are we going to talk about it or just keep pretending we aren't being stalked?" Archie asked.

"I vote for pretending we haven't noticed," Ryan said as he took a bite of jerky.

"We could shoot off a few rounds in the direction of the noise. I hate to waste ammunition, but maybe it will scare whatever it is off," Fiona suggested.

Caleb looked around. He didn't hear or sense anything at the moment, but he had a good idea from which direction the occasional crunching leaf or broken twig was coming from. He didn't know if he could really feel the footfalls and hear the heavy breathing or if it was his imagination, but there was definitely something out there.

"Since you're at the back of our train and have a lot more ammo than I do, the next time you hear something go ahead and take a couple shots. Be sure to give us a heads up so we can keep a tight hold on the horses," Caleb said to Fiona.

Fiona nodded and popped a few dried apple bits into her mouth.

"How's everyone holding up?" Caleb asked.

"Fine," Ryan replied, though Caleb noted the uncharacteristic nasally tone to his voice.

"I can feel blisters on my feet developing already," Archie added.

Melora dug through her pack and pulled out a small, plastic box just as Fiona did the same. They held them up and both chuckled.

"Good old government issue. When we were in the field, we had these little personal first aid kits. Graham used up everything in his own on our trek to Beartooth, but we still have ours," Fiona said.

Melora opened it and removed a small supply of moleskin. She tossed the packet over to Archie. "Put this over your blisters or hotspots where a blister is trying to form."

Archie tended to his blisters while Melora checked the GPS. Confident they were heading in the right direction they resumed the trek toward home.

After another hour of walking, Fiona held up. "Archie, take the lead rope and everyone hold on to your horses, literally."

Fiona walked ten yards toward the trees. She discharged a round from her 9mm in the direction of the loudest noises and then repeated the process a short distance behind them.

They all stood still for a moment and listened to thrashing and rumbling in the brush. The ground vibrated with each footfall and twigs snapped, and then everything went quiet.

"Whatever was out there ran, but how far it went is anyone's guess." Fiona holstered her gun and took the lead rope from Archie.

After another hour of walking in silence, they stopped for lunch.

"Did anyone hear anything after Fiona shot?" Caleb asked.

"Not a thing," everyone replied in unison.

"Well, let's hope we scared off whatever was trailing us," Caleb said as he retrieved his water and food from his saddlebags.

"I think I'll make a quick flight with the drone. I don't have a lot of battery life left, but it might help to see if there is anything out there. I'd also like to get a bearing on where we're at and what kind of terrain we have in front of us," Melora said.

By the time Melora and Fiona finished flying, the guys had eaten lunch. Melora stowed the drone, took out her map, and spread it out on a rock.

"Looks like we're about here," she said as she pointed to a spot on the map. "Using that knowledge and the GPS, I believe we're still about twenty-five miles from Beartooth as the crow flies, though we've probably covered nearly ten already today with having to hike around obstacles and across ravines."

"A little depressing, walking ten miles to be only five miles closer to home," Caleb said.

They didn't detect any sign of predators as they

continued on. The longer they walked, the more frequently they had to stop for breaks until they finally decided they'd had enough for one day.

They found a spot to camp in a small stand of large, mature aspen trees in the middle of a meadow that was slightly elevated and surrounded by pine trees. Dry grasses were plentiful along the edge where the aspen grove met the meadow. It wasn't ideal grazing, but it would sustain the horses.

"By the size of these aspen, it doesn't look like there have been any elk here for decades, so hopefully it isn't a regular haunt for predators either," Caleb said.

"How can you tell?" Ryan asked.

"When there are a lot of elk frequenting an area they browse down aspen shoots, keeping them from growing into trees of this size," Caleb replied.

"I'm just glad we have plenty of trees to secure the horses and string our tarp. The open space between us and the pine forest should also help us spot a predator before it gets too close," Melora added.

After unpacking the horses and hanging the meat in the pine trees at the edge of the forest, they led the horses to a creek on the opposite side of the meadow to drink. They found a good patch of grass and picketed the animals to graze.

Melora and Ryan stayed behind to watch the horses and set up camp while Caleb, Fiona, and Archie made another trip to the creek for water and firewood.

"Got the water yet?" Caleb called down to Archie, who had climbed down a steep embankment to refill their water bottles and the camp pot.

"Yep, I'm heading up your way now," Archie replied as he started to climb the slope with his hands full.

They had watered the horses downstream where the

banks were less steep but decided it would be best to get their own drinking water upstream from where the horses waded into the water and drank.

Just as Archie reached the top, the rock he stepped on dislodged. As it rolled, so did his ankle. He cried out in pain as he fell to his knees and dropped two of the bottles.

"Are you alright?" Fiona called out.

"Yeah, but I twisted my ankle. Luckily, I dropped the water bottles with secure lids and didn't spill the pot," he replied as he picked up the bottles and hobbled over to where she and Caleb waited.

They slowly made their way back to camp. Caleb and Fiona dropped their armloads of wood where they would build the fire.

"Looks like you downsized our shelter," Caleb said.

"We figured no more than two of us would sleep at the same time, so thought a smaller shelter would stay warmer and we could pile the extra bags on those sleeping for extra warmth," Melora replied.

"Good plan, it sure is cold up here when the sun goes down," Caleb added.

While Caleb, Ryan, and Fiona brought the horses into camp for the night, Archie retrieved his knife from his saddle bag. He hobbled back to the fire that was now blazing and set to work preparing the meat he had chunked off before hanging the game in the trees.

"The blisters hurting that bad?" Melora asked.

"They don't feel great, but I rolled my ankle down by the creek," he replied.

"If we weren't so nervous about what might be out there, I would suggest we soak the ankle in the cold creek water and wash the blisters. Instead, let's just wash any exposed craters here and use one of my little packets of antibiotic ointment. Hopefully it's not too outdated and will keep your wounds from getting infected," Melora offered.

"I'll elevate the ankle. That should help with the swelling, and I'll take you up on the ointment for the blisters that broke. I'd rather take my chances with swelling and infection than leave camp at dusk," Archie replied.

By the time they finished dinner, the sun had set. There was a little wind, and as soon as the sun went down, the temperature plummeted.

Melora retrieved her first aid kit and a bottle of water. She washed Archie's blisters, put ointment on them, and elevated the twisted ankle.

"I feel a little vulnerable like this. Hand me my rifle."

Ryan got up and handed Archie his rifle and threw a couple more logs on the fire.

"Don't we make a pair, a black eye, broken nose, raw blisters, and a sprained ankle," Ryan muttered.

"Sounds like you two should sleep first, you probably need it the most," Caleb said.

After enjoying the heat for a bit longer and discussing the plan for the next day, Archie and Ryan left the fire to try and get some rest. Fiona took Archie's rifle, and she, Caleb, and Melora spread out around camp.

Caleb stared out into the darkness toward the tree line. The longer he stared into the night, eyes diverted from the fire, the more his sight adjusted to the scant light. He spotted reddish-yellow orbs in the trees. The color could belong to a cougar, but from this distance a cat's eyes would be barely discernable, if at all. These eyes belonged to something much larger.

"Fi, Mel, come check this out."

The two women joined him.

"What do you think it is?" Melora asked after a couple minutes of staring into the darkness.

"I was hoping you'd tell me," Caleb replied.

"Well, the reddish-yellow lights are moving, so we know they belong to an animal. I spot six, so we've got three animals at least, more could be in the trees," Fiona said.

"Should we wake Ryan and Archie?" Melora asked.

"They just went down, let's wait a bit. We all need sleep, especially them. It's been a rough day. Go back to your posts and watch. I'll keep an eye on the eyes. If they vocalize or get any closer, we'll wake the others."

Caleb stared at the moving lights in the dark spaces between the trees until his eyes hurt. Occasionally, one set would disappear but would soon return. The animals were patient. For over an hour, they stayed together at the edge of the forest and made no move into the open meadow.

He was starting to get a sick sensation deep in his gut. He hoped an hour and a half of sleep would be enough to keep Archie going, but he'd feel more comfortable if Achie was awake and at the ready with his rifle.

"Hey, Fi, go ahead and wake Archie. We'll post him here, and if any of these animals expose themselves in the meadow, maybe he can get off a shot before they get close," Caleb said.

Five minutes later, Archie hobbled up with his rifle. After his eyes adjusted, he could make out the reddish-yellow orbs moving slowly through the trees. "Not loving this. What's the plan?"

"They'll disappear into the trees but aren't gone long before they reappear. They seem to be moving a little more, so I wanted you to be ready in case they lose patience and try to cross the meadow," Caleb replied.

"I can't stand all night with this bum ankle. Maybe grab a couple sleeping bags and roll one out so I can lay on my stomach. The other we'll leave rolled up to give me a shooting rest."

Caleb disappeared, leaving Archie to watch the eyes dancing through the trees. He returned a few minutes later with the requested items and helped Archie get comfortable.

"I don't know how long I can lay in this position, but I can watch them for a while. We've got a little moonlight keeping it from being a pitch-black night, but it would be tough shooting in this light, especially since whatever they are, they're nearly black. I can see the eyes and the shape of their enormous heads. It's something feline, but the rest of the body blends into the darkness," Archie explained as he trained his rifle scope on the animals.

"Enormous heads and freakishly large paw prints? Not a good combo," Caleb replied as he left Archie to find Fiona.

Caleb asked Fiona to wake Ryan and then try to get some sleep. He was no longer comfortable with sleeping two at a time. They probably still had at least six hours of darkness left, so that would give them each two hours if things stayed quiet.

With four of them now spread out, it would be more difficult for an animal to slip through undetected. Caleb continued to pace the width of his approximate zone until he heard Archie whistle. He quickly made his way over to him.

"One set of eyes disappeared about ten minutes ago and hasn't returned, and another just went dark," Archie reported.

"Keep an eye on the last one. I'll wake Fiona and throw some more wood on the fire. Most animals don't like fire, I hope this is like most animals," Caleb replied.

Caleb ducked his head under the tarp. "Sorry to wake you early, but we're missing two sets of eyes."

Fiona scrambled out of the sleeping bag and slipped on her shoes. She checked the safety on her sidearm and was just about ready to slide it in its holster when one of the horses let out a panicked neigh.

They both took off running toward the horses. Caleb yelled to Ryan and Archie to hold their positions.

"The last set of eyes disappeared," Archie shouted as Caleb and Fiona ran by.

"Keep watching anyway, and shoot anything that moves," Caleb replied.

By the time they reached the horses, all the animals were in full-blown panic. Caleb hoped they had secured them well enough so they couldn't break away. The horses would likely have no chance if they ran. A predator would give chase.

Felix was the closest. He was rearing up, trying to break free, so Fiona paused to try and calm him down. Caleb kept running. At least one horse was in immediate danger.

He pulled an arrow from his quiver as he ran. He could hear Melora and Fiona not far behind him. A deep, guttural roar reached his ears before he saw the beast, barely discernable in the faint light provided by the nearby fire. He wasn't sure what it was. It was some sort of cat, but unlike anything he'd seen in the wild or in any of his North American wildlife books.

A huge animal had Luna by the throat, and another had sunk its teeth into her flank. She kicked, fought, and vocalized her terror. Caleb, Fiona, and Melora yelled, but the animals didn't seem to notice, completely focused on the kill.

Caleb pulled up and shot at the animal whose jaw was

clenched on Luna's throat. With it flailing under Luna's desperate struggle, the arrow hit further back than he intended, embedding in the cat's hind quarter.

He pulled another arrow and let it fly. The arrow struck the shoulder and stuck into the bone, missing anything vital. The shot got the cat's attention, and it let go of Luna's throat and turned to face him. Caleb froze as he and the big cat stared each other down.

"Get back. You can't save her," Melora shouted from behind and to the side of Caleb.

Melora's voice broke through. He turned and ran. Shots rang out from Fiona's gun. He assumed she was shooting at the second animal clenched on Luna's flank. The boom of the shotgun discharged at close distance nearly deafened him. But the heavy footfalls kept coming. Another shot rang out just as Caleb was hit from behind by the massive creature.

The air was forced from his lungs as he slammed into the hard ground. Excruciating pain emanated from his lower back and down his thigh, stopping just short of the back of his knee.

He didn't move, his face plastered into the dirt as he heard Fiona fire several more times. When the shots stopped, he rolled over and sat up, gritting his teeth. He could see a massive, dark mound next to him.

"Are you okay?" Melora asked as she approached after quickly reloading her shotgun and verifying the animal was dead.

"Did Fiona get the other cat off of Luna in time?"

Melora shook her head. "Luna's alive, for the moment."

Caleb closed his eyes and thought about Ash. She loved the little mare.

Fiona approached. "I know I hit it a few times, but it

wouldn't let go of Luna's flank until Melora put down its partner. Between the dark night and black cat, I don't know how many times I hit it or if any of the shots might be fatal."

"Help me up," Caleb said as he extended both arms.

Melora and Fiona each took an arm and helped pull Caleb to his feet. He grimaced as he slowly stood. He stared down at the strange animal for only a moment, his chest heaving, and then made his way over to Luna.

"Oh my God, your jacket and your pants are shredded and covered with blood," Melora said as he walked away.

"Are you sure you're alright?" Fiona asked.

"I think so. It felt like it's claws just grazed me, but the hit knocked the wind out of me."

"What's happening over there?" Archie yelled.

"Tell Ryan to keep patrolling and then go relieve Archie. If he's still lying on his stomach, he's probably lost all feeling in his legs. Send him this way," Caleb said to Melora.

Melora jogged off to get Archie. Fiona joined Caleb next to Luna. Caleb pulled a flashlight out of his pocket and ran the beam across the mare's neck and flank. With each gasping breath, blood shot out of a hole in her neck. He had no idea how she was still standing.

"Ash will be devastated. She loves this horse," Caleb said as he ran his hand down her neck and spoke softly to her, trying to calm her down. He untied the lead rope from the tree. "See to the others."

Fiona nodded and walked to the next closest horse. Thankfully, it was June. If it was Felix or one of the geldings, it would have broken free and been chased down as prey.

"What happened?" Archie asked as he hobbled

quickly to Caleb's side, glancing only briefly at the large, dark, mound on the ground as he passed by.

Archie stopped next to Caleb and shone his light on the horse. "Do you want me to do it?"

Caleb shook his head, "No, but I could use your help if your ankle will hold up. Fiona, are the horses calm enough to move?"

"I think so."

"Help Fiona move the horses to the other side of camp so we don't get a stampede when I shoot. Fiona wounded one of the cats, but we don't know how bad, so keep an eye out for an angry predator. It and the third may still be out there, close by. Once the horses are secure, let me know."

As Archie and Fiona moved the horses, Caleb continued to comfort the little mare the best he could. She wanted to follow the rest of the horses, but when she took a step, she went down to her knees. Caleb urged her to the ground and onto her side. He spoke softly in her ear. By the time Archie returned, Luna was calm but taking shallow breaths.

Caleb looked up at Archie, and then back to Luna. Her eyes were closed. He placed the barrel of his 9mm in the middle of her forehead and pulled the trigger.

SIXTEEN

WITH TWO MASSIVE predators still out there, no one could sleep. They tossed more wood on the fire and spread out around the flames, trying to stay warm.

"We need to do something about your wounds," Melora said as she retrieved her small first aid kit and a bottle of water.

Caleb took the items from her hand. "Since you, Archie, and Fiona have the most fire power, Ryan can help me while you keep watch. Besides, the location of some of my wounds may show you more than you want to see."

"I doubt that," Melora and Fiona said in unison. They looked at each other, chuckled, and followed Archie away from the sleep shelter.

Caleb removed his jacket. It was ripped up pretty bad, but he spotted only a little blood on the inside, and it hadn't soaked through to the outside. He took off his shirt. The back was shredded and soaked with blood. He ripped the sleeves off since they were relatively clean and several strips from the front, and then tossed the rest in the fire, thankful he'd brought a spare.

"I don't know much about first aid," Ryan said, wincing at the sight of all the blood.

"We don't have much to work with, so it won't be too complicated," Caleb responded as he removed his boots and stripped down.

Ryan adjusted his headlamp and looked at Caleb's backside. "Holy cow! What do I do?"

"Pour water over the cuts to wash them up as good as you can. Then tell me what you see."

Caleb flinched as Ryan slowly poured water down his back, over his buttock, and down his leg. Ryan then dapped at the wounds with a rag torn from Caleb's destroyed shirt until the cuts and punctures were mostly dry.

"The ones on your back aren't deep and have already quit bleeding. There are four, closely-spaced, deep wounds on your butt that look more like punctures than scratches and three gashes on your upper thigh. All those are still oozing blood," Ryan said as he pressed a cloth over each group of wounds.

Caleb groaned, partially from pain but also from the thought of Ash seeing the new wounds, assuming they made it out of here alive.

"Lay down on your stomach on your sleeping bag," Ryan said.

Caleb dropped to his knees and then laid down as Ryan suggested.

"Can you reach back and keep pressure on this rag while I see what's in the first aid kit?"

"How's it going over there?" Melora called out.

"I've cleaned the punctures and scratches. Some won't stop bleeding. We got pressure on them now," Ryan replied.

"Put the last of the antibiotic ointment on the wounds,

starting with the deepest. There should be some closure strips in the first aid kit that you can use to close up the bleeders," Melora said.

Ryan found the items. He did as Melora instructed and then used the sleeve torn from Caleb's ruined shirt to secure a gauze pad over the wound-closure strips on his thigh.

"Everything looks pretty good, but if the closure strips on your butt cheek fall off and you start to bleed, I'm not sure what we can do about that. It would be difficult to wrap," Ryan said.

"Let's start with not talking about wounds on my ass," Caleb grumbled.

With Ryan's help, Caleb struggled to his feet. He had a clean shirt in his saddlebags, which he put on. He donned his jacket. The back was shredded, but free of visible blood on the outside. He hadn't brought spare pants, so he put the bloodied and torn pants back on.

He had just finished buckling his belt and securing his gun in its holster when Melora returned.

"Sorry, there's not much left in here," Ryan said as he handed her the depleted first aid kit.

"I hope Fiona still has some ointment, and this isn't too outdated to be effective. If I had any idea anyone would come into contact with claws, I wouldn't have used up a packet on Archie's blisters," Melora said as she stowed the kit.

Caleb grimaced as he took a step. His back tingled, but the pain in his buttock and thigh nearly sent him to the ground.

"Do you need to sit and rest for a while?" she asked.

"No," he blurted out more forcefully than he intended.

"Geez, sorry for wanting to help," Melora mumbled.

"I mean, I couldn't sit even if I wanted to. It hurts like

hell, and I feel like predator bait with my pants soaked with blood, but I'll live."

"I hope so or Ash will kill the rest of us," Melora replied.

Caleb, Ryan, and Melora re-joined the camp patrol. Even though the rest of the night was uneventful, they were all relieved when the sun finally rose over the trees. In the daylight, they could see across the meadow in all directions. They spotted nothing and felt relatively safe for the moment.

"With those nearly black coats, they're hard to see at night, but they'll be easier to spot in the daylight," Fiona said as they walked to where the dead cat and Luna lay on the ground.

"Any ideas what it is?" Caleb asked.

"It kind of looks like a jaguar. They usually have pale yellow to tan fur covered by spots that transition to black rosettes, but this animal also has faint stripes. In rare instances, jaguars can have a melanistic black coat, which I'm assuming that's what we have here, even though some of the fur has a brownish-orange tint to it. I think finding three, melanistic, black jaguars together would be extremely rare, especially at this latitude. Their normal range has traditionally been Central America, Mexico, and occasionally they've been spotted in the far southern part of the U.S., and I'm pretty certain they don't get this big. I believe adults are about six to eight feet from nose to tail and generally less than three hundred pounds. I'd bet this one is around nine feet from nose to tail, weighs over four hundred pounds, and stands four feet high at the shoulders," Melora said.

"I saw a jaguar along with a number of other exotic wild cats in a zoo once when I was a kid. I remember the jaguar as kind of an orangish-yellow with black rosette-type spots, but it was about half this size," Fiona added.

"I never made it to a zoo. There weren't many left when I was young since most had been shut down decades earlier after hundreds of animals escaped from coastal zoos when the sea level rose, inundating cities and forcing large areas, including zoos, to be abandoned," Melora said.

"The zoo I went to was one of the last still functioning in the country. I went there when my family was visiting relatives in Nebraska. I sure hope my folks made it there and are safe," Fiona said, suddenly overcome with emotion.

"I'm sure they are," Melora replied as she squeezed Fiona's shoulder.

Sometimes Caleb forgot that Fiona was one of the few residents who left family behind who were now trapped in a country in crisis. "I'm sorry," was all he could think of to say.

Fiona nodded. "Aside from the color and size, it seems like there are other characteristics that are off, but it was a long time ago, and I didn't spend a lot of time viewing the non-native big cats. I was more curious about the wildlife I might encounter in our area."

"Maybe they've gotten really big since they have larger prey like elk, moose, and deer in the mountains here. I suppose it's possible the greyish-black coats helped them blend in at night or while in dark pine forests. If it weren't for their eyes, they'd be nearly impossible to spot. The melanistic cats would have had a much better chance of making the long journey north without being spotted than orangish-yellow cats," Caleb pondered.

"Until we determine otherwise, I guess we'll assume

they are some sort of mutated or hybrid melanistic jaguar," Melora said.

Fiona pulled out her phone and took photos of the dead animal while everyone else continued to stare in disbelief.

"What should we do about Luna?" Ryan finally asked, breaking the silence.

Caleb looked over at Ash's favorite horse. He would have been sad if any of the horses were injured or killed, but Luna was special. He stared at her and the jaguar for several minutes before looking up and meeting the gazes of his companions.

"I hate saying everything I'm about to say, but I think we spend another night here."

"You've got to be kidding," Ryan gasped. "We should ditch the meat and ride as fast as we can for Beartooth."

"First of all, I don't think I'm sitting in a saddle anytime soon, so I won't be riding anywhere. But what I fear is that the remaining two jaguars may follow us home. They clearly trailed us all day yesterday. We can't lead two oversized predators to our community where the only sources of food are livestock and people," Caleb replied.

Ryan looked like he might get sick, Archie exhaled loudly as if accepting the logic, and Fiona stared at the dead predator on the ground, shaking her head.

"So, what's the plan?" Melora asked.

"I'm open to suggestions. All I know is we can't lead the cats back to Beartooth," Caleb replied.

"My first two shots hit the second cat, and it barely flinched. I fired a couple of more times, and it still got away. Granted, it was really dark out, and I was shooting at a black object that was getting flung around by a frantic black horse, but I know a few shots connected. Caleb hit the one latched onto Luna's neck twice, and it still took both barrels of Melora's shotgun to bring it down," Fiona said.

"They were both bad shots," Caleb admitted.

"My hunting rifle has more stopping power than a shotgun and accuracy at greater distances so how do I get a clean shot?" Archie asked.

"We haven't seen any game around here, so I doubt they went far. I'll be surprised if they don't come back tonight in search of food. They found meat but went hungry. Somehow, we need to ensure their only meal option is a dead horse or their fallen comrade, so they don't go after the rest of the horses or us," Caleb said.

"If we could drag the carcasses into the meadow, maybe we could lure them to a place and distance where our chances of a kill shot are vastly improved over last night. We could build multiple fires, creating a ring of flames around the horses in order to protect them better. If we place the bait at the right distance in the meadow, maybe we could take the cats out when they're feeding in the open," Archie offered.

"At what distance are you accurate?" Caleb asked.

"I'm pretty accurate up to a couple hundred yards with a lot smaller target than those monsters, though closer would be better, especially in low light," Archie replied as he glanced over at Melora.

"Seventy-five yards would be pushing it with my twelve-gauge, fifty would be more realistic," Melora added.

"If both cats come in on the carcasses, we'll have one chance to take them out. If one shot misses, they'll bolt. Unless anyone can come up with a better plan, let's build a shooting platform for Melora and Archie and gather a lot of firewood."

Caleb studied his companions as they all mulled over the plan. If Archie or Melora missed, hopefully they'd still take out one of the big cats, which would be better than nothing, but he still wouldn't feel comfortable heading home. Since he didn't have a better idea at the moment, they'd just have to cross that bridge if it came.

They spent the rest of the day preparing. Melora and Archie scanned the aspen grove and located a place facing the forest that would provide a slightly elevated perch to enable them to see the meadow better. About twenty yards behind that vantage point was a cluster of sturdy aspen trees where they would secure the horses before nightfall.

While Archie and Melora arranged sleeping bags to create a comfortable place to wait and a shooting platform, the others gathered firewood. They stacked the wood in five locations which would create a semi-circle of fires behind Archie and Melora and around the far side of the horses, basically corralling the horses in a ring of fire.

Ryan and Fiona would position themselves to the sides of Archie and Melora, where they could ensure nothing approached from the sides, and they'd be able to tend two of the fires. Caleb would be at the opposite side of the semi-circle as Archie and Melora to make sure nothing sneaked up on them or the horses from behind. He could also feed the remaining fires as needed.

The last task was the one they were all dreading. Caleb saddled Felix with the old, heavy-duty, roping saddle that he usually used. They secured a rope around the dead jaguar, and he dragged it out into the meadow where Archie indicated. As much as Felix strained to get the job done, Caleb figured Melora's estimate of about four hundred pounds might be a little light.

None of them could bear the thought of the predators

feeding on Luna while looking like Luna, so they removed the hind quarters and moved them to the meadow for additional bait in case the cats were reluctant to feed on their own. They dragged the rest of her into a low spot and spent hours carrying rocks to cover the remains of the beloved horse.

By the time Luna was buried under a mound of rocks, they were all emotionally and physically drained. Nightfall was still hours away, and since the predators had yet to show themselves in the daylight, they decided to try and sleep in shifts. Archie, Caleb, and Fiona slept first. After two and a half hours, Ryan woke them up, and he and Melora settled down to rest.

As Caleb paced the perimeter of camp, all he could think about was Ash and Sara. He prayed they would survive the night, and he would find his way home to his family.

SEVENTEEN

BY THE TIME Ash dropped Sara off with her grandparents and Dillon and Miranda helped her carry the spare archery equipment to the range, a crowd had already gathered.

"Wow, I didn't expect such a turnout," Ash said.

"Beth needed a break. The boys miss their dad, and she's worried sick about Archie, so I brought my nephews along with my daughter. The kids haven't shot much, but they have mine and Archie's hand-me-down bows. Dad started us out young," Dennis said.

"When Evelyn suggested I organize this activity, I was thrilled. I needed something to think about other than Caleb's safety. Apparently, we all need a distraction," Ash replied.

"Everyone's worried. The hunting trip has made me realize that I need to brush up on my skills. I haven't wanted to get back out there since Dad's accident, but I need to step up. I can't leave it all to my brother and others," Dennis added.

Ash spotted Dillon helping Evelyn get situated on a

log away from the targets. He leaned over and kissed her, and she smiled up at him with such love and adoration that it melted Ash's heart. With Evelyn's visual impairment, life was tougher for her than most living on this remote, rugged mountain with few flat surfaces and no access to vision care.

"Ready whenever you are," Dillon said as he joined Ash.

"Since we have such a wide range of ages and abilities, let's divide up into three groups. I'll take everyone ten and under with me. We'll head back closer to the community, where it'll be safer for our lessons, and the targets are closer together. Anyone who has shot before but could use more training, go with Dillon. Those who mostly came to knock the rust off and practice, go with Dennis," Ash explained.

Dennis headed for the targets set up furthest away. Miranda, Gavin and Aiden Winters, Gabe Phillips, and Sam Ferguson went with him. Zane Ferguson, Lauren Adler, Jacob Thorn, Joy Garland, and Daniel Gallegos followed Dillon.

"Are you good here or would you like to help me with the little ones," Ash asked Evelyn.

"I'd love to help if there is something I can do," Evelyn replied.

"There's plenty, and I have an idea to run by you when we get to the targets."

Evelyn called to Dillon to let him know that she was going with Ash. They made their way toward the residential area with the children ranging in age from six to ten.

"I was wondering if you want to learn to shoot," Ash said.

"How can I shoot? I can barely see my hand in front of my face."

"I've noticed that you are very good at honing in on sounds. When Dillon calls to you, you always walk straight toward him, even when he's far enough away that I'm sure you can't see him."

"As my sight has worsened, I've relied more on other senses, especially hearing."

"I'm not sure what we could use for a sound device yet, I just came up with the idea a few days ago. Anyway, I thought we could place a noisemaker right behind the target and see if you can hit it that way. If you could get proficient with that, you might be able to shoot something that made noise like a turkey or rattlesnake, but mostly I think it might be fun."

"That would be exciting. I've felt so left out most of my childhood. Dillon has introduced me to so many new things that my folks would have never allowed. I'm game to try anything."

When they reached the spot Ash had in mind, she gathered the kids and Evelyn around her. She and Evelyn helped the kids put on their arm guards and shooting gloves. Ash explained the equipment, how it was used, and then demonstrated the process. She helped each child pull the bow string back and ease it forward, like Caleb did for her when he taught her to shoot.

They practiced the motion until Ash felt comfortable the kids understood. Once they learned how to stand, nock an arrow, and aim, they took turns shooting at a target ten yards away. Ash was surprised how quickly they caught on. More importantly, the kids were having fun.

Before long, the adults wandered in their direction. Dennis took his daughter and nephews and left, and others escorted the rest of the children home.

"We'll drop this stuff off at your cabin. I'll see you at

Mom and Dad's when you pick up Sara," Miranda said as she, Zane, and Lauren grabbed the extra archery equipment.

"What are you doing?" Dillon asked Evelyn.

"I followed along with the kids as Ash taught them to shoot until we got to the actual shooting part. She thinks that we might be able to put some kind of noise maker behind the target, and I can hone in on that and actually shoot."

Ash hoped she hadn't gotten Evelyn's hopes up for nothing. She sounded so excited to be included.

"Come stand here," Dillon said as he grabbed a small bow, walked up behind Evelyn, and put his arms around her.

He placed his hand on the bow below hers to help steady the bow. He then nocked an arrow and helped her place her fingers in the correct spot to pull back.

"Now pull the string back to the corner of your mouth. I'll help you aim," Dillon said as he helped Evelyn line up her arrow with a target she couldn't see.

"Release. How did that feel?"

"Amazing, did I hit it?"

"Let's go see." Dillon handed the bow to Ash and winked.

The three of them walked up to the target and found the arrow stuck in the outer edge. Dillon guided her hand to the arrow so she could feel it.

"I think Ash's idea might work," Dillon said.

"I hope so. It would be a lot of fun if I could tag along and actually participate when you all go practice."

"I just love having you with me, whether you shoot or not," Dillon replied.

Evelyn smiled up at Dillon, stood up on her tiptoes, and kissed him.

"Need any help before we head home?" Dillon asked.

"Nope, we've been leaving the targets set up. The only equipment left, other than my own, is Evelyn's."

Evelyn thanked Ash for the lessons, and she and Dillon left, hand-in-hand, for home.

Seeing them like that made Ash happy, but it made her miss Caleb all the more. Dillon was three years younger than Caleb, but the brothers shared a lot of physical traits. Both were over six feet tall and of similar build, though Dillon outweighed Caleb by probably ten pounds. Both had dark brown hair, olive complexions, hazel eyes, and wonderful smiles. Both were strong and reliable, but Dillon was not adventurous like Caleb. Caleb loved exploring, and Dillon was happy to stay close to Beartooth and the farm. Caleb helped with the farm, but being tied down to it would have bored him to death.

There were other differences between the brothers. Dillon always kept his hair much shorter, he liked to joke, and they had different mannerisms. Miranda was obviously a Solomon, but her hair was much lighter, her features softer, and her eyes darker than her brothers'. And, while the brothers didn't ruffle easily, Miranda was prone to melodrama.

Thinking about Caleb's adventurous spirit, which often led to somewhat reckless behavior, made fear for his safety surge to the surface. He had been gone for four days and three nights. They all knew that the group would have to travel further than they ever had before in pursuit of the herds, but she had desperately hoped he would be home by now.

She tried to shake off the bad feeling in her gut. Sara was so young, but she was perceptive. If Ash didn't hide her worry well, she had no doubt their daughter would sense it.

EIGHTEEN

THE SUN WAS STARTING to set. Caleb woke Ryan and Melora while Archie and Fiona brought the horses in close to camp. They had heard nothing all day from the remaining jaguar-type predators, but Caleb suspected that would soon change.

After a simple dinner, the group lit five fires and took up their positions. The fires helped keep the cold at bay, and they hoped the flames would discourage the massive cats from coming into camp for the horses.

Despite little sleep, they were alert and ready, and the moon illuminated the meadow just enough to give the shooters a decent view of the bait. Caleb paced along the outside perimeter of his assigned section of the half-circle. Archie and Melora had to move around some to keep from cramping up but didn't venture far from their shooting platforms. Ryan and Fiona guarded their flanks.

Three hours passed without any sign of the big cats. Caleb had felt certain they would return with the lure of meat but was starting to have doubts. They didn't have a

Plan B, so they'd stay the course until something happened or morning came, whichever came first.

"We have two pairs of eyes in the trees. They're hunkered down together at the edge of the forest, watching," Archie reported.

Caleb, Ryan, and Fiona threw more wood on the fires. Caleb hated the waiting but they had to be patient. Archie watched through the scope of his rifle and would provide them with updates. Until the animals made a move, there was nothing more they could do.

"One will disappear into the trees for a few minutes and then return. They seem to be losing their patience," Archie said.

Caleb wasn't sure if that was good news or bad. The previous night, when the predators started the retreat and return behavior, two of the three eventually found a way to flank them and get to Luna. They couldn't afford another loss, but they needed to lure the animals out of the trees. Hopefully, the prospect of an easy meal would make them less cautious.

"One set of eyes has disappeared. The other is crouched low and slinking toward the bait."

Adrenaline coursed through Caleb's veins. He quickened his pace, not wanting any part of his zone to be unwatched for any longer than necessary.

"It's risen up, and it's stalking toward the meat cautiously. The big cat is about halfway between the forest and the bait and has a limp. It must be the one Fiona injured, so it's probably more desperate for an easy meal," Archie relayed.

Caleb wished the uninjured jaguar would show itself. Not knowing its whereabouts was concerning.

"The jaguar is crouched on the ground behind the bait, tearing off chunks of meat. It's keeping its body low behind the dead jaguar, so I can't get a good shot," Archie said.

"Keep waiting for the other to show. If you shoot now, we'll have no chance of luring the other out," Caleb replied.

They continued to wait, tension rippling through the air. If they waited much longer the injured cat might eat its fill and leave.

"We're in luck. The other has just reappeared about thirty yards south of where he was originally. Looks like he's heading in the direction of his buddy," Archie reported.

Caleb knew that it was about to get exciting when a terrifying roar pierced the night.

"Apparently, the first doesn't want to share. It's up, looking ready to fight," Archie said.

Both cats vocalized, sending bold and terrifying sounds into the darkness. Neither appeared willing to share the prize.

The noise sent chills racing up Caleb's arms. It was so unnatural for the area and more menacing than anything he'd ever heard before. If the huge animals were willing to turn on each other for the meat and feed on their own kind, he had no doubt they would welcome a chance to dine on a warm-blooded human.

"We don't have great shots, and they're moving. I think it's now or never. If one chases the other off, we may not get another chance," Archie said.

No sooner had the words reached Caleb's ears, than two shots rang out simultaneously. In the still night, sound carried well. Caleb heard the action of Archie ejecting the used shell and jacking another into the chamber, followed by another blast.

"The injured one is down, but the other fled. I'm pretty

sure I hit it, but if I did, it apparently wasn't a solid kill shot," Archie shouted to the group.

Caleb knew Archie and Melora had done their best, but he had hoped to end the threat tonight. He wanted nothing more than to go home to Ash and Sara, but he feared leading danger back to the community and his family.

They held their positions, kept feeding the fire, and waited until the sun slowly rose above the trees. Caleb finally left his post and called the group together.

"We likely have an injured animal. It may be in self-preservation mode and is long gone, or it may stay and fight. I wish I knew what to expect," Caleb said.

"What do we do now?" Ryan asked, rubbing his cold hands together and blowing on them for warmth.

Caleb thought for a moment. He looked around at the group. They couldn't stay out here forever. They had no idea if the third cat was even still in the area. He knew everyone was just as anxious to go home as him.

"Let the fires die. I guess we might as well eat some breakfast and break camp. I doubt the jaguar will come back again, at least not until dark. I don't see the point in sitting around for another day. Let's just pray it was hit bad enough to succumb to its injuries," Caleb replied.

After packing up camp, they led the horses into the meadow. An examination of the carcass revealed multiple injuries. Fiona had apparently connected a number of times in the front shoulder the night before, but none of her shots were fatal. Archie's first shot in its chest had finished the job. Melora had attempted a head-on shot at the other beast since that's all the second cat gave her. She didn't know if she connected. Archie also took a shot, but the animal had already turned to flee.

As they studied the area around the carnage, Caleb

located a blood trail leaving the scene. After seeing all they cared to and taking more pictures of the unusual animal, they followed the trail from the meadow to the trees. It led to where they had hung the elk and deer the day before. The area around the base of the trees was packed down with huge paw prints, and claw marks marred the bark about eight feet up the trunk.

"Maybe they're too heavy to climb," Melora observed.

"Even if they could climb that high, the branches we hung the meat on wouldn't have held their weight, and maybe they sensed that," Archie added.

"It's losing a lot of blood. It might die from the gunshot, but I'd like to be sure. I want to track it, but that would mean splitting up. Five people and eight horses couldn't sneak up on anything," Caleb said.

Caleb looked around at the group. Ryan's eye seemed to be getting blacker and, despite Melora's effort to straighten his nose, it was crooked. Between the blisters and sprained ankle, Archie would have a difficult enough time making it home on foot much less going after an injured predator. And his entire backside throbbed. He believed he could walk all he needed to, but encountering a huge, hungry cat with dried blood covering half of the back of one pant leg didn't sound like a great idea.

"We have a few possible scenarios here. The jaguar will wait until we leave and come back to feed on its buddies. But eventually it will need to find new prey, and it could probably follow our trail back to Beartooth even after a few days. It might just follow us right out of the gate. Or, if we're lucky, it could succumb to its injuries," Melora explained.

"I'm not feeling very lucky," Fiona muttered.

"Me neither. If Caleb's leg will hold up, I suggest we leave Ryan and Archie here with the horses. If the cat shows up, Archie can handle one in the daylight with his rifle, and Ryan still has my 9mm for backup if needed. The three of us can go on the offensive," Melora said.

"I can walk, and if we're trying to attract a predator, the large amount of blood soaked into my pants isn't an issue," Caleb replied.

They secured the horses to a trio of sturdy pines. Caleb rolled a log into a position where if Archie and Ryan sat down back-to-back, facing opposite directions, it would be difficult for anything to sneak up on them.

"There isn't a lot of battery left on the radios, but hopefully enough where you can call us if the injured cat shows up," Melora said.

She handed Ryan her radio and a box of ammunition for her gun that he still carried. Without further discussion, the trio walked away, leaving Archie and Ryan to guard the horses in case the huge predator returned.

NINETEEN

AFTER THIRTY MINUTES of following the blood trail, they reached a drainage filled with large irregular rocks and a few rounded boulders. They picked their way to the bottom, which was covered with brush and smaller rocks.

"It's getting tougher to follow the trail in this brush," Caleb said as he knelt down to study a large drop of blood soaked into the dirt.

Fiona and Melora knelt down next to him and looked at the spot of blood.

"The trail disappears at this fork in the ravine. The jaguar could have gone either direction or maybe even climbed back out," Melora replied.

They fanned out. Caleb took the left fork, and Melora took the right. Fiona climbed over a couple boulders until she was fifteen feet above the bottom of the drainage in order to give her a better view of the area.

Caleb stopped and turned back toward Fiona. He didn't like her position. There were too many places for a big cat to hide.

As he studied the terrain on the opposite side of the drainage, a rock rolled down the steep slope behind Fiona. He looked in the direction of the noise and saw Fiona pull her gun from her holster and slowly turn.

Caleb froze in place, holding his breath. For a moment neither Fiona nor the beast moved or made a sound.

Chills ran down Caleb's spine as a rumble deep in the huge cat's chest resonated, followed by a growl and roar that exposed fangs at least three inches long. He pulled an arrow from his quiver and snapped the nock onto the string, but he knew he was too far away to do much damage.

The sounds from the jaguar echoed between the ravine's steep walls. He could hear Melora's footsteps racing toward him as he backtracked to where the ravine forked.

He saw Fiona aim, but she hesitated. Not only would an accurate, head-on shot uphill be difficult, they already learned that the 9mm didn't have enough power to bring the massive predators down, though this one had lost a lot of blood and might be weakened.

"I sure hope Melora gets in range soon with her shotgun, but I'll shoot if it moves," Fiona called out without taking her eyes off the beast.

For a terrifying moment, woman and predator stared at each other, neither backing down. After several seconds, the jaguar let out another threatening roar and leapt.

Fiona pulled the trigger multiple times, but it kept coming. She dove off to the side just as the jaguar reached the spot where she had been standing. She landed hard on her shoulder on a rock. She bounced and rolled until she came to rest at the bottom of the ravine with the cat not far behind her.

"Stay down," Caleb shouted as he and Melora closed the distance between them and the rapidly advancing jaguar.

Melora stopped, took a wide stance, and fired. She fired again, and the animal crumpled to the ground.

"Are you okay?" Caleb asked as he reached Fiona's side.

"I might have broken my arm, and I definitely dislocated my shoulder. I nearly blacked out from the pain in my left arm and shoulder when I hit the boulder. Did Melora get it?"

"Probably, she's checking to make sure it's dead."

"Help me up, just don't touch my left side."

Caleb extended a hand and helped her to her feet. He slipped his arm around her waist and kept a hold of her as they made their way to Melora, still standing over the corpse.

"I've never seen a wild cat with five fully formed toes. Some species have four toes and a fifth dewclaw, but this is different," Melora pondered.

"I can't believe it's over, and we can go home," Fiona gasped through painful breaths.

"Unless there are others," Melora replied.

"Don't even say that out loud," Caleb added. "We can't take much more."

Fiona pulled her phone out of her pocket and took more photos, while Caleb knelt down and examined the animal.

"It's a male."

"Not surprised. Males are often larger than their female counterparts. This one probably outweighs the other two by nearly a hundred pounds," Melora said.

"So, we have a male and two females traveling together. Is, that common?" Caleb asked.

"I'm no jaguar expert, but I think they are usually solitary except to mate," Melora replied.

"Maybe another adaptation they've made in order to successfully migrate from the southern U.S. to the northern mountains."

"As fascinating as I find this wildlife biology discussion, we need to get back to Ryan and Archie, pack up the game, and get out of here. First though, I'm going to try and pop my shoulder back in, so if I pass out from extreme pain, do something," Fiona said.

Caleb cringed as he watched her lift her arm over her head, touch her hand to the bottom of her neck, reach over the opposite shoulder, and push down. She screamed out in agony.

"Did it work?" Melora asked.

"The shoulder popped back in, but I'm more confident now that I have a break in my forearm."

"I thought Ash was the toughest woman alive, but I may have to reassess," Caleb said as he shook his head.

"Thanks, but I'll be crying like a little girl if we don't get the arm splinted soon. Every movement I make hurts like heck," Fiona replied as they left the dead animal behind and headed back to Ryan and Archie.

The hike to where Archie and Ryan waited with the meat and horses went quickly since they weren't trying to be quiet, nor were they watching the ground for blood or tracks.

"We heard shots. Did you get it?" Ryan asked as they approached.

"Yes, but not without more injuries. Melora, check Archie's ankle and get a splint on Fiona's arm and Archie's ankle if needed. Ryan and I will lower the meat and start packing up," Caleb replied.

By the time Caleb and Ryan got the meat out of the

trees, and saddles and pack trees on the horses, Archie and Fiona were patched up.

"We're short a horse, but all Luna was carrying were the antlers and hides. All of the horses could pack a little more. We could leave the hides, antlers, and a little meat to free up a horse for Archie or Fiona to ride," Caleb offered.

"The arm is secure now, so I'm good to walk. In fact, walking would be smoother than riding, and it would be difficult to get on anyway," Fiona replied.

"The splint is allowing me to put weight on the ankle. I'll give it a try and let you know if I can't handle the pain," Archie added.

"What about your thigh?" Melora asked.

"It hurts, but I don't think any of the cuts were deep enough to damage the muscle, and sitting in a saddle is out of the question," Caleb replied.

Melora took out the map and GPS and determined where they were and which direction they needed to travel.

"It's almost noon already, but I say we walk for a few hours, take a late lunch break, and try to put another four or five hours in this afternoon if our bodies hold up," Caleb said.

They all nodded. Melora took the lead since she had the best idea on which way they needed to go. Caleb fell in line last so he could keep an eye on everyone and make sure no one fell behind.

As they started walking, Caleb didn't look back. He had no desire to ever see the area again that had haunted them for two nights.

TWENTY

ASH WOKE up early with an idea on how to help Evelyn shoot a bow. Not only was Diane Garland an amazing potter and painter, but she had also given guitar lessons before coming to Beartooth. She played for the community occasionally and gave lessons until she was down to her last guitar string. Ash thought she might have a metronome they could borrow.

After she showered and dressed for the day, she peeked in on her daughter. Sara looked like an angel, sleeping soundly in her crib with a faint smile on her tiny lips. Ash adjusted her blanket and quietly left the room.

Ash heard a light tap on the door. She walked over and opened it to find Miranda on the other side.

"Sorry I'm so early, but I couldn't sleep. I'm worried sick about Ryan and Caleb. They've never been gone this long. Should we try to organize some sort of search party?"

"I'm worried too, but we don't have any idea where they went in search of the herds. It would be foolish to go after them," Ash replied as she put a kettle of water on to heat.

"I figured you'd say that, but I was tired of hearing Mom and Dad tell me the same thing. I hoped you had an answer I liked better."

"Sorry, I wish I did."

When Sara called out, Miranda followed Ash into the toddler's room. Sara smiled when she saw her aunt. Miranda plucked her out of her crib and cuddled her.

Ash was happy for the distraction. She was so worried about Caleb and missed him so much her heart ached, making it difficult to console Miranda. She tried to put on a brave front, but she was barely holding it together.

"Do you think Diane is up for visitors? I was hoping she had a metronome I could borrow to possibly help Evelyn learn how to shoot, but I hated to go over there just to ask her for a favor when she's been so sick."

"She's doing much better, so probably wouldn't mind visitors, but I'm going over there after I leave here. I can ask about a metronome then. I haven't looked in on her in days and thought I should see if she's still heading in the right direction."

"That would be wonderful. Thanks. Do you have time for tea?" Ash asked as she took Sara, gave her a hug and kiss, set her on her feet, and watched as she toddled out of her room, clutching her stuffed bee.

Miranda stayed for tea, but neither could think of anything positive to talk about. It was difficult to focus on anything except how long Caleb and Ryan had been gone.

After Miranda left, Ash bundled Sara up, grabbed an empty canvas bag, and went outside. She checked the thermometer at the back of the cabin. It read forty-two. She looked at the minimum overnight reading and was pleased to see it had stayed above freezing for the third consecutive night.

As Ash and Sara walked toward the storehouse, Beth Craig fell into step alongside them.

"Thanks for working with the kids yesterday. The archery clinic helped to take their mind off Archie for a few hours and allowed me time alone to cry. Evelyn and Gretchen have done a great job keeping the kids busy at school, but I knew the weekend would be difficult," Beth said.

"I wonder if I could join Gretchen's class. I really could use something to take my mind off of Caleb and the rest of the group."

Beth chuckled. "The only thing holding me together is the kids. I have to project a calm, confident, worry-free attitude for them."

"Sara is young, but she can sense it when I'm sad, mad, or scared, so I'm trying to act like everything is normal."

Beth nodded, and they walked the rest of the way to the storehouse in silence. Tony was busy rearranging stock in the coolers when they entered. He stopped and helped Ash load dried beans, cornmeal, oats, eggs, and a small serving of pork into her bag. She said goodbye to Tony and Beth and left.

After putting away her food and getting Sara down for a nap, Ash positioned herself in front of the radio. She quickly found a broadcast in progress. The reception was much clearer than it had been the last time she caught the station on-air.

"Due to the severe damage inflicted on the capital during the multinational bombing campaign, followed by nearly six inches of volcanic ash falling on the city, President Steele has moved the nation's capital to Oklahoma City," the newsreader stated.

After only five minutes the broadcast ended with a promise to broadcast daily. The newsreader suggested listeners check back frequently since there were rumors President Steele was planning to unveil a new program to address multiple concerns plaguing the country.

When Sara woke up, Ash dressed her warmly, and they went outside. Before they got off the porch, they saw Miranda approaching.

"Diane had a metronome and was happy to lend it out. She said not to worry about it if it gets broken when I explained why you wanted it." Miranda handed the device to Ash and picked up Sara.

"How's Diane doing?"

"She's on the road to recovery. I was a little nervous early on that she might not make it, but her lungs sounded much better today."

"That's a huge relief," Ash said.

They sat down on the porch and Miranda bounced Sara up and down on her knee. Sara giggled and kept asking for more. It warmed Ash's heart to hear her little girl laugh.

"So, how's the metronome going to help Evelyn shoot?" Miranda asked.

"If it's ticking behind a close target, maybe Evelyn could aim at the noise rather than the physical target. I hope it works because she was so excited by the idea."

"That would be cool. I've grown to really like her. I never had any doubt about you and Caleb, but I worried about Dillon finding someone. I can't help feeling very protective of my older brothers, but I'm happy about how everything has worked out."

"Me too. I adore Evelyn now. There was a time when I

thought she had her sights set on Caleb so I didn't like her very much, but apparently, I misread the situation, and she was always interested in Dillon."

Miranda laughed. "I can't believe you ever had doubts about Caleb. It's you, and it always has been."

"Yeah, he tells me that a lot, and I feel the same way," Ash replied as a tear slid down her cheek.

"He'll come home," Miranda said as she stood to leave.

"And so will Ryan," Ash added, while forcing a weak smile.

Miranda set Sara down, and Ash took her hand to keep the toddler from wandering off.

"I was pleased when Caleb and Ryan started doing things together. I don't know who wanted Caleb's approval more, me or Ryan. Nothing made me happier than my brother and the love of my life spending time with each other, but I never envisioned then that they would go to Pryor together and now this. I try not to think about how much I could lose if something bad happened, but it's hard not to."

Ash turned and pulled Miranda into a one-armed hug. "I'm sorry. I've been so consumed with my own worry that I didn't realize how much worse it is for you."

"Worry is worry, no one's is better or worse than the other," Miranda said.

Sara let go of Ash's hand and wrapped her tiny arms around Ash and Miranda's legs. Ash looked down and smiled at her precious little girl.

"A lot of us in Beartooth are worried, but we can't forget about how many blessings we still have in our midst," Ash said as she glanced down.

Ash let go of Miranda and picked Sara up. Miranda kissed her niece on the cheek and left.

TWENTY-ONE

BY THE TIME they stopped for the night, Melora figured they had traveled ten miles, but were still fifteen from home. Due to the terrain and injuries, the going had been slow all day.

Everyone in their group, except for Melora, was nursing an injury of some sort. But they needed to remain cautious, which meant they had more work to do before they could call it a night.

Caleb, Ryan, and Melora hung the meat high in the trees a quarter mile from camp and tended the horses. Archie and Fiona gathered firewood, set up camp, and got a blazing fire going.

"Here's a chunk of elk. Sorry if I cut it wrong, but thought we'd all appreciate a little protein," Caleb said as he handed Archie a chunk of raw meat.

Melora stood by the fire, rubbing her hands together. "I'd complain about the cold, but we need it to keep the meat from going bad until we get home, so I'll live with it."

"Agreed, I'd sure hate to lose any meat after everything we've gone through to get it," Caleb added as he rolled a log close to the fire and sat down near the end so that his injured side didn't touch the wood.

"How's everyone holding up?" Melora asked.

"My nose still hurts, and I'm afraid to see what my eye looks like, but I'm okay," Ryan replied.

"My back feels better. My butt and thigh still throb, but I'll live," Caleb added.

"As long as I don't jostle the arm, it doesn't hurt too bad, and the shoulder hasn't popped back out," Fiona said.

Melora chucked. "I feel a little guilty being the lone uninjured party member. Everyone back home will think I didn't pull my weight."

"Archie?" Caleb asked.

"I'd be lying if I said that hiking all day on uneven terrain didn't hurt like crazy. But I'm sure after a few hours of sleep, I'll be able to keep going in the morning."

As soon as the elk steaks were cooked, they ate. Fiona, Melora, and Ryan crowded together under the tarp to sleep. They had seen no sign of predators all day but were too nervous to leave the camp unattended.

After two hours, Archie switched places with Ryan, and two hours later Caleb woke Melora. He lay on his stomach on his bag and Melora threw hers on top of him to keep him warm as the night continued to cool. Despite being nervous about what else might be lurking in the forest and his uncomfortable position, Caleb was so exhausted that he quickly fell asleep.

———

They kept the fire going all night, and fortunately, nothing dangerous visited camp. They let Fiona sleep all night since she had the newest and worst injury. Everyone else got between two and four hours of sleep and felt rested enough to push on as the sun crested the mountain peaks.

After breakfast, they spread the map out and studied it.

"We're about here," Melora said as she pointed to a spot on the map.

"Some of these creeks, trailheads, and peaks are starting to sound familiar. I think if we follow this drainage we can reach this lake by noon. We can take a break there, and if all goes well, we might make it back to Beartooth by late afternoon," Caleb added.

"That's what I'm thinking. I hope our calculations are on target. I miss Tyler, and I'm sure he misses me more than he'll let on."

"I bet Beth is out of her mind with worry. Ash is a little more used to Caleb's adventures, but until the stratospheric aerosol injections began, our electricity system needed replaced, and a massive volcano erupted making life in Beartooth a lot more difficult, I was happy being a boring husband and dad," Archie said.

"Ash worries, she just tries not to let it show. I hate doing this to her. She is my world. I don't know if I could survive without her. And now there's Sara. I don't want to leave Ash alone with the sole responsibility for our little girl. Ash doesn't want Sara to grow up like her without a dad."

"I'm sure Miranda is beside herself with worry and letting everyone know about it. You may not know this, but she can be a little melodramatic," Ryan said.

Caleb burst out laughing. "A little? I hear that at one time, before the country fell apart, they used to give awards for Miranda's dramatic ability."

"But she can be strong too, and I love her a lot," Ryan added.

Caleb slapped him on the back. "Don't worry, I'll never tell her that you've noticed her flair for melodrama."

"Thanks," Ryan smiled sheepishly.

"I imagine Graham is a little concerned about me, but it isn't the same as having someone who loves you so much it hurts," Fiona added sadly.

"Maybe you need to put a little more effort into Jacob when we get back. It's obvious he's really into you, but you seem to be keeping him at arm's length," Melora said.

Fiona just nodded her head.

Hesitant to leave the warmth of the fire but anxious to get home, they broke camp and retrieved the horses. By the time they packed up and got on the trail, it was mid-morning. Despite the chill in the air and injuries all around, they set off at a strong pace.

"Your limp isn't too bad this morning," Caleb said.

"The thought of sleeping in my own bed tonight curled up with Beth is giving me a little more strength," Archie chuckled.

"Me too. I can handle anything, as long as I can make it home to Ash and Sara today."

"Hey, a little less talking and a lot more walking," Melora called from the front of the line. "I'm not slowing down. I'm going home today, with or without you."

Caleb couldn't help but smile. Melora would never leave anyone behind, but her tough talk was just what they needed. They were tired, injured, and morale was low, but her words made them all smile, and they picked up the pace.

TWENTY-TWO

ASH SLEPT VERY little and got up well before dawn. She stood on the porch, cradling a cup of hot tea in both hands. The temperature was only in the upper-thirties but it would hopefully reach fifty by afternoon.

Caleb and the others had now been gone for six days. It was the longest they had ever been apart. She prayed he was okay and would come home soon. He had been a part of her life ever since she could remember, and she couldn't imagine life without him.

"You're up early," Dan said as he walked up to the porch.

"I didn't sleep much."

"Too worried?"

Ash just nodded. "Can I get you some tea?"

"No thanks. I was just out walking to clear my head. Libby stayed with Beth and the grandkids last night. Beth is scared, and Libby thinks we should do something, but I don't know what."

"Miranda stopped by yesterday and suggested we organize a search party. I told her we have no idea where they went. We know the direction they were heading, but if they located the deer or elk herds, they could have followed them anywhere."

"And they took all but four of our horses with them. Star isn't broke, Misty is young and green, that leaves Ivy and Thor, who no one wants to ride. We can't mount much of a search party with one well-broke horse, one green-broke, and a cantankerous stud barely fit to ride."

Ash cracked the door to the cabin so she could hear Sara if she woke up and then returned to Dan.

"So, we just wait?" Ash asked.

"Unless you or anyone else has a better idea," Dan replied.

"Is it worth pulling the CLB together?"

"Couldn't hurt. I'll make the rounds and set something up for two this afternoon. Since school will still be in session and our group will be smaller than usual, let's meet at the mill."

Ash watched as Dan walked away. She continued to stand on the porch, staring to the north, willing Caleb to ride up. Nothing.

"Mama!"

The summons was a welcome interruption from her thoughts. She went back inside the cabin and retrieved her daughter. She pasted a smile on her face and cuddled her little girl.

"Where Daddy?"

Ash wasn't sure how to respond. Sara asked for Caleb many times each day, but it was getting harder to answer and sound like everything was fine.

"He went with our friends to get food for us and everyone in the community," Ash said with a comforting smile.

"I want Daddy." Sara buried her face in Ash's shoulder and cried.

"I want Daddy too. I'm sure he'll be home soon," Ash whispered as she stroked Sara's hair.

It didn't take long to divert Sara's attention. She was hungry, so breakfast distracted her. By the time Ash gave her a bath and got her ready for the day, Miranda showed up.

"Do you think you could watch Sara for a bit this afternoon. Dan has called a CLB meeting for two to talk about what, if anything, we can do."

"Absolutely, but the reason I'm here is that Mom asked me to come over and invite you to lunch. She's stress baking and needs someone to share the goodies with. Having you and Sara will perk her up, and then you can leave Sara there when it's time to go."

"Thank you. I wasn't sure how I was going to get through the day, so being around family will help."

"Does Dan have a plan?"

"No, but we thought it couldn't hurt to get the board together. Maybe someone will have an idea," Ash replied.

"I need to go check in with Emily. I'll see you at the farm later."

Ash and Sara walked Miranda out. Back inside the cabin, Ash played with Sara, washed dishes, and swept the floors. Sara hadn't been taking a mid-morning nap lately, but she was relieved when she did so today since Ash wanted to check for news on the radio.

They seldom turned the radio on when Sara was awake and in the room. It would be difficult to explain that there was a whole other world out there, full of hate and violence. To Sara, the world was no bigger than Beartooth, which in her eyes was a happy place full of love.

Ash placed the radio on the kitchen table and quickly found the broadcast. She sat close and kept the volume low.

"The President announced the rollout of her FOCUS initiative, which stands for Food, Oil, Climate, Unity, and Security. The FOCUS initiative will address the multitude of issues facing our country. She hopes the plan will ease tensions around the country and rebuild relationships with our neighbors. President Steele stated that she has negotiated a cease-fire with the multinational forces south of the border, contingent upon a deal with Canada to repair the rail destroyed by the annexed areas and the U.S. providing protection for food shipments from Canada to the southern border," the newsreader stated.

Ash found the information hopeful but couldn't take her mind off worrying about Caleb. She also wondered if the ambitious plan could possibly work and if the cease-fire would hold.

The newsreader then went on to explain that the President partially rescinded the Continuity in Crisis Bill, allowing states to hold elections to replace those senators and congressional representatives executed by the former President. However, she did not state when a new presidential election would be held, citing that trying to regain control of food distribution channels was the priority, and the next presidential election would be addressed once people were no longer starving or being killed in the streets.

The broadcast abruptly ended with no warning. Ash turned off the radio and returned it to its usual spot near the sofa. She went into Sara's room and saw that she was awake, but entertaining herself with her stuffed bee.

"Do you want to go to Grandma and Grandpa's?"

"Grandma, Grandpa," she exclaimed as she stood up in her crib and held her arms out to Ash.

Ash lifted her out of her crib and dressed her warmly. The temperatures were still only in the mid-forties.

It took only a few minutes for Ash to walk the short distance to her in-laws' cabin. Once inside and surrounded by people she loved, it was easier to control her fear. She told them about the radio broadcast while they sat in the living room entertaining Sara.

"It sounds like a step in the right direction, but it seems like once someone gets into power, they are never too keen on letting it go," Owen said.

After a late lunch, Ash kissed Sara goodbye and left for the CLB meeting.

The group gathered in the mill and storage area at the back of the storehouse. With three of their ten members missing, they were able to sit in chairs arranged in a small circle in the center of the room.

"I'm not exactly sure why I called this meeting, but I felt I needed to do something. Everyone is desperately worried about how long our hunting party has been gone. We don't know where they might have gone in pursuit of the herds, so I'm not sure how feasible it is to search for them. Any ideas?" Dan asked.

"Don't forget, only three ridable horses were left behind, and calling them ridable is being generous," Bob said.

"If we don't know where to look and don't have the horses needed to mount a search, what can we possibly do?" Maria asked.

"I doubt there is much we can do for them, but they are a very capable group. We shouldn't assume anything is wrong, but rather they had to travel a long distance in search of the herds," Dan said.

"I agree, but what we can discuss is food. I've talked to Mark. He has no male goats or llamas to butcher, and losing any females would set his breeding program back. At my place, we've butchered all but a few roosters already, and I'm hesitant to take any hens because eggs are a renewable resource. A dead chicken isn't. I still have five pigs and six sheep we could butcher, though I'd like to fatten them up a bit more. If we don't get wild game to supplement our protein supply soon, that won't last an entire community very long," Bob reported.

"Caleb thought we could start fishing again now that the fallout has stopped. Henry said the water quality is good. We could get a group together and give it a try," Ash added.

"Tony said the grains in the storehouse are holding up well, but when we determined how much we needed in order to survive this winter, a bad summer, and another winter, we didn't take into account upping consumption to compensate for little to no meat," Maria added.

"I hope we can figure something out," Tyler mumbled. "Caught a radio broadcast yesterday that said countries in Europe with confirmed possession of nukes are all threatening each other. The U.S. claimed it can't get involved due to a serious shortage of fuel for planes and ships. They can't even cross the Atlantic."

They sat in silence for a moment, no one knowing what else to say, but hesitant to end the meeting with no answers or plan. Dan cleared his throat to speak just as they heard someone enter the front of the storehouse. The open door revealed lots of shouting and noise outside. As Dan stood to go and find out what the ruckus was about, Tony burst in.

"They're back," he shouted as he turned and ran out of the room.

Ash stood up so quickly that her chair toppled over and skidded across the floor. As she darted out of the room, through the storehouse, and out the front door, she felt the rest of the group on her heels.

She pushed past the crowd gathered out front and saw Melora in the lead. As she ran past Melora, then Ryan, Archie, and Fiona, she barely registered the splints and limps. Her eyes were focused solely on the man at the end of the group.

Caleb stopped and Ash threw her arms around his neck. She held him for several moments, enjoying his warm breath on her neck and his arm wrapped around her waist, pulling her tight to his chest.

"I was so scared," she said as she finally looked up.

His lips descended on hers. He kissed her until she was breathless.

"I missed you so much it hurt," Caleb said as he ran his hand down her cheek and looked into her eyes. "Don't cry, I'm home."

"These are tears of joy."

She took Caleb's hand, and they walked to where the rest of the community was gathered. Ash could feel the relief around her as everyone reunited with their loved ones. She spotted Miranda clutching Ryan as they made their way over to them.

When Miranda saw them, she released Ryan and hugged her brother. Ash gasped at the sight of Ryan's black eyes and crooked nose.

After the initial shock, Ash gave him a hug. "Too much togetherness?" she asked.

"It's a long story, but we made it back and that's all that matters. All of us, except Melora, are a little worse for wear," Ryan replied.

Miranda let go of Caleb and returned to Ryan's side.

Ash let her eyes wander from Caleb's face toward his boots. If he was injured, it wasn't obvious. She heard someone standing behind Caleb gasp. Ash slowly walked around and saw the ripped back of his jacket and shredded and bloody back half of his pants.

"The cuts aren't very deep. Melora had some wound closure strips and a little antibiotic ointment. I'll be fine."

"Did you run into mountain lions again?" Ash asked.

"No, whatever these beasts were, they killed the lions before we tangled with them," Caleb replied.

Ash felt her knees go weak. Dillon ran up and pulled Caleb into a strong hug, making him gasp and wince, which didn't help her worry.

"Sorry. I should have guessed you would return beat up."

Dillon took Felix's lead rope from his brother's hand, allowing Caleb to wrap both arms around Ash.

"We survived and brought home a lot of meat, that's what's important," he said.

Ash stepped out of his embrace, but the arm draped over her shoulders hung heavily on her.

"Can I get everyone's attention for a moment?" Dan yelled from the storehouse steps.

The crowd quieted down and edged in closer so they could hear him.

"These five and their families need to go home. So, we need volunteers to hang as much of this meat in the walk-in cooler in the storehouse as we can. The rest we can hang in the trailers in the bone yard. Once that's done, take the horses to Bob's. He and Jacob will be waiting to take care of those. Emily will tend to Fiona's broken arm and then go visit the rest of the group at their cabins. Apparently, Melora is the only one who returned unscathed."

The crowd immediately dispersed, some jumping to the tasks Dan described, the others walking with the returnees toward their cabins. Ash and Caleb hadn't walked far when Owen and Olivia rushed up to them. Olivia had Sara bundled up and secured in her arms.

"Daddy!" Sara screamed when she saw Caleb.

Caleb took her from his mom and held her tight. Owen patted his back, catching a glimpse of the dried blood but saying nothing while Oliva clutched her son's arm and cried.

"Glad you're home, son. I'll help with the meat and horses now. I'll be by later to see if you need anything," Owen said.

Caleb just nodded and continued on toward home, holding his little girl tight.

TWENTY-THREE

DAN GAVE the group only one full day to rest and recover from their ordeal before calling a CLB meeting. He was clearly anxious to find out what happened before the rumor mill kicked into high gear.

Even though Caleb told Ash what happened, she was still a little apprehensive. She hadn't seen Fiona's photos and suspected he'd left out a few terrifying details. He answered her questions but offered up little else. He was understandably tired, but Ash felt there was more to his reluctance to share everything that happened with her.

After they dropped Sara off with Olivia, they headed toward the schoolhouse. She could detect a slight limp, but after seeing the injuries to the back of his thigh, she was surprised it wasn't worse. Even though he had just gotten home, the punctures and scratches occurred enough days ago that with no sign of infection, she felt confident his physical wounds would heal in time. She hoped any emotional scars were no deeper.

"How's the leg feel today?" she asked.

"Better. The way you gently massaged the honey all

over my wounds for the past two nights probably helped more than anything," he replied, smiling mischievously at her.

Ash was pleased to see him smile. She loved his smile, and it had been absent for a while, even before the hunting trip.

When they reached the school, the rest of the board members were already there, along with Archie and Fiona. Melora and Fiona were setting up the projector, which was connected to Fiona's laptop.

Ash pulled a chair away from the table and sat in the corner near where Caleb stood. Dan looked at them curiously but didn't question Caleb's decision to stand.

"First, I want to thank you five on behalf of the entire community. We all feared this might be a dangerous mission, but it sounds like you encountered something none of us could have imagined. Before we talk about your ordeal, I just want everyone to know that if doled out judiciously, the elk and deer meat will be enough to last the community for nearly two months without butchering any livestock," Dan began.

"That much time will give us the opportunity to fatten up what few animals we have so the meat will go further," Bob added.

"Maybe the deer herds will return by then. We can also try fishing in the lakes and streams. If we add some fish to our diet we can delay butchering even longer," Caleb suggested.

Ash noticed that Caleb didn't look at Bob when he spoke, even though he was tagging on to Bob's comment. Apparently, Bob noticed too.

"It's okay, Caleb. I loved that horse, but I'd much rather lose her than one of you," Bob said.

Ash's mind flipped through the images as she ran

down the line of horses when the group returned home. She remembered the geldings, Caleb was leading Felix, June was packed as usual. Closing her eyes, she pictured Bella and Sierra.

"Luna, no," Ash mumbled, choking back the tears.

"I'm so sorry, Ash. I did everything I could to save her," Caleb said as he squeezed her shoulder.

"It was the same animal that attacked Luna that injured Caleb when he tried to get it off her," Melora added.

Ash bit her lip to keep from crying, not wanting Caleb to feel worse than he already did. She had no doubt he did all he could.

"I just hate that you got a bunch of new scars trying to protect her," Ash said as she looked up at him, forcing a weak smile and blinking back the tears.

Fiona turned on the projector and clicked to the first photo. Nearly everyone in the room gasped.

"We aren't completely sure what they are. Fiona and I think they're similar to jaguars we've seen in books and zoos, but they're much larger and have a melanistic coloring, which is fairly rare. It seems remarkable that all three exhibited the trait," Melora said as the group stared at the first dead cat.

Henry stood up and walked closer to the wall. "They have the black rosettes characteristic of jaguars, but they also have faint stripes and short manes which aren't. How much do you think it weighed?"

"This is one of two females we encountered. The females were probably around four hundred pounds, and we believe the male was closer to five," Caleb responded.

"Geez, do you think there are more out there?" Bob asked.

"We didn't see any other sign, but if there were three,

there's no reason why there couldn't be more," Fiona replied.

"Were they just driven by hunger to attack your camp, or are they extremely aggressive?" Maria asked.

"I'd say aggressive," Fiona replied as she flipped to the images of the dead mountain lions. "They didn't eat much of the cougars, and the way the carcasses were dragged around, it looked like the giant cats had killed for sport."

Fiona slowly flipped through all of the photos she took and downloaded onto her computer.

"The canine teeth are exceptionally long, and the track has a fully-formed fifth toe. Did it also have a dewclaw?" Henry asked?

"No," Melora replied.

"Most wild cats only have four toes, and some species not native to North America have a fifth, but it's more of a dewclaw," Henry explained.

"Fiona has seen a jaguar in a zoo when she was younger, and we've both seen pictures of non-North American wildlife in books in school and college, as I imagine some of you have before moving to Beartooth. We're leaning toward a theory that these creatures are melanistic jaguars that were making their way north as temperatures warmed and food got scarce. They may have encountered other big cats that escaped from zoos, and through cross-breeding, we ended up with this giant, melanistic, jaguar-tiger hybrid," Melora explained.

"That explanation is as good as any. Not only would breeding with tigers increase their size, but having access to large prey like elk might have increased the likelihood of larger individuals surviving, spurring an evolutionary response geared toward larger individuals. It was once believed that evolution took hundreds of thousands of years, but over the last century, we've seen rapid evolution in which significant changes occur within a single generation," Henry said.

"The animals were most active at night, so the nearly black color made them difficult to see. This coloration may have helped the jaguars make the journey here from wherever they came from if they traveled at night, increasing the chances of survival for cats with the melanistic coloring," Caleb added.

"Marine life was my specialty before coming to Beartooth, but my background in wildlife biology makes this a terrifying, yet intriguing discovery. I'm baffled by this creature, but I suppose we'll just call it a jaguar since those seem to be the most dominant traits," Henry said.

"I guess we'll add this to our growing list of threats to our community, but what do we do about it?" Bob asked.

"Melora and I took all the cameras down when the volcano erupted in order to avoid damage to the equipment from abrasive and corrosive fallout. We'll put them back up and continue regular surveillance with the drone," Tyler replied.

"I've told Dennis he needs to be ready if we see any sign of these massive predators. He's a much better shot than me. Caleb's bow didn't do a lot of damage, though he didn't have the opportunity for a good shot in a vital area. Fiona's sidearm pretty much just pissed it off. Big game hunting rifles will be the most effective at bringing them down. The shotgun will do the job, but it doesn't have as much accuracy at a long distance, and believe me, the more distance between these animals and us the better," Archie said.

While Fiona powered the equipment down, Dan asked how everyone was healing up.

"Emily didn't see any sign of infection. The punctures were already starting to close up by the time we got home.

With Ash tending my wounds, I'm sure I'll heal fast. She's got just the right touch," Caleb said.

Fiona and Melora chuckled, Ryan smiled, and the rest in attendance looked confused.

Archie cleared his throat and suppressed a smile. "The short time I've been off the ankle has already done wonders. It just needs time."

"Even though Melora tried to straighten my nose, it'll always be a little crooked, but Miranda thinks it makes me look like a badass, so I'm okay with it, and the black eye is starting to fade," Ryan reported.

Dan shook his head and chuckled. "Fiona?"

"It hurt like heck when Emily set the fracture but thank goodness she still has a stash of pain relievers. It'll mend."

"Thankfully, Melora came out of this unscathed since Tyler was apparently in a lot of pain in her absence," Dan joked.

The comment lightened the mood somewhat. Tyler blushed and Melora gave him a loud kiss on the lips, making everyone laugh. Ryan looked terrible, but as long as Miranda liked it, he was happy. Maria still seemed in shock, and Ash could tell Henry's scientific mind was running through the discovery of the oversized jaguar-type animals with a rare melanistic coloring and other anomalies, all traveling in a group far north of what should be their home range.

"After seeing and hearing what you encountered, I hope the herds return. I can't in good conscience encourage another such trip," Dan stated.

"I doubt rounding up volunteers will be as easy if there is a next time," Caleb said.

"When and if the need arises, count me out. Becoming

a vegetarian doesn't sound as bad as it used to," Fiona added.

"Anything else before we move on?" Dan asked.

"Dennis is cutting up meat as we speak. I'll join him when the meeting is over so we will have venison in the storehouse coolers by the end of the day," Archie said.

"Just in the nick of time. Tony told me this morning that there's only about fifteen pounds of pork left in the coolers. I was going to have to slaughter a hog or sheep that could use a lot more fattening up, but this will buy us some time to make better use of our animals," Bob added.

After finishing the discussion of the hunting trip and the status of their food stores, they talked about what many of the residents heard on the radio.

"It sounds like there is reason to be hopeful, but I'm still glad we're here and not living among the chaos below the mountain," Maria said.

"That's what I thought too. I gather that people are already a little nervous that the new president is dragging her feet on scheduling a presidential election, and I would have loved to hear some news out of Pryor," Dan added.

Everyone nodded their heads in agreement, feeling cautiously optimistic about the future of America, but still happy to be far from the fray. What was happening in the rest of the country seldom touched their lives, and they had no control over events below the mountain, so they didn't spend much time on the topic.

Dan adjourned the meeting, and everyone filed out. When they got outside, Caleb stopped and pulled Ash into his arms.

"I'm so sorry about Luna and sorry I didn't tell you. I just didn't want to see you sad."

Ash looked up at him. "I have no doubt you did all you could. All that matters to me is that you made it home in reasonably good shape. As much as I loved that little horse, I'll get over it. I could never get over losing you. Let's get our daughter and go home. She missed her daddy a lot."

She stepped out of his arms and took his hand. As they walked toward the farm, Ryan caught up to them and fell into step.

"Miranda said your folks gave their blessing for us to get married."

"So, it seems," Caleb replied.

"What about you? Are you good with me and Miranda?"

"If my baby sister has to get married, I'm happy it's you. Besides, since someone other than Ash had to treat my wounds, I'm glad I could keep it in the family," Caleb conceded.

Ash assumed it was Melora who tended to Caleb since she had administered first aid to everyone else. Ash hadn't asked Caleb, fearing she would sound jealous or insecure, but she was pleased to learn she was still the only woman to have seen and touched all of him. The knowledge made her want to hug Ryan.

"And, if she thinks those black eyes and crooked nose are sexy, she's obviously so in love that nothing will ever tear you two apart," Ash added, making both men laugh.

Caleb slapped Ryan on the back as they walked up the steps to the Solomon cabin. "Welcome to the family, brother."

TWENTY-FOUR

IN THE WEEKS following the deadly hunt, life slowly got back to a somewhat normal rhythm. The Solomons continued to prepare for spring planting like they did this time every year, even though planting would be delayed until the temperatures warmed.

With the storehouse coolers stocked with wild game and more still hanging in the trailers in the boneyard, temperatures no longer dipping much below freezing at night, and Beartooth's citizens on the mend, morale was much higher than it had been since the volcano erupted.

Tyler and Melora flew the drone every other day. So far, they had seen no sign of predators or the deer and elk herds, but they could see the volcanic deposits were settling and grasses were starting to break through the gray blanket cloaking the ground. Everyone was hopeful that if grazing returned so would the wild game, but Ash feared the herds would also bring predators.

Most of the ewes, sows, nannies, and llamas had given birth. Assuming the grasses continued to force their way through the ash-covered pastures, livestock levels would be restored going into next winter. Overall, the residents of Beartooth felt hopeful.

Ash couldn't help smiling as she and Sara went about their morning ritual. Sara was seldom grumpy. She was definitely a morning person like her daddy, even at such a young age.

"Are you sure this is a good idea?" Caleb asked as he assembled the archery equipment they would take.

"No, but it's worth a try. Henry and Gretchen did what they thought was best to protect Evelyn, but I think they underestimated her. I love seeing the joy on her face when she gets to experience something new," Ash replied.

"You're a good sister-in-law."

"I try. I love Miranda and Evelyn as if they were my true sisters."

Carrying Sara and all the gear they would need, they set out for the Solomon farm. Dillon, Evelyn, and Olivia were waiting on the porch when they arrived. Ash handed the toddler to her grandma, and they headed for the archery range.

"I'm so excited. I always felt left out when everyone else went shooting. Dad wouldn't even let me go with you all because he thought I might get in the way and someone would accidentally shoot me with an arrow," Evelyn said as she held on to Dillon's arm as they walked.

When they reached the closest targets, Dillon helped Evelyn put on a shooting glove and arm guard. Caleb strung a lightweight bow while Ash set up the metronome behind the target.

"Walk toward the target until you can hear the ticking," Ash said.

Dillon guided her to a spot only ten yards from the target. He stood behind her with his arms around her and went through the motions of helping her pull the bow string and ease it forward. He showed her how far back to pull the string and where to place her fingers.

"Now, hone in on the sound," he whispered in her ear.

Evelyn nodded. "I can visualize where it is, but how do I aim?"

"Point the tip of the arrow at the sound, pull back, and release. I'll help you pull," Dillon said.

She did as Dillon explained and the arrow flew wide. "Did I hit anything?"

"No, but your release was smooth, and you had the distance," he replied.

Evelyn tried ten more times but never hit the target. Ash could tell she was getting frustrated.

"Let's take a break. You don't want to overdo it on your first day. Archery requires muscles you don't always use," Ash said.

"I'll bet you hit the target on your first dozen tries," Evelyn grumbled.

"I don't remember. When Caleb was teaching me to shoot, I was so distracted with his arms around me that I couldn't really focus."

"You did hit the target right away. I was a little disappointed that you mastered it so soon and didn't need my help. I was looking for any excuse to touch you back then," Caleb replied as he pulled Ash into his arms for a long kiss.

"Fortunately, you no longer need an excuse."

"That's all cute and everything, but it doesn't help me out much," Evelyn said as she picked up her bow and walked back toward the target.

Evelyn, with Dillon's help, tried six more times with the same result.

"Hold up a minute," Ash said as she pulled an arrow out of her quiver. "Try this one. It has a black rubber blunt on the tip. I dyed the shaft black and used red feathers so I could easily retrieve it from my quiver without pulling each one out to check the tip. Turkey feathers on a natural wood shaft have to be hard to see."

Dillon helped Evelyn nock the arrow.

"Yes, that's better. The tip is still fuzzy, but I can see something is there, and I can follow the shaft further down the arrow," Evelyn replied.

"Back up as far as you can while still hearing the metronome. If you hit the target, the arrow may bounce back," Caleb said.

Everyone remained silent as Evelyn honed in on the noise, sighted down the black arrow with the black blunt on the end, pulled back, and released. The rubber blunt hit just outside the furthest ring and bounced only a few feet back and to the side.

"I hit it! I could hear it," Evelyn exclaimed.

"Congratulations," Ash said. "This is probably enough for today so you don't get sore. I'll make you some new arrows with dark, bold colors, but with regular tips painted black so the arrow will stick in the target."

Evelyn handed Caleb the bow and hugged Ash and then Dillon. "Thank you so much. I've always wondered what it would feel like to shoot a bow like everyone else. I know Mom and Dad were just trying to protect me but keeping me from trying so much made me feel like an outcast."

On the short walk back to the farm, Evelyn described how it felt to hold the bow, pull the string back, and shoot. Ash couldn't help but notice that Dillon was smiling nearly as much as Evelyn. He was clearly happy that his wife was so happy.

"So, I take it you kids had fun?" Owen asked as they entered the Solomon cabin.

"It was great," Evelyn said as she once again described every detail of the experience.

"I'm happy it went well, but if you boys are done playing around, we've got one more field to plow," Owen said.

Ash offered to walk Evelyn home. Caleb left for Bob's to get Thor. Dillon and Owen went out to the barn to get the plow ready.

Sara squirmed in Ash's arms until she set the toddler on her feet on the ground.

"She doesn't like to be carried much anymore unless she's tired or trying to get Caleb's attention," Ash said as they slowly made their way across the community toward Evelyn and Dillon's cabin with Sara in the lead.

"She's definitely going to be as curious as you and Caleb. Most of the residents in Beartooth are happy to keep close to home. Caleb has always been different, and he found his soulmate in you. I bet it's hard staying behind now," Evelyn replied.

"I do miss going with him sometimes, but I don't regret Sara. She brings me so much joy. In fact, I'd love to have another baby if I wasn't so worried about the survival of Beartooth. I want her to have brothers and sisters. Being an only child was kind of lonely. I'm thankful to have you and Miranda for sisters now, but it would have been nice to have a sibling growing up."

"Along with the current environmental crisis and dissolution of humanity, imagine being nearly blind. It all makes the thought of having a baby extra terrifying for me."

"I'm sorry." It didn't seem sufficient, but it was all Ash could think of to say.

"Don't be. I'm happy, and my world has definitely expanded since marrying Dillon. Heck, I never thought

I'd shoot a weapon, and I did that today. Maybe I'll try fishing next. I love children, and I can see by the way Dillon interacts with Sara that he would be a great father. It would probably be a bad idea to have a baby, but we haven't discounted the idea totally."

"I'm glad you're happy."

"You know, I don't need you to walk me home. Since I lost most of my sight gradually, I made adjustments as it worsened, and the placement of our cabin is perfect. If I go out my front door toward the school, turn left and head straight toward the Craig brother's duplex, and then turn right as I get close, I can reach nearly every cabin by keeping each fuzzy blob to my left and walking clockwise around the community. I got turned around that once, but generally I get around Beartooth really well."

"Sorry if I offended you. I have no doubt you can find your way around. It just seems like Dillon worries a lot when you're out alone. Besides, I enjoy the extra time with you," Ash replied.

"I'm not offended. I just wanted to make sure you knew I wasn't as helpless as some people think."

As Ash watched Sara toddle, she was surprised at how much distance she could cover so quickly. She glanced over at Evelyn and saw her sister-in-law in a whole new light. She was smart, resourceful, and fearless. Life in a remote area like Beartooth had to be difficult, but she faced each challenge head-on and never backed down or complained. Ash couldn't help but admire her even more.

TWENTY-FIVE

ASH CRADLED A STEAMING cup between her hands and made her way out to the covered work area behind the cabin. She glanced at the thermometer. It was already up to fifty-three degrees. She had faith it would reach sixty today for the first time since last fall.

The overnight low had only dipped down to forty-two. Lows hadn't dropped below freezing in weeks, so the outlook was promising. If the slow warming trend continued, they could start planting cool-loving plants in sunny areas in a few weeks and the rest soon thereafter. In that scenario, they would have a short growing season this year, but it was better than nothing.

When she walked back into the cabin, she found Caleb making French toast and Sara riding the small wooden rocking horse Archie loaned them. The old horse had entertained countless toddlers in the community over the years until they tired of its simplicity or outgrew it, and then it was passed on to the next youngest.

"I think we'll hit sixty degrees today," Ash said as she

walked up behind Caleb and wrapped her arms around his waist.

He turned around and pulled her closer. He smiled as he looked down into her eyes and gently brushed her hair behind her ear. "Somedays, I still have to pinch myself to prove I'm not dreaming," he said as his lips descended on hers.

"I still haven't gotten used to that talk, but I'm not complaining." She plucked Sara off her horse and sat her in the highchair. She fed her the cereal Caleb made earlier while he finished making their breakfast.

"I'd like to visit the hives today and see if I can detect any more activity. I'd also like to drop off the arrows we made for Evelyn. I hope they work better for her," Ash said.

"I'm helping move Emily and Fiona this morning, but if you want to wait until this afternoon, I'll go with you."

"I feel a little guilty not helping with the move, but I hate imposing on your mom to watch Sara again."

"Don't worry, we've got more than enough help. Since the cabin is for Miranda and Ryan, me, Dad, Dillon, and Ryan's folks and brothers are helping. Archie and Dennis plan on being there to move Emily, and Graham, Melora, and Tyler offered to help move Fiona. Bob and Jacob are bringing the wagon to haul any heavy furniture. With that many volunteers, I think we'll have everyone moved in an hour."

"Now it's starting to sound like a party, so maybe I will wander by before I check in with the mothers to see if they need any help with wedding arrangements. Things are moving fast since Miranda is determined to be married before her nineteenth birthday."

"She has always been stubborn. Even though she'll

only beat her birthday by a couple of days, I'm sure she'll feel like she bested Dad," Caleb chuckled.

Caleb put Sara back on her horse. He gathered up the breakfast dishes while Ash retrieved the radio. She set it on the counter next to the kitchen sink and found their usual station.

She kept the volume low and glanced over her shoulder at Sara. She seemed thoroughly engrossed with the wooden horse. Ash grabbed a dish towel and dried while Caleb washed.

"The cease-fire continues to hold, allowing rail shipments of grain to move from Canada, across the U.S., and to Mexico. According to sources inside the new administration, food distribution warehouses on the new East Coast and the middle of the country are once again under government control. The flow of food to warehouses in those areas has been restored, and grains and other consumables are being distributed in an orderly manner by military personnel. President Steele has informed the western governors that she will not risk sending limited food supplies to rebellious regions until those states restore law and order. She has also demanded that those governors address the reports of extreme human-rights violations by rogue governments like that of Jonah Bennett and his Freedom and Morality Alliance in Pryor, Wyoming," the newsreader reported.

"Good luck with that," Caleb mumbled as he drained the dishwater from the sink.

"The President's FOCUS program has made progress in improving food availability by mending relationships with our neighbors to the north and south, but until security is restored across the country, it will be difficult to address the climate crisis and restart oil extraction and refining, worsening current fuel shortages."

The radio went silent.

"I wish the newsreader would say if that was all so we'd know whether the broadcast was over or we lost reception," Ash said as she returned the radio to the living room.

"I'm just thankful we're getting some news. Maybe the President withholding food from those states harboring dangerous and delusional groups will finally force the governors to do something," Caleb said.

"We can only hope. As long as Jonah Bennett and his FAMA militia are still functional, I'll worry. I just hope Melora is right about us being safe now that their helicopter has been destroyed."

"Her guess is the best guess we've got when it comes to the FAMA fanatics."

Ash prayed Caleb was correct. Not a day went by that she didn't think about Neal. He was a founding father of Beartooth but now he was gone. The only time the FAMA militia reached Beartooth it had cost Neal his life and shattered everyone's illusion of safety and security.

"Let's go," Caleb said, breaking into her thoughts.

When they reached Emily's cabin, most of the volunteers had gathered. Emily and Fiona were moving to the other side of the duplex that Dillon and Evelyn occupied. Miranda and Ryan would move into the cabin that Emily and Jon had raised their family in. After Jon died and their sons married and moved out, Emily had been lonely and was more than happy to downsize. As Miranda was slowly taking over as the nurse for the community, it only made sense that she and Ryan would occupy the cabin next door to the clinic.

"Where's Miranda?" Ash asked as she approached Ryan.

"She's packing up her room. As soon as Emily and Fiona are out, we'll move her stuff over here."

Ash left with Sara and headed for the farm to help Miranda. When she reached the Solomon farm, she found Olivia sitting in the living room crying.

"I can't believe my baby is leaving. It will be so lonely here," she sniffled.

"Gramma sad," Sara said as she crawled up onto Olivia's lap and hugged her.

"Not anymore, now that you're here," Olivia replied as she nuzzled Sara.

Ash slipped away to help Miranda. It didn't take long. Residents of Beartooth possessed few material goods. Items brought by the original settlers were used until worn out beyond repair. Anything new was handcrafted.

"This is kind of the opposite as when you got married. We moved your mom's belongings out, so you and Caleb could have your furnished cabin. I can't imagine Emily will leave anything, so the cabin is going to be empty," Miranda said.

"You'll be surprised by how quickly it will feel like home," Ash replied.

The cabin door opened, and it sounded like a horde of people heading their way. Caleb, Dillon, Owen, Ryan, and Ryan's dad and his two brothers each took the items Miranda pointed out. In just a few minutes and only one trip, Miranda's old room was empty.

Miranda followed the guys to the home she would soon share with Ryan, and Ash stayed behind with Olivia and Sara.

"I didn't realize how difficult this had to have been for your mom," Olivia said as she sniffled.

"Mom was nudging Caleb and I pretty hard to get married. We didn't know at the time that she was terminal, so I was a little sad my mom was so anxious to move out. Looking back, she just didn't want me to face the future alone. I'm so thankful she made sure I had you all in my life before she passed on," Ash said as she sat next to Olivia.

"And, I'm so glad you and Caleb gave us this little angel before I had to let go of my baby girl."

"We're pretty pleased with her too."

Before long, Owen and Caleb returned.

"How's it going?" Olivia asked.

"Emily and Fiona are moved out, and Miranda's stuff is moved in. The Fergusons said they don't need any help with Ryan's belongings since he doesn't have much, but I think Miranda could use her mom about now. She was getting pretty emotional," Owen replied as he wrapped his arms around Olivia and held her while she cried.

After several minutes, Olivia pulled herself together and left for Miranda's new home.

"Need anything from us, Dad, before we head out?" Caleb asked.

"No, I think I could use a little time alone. We were all starting to worry that you were too clueless to see what was right in front of your eyes by the time you finally got around to marrying Ash. I still see Dillon every day on the farm so it's not like he actually left, but it's harder than I thought it would be to let my little girl go."

Caleb picked Sara up and held her in front of him. "I get it, Dad, no man will ever be worthy of my little princess."

Owen chuckled. "I didn't say Miranda was a princess, but this cabin is going to be mighty quiet without her. Despite her stubborn streak and tendency for drama, she was definitely an easier kid than you and Dillon. She never fought with her brothers, seldom came home injured, or scared us like you often did."

"And, he's still doing it," Ash added as she took Sara from Caleb and headed for the door.

Caleb grabbed his bow and quiver that he left at his folks' cabin that morning. They walked to the bee storage shed near the Ferguson orchard in silence. All the moving and wedding fuss made Ash think of her mom. She still missed her every day, but she had died content in the knowledge that Ash had Caleb in her life.

"Whatcha thinking?" Caleb finally asked.

"How lucky I am to have you in my life, how much I miss my mom, and how at peace she was once we decided to get married. What about you?"

"I was thinking about how you took my breath away when you walked down the aisle in that dress, and how much fun it was to get you out of it on our first night together."

Ash smiled at the memory. The dress was her mom's wedding dress. She had never seen it until the day before she and Caleb married. Ash had very few clothes that weren't patched and faded, so the dress had made her feel beautiful. Mostly, though, she loved the effect it had on Caleb.

"If I was a good sister-in-law, I would have offered it up to Miranda for her big day."

"I'm glad you didn't. It would have ruined my fantasies to see my sister in that dress."

Ash chuckled and waited while Caleb opened the door to the storage shed. She stepped through and walked up to the hives. Sara was making nonsensical noises and then laughing at her made-up sounds.

"Shush, listen closely," Ash whispered in the toddler's ear.

Sara stopped and stared at Ash with big eyes. After a moment, a smile grew on her face. "Bees."

"Yes, bees, lots of bees."

As they stood in the dim light inside the shed, bees slowly left the hives and flew out the small opening near the roofline. After a short time, some returned.

They watched the coming and going of the bees until Ash heard a high-pitched animal squeal outside. It took her a moment to place the sound.

"Daddy has apparently found what mommy calls creative cuisine."

"Daddy, bees," Sara said with a smile.

"Yes, Daddy, bees, and bunnies. Life is slowly returning to Beartooth. We're going to be just fine."

TWENTY-SIX

ASH, along with the rest of the Solomons and Fergusons, had been working hard all week to pull everything together for the wedding. For her wedding, she had left everything to her mom and Olivia. She probably didn't appreciate all their effort as much as she should have at the time. Now she had a whole new respect for what went into planning even a simple wedding.

Through marriage, Miranda would be related to nearly everyone in the community so they invited everyone. Since the entire population of Beartooth planned to attend, the reception turned into a potluck, which helped a lot.

The wedding would take place outside, so there was no need for decorations. Ash found a small patch of wildflowers. She picked flowers and arranged them for a colorful bouquet for Miranda to carry, while Miranda's and Ryan's brothers set up chairs and tables.

With all the preparations done, all Ash had to do was keep Miranda from stressing about tripping or forgetting her vows. As Ash thought back on the events that nearly destroyed her wedding day, it was impossible to focus on Miranda's melodrama. No matter how hard she tried to forget the morning of their ceremony, she couldn't push it out of her mind.

Tyler had tried to stop her marriage to Caleb. He cornered her while she was checking the hives far away from the community the morning of her wedding. He wouldn't take no for an answer. He pulled her to him, kissed her, and tripped her to the ground when she tried to get away. She managed to grab a tree limb as she tumbled to the forest floor and hit him so hard alongside the head, she thought she'd killed him.

By late afternoon, the temperature had finally reached sixty, which everyone was grateful for. Miranda decided Ash and Evelyn would be co-maids-of-honor. Ryan decided his brothers Sam and Zane would then be co-best-men.

Ash and Evelyn, escorted by Sam and Zane, followed Miranda and Owen down an aisle created by the arrangement of the chairs until they reached Ryan. Watching Owen with Miranda reminded Ash that she had walked down the aisle alone. The memory allowed her fear that she might lose Caleb someday slip into her mind. She didn't want Sara to grow up without a father or siblings, but sometimes things were beyond a person's control.

Owen handed Miranda off to Ryan and then took a seat next to Olivia, who was already crying. Dan presided over the short and simple ceremony. When Ash turned to follow the couple back down the aisle, she saw the entire community of Beartooth watching them, making her thankful that she and Caleb had been able to have a small wedding with just immediate family.

As soon as it was over, Ash found Caleb. The festivities

didn't last long. As the sun started slipping below the trees, the temperature quickly dropped.

"It's getting too cold to keep Sara out here much longer," Ash said.

"I think we're about done anyway, so go home. I'll help with the tables and chairs and be there shortly," Caleb replied before heading off in Dillon's direction.

Ash hugged Miranda and Ryan and said goodnight. When she turned to leave, she found herself face-to-face with Tyler.

"She's really growing fast, and she's beautiful like her mother," Tyler said, looking at Sara.

"Yes, she's my greatest joy. I wouldn't have her without Caleb."

Ash feared she sounded icier than she meant to, but the day had stirred up painful memories of growing up without a dad and bad memories of the morning of her wedding. Dillon and Evelyn's wedding hadn't affected her, but she hadn't been as involved in the planning or played much of a role in the actual event.

Tyler ran his fingers through his hair and shook his head, looking uncomfortable. "How many times do I have to say I'm sorry?"

Ash just shrugged and looked down at Sara. Her daughter looked confused and a little scared, so Ash smiled at her and placed a light kiss on her forehead.

"Everything okay here?" Caleb asked as he arrived at Ash's side.

"I was afraid the wedding would bring back bad memories for Ash. I guess I was right. I thought we'd all put it behind us," Tyler replied.

"I've forgiven you for the most part, but I'll never forget. It's been a long day and Sara is tired. If you'll excuse me," Ash said as she left the two men and quickly made her way home.

By the time Caleb reached the cabin, she had fed Sara and was watching her sleep in her crib. Caleb crept up close and slipped his arm around her. They stood silently next to each other while their daughter slept.

"Did he say or do anything to upset you? I have no problem giving him the beating I should have given him then," Caleb asked as they left Sara's room.

"No, a broken nose is sufficient. I guess I haven't gotten over what he took from me. I should be able to think of my wedding day without thinking of him. I can't seem to get over what he stole from me. It took everything I had to put what happened out of my mind so I wouldn't ruin our wedding day. I was afraid if you found out, things would have spiraled out of control, and we wouldn't have gotten married that day. If I didn't have you, I wouldn't have Sara," Ash choked out as tears streamed down her cheeks.

Caleb pulled her close and held her for several minutes while she cried. "You do have me, and we've been blessed with a perfect baby girl. That will never change. I promise."

Ash stepped back out of his embrace and looked up into his hazel eyes. "Please don't make promises you can't keep."

"Don't say that, Ash. I love you more than anything in the world. I always have, I always will."

"I know, and I love you too. I always will. But as I've often been told, I'm a realist. I'm pragmatic. I can be happy with what you can give me, but if anyone needs you again, you'll leave. Someday, you might not return."

"I love you so much," he whispered. He wanted to

argue with her, but he feared she was right, so there was nothing else he could say.

TWENTY-SEVEN

ASH SLEPT in later than usual. She didn't know if it was all the work leading up to the wedding or if she had been emotionally exhausted. When she left the bedroom and walked out into the living room, she was surprised to find Caleb gone.

She couldn't imagine he would leave the cabin with her sleeping in case Sara woke up, but maybe she had hurt him with her words last night, and he needed time alone. She walked into Sara's room, and she was gone too. Ash let out a sigh of relief, clearly Caleb had taken Sara so that she could sleep.

Ash heard the cabin door open as she left Sara's room. Caleb set a canvas bag on the table as he walked over to her and pulled her into his arms.

"Did you sleep well?"

"Yes, I didn't even hear you or Sara get up. Where's Sara?"

"I took her to Mom's. I thought we could spend the day together, just the two of us. We can go fishing, ride horses, or do whatever you want to do. Mom sent leftovers from the reception so we have a ready-made picnic lunch, including cake for dessert."

"That was very thoughtful of her, but you really didn't need to go to all of this trouble. I'm sorry if I hurt you."

"No, I'm sorry. I know it's hard to believe sometimes by my actions, but you and Sara are my priority. You have always been so strong and capable that sometimes I take you for granted. All I think about when I'm gone is getting back to you."

"I'm sure I was just overly emotional yesterday. Life is seldom perfect, but I wouldn't trade a moment of it with you for anything in the world," Ash replied.

"I feel the same. Now, what will it be, fishing, riding, or I'd even be happy to go punch Tyler in the face again?"

Ash chuckled. "I don't think that will be necessary. Let's go back to bed, and maybe we'll go fishing later."

"I love the way you think," Caleb replied as he scooped her up and carried her into the bedroom.

By the time they left the cabin, the morning had started to warm up nicely. Caleb carried his longbow, fishing pole, a quiver of arrows over his shoulder, and the 9mm holstered at his hip. Ash carried her pole and their picnic.

"Is it my imagination or are there a lot more birds in the trees today than there has been?" Ash asked.

"I think you're right. Let's swing by the hives on our way and see how they're doing."

When they reached the small building housing the hives in the Ferguson orchard, they watched as bees flew out of the top of the shed. They opened the door and listened. Ash was pleased with all the activity. They shut the door and walked over to the nearest cherry tree.

"I see buds," Caleb said as he reached up and pulled a branch down for Ash to inspect.

"Let's move half of the hives out of the shed and into

the orchard in the next couple of weeks. It hasn't gotten much below forty-five overnight in a week. With buds on the trees, the bees will have a source of nectar and pollen soon. They can survive a little cold for a short duration. We can leave the rest of the hives protected in the shed until your dad's crops are up. That way if the temperatures drop significantly, we won't lose all the bees."

"Sounds like a good plan. I'll check with Miranda and Ryan. We have enough suits for the four of us, and we can easily move half the hives such a short distance without more help."

The idea of getting the bees out of the shed and having pollen sources available made Ash hopeful the community would survive even if the next winter was as bad or worse than what they had been experiencing.

By the time they reached the lake it was already lunchtime. They headed straight for *their rock* and sat down next to each other.

Ever since Ash could remember, whenever they came to the lake she and Caleb would sit on this large boulder along the shore. Sometimes they wouldn't even talk, they would just sit, shoulder-to-shoulder, enjoying the solitude and scenery. It was here that their relationship had moved past childhood friends.

"Did you see that fish jump?" Ash asked as she finished off the potato salad.

"No, but I'll take your word for it. When it comes to fish, I never question your eye."

"That was delicious, but I now have a hankering for a trout dinner." Ash put everything back in the bag and retrieved her gear.

"That does sound good," Caleb replied.

Within ten minutes, Ash pulled in an eighteen-inch trout. Caleb reeled in a slightly smaller one by the time she took the fish off, put it on a stringer, rebaited her hook, and tossed her line out. In just over an hour, they had a dozen large trout.

"We better stop there. As big as they are, they'll be heavy to carry back to Beartooth," Caleb said.

"I wonder how much fishing pressure the lake can handle without degrading the stock? If the herds don't return, maybe we can supplement our protein supply with fish."

"We'll just have to gauge it. If it starts getting difficult to catch fish or we notice a serious decline in size we'll need to back off. I don't know if we can catch enough to alleviate the pressure on the livestock, but it's worth a try," Caleb replied.

They hadn't seen anything larger than a rabbit in the area for months, but out of habit, Ash stood with her back to the lake to watch the forest for danger while Caleb knelt at the water's edge and started cleaning the fish.

A sound caught Ash's ear. She didn't see anything, but she was sure something was passing in the trees.

"Caleb," Ash whispered. "I hear something in the trees."

Caleb stood, watched, and listened.

"The movements are light and graceful like a deer not a predator. Take this and stay alert. I'm going to check it out," he said as he handed Ash the gun.

She took the weapon and stood very still while Caleb quietly retrieved his bow and quiver. She tried not to even move as he slipped into the trees. After she could no longer see him, she knelt and finished cleaning the fish, casting frequent glances over her shoulder.

He had been gone for nearly an hour, and she was starting to worry, when he finally emerged from the trees.

Ash jogged over to him. "Did you see anything?"

"I never caught sight of any animals, but I found deer tracks. It looked like only two deer. I don't know if I was closing in on them, so hated to keep going, afraid you might start worrying."

"I was starting to worry, but I think it's a very encouraging sign. It's the first deer we've detected near the community since the eruption."

"Let's head back to Beartooth. Melora can get the drone up and try to find them," Caleb said as they returned to the lakeshore.

When they reached where they left their stuff, Caleb pulled her into his arms and kissed her.

"What's that for?"

"For cleaning the rest of the fish while I was gone."

Ash chuckled. She quickly gathered up her gear and the picnic bag and followed Caleb away from the lake.

When they reached the Solomon farm, they spotted Owen and Dillon in the field. Both men raced over, excited to see the laden stringers of fish.

"Can you help Ash with the fish? We found deer tracks in the trees. I'd like Melora to get the drone up and see if she can find them," Caleb said.

Caleb handed his bow and pole to Dillon and headed for Melora and Tyler's cabin. Owen took a stringer with six large trout, and they made their way to the Solomon cabin.

As they set the fishing gear and Caleb's bow and quiver on the porch. Olivia walked out carrying Sara.

Sara's eyes got big when she saw the fish. Ash assumed they looked like scary creatures to a toddler. Sara turned her head and buried her face in Olivia's chest.

"Leave enough for us, Ash and Caleb, Dillon and Evelyn, and Miranda and Ryan, and I'll cook them up for all of us tonight," Olivia said.

They left seven of the biggest fish and then started around the community in a clockwise fashion. They distributed the rest to the Thorn and Ferguson households.

By the time they returned to the Solomon cabin, Caleb was there holding Sara.

"Did you find Melora?" Ash asked.

"She and Tyler are heading toward the lake as we speak and will get the drone up soon. It would be a huge relief if the deer returned," Caleb replied.

Ash agreed but couldn't push back the fear that with a return of the herds, predators might follow. And now they knew that the wild held predators much more deadly than any they had seen before.

TWENTY-EIGHT

ASH WAS anxious to move some of the hives out of the storage shed. Bees were venturing out more during warm afternoons, and they would need to start gathering pollen and nectar soon or there would be no honey for the community.

Miranda and Ryan met Ash and Caleb at the shed. It was early in the morning, and the temperatures were cool enough that few bees had yet to venture out, and those that had were still sluggish. Using a hand cart borrowed from Garrett, it took only two trips to move half the hives from the shed to the Ferguson orchard.

Ryan and Miranda offered to return the cart to Garrett, so Ash and Caleb headed to the farm to get Sara.

"I'm thrilled so many bees survived the winter. I won't know exactly how many until I open the hives, but it looks very promising," Ash said as they walked.

They retrieved Sara and went home. After getting the toddler down for a nap, Ash made lunch, and Caleb turned the radio on, searching for news.

"According to the Wyoming governor's office, Jonah Bennett and his Freedom and Morality Alliance are no longer in control of Pryor, Wyoming. The Guard destroyed FAMA's ammunition storehouse with armed drones, and then they entered Pryor with tanks and ground forces. When they arrived, Bennett was gone. Those who surrendered claimed that Bennett fled with only about fifty of his most faithful FAMA militia, but it is unclear where those individuals are located at this time," the newsreader reported.

Ash stopped what she was doing and joined Caleb near the radio. "That sounds like good news, but it sure would be nice to know where Bennett and the craziest of the crazies went," Ash said.

"A spokesperson for the governor's office stated they are unsure how long the Guard will remain in Pryor. Violence from competing gangs vying to fill the void left by Bennett continues, so the Guard will provide security until a stable local government and police force can be established. Authorities have also been unable to confirm if all of the women's re-education facilities have been located and shut down. In other news, keeping the rail lines from Canada to Mexico functional continues to be a challenge as rebels relentlessly hijack railcars and steal food to sell on the black market."

Ash finished the sandwiches and placed them on the table. She sat down across from Caleb as the newsreader moved on to the next story.

"Climatologists are uncertain how soon, or if, temperatures will return to pre-stratospheric aerosol injection levels. The U.S. and EU have terminated the program due to fighting on both fronts over limited resources and critical fuel shortages. Most areas around the world are reporting little temperature change and rainfall patterns continue to be erratic. The volcano that erupted in the northern U.S. remains quiet as cities and towns continue to dig out from deep ash deposits. Scientists see no evidence the eruption will resume any time soon."

"That's encouraging." Ash took a bite of her sandwich as the broadcast continued.

"On the international front, talks have broken down between the EU and the coalition of Asia, South Pacific, and Africa countries known as ASPA. The rhetoric has ramped up considerably over the past few weeks with both sides threatening nukes. Scientists in North America believe a nuclear deployment in Europe would likely have minimal impact on our continent. Any detrimental effects would depend on the size and number of bombs and prevalent winds. President Steele confirmed there would be no U.S. intervention."

As usual, the broadcast abruptly ended with no warning.

"I'll be curious to hear Heath's thoughts on winds and nuclear fallout," Caleb said.

"I'm not sure I want to know what he thinks. Heath is prone to doom and gloom. Have you heard if Melora was able to find the deer with the drone?"

"Unfortunately, no. She and Tyler haven't seen any sign of them at the lake or any other deer or elk for that matter."

"I was in the storehouse, and all of the venison is gone. There was some mutton, but Tony was doling it out in small quantities and highly recommending stews. Maybe we should organize a fishing party like we've been talking about."

"It's worth a try," Caleb replied.

"Four of the five members of the hunting party were

injured, and we lost Luna. If there is any way to avoid another hunting trip, I think we have to try."

"I'm with you. As bad as it was, it could have turned out much worse," Caleb said.

Ash had thought about it a lot, and the realization often kept her up at night.

TWENTY-NINE

ASH AND CALEB organized a small fishing party. Collectively, they hoped to catch enough fish out of the lake with hook and line to help supplement the meat supply. They gathered up their fishing gear and walked over to the Solomon farm, where everyone would meet and hike the mile to the lake together.

Ryan was already sitting on the front porch waiting. "I dug up a bunch of worms since I figured most of the others wouldn't even think about bait," he said as he lifted up a small pail as proof.

Miranda walked out the door and wrinkled her nose. "I don't have to touch those, do I?"

"I can bait your hook, and I'll take your fish off when you catch one," Ryan said.

Ash chuckled. "Now I remember why I hung out with Caleb when we were kids and not you," she said as she handed Sara off to Olivia, who had just joined them.

"Yeah, right, you hung out with Caleb because none of the girls in Beartooth liked worms and stinging insects.

Are you sure it wasn't because you already had a crush on him at age six?"

Ash smiled and shrugged her shoulders. "He was pretty cute."

"Was?" Caleb asked.

"Cute then, handsome now," Ash clarified as she leaned up and kissed him.

Miranda rolled her eyes and shook her head.

Olivia smiled. As she started telling stories about Caleb and Ash as kids, others slowly trickled in. Dillon, Evelyn, Lauren, and Zane were the next to arrive. Ash was happy to end the stream of embarrassing childhood stories and return to the topics of hunting, fishing, and archery.

"I've been practicing quite a bit, and the new arrows you made me have helped a lot," Evelyn said.

"Dad set up a target behind our cabin so that Evelyn and I can practice whenever we want," Lauren added.

"Wow, that's surprising. I kept expecting an unpleasant visit from Henry, scolding me for encouraging Evelyn to shoot a weapon," Ash said.

"I think he's finally given up," Evelyn giggled.

A few minutes later, Gavin Winters walked up. Ash was a little surprised to see Gavin. He fell in the middle of the age group assembled, but he had always been kind of standoffish. In the last few years, he had taken archery a little more seriously, so maybe Ash should have expected him to be interested in fishing as well.

"I have a couple extra poles if anyone needs one. I also grabbed this plastic tub out of the storage trailer. I thought it might work to hold the fish you catch," Owen said as he walked up to the group with his hands full.

"I was hoping you had extras. Evelyn and Lauren need poles." Dillon took the rods from his dad.

"Great idea, Dad. It'll hold dozens of fish and make it easier to carry our bounty back," Caleb replied.

Olivia and Sara waved as the group walked away from the cabin. "Have fun and be careful. Don't hurry back, Sara and I are going to make cookies today, so we'll be thoroughly entertained."

The trail leading to the lake started between the Solomon farm and the Thorn ranch. As they passed by the Thorn ranch, Fiona and Jacob jogged out and joined the group.

"Do you want another team competition?" Ash asked Jacob.

"No, Dad said if I bet against you again, he'd make me muck out the stalls alone for the rest of the month."

They talked and laughed as they continued toward the lake. Ash noticed that Caleb and Fiona both wore sidearms, and she had her bear spray. They had only detected a few deer and rabbits, but no predators since the volcanic eruption. Even if a predator did happen by, Ash doubted anything would approach a group this size, so she felt confident they had plenty of weapons.

Once at the lake, Ryan baited his and Miranda's hooks with his worms and offered up the bait to the others. Dillon headed to the lakeshore with Evelyn, Lauren, and Zane in tow. Ash couldn't help but smile as she watched Dillon explain fishing to Evelyn and help her cast her line out into the water.

"Don't anyone go near that rock, its's ours," Caleb said as he pointed to a large boulder in the opposite direction as Dillon took his small group.

After everyone's equipment was ready, Ash followed Caleb to their rock. She climbed up and cast her line. Within ten minutes, she pulled in her first trout.

Shortly thereafter, one after another in their group

reeled in fish. She listened to all the laughter and shrieks of delight, and it warmed her heart. She spied Miranda hopping around, trying to avoid the flopping fish on shore she just reeled in. Ryan brought his line in, took her fish off, rebaited her hook, and threw his line back out.

Gavin, Jacob, and Fiona had gone the furthest around the lake. Ash hoped that Gavin wasn't interested in Fiona. Gavin was definitely attractive, and unfortunately, he knew it. Jacob was a much nicer guy.

Ash noticed that Lauren and Zane had wandered off from Dillon and Evelyn. It was difficult for teens to find ways to spend time alone together in Beartooth, so Ash assumed this was as close as they'd get to a date.

It always surprised Ash how different Lauren and Evelyn were, not just physically, but in their mannerisms and personalities. Evelyn was a petite woman with curly blonde hair, dimples, and a sweet, nurturing disposition who made friends easily. Lauren was her complete opposite. She was taller and stronger, sported long wavy brown hair with steaks of strawberry blonde, loved the outdoors and being active, and was often moody.

Dillon stayed close to Evelyn, which didn't surprise her. He was protective of those he loved, especially Evelyn. As Ash watched them, she chuckled and shook her head at a memory of her mom.

"What's so funny?" Caleb asked.

"I was just thinking about that time when I was telling mom about one of our adventures, and she said it was lucky that you chose a strong partner who can share in your adventures rather than a petite girl like Evelyn. That's when I accused mom of making me sound like a lumberjack."

"You are many things—beautiful, strong, resourceful,

sexy, but you are no lumberjack," Caleb replied with a playful smile.

"I'm glad you think so."

Evelyn squealed with delight. They watched as Dillon slowly reeled in his line. Even though they couldn't hear them, he was clearly instructing Evelyn on what to do. By the time Evelyn got the fish to shore, Dillon had his line out of the water. He picked up Evelyn's fish, removed the hook, and held it close to her face so she could see it. She ran her fingers down the length of the fish and then smiled up at Dillon.

"She is sweet and adorable, but I can't picture her carrying one end of a pole with a dead deer strung on it for two miles," Ash said.

Caleb threw his head back and laughed. "No, I can't either, in fact the only woman I ever picture doing anything like that is you. Reel your line in and just sit with me."

Ash reeled her line in and set her pole down. She scooted close to Caleb on the rock, and he draped his arm around her, pulling her close. She tilted her head over until it rested on his shoulder.

"This has always been my happy place," she said as she gazed out over the glistening lake surrounded by thick forest and majestic mountains.

"Me too. Even though we're surrounded by friends, it still feels like it's just the two of us."

Ash looked up at him and smiled. He lowered his head and kissed her.

"Hey, that kind of behavior isn't going to feed the community," Ryan yelled as he headed in their direction.

Caleb slowly ended the kiss, stood up, and extended his hand. Ash took hold and let him help her to her feet. He wrapped his arms around her and held her for a few more minutes before they climbed down from the boulder.

"We've probably got about all we can carry, so let's get them cleaned and head home," Caleb shouted to the group.

Nearly everyone pitched in to help clean the fish. Between the eleven of them, they had over fifty large trout.

"That was a lot of fun. I'll bet Mom and Dad will be surprised that I caught dinner," Lauren said.

"These are big enough that we have more than enough for the entire community. Maybe we should organize an impromptu community fish-fry when we get back," Ash suggested.

Everyone loved the idea. As they walked back, they formulated a plan on how they would get the word out, what else they would cook, and how they'd cook the fish.

The entire community turned out, contributing whatever they could to the meal. As usual, Archie jumped in to do the cooking. They built a fire in the middle of the common area. They cooked potatoes in the cooler coals near the edge of the fire and fried the fish in large cast iron skillets.

Those not cooking stood close to the fire to stay warm as the sun slowly sank behind the tall mountain peaks. As everyone visited with family and friends while waiting for the fish and potatoes to cook, Dan jumped up onto the flatbed trailer.

"I'd like to thank everyone who went fishing today. As I understand, Ash caught the first fish, which I'm sure is no surprise to anyone, but Lauren edged her out by one in the total number caught. Be careful, Ash, you may have some competition," Dan said to laughter.

Ash smiled and shrugged her shoulders.

"I'm sorry. If I hadn't distracted you, maybe you could have pulled in one more there at the end," Caleb whispered in her ear.

"I'd prefer your distraction to victory any day," Ash replied.

"This get-together comes at a good time. I know some of you are nervous about the future. Only time will tell if the temperatures warm up enough and in time to have a productive growing season and if the deer herds will return. Beartooth skated along nicely for a quarter of a century, but a lot has changed in the past few years. These are trying times for not only us, but for our nation and the world as we as a species struggle to overcome unprecedented natural and human disasters. But I have complete confidence that we will persevere. So, enjoy this bounty provided by your friends and family, and keep the faith," Dan stated.

Everyone cheered as Archie started doling out fish and baked potatoes. Ash looked over at Caleb holding Sara. He smiled and then leaned over and kissed her lips. Standing here on this cool, but beautiful night with the people she loved most, she believed Dan.

THIRTY

THE PAST SEVERAL weeks had been busy. Ash and Caleb, with help from Miranda and Ryan, moved the rest of the beehives out of the shed and into the fields. As the temperatures warmed, covering the fruit trees with fragrant blossoms, the bees had become more active. Wildflowers and weeds also poked through the volcanic deposits, adding an additional source of nectar and pollen for the bees and color to the gray landscape.

Caleb worked at the farm with Owen and Dillon from dawn until dusk to sow seeds in the fields, though three weeks later than the previous year. The crops were vital for the community. They would help sustain them through the coming winter, assuming the growing season was long enough for the crops to mature.

While Caleb worked in the fields, Ash planted their garden and helped Evelyn plant one for her and Dillon.

"I feel guilty letting you and Lauren plant my garden," Evelyn said as she sat nearby in the shade, playing with Sara.

"Don't. I wouldn't have even been able to plant mine

without your help. The more mobile Sara gets, the more difficult it is for me to do projects like this," Ash replied.

"But entertaining Sara is fun, digging in the dirt, not so much."

Ash laughed. "That's a matter of opinion. I love digging in the dirt almost as much as I enjoy tending to stinging insects. In fact, I need to check them as soon as we're done."

"Can I go? It's a nice day for a walk," Lauren asked.

"Me too," Evelyn added.

"I'd love the company. I miss Caleb when he works such long hours. This year is even worse because Sara is old enough to express her displeasure with Caleb's absence as well."

"I miss Dillon, too, but I knew what I was getting into when I married a farmer," Evelyn said.

When they finished both gardens, they walked to the clinic to see if Miranda wanted to go with them.

"Heck yes! I've got no patients today. Ryan is in the vineyard pruning vines and probably won't be done until dinner," Miranda replied.

The five of them walked the short distance to the hives. Ash loved the new location, and Caleb had no issue with her and Sara checking the bees alone. From the hives near the farm, she could usually see or hear a Solomon, and from those located in the orchard, she was almost always within sight of a Ferguson.

"Sara already seems to have a rapport with the bees. Even when she's noisy, they don't seem concerned by her presence," Miranda commented.

Ash watched Sara. It was true, the toddler was fascinated by the insects. Seeing her little girl with the bees made Ash happy.

"Your other grandma would be so proud if she could

see you now. I have no doubt you will carry on the family beekeeping tradition and find joy in the task," Ash told Sara as they watched the bees coming and going from the hives.

After Ash verified the hives were undisturbed, the group headed back to the residential area and went their separate ways. Sara was clearly worn out. Inside the cabin, the toddler grabbed her stuffed bee and crawled up onto the couch. She made flying motions for a few moments but then drifted off to sleep. Ash gently picked her up and carried her to her room.

Once Sara was settled, Ash poured herself a glass of tea and turned on the radio. She tuned into an interview with a climatologist. The woman explained that a warming trend had been observed in a number of countries who had already been experiencing extreme temperatures and severe drought. She had no doubt that without continued stratospheric aerosol injections, temperatures would slowly creep back up to pre-SAI levels.

The newsreader then segued into President Steele's lack of progress on increasing oil extraction and refinement and addressing climate change as outlined in her FOCUS initiative. Securing food-distribution channels and rebuilding key government facilities and national infrastructure wasn't going well either, while fighting with rebel factions running rogue throughout the country and monitoring the southern border.

Ash finished her tea. As she stood to go refill her glass, a live report from Pryor made her pause.

"The National Guard remains in Pryor, trying to restore order. There is still no word on the whereabouts of Bennett and an estimated fifty of his most loyal militia."

Ash sat back down and listened.

"Pryor is now little more than a collection of derelict

buildings lining dusty, dirt streets. The residents, who have just started to venture out under the protection of the Guard, appear extremely malnourished and frightened. A spokesperson for the Guard said that progress has been made, but it will take time to restore order, and it remains dangerous to be out after dark as gangs continue to fight for control of the city. All of the women's re-education facilities have been located and shut down. Over a thousand women were held in four facilities where they were starved, beaten, and raped by their guards repeatedly while being forced by the same guards to attend hours of morality education each day. Approximately thirty women were flown out of Pryor in Guard helicopters to receive medical treatment beyond what could be provided locally. Grains stored in FAMA warehouses have been distributed to the residents, temporarily alleviating suffering caused by a food shortage in the city."

The reporter stated the sun was setting, making it necessary to quickly return to his bunk in the military's camp, so he would be off air until it was safe to continue reporting.

"Daddy?" Ash heard Sara cry from her room.

Ash turned off the radio and retrieved Sara from her crib. "He's still working, but let's go to grandma's and wait for Daddy, Grandpa, and Uncle Dillon. Maybe Aunt Evelyn will be there too."

Sara's face lit up.

"Daddy."

She knew there was no point in delaying. When Sara wanted something, she was relentless, and right now she wanted Caleb.

THIRTY-ONE

SEEDS for the farm fields and personal gardens had been in the ground for nearly a month. It hadn't rained, so Owen, Caleb, and Dillon cleaned the volcanic fallout from the ditches and irrigated their crops. Everyone else hauled water from the creeks for their gardens.

Temperatures had only exceeded seventy degrees several times so far, but at least the overnight lows were holding in the low fifties. Plant growth was slow, but everyone was relieved to see green shoots, verifying that the seeds had germinated, and there would be grains and vegetables given enough time.

Everyone now had their own salad greens and spinach, and the stored grain from the previous year was holding up well. Between fishing, an uptick in egg production, and more goat milk to make cheese, the rate of meat consumption had slowed, giving livestock time to mature and fatten up. They still hoped to locate wild game closer to the community, but the immediate meat crisis had eased.

Melora and Tyler flew the drone every three days to

the north and east, looking for the herds, but with no success. They made several flights south of the community as well, but after what Ash and Caleb experienced in the wild, no one was any more eager to head south than north.

Caleb was back to helping with the farm as needed and no longer worked dawn to dusk. Ash was happy to be able to spend most days together. They worked in the garden, checked the bee hives, made arrows, shot their bows, and fished in the creeks on days they didn't have larger projects.

"Are Dillon and Ryan still available to help move my honey harvesting workbenches today to the new hive locations?" Ash asked as they finished up with breakfast.

"Yep, I'm going to go get June and the wagon to gather up the workbenches. We'll move one to each of the two hive clusters at the farm and the orchard, and put the third behind our cabin," Caleb replied.

"Sounds good. I hope I don't have too many hives in too close of a proximity to each other, but I don't see any point in moving them so far from the farm and orchard just to move them back into the storage shed in a few months. Maybe someday I'll want to return them to their old locations, but I do feel more comfortable taking Sara to the hives now that they're closer."

"Why were the hives so far away before?"

"When Mom first brought the hives, people were frightened of the bees and didn't want them too close to the community. There were lots of great pollen sources where Mom located the original hives, and it was a quiet, conducive environment to grow the apiary."

"Makes sense. How soon do you think you can harvest honey? I'd like to schedule another group fishing event before then."

"I talked to Miranda, Evelyn, and Lauren. They're available to help me next week. We're going to open hive one first, and if it looks ready, we'll harvest from another hive every other day until we're done with the first harvest of the year. With eight hives, it should take a little over two weeks to get through them all," Ash replied.

"Let's plan on fishing later this week then. I'll see how many people we can gather up."

Ash, Sara, and Caleb walked to Bob's ranch. Jacob had let all of the horses out to graze in the pasture except June. He even had her harnessed and hitched to the small wagon.

"Thanks for getting June ready for us," Caleb said.

"You bet. Do you need more help moving Ash's workbenches?"

"No, there are only three, and Dillon and Ryan are helping. But if you're free later this week, we're planning another group fishing trip," Caleb replied.

"Sure, I'll check with Fiona," Jacob said as they drove away.

They stopped the wagon where Dillon and Ryan were already waiting. Ash took the reins while Caleb jumped down and helped load the workbench. Once it was secure, Dillon and Ryan climbed into the wagon bed. Caleb returned to the driver's seat, took the reins, and headed toward the farm.

Once at the farm, they unloaded the workbench near the hives, and then they threaded their way to the next area. After retrieving the second bench, they moved it near the hives in the Ferguson orchard. They hauled the last bench to Ash and Caleb's cabin.

"Thanks for all the help," Ash said as they left Dillon and Ryan to return the wagon and June to the Thorn ranch, making several quick detours along the way.

"Done already?" Jacob asked.

"It wasn't a big project," Caleb replied.

"Fiona said she'd love to go fishing, so count us both in."

"Great, we've got the same group as last time, minus Miranda. She's covering the clinic this week, and Emily will cover next week so Miranda can help with honey harvest," Ash said.

"So, Gavin's going too?"

"Sorry, but I hated to exclude him. Other than me, Ash, Dillon, Ryan, and Archie, he's the only other person in the community who's killed a deer, so we need to keep him in the loop for fish and game harvesting," Caleb replied.

"I'll keep practicing and as soon as the deer return, I'd like to go hunting," Jacob said.

"We can go shoot anytime, just say the word," Caleb offered.

"Thanks. I need all the help I can get."

Ash took one of Sara's tiny hands and Caleb took the other. It was slow going, but Sara was already showing an independent streak and didn't like to be carried all of the time.

"I can see so much of you in our daughter. I bet you were stubborn and independent too when you were her age," Caleb said.

"I've never been stubborn, and I'm only as independent as I need to be."

Caleb chuckled. "Have you ever heard Mom tell the story about how when you were like six, you insisted on cleaning your own fish when a group of us went fishing even though I tried to do it for you. You cut yourself with my knife. Dad made me do mine and Dillon's chores for a month for giving a six-year-old a knife."

"Everyone thought I was too young to go, especially

since I was a girl. I thought I had to prove I could do anything any of you boys could do. Mom gathered my bugs to use as bait so I could catch more fish, and she understood when I explained the cut. I'm sorry you got into trouble on my account. I didn't know."

"I didn't want you to feel bad, and since you let me clean your fish the next time we went, I got over it. I liked doing things for you, and I still do."

"Well, I may be stubborn, but I'm not stupid. I cut myself and learned a lesson. Besides, for some reason, most of the boys seldom went with us after that so I had less to prove."

"They couldn't handle being out-fished by a girl, and as we got older, I may have punched anyone who looked at you."

Ash laughed. "You mean there were more than Jacob and Sam?"

"Lots more," Caleb said as he scooped up Sara. "And, I'll do the same for my little angel when the time comes."

Ash shook her head and smiled. "Wouldn't it have been easier to just tell me how you felt?"

"Maybe, but when it came to you, I always had a difficult time thinking with the right part of my body."

"How about now?"

"I still do, and that will never change. It's always been you, Ash, and it always will be."

A tear slipped down her cheek. She felt the same. She prayed that they could be together forever, but every time he left without her, she feared he might not return.

THIRTY-TWO

ASH WAS anxious to open a hive for the first time in the season. It was just over two weeks later than last year's first honey harvest, but still a week earlier than she originally estimated so she was hopeful.

After the fourth stratospheric aerosol injection, coupled with a nearly simultaneous volcanic eruption, they experienced the longest and coldest winter in Beartooth's short existence. It had taken longer for grasses and wildflowers to poke through the thick layer of volcanic deposits, and they were delayed in planting fields and gardens. Fortunately, the Ferguson's fruit trees were covered with blossoms, only slightly later than usual, providing a source of nectar and pollen for the bees.

Miranda, Evelyn, and Lauren arrived at the cabin early. They gathered up the equipment and walked to the cluster of hives in the Ferguson's orchard.

"It's nice that we don't have to go as far to reach the hives as we used to," Miranda said as they set up their equipment on the newly arrived workbench.

"I feel safer, especially when I bring Sara, though I thought it was best to leave her with Olivia when we opened the hive today," Ash replied.

Ash, Miranda, and Lauren donned their protective clothing while Evelyn waited a safe distance away.

"Let's set the top box aside and check the lower honey Super first," Ash instructed.

Ash and Lauren gently moved the top box to the side while Miranda waved the smoker near the hive entrance to calm the bees. Ash then pulled a frame out and held it up.

"I think we are going to get a good harvest if this frame is any indication," Ash said as she inspected all ten frames in the Super.

Miranda kept the bees from following while Ash removed the fullest frame and took it over to the workbench. Lauren cut the wax caps off with a knife, and the wax dropped into the bucket. Ash then secured the frame in the extractor. They repeated the process with three more of the heaviest frames.

When the extractor had four frames secured inside, Ash spun the frames to remove the honey while Miranda kept the bees away from the work area with the smoker.

Ash returned the frames to the box, took four more, and repeated the process. They drained off enough honey from the extractor into an extra bucket so they would be able to add frames from the top Super without submerging them in honey. Once all the honey was extracted from the eight fullest frames in the top Super, they reassembled the hive and returned to the work area.

They took off their suits and gathered up their gear. Looking at the amount of honey and wax, Ash was pleased by the harvest, but she was even more pleased when Caleb and Ryan walked up.

"Perfect timing. We're done harvesting, and we have a lot of honey and wax to carry back. If you hadn't showed up it might have taken us two trips," Ash said.

Ash and Caleb each took a handle on the extractor and started back toward their cabin. Ryan, Miranda, Lauren, and Evelyn grabbed the wax, additional honey bucket, and all of the equipment and trailed close behind.

"You should have moved the hives years ago. The new location has probably cut the distance we have to carry the honey in half," Ryan said.

"I guess it just didn't seem necessary to change something that had been working for so long. But, I agree, this is much easier," Ash replied.

Once they reached their cabin, Ash and Caleb set the extractor on the table with the spout hanging over the edge. Below it, they placed a sieve on top of another collection vessel to strain out bits of wax, bee parts, and other impurities. Once everything was set up, Ash opened the spigot and honey slowly flowed out of the extractor, through the sieve, and into a clean bucket.

"Need anything else from me?" Caleb asked.

"No, I've got plenty of help, but thanks for showing up just in the nick of time to help carry everything back. I didn't expect to get so much honey after all the setbacks we've experienced."

"I was thinking positive and hoped you'd need help. I'll catch up with Dad and Dillon so we can get the last irrigation set running, and then I'll get Sara from Mom and be home in time for dinner," he said as he pulled Ash into his arms and gave her a long, passionate kiss that left her breathless.

"Sounds good," Ash said as she watched him walk out the door.

Ryan gave Miranda a peck on the cheek, and then he

and Lauren left to return to the orchard where Zane was helping their folks, leaving Ash with Evelyn and Miranda.

"Would you like some tea. It's slow going from here. We just need to keep scraping the edges of the extractor so we don't leave any honey behind, and when the level goes down, we'll start adding more honey from the extra bucket."

Evelyn and Miranda didn't have anything else going on, so Ash made tea. She sat down at the table with her sisters-in-law. They sipped their tea and watched as the thick golden liquid slowly drained out of the extractor into the sieve.

"It kind of sucks that my two best friends are married to my brothers," Miranda said, finally breaking the silence.

"Why is that bad?" Evelyn asked.

Ash and Evelyn watched Miranda fidget, wrapping her blondish-brown hair around her finger. Her eyes remained focused on her cup.

"Something wrong?" Ash prodded.

"I really need some advice on, well, I could use some ideas about…oh heck, I'd like to talk to someone about sex, but I wish there was someone other than the women sleeping with my brothers."

Ash and Evelyn burst out laughing.

"I'm serious," Miranda pouted. "Don't laugh at me."

It took Ash and Evelyn several moments to stop giggling.

"I'm sorry, what would you like to talk about?" Ash asked.

"Ryan doesn't kiss me in private as passionately as Caleb just kissed you in front of everyone. Is there something unappealing about me, or am I doing something to repulse him?"

"You are adorable. You have beautiful hair and eyes, a great shape, and an infectious smile," Ash replied.

"And you're sexy. How would you like to have overly-curly, blonde hair, baby-blue eyes, fair skin, dimples, and a height of barely 5'2." I wasn't sure if any guy would ever take me seriously," Evelyn said.

"At least you're not a lumberjack," Ash added.

"Lumberjack? That's ridiculous, you're only, what 5'7"? Where did you come up with that?" Evelyn asked.

"Once Mom said that Caleb was lucky that he chose a strong partner who can share his adventures rather than a petite girl. I accused her of making me sound like a lumberjack, and the joke kind of stuck," Ash replied.

"Okay, you're both beautiful. Ash with her long, luxurious, dark hair, long legs, and gorgeous skin. She exudes fitness and strength and makes every guy drool over her. And then there is petite Evelyn, flouncing around with her curly, blonde hair, blue eyes, and dimples, making every man want to scoop her up and take care of her. But this is about me," Miranda huffed.

"I don't flounce," Evelyn said, sounding offended.

"And, I certainly don't make anyone drool. That's disgusting," Ash added.

"See what I mean, you two are no help at all. You're just making fun of me and not taking me seriously."

"We're sorry," Ash said as she looked over at Evelyn. "So, Ryan isn't much on public displays of affection. As long as he's affectionate and romantic behind closed doors, I wouldn't complain."

"But he isn't."

"You've, uh, consummated your marriage, haven't you," Evelyn asked, unable to disguise her shock.

"Yes, of course, but not much else or very often."

"What do you mean by not much else?" Ash asked.

"He's very conservative, polite, gentle, and unimaginative," Miranda replied.

"I imagine there are plenty of women in this world who would think that's endearing," Evelyn added.

"But I have to practically throw myself at him to even get that. What can I do to make Ryan look at me like Caleb and Dillon look at you two? Most of the time when Caleb looks at Ash, it makes me uncomfortable, like I need to leave the room and give them some privacy."

"Well, that's embarrassing. I hope no one else thinks that," Ash responded.

"Yeah, it's kind of like that," Evelyn added.

Ash's cheeks turned red. She picked up her cup in both hands and took a long sip to hide her blush.

"So, how do I make Ryan look at me that way, at least in private?"

"I don't know how to make Caleb do anything, but he does get a little crazy when I put on my wedding dress, which I've only done on two of our three anniversaries. He also seems to really like it when I wear one of his button-up shirts with nothing else on."

"Dillon is easy. I'm not nearly as helpless as I let him believe sometimes. He thinks he needs to protect me from the world. It annoyed me at first, but then I realized he only does what he does because he loves me. So, when he wants to pamper me and hold me, I let him. Once he gets his hands on me, one thing usually leads to another, and he forgets about treating me like a child and realizes I'm a woman."

"None of that is helpful. I doubt putting on one of Ryan's shirts and batting my eyes at him would get him excited. For one, he's not much taller than me, so his shirt wouldn't cover what it's supposed to, and I would look stupid, not sexy. And, if I bat my eyes at him, he'd probably ask me if I had something in my eye."

Ash was trying hard not to laugh, and she could tell Evelyn was struggling as well.

"Have you tried just talking to him and telling him how you feel? You two have known each other most of your lives, and he's always been afraid of your big brothers beating him up if he so much as looked at you. Maybe he's having a hard time moving from admiring the lovely little Solomon sister and trying not to anger her brothers, to throwing you over his shoulder and carting you off to bed to have his way with you," Ash offered.

"I'd be mortified. What would I say?"

"I don't know exactly, but when Caleb and I decided to get married, he would barely kiss me at first, and definitely not like I wanted him to. He said he didn't know if the engagement instantly flipped a switch on our relationship and gave him the right to just kiss me anytime he felt like it. I told him it did, and he's been kissing me like he did today ever since."

Ash got up, scraped the sides of the extractor, and dumped more honey into it to strain. She poured them each another cup of tea and sat back down.

"You know, maybe you and Ryan need a dramatic event or adventure. When I got off track, got turned around, and ended up falling down that steep slope, Dillon is the one who found me. He rescued me and carried me home. Things changed that day. I think he was as afraid as all the other men in the community about getting involved with a nearly-blind girl, but he said that when I was missing, all he could think about was all the time we had already lost not being together. And I'm sure Ash and Caleb's honeymoon from hell in the wild strengthened their bond even more. They will always have that shared experience where there was no one else to depend on except each other," Evelyn explained.

Ash thought about what Evelyn said and there was a lot of wisdom in her words. Often a person doesn't realize what they have until they're in a situation where they might lose what they love the most.

"I don't want anything bad to happen to either one of us, just to bring us closer together and spice things up, so I'm not sure what to do," Miranda said in defeat.

"Talk to him, love him, and be patient. I know Ryan loves you, but we go from youth to adult in a very different way than people in the rest of the country, and it can be a difficult adjustment. Sometimes when I talk to Fiona or Melora, I realize that life may be simpler here, but it's different and kind of ambiguous in some respects. Fi and Mel grew up where society provided milestones for when you moved on to a new phase in life. There were school graduation ceremonies, young adults went to college, they graduated from college, they got jobs, they left home, and built careers. How we transition from child to young adult to adult here is a lot fuzzier, and everyone handles those changes differently," Ash replied.

"I guess I do feel better, thank you," Miranda said as she took Ash's hand in one hand and Evelyn's in the other and gave them a firm squeeze.

"Good. When you said you wanted to talk about sex, I thought you wanted to know what I do to your brother to drive him out of his mind when we make love. I'd be happy to share that with you in detail if it will help, and I'm sure Ash can enlighten us both," Evelyn stated with a serious look on her face.

"Oh, heavens, no. Even the thought of hearing that makes me a little nauseous. I think that's my cue to leave.

I'll see you the day after tomorrow to collect honey from the next hive. And, not a word of this to my brothers, or I will haunt you every day for the rest of your lives," Miranda said as she stood and darted out the door.

Ash lifted her cup and tapped it to Evelyn's in a toast. "That last bit was cruel, but hilarious. I never would have thought you had it in you."

"I feel a little bad, but I couldn't help myself. It was too easy," Evelyn replied as they both burst out laughing.

Ash and Evelyn were still laughing when Caleb walked in the door carrying Sara.

"Everything okay here? I just passed Miranda. She wouldn't look at me and was nearly running. Then I come in here and you two are practically rolling on the floor with laughter."

"We had a great time and an enlightening visit, but if we share any of it with you, Miranda vowed to kill us," Ash said as she tried to quit laughing.

Caleb shrugged his shoulders. "If you're ganging up on Miranda, I guess that's nothing Dillon and I haven't done our entire lives, so who am I to judge."

Evelyn got up and walked to the door. "Is Dillon still working?"

"Nope, he headed out the same time I did. I imagine he's home by now."

"Good, I'm all of sudden in the mood to go home, bat my eyes at Dillon, and have him tend to this little cut I got while helping with the honey," Evelyn said as she held up her finger, showing a tiny cut on its tip.

"Yeah, and this shirt may be a little dirty after all of our hard, sweaty work. I think I better change after we put Sara to bed."

Evelyn chuckled as she walked out the door.

When Ash turned around, she could see Caleb

studying her with an amused smile on his lips. He set Sara down and walked toward her. He pulled her into his arms and kissed her.

"If you're short on clothes, I have a shirt in the closet you'd look great in," he said with a wink as he turned and headed for the kitchen.

THIRTY-THREE

DAN CALLED A CLB MEETING. Ash had no doubt it had to do with Melora spotting deer while flying the drone south of Beartooth the day before. Ash felt sick to her stomach. She had no doubt Caleb would be leaving again.

When they reached the school, Ash and Caleb took seats between Ryan and Melora.

"I know this is short notice but all of the sudden it seems like we have a lot to talk about," Dan said to open the meeting. "Let's start with Ash. Tell us about the honey harvest."

"We completed the first harvest a couple of days ago. We got more honey and wax than I expected. I've already taken all the honey to the storehouse. I haven't worked up the wax yet, but with the long days, candles aren't a huge need right now, and I've moved away from using wax in the soap as much as I can."

"So, what does that mean going into next winter?" Maria asked.

"It's very doubtful we'll get any sort of third harvest

this year, so even though we got a lot more honey than I normally do with a first harvest, we're still going to be down from last year."

"We need to make sure everyone knows to start rationing now," Dan stated.

"While we're on the topic of food, I've weaned all of the lambs and piglets, so right now we're focusing on fattening everything up while we have decent grazing. With the fish and gardens, community meat consumption has slowed considerably. The hens are laying well at the moment. As far as the horse herd goes, Jacob has been working with Misty and she's ready to take Luna's place in the herd," Bob said.

Ash didn't want to make Caleb or Bob feel bad, so she kept her eyes diverted when he mentioned Luna. She still teared up every time she thought of the little mare and how she died.

"Sounds good, Bob. Ryan, how's everything going at the Ferguson place?" Dan asked.

"We've got a good crop of kid goats, and they're weaned as well. Goat meat has never been a huge part of our meat supply, but we'll have a few going into winter as usual. It looks like we'll have an average crop of apples, cherries, and grapes this year despite the late start."

Heath reported that Diane had finally recovered from her respiratory infection and was back to work if anyone needed dishes or food storage vessels. Henry said the water quality continued to improve since the eruption. Maria said she had nothing to add.

"Okay, Tyler, you're up," Dan said.

"I've used parts from one of the commercial dryers to build a food dehydrator. Since we haven't been using the commercial washers and dryers since prior to installing the micro-hydropower system, Tony didn't think one dryer would be missed. The Solomons have traditionally harvested their pinto beans after the beans have dried in the field. Since that likely won't be possible this year with our abbreviated growing season, we may have to dry them once harvested. I'm also working with Graham to see what we might be able to dry from the greenhouse now that everyone's gardens are taking pressure off the vegetables he's growing. So far, we've found carrots, tomatoes, and peas dehydrate well."

"I love the innovative thinking around here. It's what's made this community successful and able to quickly adapt to change," Dan added.

"Melora and I have also gotten all the cameras back up and running. So far, nothing larger than a rabbit has come into view. Lastly, I've recruited Joy Garland as an apprentice. She's expressed interest in learning about the micro-hydropower system, other infrastructure, and all the other equipment and gadgets I build and maintain. It's probably wise to train someone who can step in if something happens to me or if I get too old to do it all. Fiona is back-up for me and Melora on the cameras."

Ash sometimes forgot how vital Tyler was to the community. It was fortunate that he and Melora hit it off. Melora helped ease the strain between them.

"So, Melora and Caleb, let's talk hunting," Dan said.

Caleb nodded to Melora to begin.

"Tyler and I flew the drone to the north and east and spotted nothing. Yesterday, we flew south of the road and saw a small herd of deer about four miles from here, but still north of where Ash and Caleb felt they were no longer being stalked. Since their trip south was over three years ago, there's no guarantee that the predators haven't moved closer, but we didn't see any when we flew the drone."

"I looked at the footage. I think it's one of the herds that used to frequent this area. There's a distinctive buck with an atypical rack that I've kept an eye on for years," Caleb added.

"Do you think they're heading this way?" Ryan asked.

"I doubt it. Looking at the grass in the meadow close to the lakes where Caleb and Ash sensed they were no longer being hunted, it looks better there than here, so if they aren't being preyed upon, I see no reason why they'd head further north," Melora replied.

"So, what do you suggest?" Dan asked.

"I say we go after them. But this time we're more familiar with the area. We'll only track them as far as we can while allowing us to get back the same day," Caleb replied, glancing over at Ash.

She gave him a weak smile. As much as she didn't want him to go, this trip would be different and much shorter.

"How many horses do you need?" Bob asked.

"I don't think we need Fiona this time. I believe we're capable of packing the horses without her, and I know she isn't interested in going anyway. If Melora would bring the drone and her shotgun, and Ryan and Archie are willing, I think that's enough. So, if we could take Felix, the three geldings, Sierra, Bella, and June, that would give us four to ride and three to pack. Since we're not anticipating any elk this time, we'll likely be able to pack anything we harvest on three horses so we can ride home and make it back the same day," Caleb replied.

"Beth isn't going to be happy, and I doubt Archie will be too excited either, but I'll ask. When do you want to go?" Dan asked.

"If Archie is in, I think we should head out first thing in the morning," Melora replied.

Caleb looked over at Ash. As much as she struggled with her fears of raising Sara alone, she had to believe this wouldn't be like last time.

"Tomorrow's as good as any," she said with a smile.

Everyone filed out of the room. Dan said he'd check with Archie and let Melora know. Melora would tie in with Caleb later in the day.

"As we rode home from our trip into the wild, we finally felt safe when we reached the area we'll be hunting tomorrow. You and I rode there with Tyler and Melora once to fly the drone and there was no sign of predators. I don't see any reason you can't come with us tomorrow. I'm sure Mom will watch Sara," Caleb said as they headed for the farm.

Ash was surprised that Caleb suggested she go with him. She missed hunting with him, but it was always possible they could encounter something unexpected despite what Melora saw with the drone. She hadn't shot a deer since before Sara was born, and she hadn't ridden a horse in ages. And, she'd only ever ridden Luna.

She took Caleb's hand and pulled him to a stop. She wrapped her arms around his neck and smiled up at him.

"Thank you. If you feel it's safe enough for me to tag along, maybe I won't worry all day about you. But I haven't ridden a horse in a very long time, and I haven't shot a deer in even longer. Meat is too important for the community right now for me to squander an opportunity or take up a horse that should be packed."

"I do think it will be safe, and I have complete confidence in your riding and hunting ability. I miss hunting with you, but the decision is yours."

"I'll think about it," Ash said as she kissed him.

He pulled her tight to his chest and deepened the kiss.

"Take it home," Dillon called out as he walked up and slugged Caleb on the arm.

Ash stepped back and smiled up at Caleb. "You can still make me forget where we are."

Dillon fell into step with them as they made their way to the farm. "So, what happened at the CLB meeting? Are you going hunting again?"

"We'll head out in the morning. We plan to be back before dark. If you and Dad weren't still irrigating, I'd rope you in," Caleb replied.

"I'll pass. Bad things generally happen when people go into the mountains with you."

Caleb punched his brother and glanced at Ash.

"Hey, what was that for? It's not like Ash doesn't know. She was with you the first time you nearly got yourself killed."

"This time is different," Caleb replied.

"If you say so," Dillon said as he veered off toward the barn.

Sara squealed with delight when she saw Ash and Caleb approaching. Olivia carried her off the porch steps and set her on her feet on the ground. Sara ran as fast as her toddler legs would carry her with her arms outstretched toward Ash.

Ash scooped up her little girl and hugged her tight. She placed kisses all over Sara's plump cheeks, making her giggle.

"I think I'll take a rain check on tomorrow," Ash said.

There would come a time when she might have to take a risk but tomorrow wasn't one of them. Sara needed her, and the thought of leaving her when there were still a lot of unknown variables out there just didn't feel right.

THIRTY-FOUR

THE LAST FEW weeks in August flew by in a flurry of activity. The day after the CLB meeting, Caleb, Melora, Ryan, and Archie went in search of the deer herd that Tyler and Melora found while flying the drone south of Beartooth.

Riding and leading three pack horses, they followed the route Ash and Caleb had covered when they barely made it out of the wild alive over three years ago. This time, no predators stalked the hunting party, and they returned with five deer.

The group had been able to make the hunting trip in a long day. Everyone in the community thought that was a positive sign and held out hope that life after the volcanic eruption would eventually return to a more survivable state.

Crops were growing, but at a slower rate than before. Heath's best estimate was that they had only thirty more days left before overnight temperatures dipped into the low forties, signaling an imminent end to the season. For most crops that would be enough time to reach maturity, but for others, they would be cutting it dangerously close.

The occasional rains seldom provided much benefit. Fortunately, Beartooth's location between a number of creeks allowed them to irrigate their crops and haul water for gardens. The task made everyone's workday a little longer, but as typical with the residents of Beartooth, no one complained.

Between tending the bees, gardening, hauling water, fishing, helping at the farm, spending time with family, and taking care of Sara, Ash and Caleb stayed busy.

"In another couple of months, the long workdays will be behind us," Caleb said as he cleared the table after dinner.

"I hope so, but it seems like every time we think we have everything under control, some new challenge arises," Ash replied as she picked up Sara and left the room.

By the time Ash had Sara ready for bed, Caleb joined them. Ash handed her to him so he could tell her a story as he rocked her in his arms. He kissed her goodnight and tucked her into bed. Ash wasn't sure who enjoyed the ritual more, Caleb or Sara, and she loved watching them.

Once Sara fell asleep, Ash followed Caleb into the living room. She found a broadcast in progress on the radio. The newsreader was wrapping up a report on the political situation abroad. It sounded like a regional war was imminent. And, like the U.S.'s desert southwest, Africa was seeing a gradual increase in temperatures and a decrease in rainfall, while other areas around the world continued to experience unprecedented flooding.

"Little progress has been made in restoring law and order in the U.S. All states whose senators and congressional representatives were executed by the previous administration have held elections. The new elected officials will report to the capital when the sessions resume after the first of the year," the newsreader stated.

"That's months away. I wonder why they don't call a legislative session immediately? The sooner people feel represented, the quicker the government will be able to restore a little confidence in democracy," Ash said.

"Allowing elections is probably just a smokescreen, and the new administration will be just as power-hungry as the last," Caleb replied.

"The cease-fire continues to hold. Despite disruptions to the railway by rogue gangs hijacking grain shipments, commodities from Canada are making it into the U.S. and to countries south of our border. Food distribution to all but Wyoming, Montana, North Dakota, and South Dakota have resumed. The President reiterated that food supplies are still too limited to allow it to fall into criminal hands. Until these states eliminate the rebels and address human rights violations, resources will be directed to other areas where resources will not be wasted."

Ash shook her head. "I understand the reasons, but withholding food has got to be causing undue suffering in the affected states. It seems like a lot of people are being punished over the actions of a few dangerous and delusional groups."

The newsreader then cut over to a reporter in Pryor. "Conditions on the ground in Pryor have improved, but it is still dangerous for citizens to be out after dark. There has been no word on where Bennett and about fifty of his FAMA followers are located but authorities believe they are still in the area. There have been reports of raids on ranches and small communities by heavily armed groups ranging from four to six individuals wearing the FAMA insignia. The raiders have stolen food, weapons, and have kidnapped women. More than a dozen people have been killed while trying to protect their food supplies and families."

"That's disturbing. They came here once. What would stop them from coming back?" Ash asked as she looked over her shoulder at Caleb.

"Hopefully, the lack of a helicopter and no passable roads."

"That may have been enough before, but they've been booted out of Pryor and may be looking for a new home."

Caleb said nothing. Clearly, he had the same fear but no answer to ease her apprehension.

"A spokesperson for the Guard stated that efforts to install a local government and police force to keep the gangs vying for control of the demoralized city from gaining traction is proceeding slowly. Of the thirty women with the most severe injuries who were rescued from the re-education facilities and flown to a hospital in Nebraska, four have died, but the others are expected to make full recoveries. The state has sent in resources to help the remaining women with their medical needs, including prenatal care, and counselors to help deal with the emotional and psychological trauma endured at the hands of FAMA."

"I think I've heard enough for one day," Caleb said as he stood up and turned off the radio. Ash and Caleb went outside. They sat close to each other on the porch swing.

"It warmed up nicely today, and I think the sky is lightening up some," Ash said.

"You're right about the temperature, but it's probably a bit of wishful thinking on the sky."

"You've got to admit that there is only a hint of smoke still lingering in the air, and the air quality has vastly improved in the last few weeks."

"I suppose so. I can't help but wonder how far and

how fast a wildfire could travel in this dry forest. Seeing and smelling smoke since shortly after the eruption started has been a bit concerning."

"Fortunately, we have an evacuation zone in a rocky area with little vegetation on the ground and located close to a lake we can retreat to if a wildfire reaches us."

"If fire was the only thing that I feared might reach us, I'd sleep better at night," Caleb responded quietly as he stared out at the waning light.

Ash wasn't sure if he was still thinking about Jonah Bennett and the missing FAMA militia or his encounter with a new predator, but it was a beautiful night, and her family was home and safe. She decided to let it drop and snuggled closer to Caleb.

THIRTY-FIVE

DAN CALLED a CLB meeting out of the blue. It had only been a couple of days since Ash and Caleb heard the latest disturbing report on the radio, and she wondered if the two were connected, doubting the timing was a coincidence.

Ash and Caleb walked into the school with Ryan and found seats. Dan wasted no time calling the meeting to order.

"We have several topics to discuss. Let's start with food. Bob, how's it looking at your place?" Dan asked.

"The fishing and hunting have taken a lot of pressure off butchering livestock. We had a good crop of piglets and lambs this year, so given time to mature, we're approaching winter in decent shape."

"The community doesn't rely on us to provide much meat, but we've got more goats than usual, and they're fattening up nicely. We all love the llamas, but llama meat could also be incorporated as a source of protein. Last year's cria included two females and three males. Dad thinks we should keep the females and one male in case something happens to Bruce, but we really don't need all of the males," Ryan stated.

No one said anything. Like Ash, they probably didn't like the idea, but there was no reason not to eat llama meat.

"Caleb, what's the farm look like?" Dan asked.

"We think we'll need to start harvest three weeks earlier than last year. The plan is to get ready and watch the weather closely to get as much out of the season as possible. When we see the overnight lows drop to a certain point, we'll need a lot of volunteers on very short notice. We'll have a slightly lower yield than last year, but since last year's harvest was way up, we should be well stocked going into winter."

"What about fish and game?" Dan added.

"So far, the lake fishery is showing no sign of any detrimental effects from our bi-monthly group fishing events, so we'll keep that up. As far as the herds, Melora is searching. Hopefully, some game will wander through the area soon. No one wants a repeat of the big hunt."

"Tony said that Archie and Dennis have perfected their method for smoking trout. He's starting to get a decent amount of the smoked trout stockpiled that he'll incorporate into the meat supply," Maria added.

"Food-wise, it sounds like we're in decent shape for what will likely be our longest winter yet. If the volcano stays quiet and the government doesn't restart the SAI program, next year's growing season should be better. I'll call a community meeting soon and let everyone know to be ready on short notice to help with the harvest. Anything else before we move on?" Dan asked.

No one spoke up, so Dan continued. "The main reason I called this meeting is because I was visiting with Melora and she has been looking at some possibilities for where

Bennett and his FAMA followers might be located. We don't know anything for sure, but we thought it wouldn't hurt to throw it out there to the group. Melora can explain."

Melora projected a section of a map on the white wall. "I'm sure many of you have heard that ranches and communities have been raided by tight groups of FAMA militia. Since the attacks have been small-scale so far, I'm assuming that Bennett is sending out scouting parties to look for resources. If his fifty militia took over a town, the Guard would just roll in and re-take it. So, I got my map out. It has a lot of ranches marked on it, like here." She pointed out a number of ranches near or just inside the boundary of the forest.

Ash studied the map. As the crow-flies, a number of these ranches weren't far away, and there were some old dirt four-wheel-drive roads and a number of established trails cutting through much of the rough terrain. She glanced over at Caleb and knew he was looking at some of the features that caught her eye.

"When Ash and I rode into the wild, we left the paved road here. We then rode on this trail. If we wouldn't have stopped so much the first day, we could have easily ridden to this lake in a day. The lake was nestled at the bottom of a deep gorge, so we just looked down at it and then rode west until we tied into this dirt road," Caleb said.

"If you look east of the lake, you'll see a trail that follows a creek and eventually ties into another dirt road that leads to this ranch." Melora pointed to the features on the map.

"But Bennett and his militia could be anywhere," Henry stated.

"Yes, they could, but I'd bet they've commandeered a

ranch near or just inside the border with the forest. If no one lived there or was able to escape to alert the Guard, the authorities don't have the resources to search for the militia, property-by-property. I doubt they're all just camped out somewhere. If they want shelter, they are likely in this area, but I have no way to verify that."

"I thought you said that once we destroyed their helicopter, they couldn't reach us. You said they were too lazy to hike this far, the route was too rough for vehicles, UTVs, or dirt bikes, and you didn't see any horses," Maria said.

"Most of that is still true, but if they've taken over a ranch, they may now have horses," Melora replied.

"How long would it take to ride from the closest ranch to Beartooth?" Henry asked.

"Judging by how far Caleb and Ash rode in a day, I'd say it could be ridden in two days unless the terrain is rougher than it looks," Melora replied.

"What do we do?" Maria asked, fear in her voice.

"First, don't panic. The scenario Melora described is just a possibility, but we wanted to bring it up in case anyone has any ideas. She and Tyler are going to move a couple cameras to hopefully capture anyone arriving from the east and start flying the drone more in that area. And, we all need to be extra vigilant," Dan replied.

"There is a lot of ground to cover out there. If a small group tried to reach us, especially if they traveled at night, what are the chances we'd spot them?" Henry asked.

"Not good," Tyler admitted. "But we've located game by following trails. Assuming a human on horseback would also follow trails, we'll focus on those corridors. The cameras are pretty low-tech since I had to build them with cell phone parts and old cameras. They don't have infrared capability, and they don't capture wide-angle coverage of an area, so something could slip through at night or not be close enough to trigger a camera."

Ash wasn't sure what to make of the meeting. She was feeling hopeful after the food status reports and weather predictions, but they had no way to prepare for an intrusion that may or may not ever come. They had no idea if FAMA would try to reach them again. If they did, what would be their mode of transportation, where would they approach from, and what would they want?

Dan ran his fingers through his hair and took a deep breath, clearly conflicted. "I'm sorry to even bring up the possibility. I thought about dismissing the idea when Melora brought it to my attention, but we need to be alert for danger and think about what more we can do, if anything. For the next month and a half, though, we need to remain focused on food. We don't know if anyone will ever try to reach Beartooth, but we do know winter is coming."

THIRTY-SIX

IT HAD BEEN several weeks since the CLB meeting and community meeting, which followed a few days later. There had been no sign of intruders captured on the trail cameras or during drone flights. As each day passed with no hint of danger, Ash allowed herself to relax a little bit more.

She was looking forward to the second and final honey harvest of the year. Apiculture made her happy and brought balance to her life. She made arrangements with Miranda, Evelyn, and Lauren to help.

While Ash and her crew gathered honey, Caleb was busy at the farm preparing for the upcoming harvest. He worked long days. Ash missed him, but caring for Sara and spending more time with Miranda, Evelyn, and Lauren filled her days.

By the time they finished gathering honey from the last hive, Ash was ready to be done. Even though the hives were closer than they used to be, this year's honey collection overlapped with preparing for fall harvest, so they had little help from the guys, which meant a lot more trips between the hives and Ash's cabin.

As she often did when Caleb worked late, Ash took Sara to the Solomons to wait for Caleb and have dinner with the family.

"So how did the honey collection end up?" Olivia asked when Ash entered the cabin.

"It was a great harvest, but since we'll only collect twice this year, the total honey available to the community overall is down." Ash handed Olivia a large jar of the thick, golden liquid.

"I'm sure you did all you could, and I'm just happy I get the family bonus," Olivia replied as she went into the kitchen with Ash and Sara following close behind.

By the time they finished preparing dinner, Owen, Caleb, and Dillon walked in the door. Caleb kissed Ash and then picked up Sara.

"We haven't seen Evelyn, so didn't know if you were staying for dinner?" Olivia asked Dillon.

"She's eating with her folks tonight," he replied as everyone sat down at the table.

"I'll take Sara so you can eat. You've got to be starving," Ash said as she reached for Sara.

The toddler pressed her face into Caleb's chest and held on.

"I got it. I need time with my girls as much as I need food," he said as he coaxed Sara to face the table and take a bite of mashed potatoes.

With Sara on his lap, Caleb fed her while he ate. Ash felt a little guilty that he just came in from a long day in the fields and had to feed their daughter, but apparently, it was what they both wanted.

"We're done prepping for the harvest. Since the overnight lows are starting to dip into the mid-forties, we'll go ahead and start harvesting in a couple of days. I'll tie in with Dan in the morning so we can get the volunteers ready," Owen said.

"None of the field crops or gardens are blooming any longer, and the wildflowers and weeds are shriveling up and dying. Should we move the hives back to the shed before the harvest starts, just in case we get a rapid cool down?" Ash asked Caleb.

"Probably wouldn't hurt since all the activity in the fields may disturb them anyway. If Miranda and Ryan are free, we can do it tomorrow," Caleb replied.

"Need my help?" Dillon asked.

"Thanks, but it shouldn't take long. Besides, we only have protective clothing for me, Ash, Miranda, and Ryan. I didn't bother suiting up when we moved them out in the spring since the bees were still sluggish, but they're pretty active right now, so they might be a little more aggressive," Caleb replied.

No sooner had Caleb said their names, Miranda and Ryan walked in the door.

"Ryan told me Mom came over for apples today, so I assumed there would be pie," Miranda said.

Olivia chuckled. "Yes, there's pie. Sit down, and I'll go get it."

"We were just talking about moving the hives back into the shed tomorrow. Are you two free for an hour first thing in the morning?" Caleb asked.

"I'm sure we can get away," Ryan replied.

"I can't believe it's time to move the bees already. Even though I love the closer locations for the hives, I miss the days when we didn't need to move them to protect them from cold and predators," Ash mused.

"Life just keeps getting weirder. Everything is so out of whack with the temperatures, rain, and predators. And

Emily is barely engaging at the clinic anymore," Miranda added.

"What's she doing all day, every day?" Ash asked.

"She's grown a really big garden this summer, and she's taken up knitting."

Ash laughed. "I never pictured Emily as the knitting type."

"I'm not sure she is. The stuff I've seen is pretty bad. Act surprised, but she's making mittens or socks for Sara, I think," Miranda said.

"You think?" Caleb asked.

"Yeah, it's kind of hard to tell, but since there are two, I'm guessing mittens or socks."

Everyone laughed and continued to visit while Olivia served pie. As the laughter and banter continued, Ash prayed that times like this would never end, and one day the table would be even fuller with Sara's siblings and cousins.

THIRTY-SEVEN

THE NEXT DAY ASH, Caleb, Ryan, and Miranda moved the hives into the shed for the winter. The day after, the Solomon farm harvest began.

As usual, nearly the entire community turned out. Most residents between twelve and forty helped with the physical labor in the fields, while the original settlers who were slowing down with age or who possessed specialized skills in operating the mill, processed the grains and put them into storage as fast as the workers brought in a load.

Even with so many people helping, harvest would still take nearly two weeks to complete. Other than the mill, the process was done completely by hand using horse-drawn implements and manual labor.

Ash saw very little of Caleb during harvest. She hadn't been able to help much the past two seasons with being pregnant, and then having an infant, but this year she felt comfortable leaving Sara with Olivia so she could help. Olivia generally stayed at the farm to coordinate, cook, and this year, watch her granddaughter.

In order to perpetuate the skills necessary to run the milling operation in the future, Ash, Miranda, Evelyn, and Lauren worked in the mill to learn the process.

The equipment was simple to operate, but there were a few trouble-shooting techniques that Henry described in detail. At the end of each day, Heath supervised the cleaning of the equipment.

"Cleaning is kind of a no-brainer," Miranda grumbled. "I think Heath is going overboard supervising us so he doesn't have to do the actual work."

"Tony is no better. How many times do we have to fill a bag, label it with the product name and date, and carry it to the storage area before we have it mastered," Evelyn added.

"Like you've actually carried any bags," Lauren groused at Evelyn. "Dad said that me and Ash are probably the strongest of us four, so we've been stuck with that job."

"See, even Henry thinks I'm a lumberjack," Ash joked.

Evelyn and Miranda laughed, and Lauren demanded to know the story. Ash checked the dehydrator as she relayed the story about Caleb needing a strong partner. The dryer was a new part of the harvest process. This year, Tyler's dehydrator was being used to dry pinto beans since there hadn't been a long enough growing season or enough sunshine to dry the beans in the field.

Ash enjoyed working on the milling and drying since it gave her, Miranda, Evelyn, and Lauren a chance to visit, but that meant she and Caleb crossed paths only at night.

Most nights they ate dinner with the Solomons. Ash appreciated Olivia feeding them after a long day. The thought of cooking felt a little overwhelming.

Tonight, when they got home, Sara went straight to bed. Ash showered first, and then Caleb cleaned up. By the time he was done, she was already in bed, but not asleep.

"What's the timeline look like?" Ash asked as she watched with appreciation as he dried himself off with a towel.

Even with all the run-ins with predators, he still took her breath away. The scars only made him look stronger. It took her a moment to return her focus to what he was saying when he answered.

"We should be done ahead of schedule. Unfortunately, that's not good news. We've had a significant decline in yield."

"Since we still have quite a lot of grain stored from last summer, we should still be good," Ash replied.

"That's what we're all hoping. Heath seems to think we'll have a longer growing season next year than we had this year. If he's right, we'll have plenty of grains to get us through this winter, and we'll be able to replenish our stores before the next."

"And, if he's wrong?"

"We'll cross that bridge when and if it comes," Caleb replied as he crawled into bed next to her.

He rolled over to his side, facing her. "How's it going at the mill?"

"The old-timers treat me, Miranda, Evelyn, and Lauren like idiots, but the work isn't difficult, and it's been fun spending so much time together. We've decided that as soon as harvest is over, we're going to have a girls' archery day so we can practice without any critiquing from you, Dillon, and Ryan."

"You don't like hanging out with me anymore?"

"I love being with you, but I think the guys still make Evelyn nervous. According to Lauren, Henry set up a target behind their cabin, and she and Evelyn have been shooting a lot. Lauren said Evelyn is getting really good. I'm anxious to see for myself."

"Fine, but once harvest is done, I want some time with you too. I miss you," Caleb replied as he reached out and wound a long lock of Ash's hair around his finger.

She smiled and ran her hand down his muscular chest. "Well, if you're not too tired, we're together now, and I've got nowhere to go."

"I'm never too tired," he replied as he let go of her hair, ran his hand gently down her cheek, leaned over, and kissed her deeply.

THIRTY-EIGHT

A FEW DAYS ahead of schedule, the crops were out of the fields. The oats were processed and stored. Much of the wheat was milled into flour and stockpiled for use over the winter, and the pinto beans were dried and bagged.

As in years past, the community had come out in force to ensure the harvest was completed in a timely manner. They were as ready for winter as possible.

It felt good to sleep in a little after the past few weeks of harvest. For Owen, Dillon, and Caleb, there was still work to do to clean up and fix anything that got broken in the process, but Ash and the rest of the community had been released from their participation.

"Sara must have gotten as worn down as the rest of us. She's been sleeping in much later than usual the past few days," Ash said as she sat on the couch watching Caleb try to find a station on the radio.

"...and that's the current situation in Europe," the newsreader said.

"Hope it was nothing worse than usual," Ash added as the reporter continued.

"There is still no information on the whereabouts of Jonah Bennett and his followers, but the frequency of raids on ranches and nearby communities has increased, indicating Bennett is still in the area. As conditions continue to improve in Pryor, and the new police force gains control over the gang violence, some of the National Guard troops will be released to search for Bennett and his group. President Steele has indicated that once Bennett and the FAMA militia are rounded up, her administration will resume talks with the state about providing food aid," the newsreader reported.

Sara called out and Ash got up and left the room. She returned with Sara a few minutes later and the radio was off.

"What did I miss?"

"Just a rundown on which areas of the country the government believes is still under the control of gangs and rebel factions, and how they're going to increase security along the railway. Canada is threatening to suspend rail shipments if the raids continue."

"Is that all?" Ash joked. "So, what's your plan today?"

"Dad, Dillon, and I are going to bring in all of the irrigation dams for the winter and store them in our enclosed trailer like we do every year. Even though the dams are made of a heavy-duty synthetic material, they weren't made to last forever. What about you? Is the girls' archery day still on?"

"Evelyn, Miranda, and Lauren are coming over in about an hour. We'll go shoot at the closest targets for a bit, and then they offered to help me get the sauerkraut in crocks."

"Do you think the sauerkraut will be ready for the fall festival now that the date has been moved up?"

"It should be ready. I think the earlier date is a good idea since it would probably be too cold for our annual outdoor event if we wait until the weekend before Thanksgiving."

"I sure am relieved the deer are slowly returning to the area. Melora spotted a small herd that appeared to be heading this way. Ryan and I plan to get a group together and go after them in a couple of days. If we're successful, the timing should work with when Archie and Dennis plan to butcher a hog so they can make venison and pork sausage again to go with the sauerkraut."

"I'm looking forward to the festival. But first, I'm looking forward to a day with my sisters-in-law and Lauren."

"Have fun," Caleb said as he stood up, kissed Ash and Sara goodbye, and left the house.

By the time Ash got her archery equipment and Sara ready, Evelyn and Lauren arrived.

"I just love the bow that Caleb made especially for me, and the arrows you made are so helpful," Evelyn said as they walked over to the Solomon cabin to drop off Sara and meet up with Miranda.

Ash didn't think she would enjoy shooting with anyone other than Caleb but had to admit she had fun with the girls. Miranda had gotten quite good over the years. Ash had no doubt she would be capable of shooting a deer, but doubted Miranda ever would. She just didn't have the stomach for hunting, even though she had no problem eating meat.

Evelyn completely surprised her. They all watched quietly as Evelyn shot. She was standing back much further than the last time Ash saw her shoot. She quickly honed in on the sound of the metronome, pulled up, and shot. More than half the time, her arrow stuck in the three rings surrounding the bullseye.

"What did I tell you?" Lauren beamed.

"You've nailed it. Has Dillon seen you shoot lately?" Ash asked.

"No, Lauren and I have been practicing a lot, but I was afraid when I had to shoot in front of anyone else, I'd freeze."

"Hopefully, you'll feel confident now that you've shot in front of me and Ash and didn't choke," Miranda added.

"I do, but I really want to impress Dillon, and I don't want Caleb to treat my shooting as a joke."

"You're great. For the record, Dillon is impressed with everything you do, and Caleb has never thought teaching you to shoot was a joke. He admires your willingness to take on any challenge, as do I," Ash said.

"I can't thank you enough for introducing me to archery and building gear just for me. It feels good to be included and treated like an equal for the first time in my life. Let's go make sauerkraut before I cry," Evelyn said as she turned her back to her friends.

They picked up Sara from Olivia before returning to Ash's cabin. Evelyn entertained Sara while Ash, Miranda, and Lauren carried the cabbages inside and washed them. With three people cutting, they soon had the heads shredded and in the crocks.

Ash added salt to each crock and handed a wooden pounder to Miranda and Lauren.

"Fun time is over, Evelyn. I need to feed Sara, so get over here and start pounding," Ash said.

"I didn't really mean all that stuff about equal treatment," Evelyn said as she hugged the toddler.

"Too late. Here you go, just pound the salt and

cabbage until the cabbage is covered in its own liquid. Then, we just weight it down to keep the cabbage in its own juice and let it ferment," Ash explained.

With Evelyn, Lauren, and Miranda pounding the cabbage and laughing, Ash settled on the sofa with Sara. Watching and listening to them made her smile. She had everything she had ever wanted—a loving husband, a healthy baby, and sisters.

She tried not to focus on the state of the world, the environmental crisis that continued to unfold, predators, or FAMA. Those things were beyond her control. The here and now was all that really mattered.

THIRTY-NINE

EVEN THOUGH CROP yields were smaller than the previous year, no one was overly concerned since they still had plenty of grains stored from the season before. The members of the community were satisfied with what they had accomplished in such a short growing season,

Ash and Caleb organized another group fishing day. Since it had been four weeks since the last one, they upped their quota to seventy fish. With eleven in their group, it still didn't take long to catch their self-imposed limit.

Archie and Dennis were confident the group would be successful, so they had a fire ready when the group returned in order to cook for a community fish-fry. They also had the smoker geared up to smoke what the residents didn't eat, adding to their stores of meat.

A few days later, Caleb, Ryan, Dillon, and Archie successfully harvested two bucks that had wandered within four miles of the community.

"Even though I love to ride, it sure was nice to go hunting on foot yesterday. It made things feel normal,"

Caleb said as he began to slice a fresh loaf of bread to make sandwiches.

Evelyn chucked. "And it was nice that Dillon could go. He isn't overly fond of horses as you know, but he was getting tired of being left behind when you went hunting. Well, except for the really bad hunting trip where you were stalked by giant jaguars."

"Ryan agreed that it felt like the old days except the herd was much smaller and further away, and the bucks were still a little thin and scraggly," Miranda added.

"Are you two staying for lunch?" Caleb asked.

"No, I need to go home and get my bow ready and check the arrows in my quiver. Ash made me a couple more arrows in another color scheme to try out. I want to make sure I remove all the old ones that are harder to see," Evelyn replied.

"I'm going to run by the storehouse and pick up something for lunch and dinner. I hope Tony still has some of that bread left. It looks delicious. After lunch with Ryan, I need to get my archery equipment ready too," Miranda added.

They agreed to meet back at Ash and Caleb's cabin in an hour and go from there. Miranda and Evelyn departed, leaving Ash and Caleb alone. He finished making the sandwiches and set them on the table just as Ash finished feeding Sara.

"I'm surprised you've continued to shoot with those three. Miranda is pretty good, but you're in a class by yourself, so I figured you'd get bored," Caleb said as he dug into his lunch.

"Lauren isn't going today, so it will just be Evelyn, Miranda, and I. You'll be surprised when you see Evelyn shoot. She's getting very accurate and is standing back twice as far as she was the last time you saw her."

"I have to admit, I'm a little surprised your idea about the metronome worked. I'm really glad it did. She seems to be enjoying it."

"I've always loved Miranda, and once I realized Evelyn wasn't interested in you, but rather Dillon, we've gotten very close too. She's so smart, funny, and adorably cute, that I kind of misjudged her growing up. I didn't think we had anything in common except for a fondness for you, and that is not something that generally endears girls to each other."

Caleb chuckled. "Even if she was interested, it wouldn't have mattered. It's always been you, Ash."

Ash smiled. "And it's always been you."

FORTY

MIRANDA ENTERED THE STOREHOUSE. "Tony, are you here?"

Tony walked into the front of the storehouse wiping his hands on a towel. "What can I do for you?"

"I just left Ash and Caleb's. They were making sandwiches with some wonderful-looking bread. Do you have any left?"

"You're in luck, there are still a couple of loaves in the back that I haven't had a chance to bring out yet. I'll go get you one."

While Miranda waited for Tony, she went over to the refrigerated cooler and grabbed a small amount of deer salami.

She set the meat on the counter and glanced around, pleased by the abundance on display in the storehouse. She heard the door open and turned around to see who entered. Her eyes went wide.

Miranda had never seen the four burly men before who just entered the storehouse. They had scruffy beards, filthy clothes, and smiles on their faces that didn't look all that friendly.

"Who are you, and where did you come from?" Miranda asked, trying to keep her voice from trembling.

"Here you go," Tony said as he returned with a loaf of bread.

"Thanks, we're mighty hungry one of the men said as he walked up to Tony, snatched the loaf from his hand, took a huge bite, and tossed it to one of the other men.

Miranda looked at Tony. His fear mirrored hers. Normally, she wouldn't assume every stranger had ill intent, but everything about these men screamed danger. Each one had a sidearm and a menacing black rifle slung over his shoulder.

"So, where are you gentlemen from?" Tony asked.

The tallest man in the group laughed, showing several rotted teeth. "Cord, has anyone ever referred to us as gentlemen before?"

"No, Zeke, I'd have to say that's a first," Cord replied.

"We won't be staying long. We just came to check this community out. General Titus, God rest his soul, said this might be a place to relocate if a time came when Pryor was no longer in our control. Looks like he might be right," stated the man Miranda assumed was in charge.

Her mind whirled. Clearly these were FAMA militia from Pryor. The same group who murdered Neal and who inflicted unspeakable suffering upon the city, especially the women held in re-education facilities. These thugs weren't supposed to come to Beartooth after their helicopter was destroyed. Miranda wasn't sure what to do, so she just watched and listened, praying they'd take what they wanted and leave.

"We're pretty stocked at the moment, just take what you need and go. We don't want any trouble," Tony said.

"I see what I want, right here," said the man called Cord as he twisted a lock of Miranda's hair around his finger. "Can we take her, Knox?"

"Don't see why not. It's a long, cold ride back to the ranch, and a little female company would be nice," Knox replied.

Cord grabbed Miranda's arm and yanked her toward him. She struggled in his grip and slapped him across the face as hard as she could.

"You little, bitch," Cord said as he backhanded her with such force, that the blow knocked her hard to the floor.

Tony lunged forward. Knox pulled a pistol and pointed it at his head. "Stand back, old man. I don't want to kill you, but I will."

"I'm fine," Miranda said as she looked up at Tony with blood running down her face.

"Why'd you go and do that? She was so pretty, but now she's got a fat lip and blood on her face. I'll bet she'll have an ugly bruise on her cheek and a black eye too," Zeke said.

"She hit me," Cord replied. "I had to teach her a lesson."

"We're wasting time. Roy, Cord, load up those canvas bags on the counter with all the food we can carry. Zeke, go back to that cabin where we saw that little blonde gal enter and grab her. She wasn't very big, so you shouldn't have any problem. She'd make a nice gift for Jonah so don't damage her face. This one probably won't look too good by the time we get back, and Jonah likes them pretty," Knox said.

"No, please don't. She's nearly blind. She'll just slow you down," Miranda pleaded.

"I guess Zeke won't have any problems with her then. Grab the girl and meet us at the horses," Knox ordered.

Miranda jumped up and ran after Zeke. She knew it was futile, but she didn't know what else to do. She couldn't just stand there and do nothing. She grabbed the big man's arm and tried to stop him from leaving. "Please don't hurt her."

Zeke turned and grabbed her wrist. She felt like he could crush her bones in his iron grasp, so she went still.

"Please, leave her be. Just take me. I promise to do whatever you say if you'll forget about her," Miranda pleaded with tears running down her cheeks.

"I like em feisty." Zeke crushed his lips to hers. "Yeah, this is going to be fun," he said as he shoved Miranda back into the store and then walked out the door.

"I think we got all we can haul, boss," Roy said.

Knox walked over to Tony. "How many people live in this community?"

"Around fifty," Miranda said, afraid Tony wouldn't answer which would probably get him shot.

"I wasn't talking to you. Gag her and tie her hands," Knox said as he returned his focus to Tony.

Miranda stared on helplessly as Knox placed the muzzle of the gun to Tony's head. Cord took a filthy bandana from his pocket, twirled it into a roll, and put it between her teeth, tying it tight behind her head. He then ripped a sleeve off a shirt he found on a shelf and used it to tie her hands in front of her.

"Do you have a militia?"

"N, no," Tony stuttered.

"How many guns and how much ammo?"

"A couple of, of, hunting rifles and a few handguns. I don't know how much ammunition, but it can't be much," Tony replied.

Knox lowered the gun. "Let's go, this should be more than enough time for Zeke to nab the blind girl."

Roy and Cord peered through the windows before walking out the door.

"Still clear," Cord said.

Knox grabbed Miranda roughly by the arm and yanked her toward the door. She fell to her knees as Knox stumbled, releasing her arm. She whipped her head around and saw Tony struggling with Knox.

Before she could react, the gun Knox held went off. Tony slumped to the floor, clutching his abdomen, blood oozing between his fingers.

Tears streamed down her face as she stared at Tony. She prayed that Evelyn had left her cabin, but she doubted it. They had walked together from Ash and Caleb's cabin, and she had only left Evelyn moments before the men showed up.

"I'm sorry," Tony gasped.

Knox yanked Miranda to her feet and pushed her towards the door. She wanted to say something comforting to Tony, but she was gagged.

"Everything okay, boss?" Roy asked as he and Cord rushed back into the storehouse.

"For now, but we better get moving. I imagine everyone in the community heard that," Knox replied.

Miranda caught one last glimpse of Tony as she left the storehouse. Even if he lived, she feared she would never see him again.

FORTY-ONE

"I'LL TAKE Sara over to Mom's on my way to the farm. Dad, Dillon, and I are going to…" Caleb's voice trailed off.

Ash and Caleb stared at each other for a moment.

"That sounded like a gunshot," Ash said.

"It did. I can't imagine anyone shooting this close to the community unless a human or animal predator threatened," Caleb said as he retrieved his 9mm.

"Lock the door behind me. I'll go find out what's going on. String your bow and get your bear spray handy just in case you need to defend yourself and Sara. It's probably just an accidental discharge but might as well be prepared."

Ash followed him to the door. She grabbed his arm before he darted out and kissed him hard on the lips. "Be careful."

"Always am," he replied as he dashed out the door.

She didn't necessarily agree with that statement, but it didn't really matter. She wouldn't stop him from leaving even if she could. She locked the deadbolt and went into the extra bedroom where they kept their archery and hunting gear.

Ash strung her bow and brought her bow, quiver of arrows, and bear spray into the kitchen. She set the items on the table. When she turned around, she saw Sara standing in the middle of the living room staring at her with her thumb in her mouth and concern in her wide eyes.

She pasted a smile on her lips and scooped her little girl up into her arms.

"Daddy," Sara choked out.

"He'll be back soon," Ash said in a soothing voice, hoping she hadn't just lied to her child.

————

Evelyn flinched at the sound of a gunshot. She couldn't imagine why anyone would shoot so close to the community, and hoped it didn't mean danger. It had to be target practice or an accidental discharge.

She pulled an arrow out of her quiver and brought it close to her face so she could see the tip. She ran her finger over the pointed end of the new arrow Ash made for her.

As loud footsteps bounded up the porch, she started to have a bad feeling. The approaching person was heavier than Miranda or Ash. It sounded like Dillon when he came home, but he said he'd be out in the fields all day. She hoped that he had come home early to surprise her, but her gut told her that was only wishful thinking.

"Dillon?"

"Nope, I'm your new buddy Zeke. You be nice to me, and maybe you'll make it back to Jonah in good shape. He likes em young and pretty. We deliver you and we might even get a promotion."

Her mind reeled. Everyone in Beartooth knew who Jonah Bennett was, so this had to be one of his Freedom and Morality Alliance militia. She still had her bow in her left hand, hanging loosely at her side, and the new arrow in her right hand.

Fear coursed through her as she thought about the gunshot she just heard and the huge figure looming in her doorway. She prayed the shot hadn't connected to anyone. Everyone would be drawn to the noise, so no help would be coming for her. Her only idea for self-defense wasn't good, but it was all she could think of with everything running through her mind. She had to keep him talking.

"Did you see my friend outside?"

"We interrupted her shopping. She's a feisty one, which will make her a lot of fun to play with later. Not as pretty as she was before Cord backhanded her, but she had it coming."

Evelyn hoped Miranda wasn't hurt too bad, but he indicated she was still alive. She clenched her bow harder and slipped her hand into position on her arrow.

"Why are you here?"

"We came to check this place out. Last time the only person we saw was an old man. If we'd have known there were such pretty ladies here, we'd have tried to get back here sooner," Zeke replied.

"How did you get here? Have the roads been repaired?"

"We rode from a ranch we borrowed. But enough talk, come on, my buddies are waiting."

"I don't want to go with you," Evelyn replied as she honed in on his voice.

"That's not your decision. If you don't come over here now, I'll just…"

Evelyn closed her eyes for an instant. She focused on

his voice and pictured where his heart would be located in relation to his lips. She opened her eyes and squinted at the fuzzy image in front of her. In one quick motion, she lifted her bow, nocked the arrow, pulled back, and shot.

"Goddammit, you little whore. I'll kill you for this," Zeke bellowed as he looked down at the arrow lodged deep into his chest.

He staggered further into the cabin as Evelyn backed up, putting the kitchen counter between them. Her quiver was out of reach, so she had no more arrows. She grasped one end of her bow and swung it like a baseball bat when his blurry shape came within range. He grabbed hold and yanked it out of her hands and tossed it over his shoulder. It landed behind him and clattered across the floor.

She spun around and grabbed a cast-iron skillet. She swung it at him as he lunged for her. She connected but only grazed his shoulder. The momentum of the heavy skillet made the handle slip from her grasp. The skillet landed on the countertop and hit the draining rack. The dishes shattered into pieces which flew in every direction.

Evelyn ducked to avoid the shower of glass and pottery shards. Her mind pictured everything around her, and she couldn't think of anything useful. With no other weapons within arm's reach, she screamed.

FORTY-TWO

CALEB COVERED the distance between their cabin and the schoolhouse quickly. As he reached the back corner of the school, he heard loud thuds and glass breaking. He flattened himself against the side of the building and silently made his way to the front.

He peeked around the corner. Evelyn and Dillon's cabin door was wide open. He scanned the area and saw nothing else. Just as he stepped away from the building, he heard Evelyn scream.

Caleb sprinted the short distance from the schoolhouse to the cabin. He crept up onto the porch and peeked inside. Evelyn was trying to dodge a large man. He had a circle of blood on his back, and he didn't seem very stable in his movements.

Evelyn started pleading with the man to spare her life. Caleb sensed that she knew he was there and was trying to cover any sound he made and keep the man's focus on her. Caleb slipped his knife out of its sheath on his belt and crept up close to the man. With one quick motion, he raised his blade and slit the man's throat.

Caleb dropped the knife so he could catch the man before he hit the floor. With his hands under the man's armpits, Caleb drug him out the door and dropped him on the porch on his back. He stared down at the arrow protruding from his chest. He couldn't help but be impressed, but he had to stay focused. He doubted this man was alone, and he saw no evidence of a gun being fired here.

"Evelyn, are you alright?" Caleb asked as he approached her and took her in his arms.

Evelyn nodded and held onto him for only a moment. She stepped back. "I heard a gunshot. I think it came from the storehouse. I tried to keep him talking so I could aim. He said they came on horseback from a ranch, and that he was taking me back as a gift for Jonah. His name was Zeke. He mentioned someone named Cord, but there could be more. He said Cord backhanded Miranda, and I think his companions may have taken her."

"I hate leaving you after what you just went through, but I need to go. Lock the door until help arrives."

Evelyn followed him toward the door. "I tried to stop him," she said as tears ran down her cheeks.

"You did great. I'm impressed. If you had a broadhead instead of a field-tip, it would have been a quick kill shot. As is, you slowed him down, and he would have died eventually," Caleb said as he retrieved his knife from the floor and returned it to its sheath.

As soon as Caleb heard the deadbolt click, he knelt down and relieved the man of his sidearm, extra clip, and his automatic rifle. He quickly covered the distance between the cabin and the storehouse. He peeked in the window and spotted Melora kneeling on the floor over a bleeding Tony. She was putting pressure on a wound to his abdomen.

"What happened? Where's Miranda? How's Tony?" Caleb asked.

"Tony was shot trying to keep three men from dragging Miranda out of here. I sent Tyler for Emily and Dan. Tony said Evelyn is in danger too," Melora replied.

"No, we took care of Zeke, and she's behind locked doors."

Dan, Tyler, Emily, Ryan, and Zane ran into the storehouse. Emily instantly went to Tony. She instructed Melora to keep the pressure on while she quickly assessed the damage. The rest of the group looked on until Emily stood and walked over to them.

"I suggest we get Maria and their kids here immediately. We need to get him to the clinic. I have to be honest, it doesn't look good," Emily said and then returned to Tony.

"Do you think they're gone?" Tyler asked.

"I certainly hope so," Dan replied. "I'm going to get Fiona, Graham, Archie, Dennis, and Garrett since they're close by and have guns. We'll divide up into teams and check the area as quickly as we can to make sure the men left. Then we'll go door-to-door and let everyone know what happened. We'll have everyone stay behind locked doors until we can get our heads around this. Tyler, go get Maria, Serena, Isabella, and Daniel, but be careful and stay behind cover as much as you can. Hopefully, we'll be able to verify no one was left behind by the time you get them rounded up."

"I'm going after my wife," Ryan said as he headed for the door.

"Saddle two horses. From what we've put together from Tony and Evelyn, there were four FAMA militia. One is dead. They're on horseback and rode here from a ranch.

I'll meet you at Bob's as soon as I run home, let Ash know what happened, and grab my bow."

"I'd think that automatic rifle over your shoulder would be more effective than a bow," Dan said.

"Sometimes, stealth is better," Caleb replied.

"Saddle three, I'm going too," Melora said.

Ryan nodded and jogged out the door.

Caleb glanced over at Zane who looked like he might get sick. "As soon as Dan gives the all clear, go to my folks' place. Find out from Mom where Dad and Dillon are working and go get them. I hated to leave Evelyn alone after what she had to do and what she saw."

"What did she do?" Zane asked barely above a whisper.

"She shot a man with her bow," Caleb replied.

"I'm super impressed but a display of my admiration will have to wait," Melora said.

Tyler darted in the door, followed closely by Maria and her and Tony's adult children and spouses. Tony's family huddled around him and took over for Melora.

"I'm going after Bennett's men," Melora said to Tyler.

"Don't go," he pleaded.

"I have to. I'm the one who assured everyone we'd be safe if we disabled the helicopter and we weren't. I was tasked with security, and I've failed twice. I gotta go."

"I'm going too," Tyler said.

"No, we need to go lean and ride fast. Besides, you're a lover not a fighter," Melora said as she kissed Tyler and darted out the door.

Caleb pulled Sam aside, who was Ryan's oldest brother and married to Tony and Maria's daughter, Serena. "Miranda has been taken. Ryan is saddling horses now. Melora and I are going with him. As soon as Dan gives the all clear, Zane is going to find Dillon. Evelyn needs him. You'll need to fill your folks in. They'll be worried sick. Do you have enough people here to get Tony to the clinic?"

Sam nodded and clasped Caleb on the shoulder. "Good luck. I hope you find her quickly and take care of my little brother."

"I'll do my best on both counts," Caleb said as he left the storehouse and ran for home.

Caleb set the rifle on the porch, knocked on the cabin door, and called out to Ash to unlock it and let him in. She opened the door, and he pulled her into his arms.

"Where's Sara?"

"In her room," Ash replied.

"Good. Four of Bennett's men rode here from a ranch. They shot Tony, took Miranda, and tried to take Evelyn. She shot him with her bow. I finished him off, but the remaining three men and Miranda are gone. Emily doesn't think Tony will make it."

"You're going," Ash stated.

"I have to. They took my sister, and Ryan will go after her with or without me. He's saddling the horses now."

Ash nodded and followed Caleb. "What can I do?"

"I confiscated this off the man Evelyn shot," he said as he pulled a pistol out of his waistband nearly identical to the one in his holster. "And I left the automatic rifle outside. I'll leave our 9mm with you. Dan and those with weapons are currently searching the area in case there are any more FAMA militia hiding out, and then they'll go door-to-door and let everyone know what to do. Once he gives the all clear, I want you to go to Mom and Dad's and stay there until I return. Zane will go find Dillon as soon as it's safe."

Caleb placed their 9mm on the kitchen table and slid the confiscated one into his holster after checking the load and the spare clip. He got his recurve bow, broken down in its soft-sided case, and his quiver of arrows. He set the bow case down and secured the quiver over his shoulder.

He pulled Ash into his arms. "I'm sorry. I promised I wouldn't leave again."

"You have to go. Just come home and bring Miranda with you."

Caleb kissed her until she was breathless. "I love you, Ash."

"I love you too. Now go."

Caleb picked up his bow and left the cabin. He reached for the automatic rifle as he heard the deadbolt click on the door behind him. He didn't look back as he ran for the Thorn's ranch.

FORTY-THREE

BY THE TIME Caleb reached Bob's ranch, the three geldings were saddled. Ryan and Melora were mounted up. Caleb quickly secured the bow case behind his saddle and put the assault rifle in the scabbard.

Bob had a hold of the gelding's bridle close to its mouth. Caleb put his toe in the stirrup and slung his leg over the saddle.

"Good luck and be careful," Bob said as he let go of the bridle.

Caleb spun the horse around and tapped its sides with his heels. The gelding bolted, and the others followed close behind. They ran past the community and headed east, assuming that's the way the men fled based on Melora's earlier assessment of nearby ranches.

They hadn't ridden far when they spotted a horse tied up in the trees near the road corridor. Caleb assumed it was Zeke's horse but was a little surprised the men left it behind. Unless they had a spare horse, Miranda had to ride with one of the men, which might slow them down.

Caleb jumped off, handed his reins to Ryan, and checked the saddlebags.

"Find anything useful, like a trail map with the route highlighted in red?" Melora asked as she dismounted and handed her reins to Ryan as well.

"No such luck. These guys were traveling light. There's a plate, fork, cup, flashlight, canteen, and a full box of ammo for the 9mm," Caleb replied.

Caleb took the canteen, ammunition, and flashlight. He quickly stowed the items in his saddlebags.

Melora walked up and pulled the rifle out of Caleb's scabbard. "Standard issue military assault rifle. They probably got this when they commandeered the Guard's helicopter or during one of the other run-ins we heard about on the radio."

While Melora examined the rifle and removed the magazine, Caleb searched the ground for tracks.

"Since I'm the only one here with extensive experience with this firearm, I'll take it and give you my shotgun," Melora said as she swapped guns with Caleb.

"Probably wise. Looks like they headed back to the old, paved highway and turned east. I'll put money that they'll follow it until they reach the turnoff for the dirt four-wheel-drive road and then head southeast," Caleb said as he mounted back up.

They loped toward the highway. Caleb dismounted again and found more horse tracks alongside the pavement.

"How big of a head start do they have on us?" Ryan asked.

His voice almost startled Caleb. He hadn't heard a word from the young man since they rode out. Caleb wasn't surprised. As angry and frightened as he was about his sister's safety, he couldn't imagine what was going through Ryan's mind.

"Judging by when we heard the shot and when we rode out, I'd say at least thirty minutes," Caleb replied.

"If they've hurt her, I'll kill them," Ryan said through clenched teeth.

"I've been thinking about this since the moment we mounted up. If we catch up to them, we have to kill them all. No one can make it back to Bennett and the rest of the FAMA militia. If they found out we already killed, what was his name, Zeke, they'll retaliate. That's all Bennett needs to rally his militia—a score to settle, a common goal, a mission those brutal nut jobs can get behind. It would be best if none of the men returned. That could mean anything to Bennett. They could have deserted or been eaten by a bear or a pack of wolves," Melora said.

"Glad we're all on the same page," Ryan hissed.

Caleb had never seen Ryan like this. He was angry and determined. Caleb hoped he could still be reasonable. As he glanced over at the deadly weapon now carried in Melora's scabbard, he knew they were severely outgunned if the three other men were equally armed. They also couldn't afford a shootout as long as Miranda was in their clutches.

Ryan had Melora's 9mm which he'd never shot, Melora had the assault rifle, and Caleb had the shotgun, his bow, and the confiscated handgun. They would need a plan, stealth, and a lot of luck, but he feared Ryan would be thinking with his heart, not his head.

They rode for another hour. They still hadn't caught up to the men holding Miranda, but they were able to follow the group's tracks off the highway and onto the four-wheel-drive track, so they knew they were still heading in the right direction.

This time of year, night came early, especially in the mountains where the sun slipped below the tall peaks earlier than it would dip below the horizon in the flat lands. It would be more difficult to track the men after dark, so Caleb hoped they would catch up to them before then.

Once the men made camp, he feared for Miranda. His mind flashed back to the sight of the women handcuffed to a bar in the back of a truck pulling a trailer load of dead women down a dusty street in Pryor. Between that image seared in his mind and the horror stories they heard on the radio about the abuses women endured at FAMA's re-education facilities, he doubted Miranda would survive for long.

FORTY-FOUR

MIRANDA WAS EXHAUSTED, and every bone in her body ached. She had been riding in front of Cord for hours with her hands tied tightly in front of her and a filthy, stinking bandana gagging her in more ways than one.

They stopped only once for a quick break. No one offered her a sip of water when they drank from their canteens, and they didn't even turn around when they peed. When she turned her head and closed her eyes, they laughed and graphically described the futility in not looking now since she'd see a lot more later when they made camp.

She hated these miserable men so much that the hate overshadowed her fear, which was a blessing at the moment. If she succumbed to her fear, she wouldn't be able to escape if a chance arose. So far, no opportunity had presented itself, but maybe once they stopped riding for the day and it got dark, she'd figure something out.

Beartooth had sheltered her. She had never come across anyone so crass, foul-mouthed, and uncouth. They were brutal pigs. When she thought about the caliber of these men, her pity for the women once held in their re-education facilities soared.

Cord had already touched every inch of her body that he could reach while seated behind her in the saddle. He had nipped at her ears and kissed her neck repeatedly. The smell of his breath so close to her face made her nauseous. It was disgusting, but since he kept her gagged, she couldn't even tell him what a pathetic lowlife he was, which was probably for the best. If he hit her like he did at the storehouse, it would knock her off the horse, and it was a long way to the ground.

"I still don't feel right leaving Zeke behind," Cord said.

"I'm sure he'll catch up with us before long. We're backtracking the way we came, sticking to established roads and trails, so he should be able to find us," Knox replied.

"What if someone comes after us, this one here is pretty fine. Someone will miss her, and they had to hear the gunshot. They might follow the same roads and trails too," Cord added.

"If they're dumb enough to try, the guy at the store told us they don't have comparable weapons, so we'll just mow them down," Knox replied.

"He might have lied," Cord added.

"I doubt it. It was obvious how scared he was, and when General Titus landed here, he didn't find any weapons or much ammo when they searched the cabins," Knox explained.

"Maybe Zeke just kept that pretty little blonde girl for himself and rode in the opposite direction," Roy pondered.

"Even he isn't that stupid. He might have himself a lot of fun for a day or two, but then he'd be on his own. He couldn't find his way out of a latrine, much less back to the ranch once we have to go cross-country," Knox replied.

"You're probably right," Roy said as the men finally fell silent, which Miranda appreciated.

She had no doubt that Ryan and Caleb were tracking these scumbags down as they spoke. She hoped Ryan wouldn't charge into the situation and get himself shot. She loved him more than anything in the world, and she wanted to spend her life with him.

Caleb would form a plan. She had faith in her brother. Ryan had good intentions, but he was still not quite twenty, and he hadn't experienced as much as Caleb. Ryan was kind of naïve and innocent, which were some of the traits she loved about him.

Thinking about Ryan made tears slip down her cheeks. She didn't know if she could go on without him, but if he didn't come for her, that probably wouldn't be an issue. She likely wouldn't survive more than a night out with these brutal men.

FORTY-FIVE

AS SOON AS Dan stopped by the cabin and gave the all-clear, Ash packed a few things for her and Sara and hurried over to the farm. Before she could knock on the door, it opened and Olivia hustled them inside.

Olivia wrapped her arms around Ash and Sara. Ash could tell she was trying to hold it together in front of Sara, but Ash knew it had to be difficult. Dan had already been to the Solomons by the time he stopped by Ash's cabin, so they knew almost everything she knew.

"Where's Owen?" Ash asked as she stepped back and set Sara down.

Olivia looked from Ash to Sara. "Grandma made you a new toy. It's over there on the table by the couch."

Sara toddled over to the table and picked up the stuffed toy. "Bunny," she said as she squeezed the soft toy and ran to Olivia. Sara hugged Olivia's legs, then darted off to play with her new toy.

Once she was happily distracted, Olivia turned back to Ash. "He went to help remove the body from Dillon and

Evelyn's porch. He's going to bring them back here for dinner and hopefully the night," Olivia whispered.

"Good, I'll feel better when we're all together. I'm also wondering how Evelyn is holding up. Caleb said she shot the FAMA guy with her bow," Ash said.

"I didn't know that. I just assumed Caleb was responsible for the body. The poor dear, that had to be so traumatic."

"She didn't kill him, but her shot slowed him down until Caleb got there."

"Well, that's something. I hate that Caleb was put in that position. It can't be easy to take a life, even if it's justified," Olivia replied.

"I doubt they'll be able to get Miranda back without more loss of life, but they will get her back," Ash said in hopes of comforting Olivia.

"Let's just pray the loss isn't on our side."

Ash looked at Sara. She hoped her daughter wouldn't be too confused about the family slumber party at her grandma's, but without Caleb. Despite the all-clear from Dan, she couldn't have slept at home. Caleb wanted her and Sara here, and she felt much safer with family.

"Olivia, unlock the door," came Owen's booming voice.

Olivia hurried over and unlocked the door. Owen walked in carrying his rifle with Dillon and Evelyn close behind him. Olivia pulled Evelyn into her arms and hugged her. Ash was surprised that she didn't cry.

"Aunt Elfin. Look, bunny," Sara said as she ran over to Evelyn.

Evelyn reached down and picked Sara up. "That is a pretty wonderful bunny. It's soft, just like you and exactly what I need right now."

Everyone kept conversation about what happened to a

minimum in front of Sara. Ash could tell that Evelyn was relieved. She assumed her sister-in-law wasn't ready to talk about what happened.

Ash went into the kitchen and helped carry dinner to the table. By the quantity of food, she knew Olivia had resorted to stress baking and cooking the minute she heard that Miranda had been kidnapped, and Caleb had gone after her. As distraught as Ash felt, she couldn't imagine what was going through Olivia's mind.

"Dinner's ready," Olivia announced.

Everyone took their places around the table and filled their plates. Ash held Sara and fed her small bites of food.

"Are you feeling okay, Ash? You haven't touched your dinner," Owen asked.

"Just worried and distracted," she replied.

Owen nodded his understanding and went back to eating. They tried to make small talk, but it was difficult when all anyone could think about was Miranda, Caleb, Ryan, and Melora.

After the dishes were washed, the family went to the living room. Ash knew that Sara could sense the tension and was doing her best to help. She made her rounds hugging and kissing everyone in turn and offering to share her bunny.

Ash's heart broke, knowing that her little girl could sense the sadness and fear, but wouldn't be able to understand if she tried to explain. Dillon and Owen went out of their way to cheer everyone up, especially Sara, but Ash had no doubt they were just as afraid. The Solomons had always been a close family, so the fear Dillon felt for his brother and sister, and Owen and Olivia felt for their son and daughter had to be paralyzing.

"Miranda took all her furniture when she moved out, but since Ash and Evelyn contributed the most to their new households, we still have two beds. We can move Dillon's mattress into Miranda's room so Dillon and Evelyn can have privacy and use couch cushions and pillows to make a bed for Sara in the boys' old room with Ash," Olivia said.

With a task to do, they all bustled about until all the sleeping arrangements were completed. By then, Sara was exhausted, so Ash took Sara and they both went to bed. Shortly thereafter, she could hear doors shutting and then all went quiet.

FORTY-SIX

MIRANDA STRUGGLED to stay upright in the saddle, but she was exhausted and had a difficult time gripping the saddle horn with her hands tied together. She tried her best to remain centered in the saddle. If she started to lean too far one way or another, Cord righted her, and his touch repulsed her.

"We've had a long day. Let's make camp in that little clearing there," Knox said as he pointed to a spot ahead.

The small clearing was surrounded by thick trees with a low hill nearby that would provide an elevated platform to post a lookout overnight.

Knox led them to a cluster of trees, and they all dismounted. Cord grabbed Miranda by the arm and pulled her off the horse. He did nothing to lessen the impact and let her hit the ground hard, sending pain shooting through the arm and shoulder she landed on.

Miranda rolled to a sitting position and tried to move her shoulders as much as she could with her hands tied together in front of her. Severe pain in the impacted shoulder made her eyes tear up, but she didn't think it was broken or dislocated.

"Here, tie her to a tree," Knox said as he tossed Cord a length of rope. "We'll unsaddle the horses, build a fire, and enjoy some of this food we got. Once it gets dark, we'll take turns up on that hill keeping a lookout all night in case anyone decides to come after...what did the old man call her?"

"Miranda," Cord replied.

"Miranda, that's a pretty name," Roy added.

Cord wiped his nose on his shirt sleeve. He'd been doing it all day, and it only added to his uncivilized demeanor. He then grabbed her arm and yanked her to her feet. Miranda was just thankful it was the opposite arm that hit the ground a few minutes earlier. He led her over to a tree and tied her hands to a sturdy limb above her head, which made her injured shoulder throb even more.

Roy walked up to Miranda and pulled the bandana out of her mouth but left the twisted material hanging loosely around her neck. He lifted a canteen to her lips. She hadn't had anything to drink since she was taken from Beartooth, and she was parched. She took a gulp and then spit it out at his feet.

"What is that swill?" she rasped.

The three men laughed. "If you don't like moonshine, you're going to get mighty thirsty," Roy said as he lifted the canteen back to her lips.

Miranda shook her head that she didn't want anymore.

Roy went to replace the gag.

"Please don't. I promise not to scream," she pleaded.

Roy looked over at Knox.

"No one would hear her anyway. Besides, I kind of like it when they scream," Knox said.

Roy let go of the bandana and went back to unsaddling his horse.

The branch her hands were tied to was so high, she nearly had to stand on her tiptoes. Her arms ached and she was exhausted, but if she sagged even a bit, she'd be hanging by her arms. With no other option, she stood tall as she watched the men, looking for an opportunity.

The men ignored her as they unsaddled the horses, gathered wood, built a fire, laid out their bedrolls, and unpacked the food.

They got a roaring fire going and devoured some of the food they'd stolen from the storehouse. After eating their fill, Roy took a long drink from his canteen and passed it to Cord. The men drank and passed it around until it was empty.

"Pretty women and good food, I can hardly wait to report to Jonah," Knox said as he stood up and walked over to Miranda. He ran his hand down her cheek and neck.

Miranda turned her head away from him, but he clenched her cheeks painfully between his fingers and turned her head back, forcing her to look at him.

"So, how many women live there?"

"Not many," Miranda replied as tears streamed down her cheeks.

"We don't mind sharing," Cord added as he leered at her from across the fire.

Miranda suspected her time was about up. They were clearly done riding for the day, had eaten their fill, and drained Roy's canteen of its vile brew.

"Since I'm in charge, I get the first go at her. Roy, take

your rifle and head up on top of that hill and keep watch. Cord, you can hold her down and have her next. Roy, we'll come get you in a couple hours, and she'll be all yours."

Miranda bit her lip to keep from crying. Nearly hanging by her hands from a tree, she didn't know what she could do to help herself.

Roy argued and grumbled about having to take the first watch but eventually grabbed his assault rifle and hiked off toward the hill. Cord retrieved his canteen which was setting on the ground next to his saddle. He took a long gulp while Knox walked over to the fire and threw another log on the flames, sending a shower of embers into the sky.

Knox turned around and walked over to Miranda. He pulled his knife out of its scabbard on his belt. He ran the tip of the knife down the length of her shirt, popping all the buttons as the blade moved downward, leaving a trail of blood from shallow nicks.

Miranda closed her eyes and whimpered in pain but refused to give them the satisfaction of crying.

FORTY-SEVEN

CALEB PULLED his horse to a stop. Ryan and Melora rode up on each side of him.

"Do you smell that?" Caleb asked.

"I'd say someone built a campfire not too far from here. We'd probably better tie up and proceed on foot," Melora replied.

They quickly got off, secured the horses, and headed toward the smoke at a run. The trail made by three horses was easy to follow, even in the fading light. Moving as quietly and swiftly as possible, they ran in the direction of the smoke.

Caleb held up a hand, indicating they all stop, and then motioned for them to join him.

"Do you see Miranda?" Ryan asked.

"Not yet. I see a blazing fire and off to the left of the fire up on that hill, I see a guy sitting there."

Melora pulled out her binoculars. "He's got an assault rifle resting in his lap just like the one Caleb took off of Zeke. I'd say we found our men."

"Where's Miranda?" Ryan asked again.

Before anyone could answer, they heard voices. They couldn't hear what the two men were saying, but they could make out laughter.

"Come on," Caleb said as he made his way through the trees in the opposite direction as the lookout.

He was the first to spy Miranda and two men standing close to her. Her arms were straight above her head, her hands tied together and secured to a high branch. As Ryan and Melora came alongside, he reached out and grabbed Ryan, afraid he would bolt out of the cover of the trees and expose them before they could develop a plan.

Melora looked through the binoculars. She grabbed Ryan's arm before handing them to Caleb.

"Let me look," Ryan demanded.

"She's alive, but if you go running out there half-cocked, she won't be for long. You can have a look, but then we'll decide what to do to get her back. Remember, they have assault rifles. If we go running out of the trees, they'll mow us down before we get anywhere near her," Caleb said as he handed the binoculars to Ryan.

Caleb was relieved to see that Melora kept a hand on Ryan's shoulder. Caleb was so angry he could hardly think straight, but he also knew they couldn't act rashly.

Ryan lowered the binoculars and took a deep breath. He closed his eyes for a second before looking over at Melora and Caleb. "What do we do to get her back?"

"Caleb, do you think you can get close enough with your bow to take the guy on the hill out before he can shoot or alert the other two?" Melora asked.

"Just give me two minutes to get in position."

"Take out the guy on the hill without drawing any attention. Then get back here. You and Ryan should be able to get pretty close to the guys and Miranda if you stay in the trees. They look drunk and, uh, distracted, so

I'm counting on you two being able to get to them before they can pick up their rifles or draw their sidearms," Melora explained.

"What are you going to do?" Ryan asked.

"Until Caleb gets back, we're going to watch what's happening with Miranda. I'm hoping those men will continue to taunt and terrify her long enough for you two to get into place. But if I have to take a shot to protect her, I will. These guys are pretty big. We'll be relying on the element of surprise and adrenaline to help even the odds. Once I'm sure you and Caleb can reach them without exchanging gunfire, I'll be right behind you. I've never seen either of you in hand-to-hand combat, but if the bullets start to fly, Miranda could get caught in the cross-fire, so let's try to avoid that, if possible," Melora explained.

"I've never been in a fight," Ryan admitted.

"I figured as much, but you'll learn pretty quickly. It's kind of instinctive. Try to hit him before he hits you," Melora replied.

Caleb leaned the shotgun against a tree and took off at a sprint, slipping silently between the trees. He didn't' like having to shoot uphill, but there wasn't enough cover to get any closer.

He positioned himself slightly to the side of the man. He'd never shot a person before, so he wasn't sure if an arrow would kill him instantly, even if he could hit where he aimed. He decided on two quick shots, one in the neck to hopefully prevent the man from calling out a warning to his companions, and a second to kill him.

With Miranda's time running out, he pulled up, shot, hit his mark, and quickly got the second shot off. The man slumped over without a sound.

Caleb raced back to where he left Melora and Ryan, set

his bow down, and removed his quiver. He had his sidearm holstered and his knife sheathed. He noticed Ryan was equipped the same.

"Leave the guns. They might get in the way in a brawl, and if there is an accidental discharge, the wrong person might get shot," Melora said.

They removed their sidearms and set them on the ground next to Melora. They nodded at each other. Caleb darted for the next tree with Ryan on his heels.

FORTY-EIGHT

"CUT HER DOWN," Knox ordered.

Cord pulled his knife out and cut the rope tying Miranda's bound hands to the limb. She fell to her knees once the tension was released. She winced in pain but held in a cry of agony that threatened to escape her swollen lips.

Even with her hands free of the tree, her wrists were still bound together, so she was unable to pull the sides of her shirt back together. She leaned forward and stared at the ground, debating about what to do. She suspected that begging for mercy would do no good and might even egg them on. Clearly, they took pleasure in torturing her.

Miranda took several deep breaths, trying to calm her racing heart. She stayed still, sitting on her heels, hunched over, looking at the ground, saying nothing.

"You got nothing to say?" Knox asked as he grabbed a fistful of hair and pulled her head back.

Miranda bit her lip and shook her head. When he released her hair, she resumed her position on her heels, bent forward, refusing to look at them or respond.

"Well, this ain't no fun at all," Cord croaked as he stabbed his knife into the tree. He grabbed the loose bandana still tied in a loop around her neck. He yanked hard, pulling her over onto her back.

Miranda reached up with her bound hands, frantically trying to get her fingers between the fabric and her neck. Cord drug her backward for a few yards, choking her. She clawed at the bandana around her neck, needing to loosen it enough to breathe. Just as she was about to lose consciousness, he let go.

She gasped for breath, unable to speak, fearing what they would do to her next. Her fingers rested between her neck and the fabric.

"Hold her arms down," Knox said.

Cord grabbed her arms and stretched them above her head. He knelt on her arms. The pain was unbearable. Between his knees digging into her biceps, the throbbing of her injured shoulder being wrenched over her head, and difficulty breathing, she felt on the verge of blacking out.

Miranda closed her eyes. She held in the sobs as tears streamed down her cheeks.

Knox kicked her in the side with the pointed-toe of his boot. He sat down on her, straddling her thighs and reached for the button on her pants.

———

After leaving Melora, it took Caleb and Ryan less than a minute to get into place not far from the men and Miranda. As Melora predicted, they were so distracted with Miranda that they wouldn't have noticed if they had walked right into camp.

The man holding Miranda's hands above her head was

the smaller of the two men but was probably still four inches taller and twenty pounds heavier than Ryan. The other man looked to be about Caleb's height, but stockier.

Caleb pointed to the smaller man. Ryan nodded. Caleb held up three fingers. When he had Ryan's attention, he quickly counted down by dropping one finger at a time to synchronize their attack. When Caleb's last finger dropped, they bolted from the trees.

Ryan made a diving tackle for the man holding Miranda's hands. The man lost his grip on her and tumbled over backwards. They rolled away from Miranda, freeing her arms.

Caleb slammed into the other man with his shoulder, knocking him off of Miranda. He stole a quick glance at his sister and saw her crawling toward the trees on her hands and knees. With Miranda putting distance between them, his focus returned to the man.

The man struggled to his feet but was unable to react before Caleb closed in and landed a powerful uppercut to his jaw. As the man stumbled backwards, Caleb hit him in the stomach, doubling him over. Before the man could straighten out, Caleb threw another uppercut, snapping his head back.

Spitting out a mouthful of blood, the man looked up at Caleb with fire in his eyes and cursed. He reached down and pulled his knife out of its sheath. Caleb followed suit. As the two men circled each other, Caleb stole a quick glance at Ryan. The other man had Ryan pinned to the ground. He couldn't help him now, so he hoped Melora was nearby.

The man lunged, but Caleb dodged to the right, evading the blade. The man whirled around and lunged again, this time leaving a gash down Caleb's arm. He didn't even register the pain as he took the opportunity while the man was off-balance and still within reach to bury his knife in the man's gut.

Caleb stepped closer as the man dropped his knife. The man's eyes went wide with shock and pain, and he gasped. Caleb yanked up hard on his blade and could see the life draining away. He pulled his knife out and stepped back out of reach. The man took an unsteady step forward and collapsed on the ground.

He stood for only a second, trying to catch his breath when he heard Ryan cry out in agony. He took a step toward his brother-in-law, but before he could reach him, Melora dove and hit the man in the back at a full run. The man rolled off Ryan and grappled with Melora.

By the time Caleb reached them, Ryan had gotten to his feet. The man had just managed to pin Melora and was lifting his fist to punch her. Caleb grabbed the raised arm, pulled him off her, and dragged him a few feet before Ryan jumped on the man's legs, immobilizing him.

Caleb knelt down, digging his knees into the man's biceps, pinning his arms above his head. "Doesn't feel so good, does it," Caleb hissed.

The man struggled under the weight of Caleb and Ryan until Melora walked up and pointed her 9mm at his head.

"What's your name?" she demanded.

The man spit at her but didn't answer.

"His name is Cord," Miranda rasped as she made her way next to Melora, limping and clutching both sides of the front of her shirt.

Melora holstered her gun and pulled her knife. She cut the fabric binding Miranda's wrists, slipped out of her jacket, and draped it over her trembling shoulders.

Caleb was so relieved to see Miranda walking and

talking, but her condition made him want to kill this man now. He tamped down on his rage. They needed answers.

"That man is the leader of their mission to scope out Beartooth," Miranda choked out as she slipped her arms into Melora's jacket, zipped it up, and then pointed to Knox. There's a man named Roy somewhere serving as a lookout."

"Not anymore," Caleb replied.

"We weren't going to hurt her," Cord finally said in a pleading voice.

"We saw what you were trying to do. I wouldn't waste my breath attempting to convince her husband and her brother otherwise," Melora said.

Caleb could see the fear in the man's eyes. He now knew the lookout wouldn't be coming to help. He could see his buddy was dead, and he was dealing with two men unlikely to show him mercy.

"How bad did they hurt you?" Ryan asked as he looked up at Miranda.

"I'll heal, and thanks to you three, they hadn't gotten around to raping me, but I'm sure I don't look very pretty," Miranda said as her voice broke.

"You're just as beautiful as ever. You said my black eye made me look tough. I think yours makes you look dangerous," Ryan said.

Miranda tried to chuckle but ended up coughing.

"Are you going to be okay?" Ryan asked.

She nodded. "I haven't had a thing to drink all day except a sip of moonshine. Add that to a lot of crying and him nearly choking me to death, and I'm not surprised I sound so bad."

"Cruel bastard," Melora said as she kicked Cord in the side.

"Where is Bennett and the rest of the FAMA militia?" Melora demanded.

"I ain't saying, and I don't like bossy women," he replied as he glared at Melora.

Melora pulled her knife and pierced the fabric of his jeans near his crotch. "I really don't need much reason to give you what you deserve."

Cord struggled, but Ryan and Caleb held tight.

"I'll ask you one more time, where's Bennett and his followers, and why are you here?" She added more pressure, drawing blood.

"Okay," he conceded. "We took over a ranch another day's ride southeast of here. Jonah sent out a bunch of scouting parties to find a place to settle and lay low until the Guard leaves Pryor. Knox, Roy, Zeke, and I were supposed to check out where General Titus flew in by helicopter and find out if there were still people here, how many, what kind of weapons, and if it looked like there would be food, lodging, and women enough for all of us."

"How many of you are there?" Melora asked.

"We had about fifty, but some have left and not come back."

"What will happen if your party doesn't return?" Caleb asked.

"Don't rightly know. Sometimes groups go and don't come back. A couple times we ran across them somewhere, and they claimed they got lost."

"Did Bennett send out anyone to look for them?" Melora asked.

"Not that he told anyone."

Melora and Caleb looked at each other and shared a satisfied look. It was possible Bennett would send someone else to scout Beartooth and look for the men, but it wasn't a given. Apparently, defection wasn't unheard of.

"What happened to Zeke?" Cord asked.

"Never made it out of the community. The woman he went after put an arrow through his heart," Caleb replied.

Cord's eyes went from shock to skepticism. "I thought you said she was blind?" he directed at Miranda who was still standing next to Melora.

"I said nearly blind, but she can hone in on sound. I have to assume he couldn't keep his mouth shut," Miranda replied.

Caleb looked up at his sister and smiled. "It was a darn impressive shot."

"Wha, wha, what are you going to do with me? Zeke was the mean one, and Knox over there was the leader. I just, just followed orders," Cord stuttered.

"I didn't hear Knox order you to backhand me to the floor in the storehouse; in fact, mean old Zeke wasn't happy you damaged my pretty face. He didn't tell you to grope me along the entire ride here, he didn't tell you to pull me off the horse and let me hit the ground, and he most certainly didn't order you to nearly choke me to death," Miranda hissed as she absently stroked her neck, once again fighting to hold back the tears.

Melora put her arm around Miranda and pulled her close. She looked at Ryan and then Caleb. "I'm taking Miranda to the fire to warm her up. I think we got all we need out of him."

Both men nodded. Melora and Miranda turned and walked away.

FORTY-NINE

CALEB AND RYAN joined Melora and Miranda at the fire a few minutes later. Night had settled in, and a chorus of howls echoed all around them. The moment Miranda saw Ryan, she walked into his arms. He gently held her while she cried.

Melora left and returned a few moments later with the sleeve off of Knox's shirt. She wrapped it tightly around Caleb's forearm. "It doesn't look too deep. This should stop the bleeding."

By the time Melora finished tending to Caleb's gash, Miranda had stopped crying. She stepped out of Ryan's arms and went to Caleb.

She wrapped her arms around her brother and hugged him. "I knew you and Ryan would come. I just didn't know how quickly you could find me, but knowing you were out there gave me the strength to endure their torture."

"I'm so sorry you had to endure anything. I wish we could have caught up to you sooner," Caleb replied.

"You're here now. How's Tony?"

"He was still alive when we left," Melora replied.

"I'm anxious to hear more about Evelyn's ordeal, but we obviously have more immediate concerns. I don't like the sound of the howling," Miranda said as she returned to Ryan's side and clutched his arm.

"Those wolves aren't very close, and we have some heavy-duty firepower if they give us any trouble. We need to make some decisions, though," Caleb said, looking over at Melora.

"We should gather up all the weapons and anything else these men had that would be of use. We might as well take the horses. We're one short unless someone rides double anyway, and they'll just end up as prey if left alone out here. So, the big question is, what about the bodies?"

"We don't have any tools to dig a hole, but I don't want to leave them for the predators. The carnivores may develop a taste for human flesh," Caleb replied.

"What about stoking up this fire until it is really big and hot?" Ryan asked.

"Probably our best bet," Melora replied.

"Do you have any injuries that need treated right away?" Caleb asked Miranda.

"No, the cuts have stopped bleeding. I don't think anything is broken or dislocated. It will just take time for the bruises to heal and the pain to go away," she replied.

"I'm so sorry I didn't find you sooner. I've always wanted to protect you and make you happy, but I've failed," Ryan said as he looked at Miranda with wet eyes.

"No, you haven't. We assumed FAMA would never make it to Beartooth without the helicopter, so no one could have predicted this. Then, I was just in the wrong place at the wrong time. But as far as making me happy, you've succeeded there. I love you, Ryan."

"I love you too," he said as he pulled her back into his arms and held her.

No one spoke for several minutes, knowing Miranda needed to be held. They had all night to take care of the men and their gear. When Ryan finally let her go, she had quit crying.

"Miranda, stay here close to the fire and take it easy. You've been through a lot. As for the rest of us, let's gather a lot of wood and stack it close by. We'll get it burning hot, drag the bodies over here, and roll them into the fire," Melora explained.

Miranda stepped back from Ryan and stood close to the fire with her arms wrapped around herself. The rest of the group spread out and started dragging dry tree limbs close to the fire. It didn't take long before they had a large pile of wood. They fed the flames until the fire was roaring and too hot to stand close to for very long.

Melora took an armload of smaller wood and led Miranda away to another clearing downwind to build a small fire to huddle around while the bonfire did its job. Miranda had been through more than enough and didn't need to see the bodies burning or smell the smoke.

Caleb and Ryan dragged the two closest bodies next to the fire. After removing anything from the men that might be useful, they rolled the bodies into the fire. Once the bodies were fully engulfed, they hiked up the small hill and brought Roy down to the fire and repeated the process.

"Why don't you go to Miranda and send Melora back. I'm sure she needs you right now. Melora and I can keep feeding the fire and pack everything up. As soon as it gets light, we'll head home. Take a couple of their bedrolls and try to get some sleep."

Ryan gathered up the bedrolls and left. A few minutes later, Melora returned.

"How's she doing?" Caleb asked.

"I think she's so physically and emotionally exhausted that she's numb right now. I imagine she'll have nightmares for a while, but she's tough. With Ryan and the rest of your family's support, she'll get through it."

"I've always been there to protect my baby sister. I hate letting her out of my sight, but I'm sure you're right."

Melora squeezed his shoulder. "I know it's hard, but she's an adult woman, and she needs her husband more than her brother right now."

Caleb nodded. "Let's go get our horses and bring them into camp with the other three. Then we can go through everything we acquired and figure out how best to pack it out. Once we get that done, we can take turns sleeping while the other keeps watch and feeds the fire."

"Sounds like a good plan," Melora replied.

After bringing all the horses together, they went through the three men's saddlebags. They were traveling light. The first two sets of saddlebags held eating utensils, more ammo, a bottle of booze, and a few personal items.

"Find anything interesting?" Melora asked.

"Nope, wait, I take that back," Caleb said as he walked over to where Melora was digging through a bag.

"Holy heck, this must have been their escape plan if the residents of Beartooth put up a fight."

"Glad they didn't use it, may come in handy someday," Caleb said as he handed the grenade to Melora. "I think you should keep this. I don't know anything about grenades except they can cause a lot of damage."

"They can. This makes me worry even more about another visit from Bennett and his militia. They commandeered a helicopter, but we sabotaged it. Now we know they have assault rifles and grenades. What other surprises might they have?"

Melora stowed the grenade in her saddlebags, and then they finished going through the rest of the men's gear. They piled together the assault rifles, sidearms, knives, and everything else that might be useful. Once they saw what they had, they repacked everything in order to haul it home with them in the morning.

"I think that's about all we can do to prepare for an early morning exodus," Melora said.

"Yep, go get some sleep. I'll head back to the fire and keep the flames burning hot." Caleb turned to walk away, but Melora reached out and grabbed his good arm, stopping him.

"I didn't want to ask in front of Miranda, and I guess it really doesn't matter, but which one of you slit Cord's throat?"

"Ryan didn't even give me a chance. I think he felt the need to do it himself. I don't blame him. If some man put Ash through what Cord subjected Miranda to, I'd make darn sure I was the one who made him pay."

"I wasn't sure if Ryan had it in him."

"Me neither," Caleb replied.

FIFTY

ASH LAY on her side in Caleb's childhood bed in the room he had shared with Dillon growing up. Worry for Caleb and the others kept her from sleeping.

Sara woke up in the middle of the night crying, so she brought her into bed with her and held her little girl until the toddler fell asleep. Ash was afraid if she moved, Sara would wake up, so she stayed in the same position most of the night, making it impossible to sleep even if she could clear her mind.

The cabin was slowly coming to life. Ash heard multiple sets of heavy footsteps crossing the hardwood floors and the exterior door open and close. She assumed Owen and Dillon had already left for the morning. A few minutes later she heard the door to Miranda's old room shut. She needed to get up but didn't want to wake Sara.

Another thirty minutes passed before Sara stirred. When her eyes fluttered open, she smiled and reached up with a tiny finger to touch Ash's cheek.

"Good morning, Sunshine," Ash said as she kissed her daughter.

"Daddy?"

"He went for a ride with Uncle Ryan so we had a sleepover at Grandma and Grandpa's," Ash replied as cheerfully as she could.

Sara seemed satisfied. After cuddling for a few more minutes, Sara was ready to get up. She retrieved her new stuffed bunny, and Ash opened the door. Sara ran out and held the bunny up to Olivia.

"I've got her if you want to get dressed," Olivia said as she scooped her granddaughter up.

Ash went into the bathroom. She tried to hurry since Evelyn might be waiting, but she was moving slowly this morning. She had gotten little sleep the night before, and she felt awful.

When she exited, Olivia looked up. By the red, puffy rings around Olivia's eyes, she had no doubt her mother-in-law spent most of the night crying for her children. Ash completely understood. The only thing keeping her tears at bay was putting on a calm front for Sara.

Ash went into Caleb's old room. She dressed and made the bed. She gathered up the furniture cushions, walked out into the living room, and put the cushions back where they belonged.

"Now you can sit down. Is that why the guys left so early? They had no place to sit?" Ash joked, trying to sound upbeat.

Olivia chuckled and sat Sara down. They watched as the toddler crouched and mimicked a bunny hopping.

"Owen took his rifle and is going with the rest of the armed residents to sweep the area once more to make sure there are no FAMA stragglers. Dillon went home to clean the floors before he takes Evelyn home. As soon as Evelyn gets up, she can watch Sara, and you and I can start breakfast."

Ash nodded but didn't really feel like cooking. They continued to watch Sara play in silence until Evelyn joined them.

"If you've got Sara, Ash and I will go start breakfast. Owen and Dillon should be home shortly," Olivia said.

Evelyn got down on the floor. Ash could hear giggles from Sara as she followed Olivia into the kitchen. Ash set the table and made pancakes while Olivia grated potatoes and made hashbrowns. Just as Ash pulled the last pancake off the griddle, she heard the door open.

By the time the food was on the table, the guys were washed up, and everyone sat down. Ash held Sara and fed her tiny bites of pancakes with a little bit of honey drizzled over them.

"Did you find anything out there?" Olivia asked.

"No, we found no sign of intruders, so the three that rode out of here must be the last of them," Owen replied.

"I did a little cleaning at the cabin, so if you want to go home after breakfast, we can," Dillon said to Evelyn.

"Thank you. I'm not sure how much help I'd have been. I doubt I could have seen the spots, and if I did, I might have lost my composure," Evelyn replied as she squeezed Dillon's hand.

"Any word on Tony?" Olivia asked.

Owen looked up and swallowed hard. "He didn't make it."

"Oh, poor Maria. She and the kids and grandkids must be devastated. I'll bake something after breakfast."

Olivia always baked when she was upset. Ash had known Tony and his family nearly her entire life. She was shattered by the news but didn't want to fall apart in front of Sara. She was also consumed with worry for Caleb, Miranda, Ryan, and Melora, and for the future of Beartooth.

They finished breakfast in silence. Between their sorrow over Tony's death and their worry for Caleb and Miranda, no one could think of anything positive to talk about.

"We really appreciate staying here last night. I'm not sure I could have slept in our cabin the way it was," Evelyn finally said.

"It was our pleasure, and we needed our family around us just as much. It was very comforting," Olivia replied.

"As soon as we help clean up, we'll get out of your hair," Dillon added.

"There isn't much mess. Ash and I can handle it," Olivia replied.

After breakfast, the family followed Dillon and Evelyn out. Hugs were given all around. Ash hugged Evelyn last. "If you need to talk, I'm here for you."

"Thank you, and thank you for teaching me to shoot. It might have saved my life. If you need a shoulder, mine may be small, but it's all yours."

When the dishes were done, Olivia hung the dishrag to dry and turned to Ash. "Have you told Caleb yet?"

Ash froze in the act of drying the last plate. "No. How did you know?"

"It's written all over you and the signs are there, your lack of appetite, time in the bathroom, and you looked nauseous at dinner last night and throughout breakfast, just to name a few."

Ash finished drying the plate, put it away, and hung up the dish towel.

"Talk to me, Ash. I know you wish your mother were here, but I'll do my best."

Ash turned around and leaned back against the sink with tears threatening to fall. "I'm so scared. I was going to tell Caleb yesterday, but then terror struck our community. How can I talk to you about my fear when I know yours is paralyzing?"

Olivia pulled her into her arms, and they both cried. When Ash no longer had any tears left to shed, she stepped back. "I'm sorry."

"Don't be. Let's not focus on our fear for Caleb and Miranda's safe return and talk about you," Olivia said as she sat at the table and motioned for Ash to sit down across from her.

Ash nodded. "Judging by the way I feel and the timing of things, I think I'm about six weeks along. I haven't been to the clinic yet because I wanted to tell Caleb before his sister found out. So far, I haven't been nearly as sick as I was with Sara."

"All that sounds like good news, but you don't seem as happy as I expected you to be. I thought you wanted a large family?"

"I do, but we didn't plan this. The timing couldn't be worse. We have so much uncertainty going into winter, and the world is crumbling around us. We've discovered a more deadly predator than anyone has ever seen, and we have no idea how many more are lurking in the wild. Worst of all, Bennett's militia has returned to Beartooth. Who's to say more won't come soon? They murdered Neal and Tony and kidnapped Miranda, and Caleb has gone after them. When he leaves, I worry a lot about raising Sara alone, but with another on the way, I'm not sure I could do it without him."

Oliva took her hands. "You will never be alone. I know a bunch of in-laws aren't the same, but we will always be here for you and our grandchildren."

"I know, but I just love him so much. I always have, and I always will."

"You don't need to tell me that. It's been obvious since you were a little girl."

Ash dried her tears. "I just want our children to know their father."

"They will. He'll come home."

Ash knew Olivia had to be worried beyond belief, but her words and expression were confident and strong. If her mother-in-law could have faith, she could too.

FIFTY-ONE

CALEB FIGURED he got about two hours of sleep. It wasn't much, but it would be enough. As the sun slowly peeked above the mountain tops, he could hear the others stirring a short distance away, where they moved the camp.

Melora joined him. They walked around the perimeter of the bonfire they had kept blazing all night long.

"I don't see anything recognizable, do you?" Melora asked.

"Nope, I guess it's time to quit feeding it and let it go out."

"How are you doing?"

"The arm doesn't hurt much," he replied.

"I mean, are you okay with what you had to do yesterday? I remember my first time. It probably wasn't as justified as yesterday. It was part of the job, but that didn't make it any easier. I'm still haunted by some of the things I've had to do in my life."

"Growing up in Beartooth was carefree. I never would

have dreamed that I'd find myself in a position one day where I had to kill someone. I'm not sure what bothers me more, that I did it or that I don't feel bad about it."

"Don't beat yourself up. There was no other option. If those men made it back to Bennett, I have no doubt they would have led the whole deranged group to our doorstep."

"Even if we weren't worried about Bennett, I'd have still done it. I didn't have time to subdue the guy trying to grab Evelyn, and he would have died anyway from the placement of her arrow. I thought it would be better for her if I put him out of his misery. And Miranda, she's my baby sister. I've always thought it was my job to protect her. Knowing how much they hurt her and what would have happened if we hadn't found them when we did, still has my blood boiling."

"If you ever need to talk, I'm here to listen. How do you think Ryan will handle it?"

"I don't know. I'm sure he matured a lot yesterday. He did what he felt he had to do, but I have no doubt it will eat at him."

Melora gave Caleb a sad smile and clutched his shoulder in a show of solidarity. They turned their back on the dying embers and joined Miranda and Ryan.

"Just in time, we've put together breakfast," Ryan said.

Miranda stood up and hugged Melora and Caleb. "Thank you both."

Caleb looked at the cuts and bruises on her face and the bruise around her neck. He took her hands and held them up. Both wrists were rubbed raw from her bindings. "I'm so sorry this happened to you."

"I'm just happy you arrived when you did, and we all survived. How long of a ride do we have back to

Beartooth? It felt like we rode forever yesterday," Miranda asked.

"We loped where we could to make up time, but occasionally we had to stop and search for tracks to make sure we didn't lose your trail. Factoring in the stops and loping, I'm guessing we can be back in five or six hours," Caleb replied.

"I'm anxious to see how Tony and Evelyn are doing, and I bet Mom, Dad, Ash, Dillon, Evelyn, Tyler, and Ryan's entire family are all worried sick. I just hope this nightmare is over for all of our sakes," Miranda said, her voice still raw and raspy.

"You're amazing," Ryan said as he leaned over and kissed her cheek. "After everything you've been through, you're worried about everyone else."

"I was hoping you'd sound a little better this morning," Caleb commented.

"I'm sure they bruised my vocal cords. Once we get home, I'll make some tea with honey and that should help."

"How about the rest of you?" Caleb asked Miranda.

"I hurt all over, but it could have been worse, so I'm not complaining."

"That's the attitude. Hopefully, you'll still be thinking positive after five or more hours in the saddle," Caleb said.

"If I'm looking at Beartooth by then, I guarantee I'll be happy. But I better limit talking so I can rest my voice."

"That won't be easy for you," Caleb joked as he ate a slice of bread.

A deep rumbling roar echoed in the distance. Melora, Caleb, and Ryan exchanged concerned looks."

"What was that?" Miranda whispered.

"It was a long way away," Ryan offered.

"Probably too far away to be certain," Melora added.

"To be certain of what?" Miranda prodded.

"It sounded like the jumbo jaguars we tangled with on the hunt, but as they said, it was a long way away," Caleb answered.

"Nonetheless, let's get packed up and out of here as quickly as possible," Melora said.

They finished eating, extinguished the fire, and saddled and packed the horses. Within twenty minutes of the disturbing sound, they were ready to ride.

Before they mounted up, Melora gave Miranda one of the sidearms taken from the men and showed her how to use it. Miranda took several practice shots since they now had more ammunition than they ever had before. It seemed like a wise use.

Caleb offered to ride one of the new horses since they knew nothing about the recent additions. Miranda, Melora, and Ryan rode the geldings, and Melora and Ryan led the remaining horses.

The stock was as nervous as the people, but after two hours of riding with no incident, both relaxed. Caleb set a strong pace, and no one had any difficulty keeping up.

They took a quick mid-morning break. Miranda had a difficult time getting off her horse, but Ryan was close by to help her. Despite her lack of complaint, Caleb could see she was in a lot of pain. The only thing he could do for her was to get them home as quickly as possible.

It was late afternoon when they approached the community from the east. No one ran out to greet them.

"Hold up. Something doesn't feel right. It's too quiet," Caleb said.

He and Melora pulled out their assault rifles. The group rode side-by-side with Ryan and Miranda in the middle. When they reached Miranda and Ryan's cabin, Ryan helped Miranda off the horse and into the cabin.

Once Miranda was safely inside the cabin, they rode on toward the Thorn's ranch. They saw no sign of Bob, Maggie, or Jacob at the ranch.

"Where is everyone?" Ryan asked.

"I wish I knew, but Zeke's horse is in the coral over there," Caleb replied.

He wasn't sure what to make of that. Likely, Dan and the armed residents found the horse while securing the area. If more FAMA militia were in the area and had taken over, surely there would be more unfamiliar horses in the corrals.

They quickly unsaddled and unpacked the horses. They put the three new ones in the corral with Zeke's horse and turned the geldings out in the pasture.

"Ryan, go home and take this food. You and Miranda stay behind locked doors while Melora and I try to figure out what's going on. I think she's hurting more than she'll admit, so I hate to leave her alone," Caleb said.

Ryan didn't argue and headed for home.

Caleb and Melora hid all the extra guns, ammunition, and supplies in Bob's barn and took off on foot. The Solomon cabin was next door, so Caleb and Melora went there first. No one was home, but Caleb could see Sara's bag, so knew they had been there. They did a quick check of cabins until they reached Melora's cabin. When Tyler wasn't home, they headed straight for Ash and Caleb's cabin. It was empty.

"What next?" Melora asked. "An entire community can't just disappear."

Caleb thought for a moment. There weren't many places that would draw the entire community.

"I hope I'm way off base, but if Tony didn't make it…" Caleb said, his words trailing off.

"Pray you're wrong, but it's the only explanation I can think of as well," Melora replied.

They quickly walked the distance west of the community to the cemetery. As they rounded a bend in the road, they spotted a mass of people with their backs to them. They quietly approached. Tyler stood near the rear of the crowd. Melora slid in next to him. He turned and wrapped his arms around her.

Caleb saw his family was near the front. He didn't want to detract from the memorial service, so he stood quietly out of sight until they lowered a simple wooden coffin into the ground. After Sam Ferguson, Aiden and Gavin Winters, Jacob Thorn, and Archie Craig finished filling the hole, everyone turned to leave.

Caleb saw Ash and quickly made his way to her. Sara spotted him before anyone else.

"Daddy, Daddy, Daddy," she screamed over and over.

Ash whipped her head around and saw Caleb. She ran to him, carrying Sara. He wrapped his arms around them and held them until he was surrounded by people.

"Did you get Miranda back?" Olivia asked.

"Yes, we caught up to them and took Miranda back. Miranda and Ryan are at home. She's pretty banged up, but it could have been a whole lot worse. If we were even five minutes later those monsters would have…"

"Glad to hear you reached her before that happened," Owen said as he pulled Caleb into a strong hug.

He could see the Ferguson family running toward the residential area. He had no doubt they wanted to see Ryan for themselves. Olivia threw her arms around Caleb and sobbed.

"I need to see Miranda," Olivia demanded when she finally quit crying.

There was a lot of chatter as the residents followed them back to Beartooth. Caleb couldn't tell what was being said, but the aura was solemn. He was sure everyone was relieved Miranda had been rescued, but there was no cheering on this day when one of Beartooth's most beloved residents was laid to rest.

As everyone drifted off in different directions, there were a lot of pats on the back for Owen and Caleb and hugs for Olivia. When they reached Ryan and Miranda's cabin, the Ferguson clan was already there.

Olivia pulled Miranda into her arms and cried some more. Owen hugged her next, and then Miranda reached for Evelyn. "I was so relieved when Caleb said you were okay, and I really want to hear how you shot that sleaze ball," Miranda said as she hugged Evelyn.

Dillon and Ash hugged her next, but when Sara got her turn, she refused to let Miranda go.

"Zane went for Emily. When he gets back, we'll get out of your hair," Tara said.

Tara and Olivia hugged and cried. Ash understood. They were mothers, and their children had been in danger. Ash couldn't even imagine the terror she would feel if Sara were ever in a similar situation.

Emily raced through the door into the cabin.

"I'm going to be fine," Miranda stated.

"You sure don't look fine, so I'll be the judge," Emily said. "Let's go have a look."

Miranda handed Sara to Ash, rolled her eyes, and followed Emily into her bedroom.

Ryan assured his family he'd let them know if Emily found anything. He admitted that Miranda had been beaten, bruised, tortured, and was in a lot of pain, but he believed she would heal. "In case you're wondering, we arrived in time to spare Miranda even more trauma."

"Oh, thank goodness," Tara said as she hugged Ryan again before leaving.

By the time Emily came out, all the Fergusons had left.

"I gave her something for the pain. She's covered from head to toe with bruises. In addition to the ones you see, she was apparently kicked in the side. Her ribs are probably cracked and are tender and she has a massive, nasty-looking bruise. We need to watch her closely, but I think we'd know by now if she has any internal bleeding. She has bruises on her arms from being roughly grabbed and one of them held her down by kneeling on her arms, so be careful how tightly you hug her or where you touch her. The cuts down her stomach and chest between her breasts aren't deep, so we'll just treat those with honey. She needs a lot of rest, but I agree with her assessment. She'll heal physically, and although it apparently could have been much worse, this was an incredibly traumatic event for her nonetheless. She's harboring a lot of guilt over Tony's death, so be patient and give her lots of love," Emily said and then left.

"Come on, Olivia. I'm sure they could use some quiet time alone," Owen said as he ushered his wife out the door.

"I guess that's our cue. Let us know if you need anything," Dillon said as he and Evelyn left.

Ryan pulled Caleb into a strong hug. Caleb seemed a little uncomfortable at first but then hugged his brother-in-law back.

"Thanks for letting me do what I had to do. I'm not sure if I could have looked Miranda in the eye otherwise."

Caleb nodded and took Sara from Ash. The toddler instantly rested her head against Caleb's chest, clearly content to have her family together. With Caleb's arm wrapped around Sara, holding her tight to him, Ash slipped her fingers through his free hand.

She raised their joined hands to her lips and kissed the back of his hand. Ash noticed the blood soaked through the unfamiliar shirt sleeve tied around his forearm. She looked up at him and their eyes met. There was no point in discussing it now, so they slowly walked home in silence.

FIFTY-TWO

SARA WAS EXHAUSTED. Ash had little difficulty getting her to bed while Caleb showered. It had been a long and emotional day, and it had to be especially confusing for a toddler. There was no way to explain to her that the nice man from the storehouse was dead and had to be buried, or why nearly everyone in the community was crying. But with everyone at the graveside, Ash had no choice but to take her along.

Once Sara saw Caleb, Ash could see their daughter's joy return. She wished she could share in such innocence and belief that Caleb's mere presence made her world safe again.

Ash was thrilled that he, Miranda, Ryan, and Melora were home, but she suspected that the ordeal would cause deep emotional wounds for all of them that would take time to heal. At the moment, she could do little about that, but she could tend Caleb's physical wounds.

She gathered up her medical supplies and set them on the nightstand on Caleb's side of the bed. Ash walked into the bathroom and found Caleb standing in front of the sink, brushing his teeth. She wrapped her arms around him and rested her head on his back until he was finished, reveling in the warmth of his skin on her cheek.

He turned around, pulled her into his arms, and kissed her deeply. When the kiss ended, she held on to him, not wanting to let go. After several minutes, she eased back and took his hand, lifting his arm. A six-inch gash ran from below the elbow to four inches above his wrist, fortunately, the cut did not hit any major arteries.

"Come lie down on your back and let me put some honey on it and wrap it so you don't ruin our only set of sheets if it starts bleeding again."

He stretched out on the bed and smiled up at her as she sat next to him. "It's not as bad as it looks."

"Maybe not, but you can't deny the severity of these," Ash said as she ran her hand down the scars along his side. "I was there when it happened, and it took a lot of stitches to close you up. Fortunately, I didn't see how you got the ones on your backside. I would love for you to come home once without injuries."

"Me too," he said as he reached up and ran his hand gently down her cheek.

She closed her eyes for a moment and leaned into his touch. She loved the intimate gesture.

"You still take my breath away every time I look at you," he said as he dropped his hand.

Ash smiled, leaned down, and kissed him. "And my heart nearly misses a beat when you touch me, but don't try to distract me. This newest addition to your collection," she said as she lifted his arm, "is a straighter, thinner, and much cleaner cut. My guess is a knife wound, not an animal encounter."

He nodded. "Very perceptive, but the other guy fared much worse."

"I figured as much since you made it home with three extra horses."

Since the cut was from a knife rather than a wild animal, Ash assumed the honey's anti-microbial and wound-healing properties would be sufficient. With her finger, she gently smoothed the honey down the length of the cut and then put a thin strip of gauze over the wound and wrapped his forearm loosely with an elastic bandage.

"Thanks, that feels much better already, or maybe it's just your touch," he said with a smile.

"I think honey will do the trick, but we should have Emily or Miranda look at it tomorrow just in case. We need to watch for infection. Medical supplies are very low, so I hate to use any of the last bit of commercial antibiotic ointment if it isn't necessary."

Ash put on her nightshirt, brushed her teeth, and crawled into bed next to Caleb. She rolled over onto her side, facing him. He was on his back, staring at the ceiling.

"Scoot over here closer," he said as he looked over at her.

She edged closer and placed her hand on his chest. She could feel his warmth, his strength, and the steady beat of his heart.

He reached over and caressed her cheek, then tucked a loose strand of hair behind her ear. His touch was so gentle, it nearly brought tears to her eyes.

"I love you, Ash," he said as he turned his head and gave her a tender kiss on the lips. "I'm sorry I had to leave you and Sara, but I had to go."

"I know. I'm just happy you rescued Miranda as quickly as you did, and you all made it home with only one night out. The community is grieving and suffering over the loss of Tony. I'm not sure if we could have withstood any more tragedy, especially me. I love you so much."

"Do you want to know what happened?"

"If it will help to talk about it, otherwise I can wait if it's still too raw," Ash replied.

"I'll probably have to share the details tomorrow with the CLB, so no since repeating them now. But just so you're not shocked, the guy trying to nab Evelyn wasn't the only man I killed."

"I assumed as much. Does it bother you?"

Caleb thought for a moment. "In my head, I know there was no other option, but I never imagined I'd ever have to take a person's life. I remember how horrified everyone was when they found out I'd punched Sam and Jacob for looking at you when we were younger, and a few others over the years. What will everyone think when they realize I killed not only Evelyn's attacker, but others?"

"Bennett's men murdered Neal and Tony, tried to kidnap Evelyn, and took Miranda who would have been assaulted, tortured, and eventually killed. You can't negotiate or reason with men like that. You did what you had to do."

He nodded and went silent again. Ash gently ran her hand across his chest, but said nothing, wanting him to know he was loved, but giving him time to process what he probably hadn't had much time to do until now.

"What happened yesterday seems like a lifetime ago already. When I saw what those animals had in mind for Miranda and what they'd already done to her, I couldn't help but wonder if there is any hope for our species.

There's just so much evil out there. But then I get home and hold you and Sara, and I see that there is also a lot of love and goodness left in the world. I'll fight for it, for you, and everyone I love until my last breath."

Ash prayed it would never come to that, because she had no doubt he would.

FIFTY-THREE

AS CALEB PREDICTED the night before, Dan called a CLB meeting first thing the next morning. A lot had changed in Beartooth in a very short period of time. No one knew all parts of the tragedy, and everyone was anxious to put all of the pieces together.

The morning was cool. Ash bundled Sara up, and the three of them headed over to the farm. After dropping Sara off, they went to check on Miranda. Ash knocked on the door and Miranda answered.

"Shouldn't you be in bed?" Ash asked.

"I'm sore all over, tired as heck, and it will take a while for the bruises to fade, but considering what they could have done to me, I feel pretty lucky. I just want to put it behind me and move on, but Dan wants me to tell the board what happened. Unfortunately, I'm the only witness to much of the horrific events," Miranda said.

Ash, Caleb, Miranda, and Ryan walked to the school-house together in silence. When they entered, everyone was seated, including Evelyn and Dillon. They took the four empty chairs between Melora and Evelyn.

"I'm sorry we're all meeting so soon, but I thought it was important to learn what transpired over the past couple of days and discuss what, if anything, we can do to better protect the residents of this community. I told Maria she didn't have to join us, but she wants to know what happened."

Ash knew that having Maria present would make this more difficult for Miranda since she already felt guilty over Tony's death.

"Miranda, I know this won't be easy, but it is important we know everything," Dan said.

Miranda looked over at Maria. "I'm so sorry."

"Don't be. You are not responsible for the deplorable and hateful actions of others. It is my choice to be here. I want to know what happened, even if it's painful," Maria replied.

Miranda looked at Evelyn and then at Ryan. She cleared her throat. "Evelyn and I left Ash's cabin. The three of us planned to meet up later to go shoot our bows. I left Evelyn at her cabin and went into the storehouse for some food. I asked Tony about the bread, and he went in the back to get a loaf. While I waited, I heard the door open. When I turned around to see who it was, the four men entered. Tony returned and told them to take what they want and leave, that we didn't want trouble."

"Sounds like Tony, always the diplomat," Dan said.

"Cord, the man closest to me asked Knox, who was the leader, if they could take me with them. Knox agreed and Cord grabbed hold of me. I slapped him as hard as I could, which in hindsight was a stupid thing to do. He backhanded me with such force it sent me to the floor and left this," Miranda said as she paused to point to her black eye and bruised cheek.

"I'm sorry, we should have asked how you're doing before we got started," Dan said.

"It'll take time to heal, but I feel fortunate to have escaped with my life so I won't complain."

"Glad to hear, continue," Dan replied.

"Anyway, Tony lunged forward to help me. Knox put a gun to his head and ordered him to stand down. I told Tony I was fine, so that he wouldn't try to do anything more. Apparently, they had been watching for a while and saw Evelyn and I walking. Knox told the guy named Zeke to go get Evelyn so they could take her back to Jonah as a gift. That's when I was certain these men were FAMA militia. I tried to convince them to leave Evelyn and just take me, but to no avail. They told Zeke to meet up at the horses once he grabbed Evelyn."

Miranda glanced over at Dillon and Evelyn. She could feel the rage radiating from her brother, but Evelyn's expression remained unreadable.

"Cord and a guy named Roy filled a couple bags with food. Then Cord tied my hands in front of me and put a rolled-up bandana between my teeth and tied it behind my head, gagging me. Knox grabbed me by the arm and dragged me toward the door. Tony tried to stop him and that's when Knox shot Tony. They forced me out of the storehouse before I could see if Tony was okay."

Miranda closed her eyes as the scene forced its way into her head. She bit her lip to keep from crying, looked around the table, and continued. "When we got to the horses, Zeke wasn't there. They rode off without him, thinking he'd catch up. They put me on a horse in front of Cord. We rode for hours before stopping for the night. I was tied to a tree by my wrists so high I had to stand on my tiptoes to touch the ground. After they set up camp and ate dinner, Knox sent Roy up a hill to keep watch.

Cord cut me down from the tree, and they were in the process of..." Miranda's voice broke off as she looked over at Ryan with tears in her eyes.

"We get the picture, go on," Dan said.

"All of the sudden, both men tumbled off of me. I scrambled away on my hands and knees and hid behind a tree. Ryan and Caleb were battling with the two men and soon Melora jumped in to help. They arrived just in time to stop them from raping me."

The room was silent. There were sighs of relief, accompanied by expressions of shock, anger, fear, and sorrow etched on everyone's face.

"Before Caleb, Ryan, and Melora pick up that thread, let's backtrack to Evelyn," Dan said.

Evelyn nodded and looked up as she spoke. "After Miranda left me, I went into the cabin to get my bow and arrows ready to go shoot. I was admiring the new arrows Ash made for me and still had my bow in one hand when I heard heavy footsteps on the porch. I knew it wasn't Ash or Miranda by the sound and assumed Dillon had come home early."

Evelyn paused for a moment and took a deep breath before continuing. "When the door opened, I turned. I can't see detail at that distance, but I knew it wasn't Dillon even before he spoke. Like Miranda, I quickly figured out who he was when he said he was taking me back as a gift for Jonah."

"They're animals, all of them," Henry blurted out.

She looked over and smiled weakly at her dad and pressed on. "For lack of a better idea, I decided to keep him talking so I could hone in on his voice. I asked questions and learned they arrived on horseback and had come from a ranch. I asked if he'd seen my friend. He told me she had been hit, but it was clear they were taking her with them so I knew Miranda was still alive. I asked him why they came and he said to check this place out. He made a reference to Neal and said if they'd have known there were such pretty ladies here, they'd have come back sooner. He told me to come with him. By that time, I had honed in on his voice and estimated where his heart would be from his lips. When he stepped toward me, I pulled up and shot. He stumbled but didn't fall and came after me. My quiver of arrows was out of reach, so I swung my bow at him. That did little to stop him. I then grabbed a skillet. I swung it at him, but it only grazed his shoulder. I thought he would take me or kill me, but then I saw someone sneak in behind him, so I kept Zeke's focus on me. Caleb should tell the rest of the story."

"I'm so proud of you," Dillon said as he put his arm around her and pulled her close.

Dan gave everyone a moment to digest everything they heard before nodding to Caleb to pick up the story.

"Like many, I heard a gunshot. I grabbed my 9mm and headed toward the sound. I approached cautiously once I reached the school. I peeked around the corner and noticed Evelyn and Dillon's door was open. I was just going to check it out when I heard Evelyn scream. As I entered the cabin, Zeke's back was to me. Thankfully, Evelyn kept him distracted. I pulled my knife, finished the job, and then dragged him out of the cabin so Evelyn could lock the door since I didn't know how many more were still out there. I then headed for the storehouse. When I arrived, Melora and Tyler were already there, and she was trying to stop the bleeding. A minute later, Dan, Ryan, and Zane entered."

"Melora, did you learn anything before Caleb arrived?" Dan asked.

"Tony said four of Bennett's men came into the store.

Three took Miranda, and one went after Evelyn. That's about all he had time to say before Caleb and the others arrived."

Dan briefed the group on what happened after that.

Maria stood up. The room fell silent. "Needless to say, our family is devastated. I really don't know how I'll go on, but somehow, I'm sure we all will in time. Since Serena, Daniel, and Isabella have helped Tony ever since they were big enough to walk, they offered to take over the storehouse if the community wants them to. We want to thank Tyler for coming for the family without knowing if any militants were still in the area, Emily and everyone else who administered immediate first aid, helped get Tony to the clinic and cared for him throughout the night, those who helped bury him, and the group who went after those responsible. And my entire family wanted me to assure Miranda that no one blames her for what happened. The results would have been the same even if no one other than Tony was in the storehouse. We know how brutal Bennett's men are. Neal didn't stand a chance and neither did Tony once they arrived. Obviously, they have no problem torturing and killing the unarmed and defenseless."

No one moved or said a word for several moments. When Miranda scooted her chair back the noise echoed in the silent room. She walked over to Maria and hugged her.

"I'm glad you don't blame me. I'm so sorry for your loss and the loss to this entire community. Tony was cherished by everyone and will be missed. I wish I could have done something more," Miranda said as she let Maria go.

"Thank you. Dan, sorry to interrupt. Please continue. I want to hear the rest," Maria said.

"Whichever one of you three wants to talk, proceed," Dan replied.

Caleb glanced from Ryan to Melora, and both nodded for him to start.

"We saddled up and rode as fast as we could while having to stop often to track them. We knew we were getting close when we smelled smoke from their campfire. We spotted their lookout on a hill, and then we saw Miranda. Even though I had relieved Zeke of his assault rifle, we didn't want a shootout for fear Miranda would get shot. I took out the lookout with my bow. Then, Ryan and I closed in on the other two men and we tackled them. The leader of the group pulled a knife on me. He got in one good swipe but got sloppy. We were able to subdue the guy Ryan tackled so Melora could question him," Caleb explained and then nodded to Melora to continue.

"After I gave him a little encouragement to cooperate, he admitted that they had ridden from a ranch a day's ride southeast of where we were. He said Jonah sent out a bunch of scouting parties to find a place to settle until the Guard leaves Pryor. Since General Titus didn't learn much when he flew in by helicopter, this group was supposed to come back to Beartooth and find out if there were still people here, how many, what kind of weapons we had, and if it looked like there would be food, lodging, and women for their group."

"Did he happen to say how many of them there are?" Dan asked.

"He said there were about fifty, but some had defected," Melora replied.

"Do you think Bennett will send more men if they don't return?" Bob asked.

"Cord wasn't sure. He said that sometimes groups go

and don't come back, and he wasn't aware anyone went looking for them," Caleb replied.

"Was he lying?" Bob asked.

"I don't think so, but I wouldn't count out the possibility that Bennett will send more men to look for this group and to verify if Beartooth could be a place to hide out," Melora responded.

"If Bennett does, we're better able to protect ourselves. We acquired four assault rifles, four sidearms, about a hundred rounds of ammo for the rifles and half that for the handguns," Caleb added.

"And, four more horses," Bob mumbled.

"I believe that's enough for today. Let's meet again the day after tomorrow in the morning and then hold a community meeting in late afternoon. That will give us a little time to let all this digest and to get word out about the community meeting. Any objections or anything else that can't wait a few days?" Dan asked.

Caleb, Melora, and Ryan exchanged a concerned look.

"Spill it," Dan ordered.

"As we were getting ready to leave the area yesterday at first light, we heard a chorus of deep, guttural roars. The call was feline, but sounded a long distance away, so it wasn't definitive. Maybe it was just mountain lions, and the distance or terrain altered how the sound carried," Caleb said.

"You're sounding like mountain lions are no big deal. After what you and Ash experienced in the wild, I'm a little surprised," Heath stated.

"Comparatively speaking, I'd take a cougar over one of those massive jaguar-hybrids any day. Three of those beasts mutilated and eviscerated five cougars, ripping out their throats and intestines, but not eating much. An animal that kills to eat is not nearly as dangerous as one that kills for sport," Caleb replied.

Dan shook his head and his shoulders shuddered. "Percentage-wise, how confident are you that you heard jaguars, or whatever in the heck those mammoth beasts were that you encountered on the big hunt?"

"Seventy-five," Caleb replied.

"I'm only going fifty percent. The sounds were far away and didn't go on for long, like maybe one animal calling out and another answering. By the time the rumbling sound caught my ear, it stopped," Melora said.

Every looked at Ryan. "That low menacing growl is etched in my memory. I hear it in my sleep. Yesterday, it was a long way away, so I won't say one hundred percent, but I will go with Caleb at seventy-five, maybe even eighty."

Dan rubbed his hands up and down over his face. "What next? How much more can we endure?'

"As much as we have to. Graham, Fiona, and I left the division, crime, political unrest, and hatred that plagued the country less than three years ago. It was bad then, and it's gotten much worse. Now, there appears to be a sliver of hope, but I have little faith this administration isn't going to end up being as corrupt and dangerous as the last. This is it. There's no place else to go," Melora said.

Everyone sat silently for a moment, watching Melora, hoping she would add something encouraging. She didn't, so the group filed out of the schoolhouse and headed home.

FIFTY-FOUR

THE NEXT DAY, Ash and Caleb stayed close to home, as did everyone in the community. Some had physical wounds to heal, and everyone had even deeper emotional scars that would take even longer to mend.

Ash was thankful that she was feeling well. It was difficult for her to keep anything from Caleb, but since everyone was reeling with grief, he didn't detect anything unusual in her demeanor. Caleb was clearly feeling like he hadn't done enough to protect his family, so now was not the time to tell him that responsibility would soon grow.

"I have a feeling tomorrow's CLB could be interesting," Ash said as she finished washing the dinner dishes.

"How do you mean?"

"We've made adjustments over the years to adapt to a changing climate, predators, the possibility of invaders, and most recently, a volcanic eruption. Now the stakes have changed. Everything is more dangerous and the margin of error for us is slim."

"That's an understatement," he mumbled as he cradled a sleeping Sara in his arms.

"We endured a long, cold winter, we've discovered predators unlike anything we've ever seen, and Bennett's militia made it here without a helicopter. They've taken two too many from our community. Tony has touched so many lives in a positive way, as did Neal, and now they are gone. Their close friends and family will never get over the losses. I can't imagine the nightmares that Miranda and Evelyn are experiencing, and taking a life can never be easy, no matter how justified."

"No, it's not," Caleb whispered as he took Sara to her room.

Once they got Sara to bed, the toddler fell back to sleep quickly. They returned to the living room, sat on the couch, and turned on the radio. A broadcast was already in progress.

"When pressed for a timeline for a presidential election, President Steele said she could not provide a specific date, but she assured the American people that as soon as law and order is restored, she will talk to her cabinet about when to hold a presidential election. The ambiguity is causing increased tension in a country already imploding," the reporter stated.

The newsreader then went on to explain that there have been rumblings from six states located west of the Missouri River about seceding from the rest of the United States. Since a large portion of the railroad from Canada to Mexico runs through a number of these states, the President warned that if they made any move to secede, the military would step in.

"I guess Melora is right, there is no place else to go," Ash said.

"There is always someplace to go. There are a lot of mountains out there and millions of acres of land where no one lives."

"But you've seen the predators. How could we move an entire community? How could we protect them from the predators and feed them in a land even harsher than it is here?"

"I'm not saying it would be possible to move Beartooth. Most of the original settlers came here for a safe and simple life. The basic infrastructure was already here, and the climate allowed year-round food production and ample wild game to harvest. We've worked to improve the community and solve problems, but if the rest of Bennett's militia comes, I don't know if they have the heart to fight or the skills to start over," Caleb replied.

"What are you saying?"

"That if you and Sara are at risk, we'll leave. Together, you and I could rebuild. Maybe a small group would want to join us, but I won't stay and fight a battle we can't win and risk losing everyone I love."

Ash was floored. She didn't know what to say. The thought of abandoning Beartooth was almost too painful to consider. She loved these people. She had known them all of her life, but if she had to choose between staying or fleeing to protect Sara and their unborn child, she would leave. She would never let Bennett or his men lay a hand on her children.

Caleb took her hands, eased her out of her chair, and pulled her into his arms. "It may never come to that. I'll do whatever I can to ensure it doesn't, but you and Sara are my life. I'll do whatever it takes to protect you, even if that means leaving."

Ash held on to him for several minutes before looking up. She felt the strength in his embrace and saw the determination in his eyes.

"I'll follow you anywhere," she whispered.

His lips descended on hers. He pulled her close and deepened the kiss, and soon all her fears melted away.

FIFTY-FIVE

AFTER DROPPING Sara off at the farm, Ash and Caleb swung by Ryan and Miranda's cabin. Miranda answered the door in her nightshirt.

"Are you feeling, okay?" Ash asked.

"I've been better. Emily doesn't think it's anything to worry about. I just need rest and time to heal," Miranda replied as Ash and Caleb followed her into the cabin.

Ryan walked out of the bedroom. Ash noticed that he had a knife sheath on one side of his belt and a holster for his newly acquired gun threaded through the other side. Caleb was similarly armed, but Caleb had always carried a knife and had possessed the gun since his dad gave it to him before their honeymoon trip into the wild. Weapons were new to Ryan.

He dished up oatmeal and set it in front of Miranda. "Eat up and try to get some rest. You were restless all night long," he said as he placed a kiss on her cheek.

"I will and don't worry. I'm black, blue, and sore, but I'm feeling better this morning."

Ryan gave her another concerned look. "I hate leaving, but we shouldn't be gone long."

"Go," Miranda said as she waved them toward the door.

Ryan didn't say a word on the short walk to the storehouse. He had always been quiet, but he had hardly spoken a full sentence since returning with Miranda. Ash still didn't know everything that happened, but she knew that four men had died. Killing wouldn't be something a resident took lightly. She wondered if Caleb shouldered the entire load or if others shared in his burden.

They entered through the back door and made their way to the milling room. It smelled of grain and always had a fine layer of dust in the air and on every surface, but it had a work area large enough to arrange chairs in a circle for meetings when it was too cold outside and school was in session. They took seats and waited for Dan to speak.

"I'm not really sure where to start. In the past couple of days, I've had nearly every resident approach me with concerns. On the upside, I think I personally told each resident about this afternoon's community meeting. All of the comments pertained to what happened on the day Bennett's men arrived. I promised a briefing this afternoon. Melora, talk to us about the new weapons acquisitions," Dan said.

"Unless anyone has objections, the assault rifles will reside with me, Caleb, Ryan, and Dan. I checked each weapon and verified we have one hundred and ten rounds of ammunition. I think we can spare a few rounds so that Caleb, Ryan, and Dan can have a little practice. The rifles we took off those men are standard military issue, so I'm familiar with them already. As far as the handguns, I've loaned mine to Ryan several times, so I thought it made sense for him to have his own. I'll teach Tyler how to shoot mine. Joy Garland, Sam Ferguson, and Gavin Winters have expressed interest in learning to shoot. Gavin has been going bowhunting, and Joy will be assisting Tyler in maintaining the infrastructure, which often involves venturing away from the community, so Joy, Tyler, and Gavin should also be armed. Not surprising, after what happened to his father-in-law, Sam has volunteered to be armed and trained. We acquired quite a bit of ammo for the handguns, so I'm going to set up a practice session so that we don't just have weapons, we know how to use them."

"Any objections to Melora's distribution and training with the new weapons?"

"Yes, but it's just with Joy's decision to carry a gun, nothing anyone here can do about it," Heath said. "Diane and I aren't thrilled, but she's a very stubborn young woman. We came here to get away from violence, but apparently our reprieve is over."

"Okay, Melora, we'll leave it up to you to organize the gun safety and proficiency training," Dan said.

"I can teach safety, but we can't spare enough ammunition to achieve proficiency. The best we can do is let everyone shoot, so if the need arises, it won't be the first time they pulled a trigger. We'll also work on scenarios for success, like maximum distance for the best chance of hitting your target, adjustments for shooting uphill or downhill, and stuff like that."

"The best you can do has to be enough. Tyler, what do you got?" Dan asked.

"Melora and I will keep flying the drone, we'll monitor the cameras and move them around as needed. The original convenience store had an alarm system on the door. I don't think we need to be able to set it when we leave at night since we never lock the storehouse anyway, but I've re-wired it so an alarm can be activated by pressing a panic button I've installed behind the counter along with another in the kitchen," Tyler added.

"Once Tyler goes live with the alarms, we need to designate a response team and develop protocols. If a situation similar to the last happened again and the alarm was pressed, we don't want everyone running in there blind. They'd probably be cut down by assault rifles," Melora explained.

"Any questions?" Dan paused. "If not, what else do we have?"

"Miranda is still pretty banged up, and she needs time to heal. With Emily wanting to step back from the clinic and Miranda the only other trained nurse, Emily and Miranda want to start training another nurse. Lauren volunteered, and we've already talked it over with Gretchen and Henry," Ryan said as he nodded over at Henry.

"I've been educating her as a biologist, but nursing is needed more in this community than another biologist, besides, her biology background will make her a better medical professional. Gretchen and I are supportive of Lauren's decision and very proud of her."

"Sorry to hear that Miranda has such a long road to recovery. Is there anything else we need to discuss today?" Dan asked.

No one spoke up, so he continued. "Unless I need clarification, I think it might be best if I'm the only speaker tonight. I can't imagine how difficult it was for Miranda, Evelyn, Ryan, Caleb, and Melora to share their stories of what happened, and Maria and her family are grieving. With this in mind, I'll present an overview of events, new and old safety protocols we're implementing or reinstating, and then we'll end the meeting with housekeeping items, specifically, we won't have a fall festival this year. It just doesn't seem appropriate. Instead, next Sunday we'll have a celebration of life for Tony using the preparations normally reserved for the festival."

He adjourned the meeting. Everyone filed out of the room and headed off in different directions. Ash and Caleb parted ways with Ryan and walked toward the farm to retrieve Sara, each deep in their own thoughts.

FIFTY-SIX

LATE THAT AFTERNOON, the residents gathered around the flatbed trailer for the community meeting. Ash and Caleb found the rest of the family and stood next to them. Caleb placed one arm possessively around Ash's waist and held Sara in the other.

Ash felt people watching them. She hoped it was just her imagination, but she wondered if the residents would see Caleb and the others in a different light after what they had to do.

Dan began the meeting with a concise summary of what transpired from the moment the men walked into the storehouse until Caleb, Miranda, Ryan, and Melora returned home. Even though he left out a lot of details concerning the rescue, Ash had no doubt that every adult had to realize that a small group of their own had killed four men.

Gasps and a low rumbling of voices echoed through the crowd gathered around the trailer. Ash knew that Caleb had killed three. She wasn't certain about the fourth but suspected it was Caleb as well.

"What happened is tragic. Now we need to heal as a community and focus on what is truly important, each other. We must help our friends, family, and neighbors, especially the Gallegos family, through our shared grief. And we need to work together to find a way to protect the community better in the future," Dan said.

He then went on to discuss the addition of weapons and ammunition and how it was distributed. He explained the other actions they had come up with, including an alarm on the storehouse, revamping the evacuation plan, increasing surveillance with the drone and trail cameras, and a warning about possible predators in the area.

"I wish there was more we could do. If anyone has any thoughts of ways to increase our security, please come to me or any of the other board members. Just because the ten of us didn't think of something, it doesn't mean someone else won't."

Ash glanced over at Ryan and Miranda. Ryan held Miranda's hand, but both were clearly not focused on anyone. Ryan's jaw was clenched, like it had been ever since they returned, and it was difficult to read Miranda's expression through all the bruising and swelling on her face.

"Maria, with help from her children and their spouses, will take over operation of the storehouse," Dan explained.

As the sun sunk closer to the mountaintops, the temperatures continued to drop. Ash glanced around and saw people with their arms around themselves and each other, trying to keep warm. Dan must have noticed it too.

"It's cooling off quickly, so let's wrap this up. We will not be holding a fall festival this year, but we will have a celebration. Sunday at noon, we'll break out the sausages and sauerkraut for a celebration of Tony's life. If anyone has anything to contribute, that would be nice."

No one spoke up, and everyone quickly headed for their cabins.

"I need to go help round up the llamas and get them inside the shed for the night. Can you make sure Miranda gets home?" Ryan asked Caleb.

"I don't need help, but if it makes you feel better, Caleb and Ash can walk me home," Miranda replied.

Ryan squeezed her hand, kissed her cheek, and then walked away.

"Can we take Sara home with us for a bit? I finished a new pair of pants, and I want to make sure they fit," Olivia asked.

Owen picked up Sara, and Caleb's parents headed back to the Solomon farm. When Ash, Caleb, and Miranda reached her cabin, she asked them to come in.

"I'm sure you've noticed that Ryan isn't himself ever since we got back," Miranda said as Ash and Caleb followed her inside and took off their coats.

"He's even quieter than usual, but he's probably still digesting what happened," Ash replied.

"He barely touched me before, but now he's sleeping on the couch. I'm not sure what to do. Yes, my body hurts, but it hurts more for him to pull further away than he was before."

"Do you want me to leave? I don't want you bursting my illusion that no man has ever touched my baby sister," Caleb said.

"No, I've already discussed that situation in detail with Ash and Evelyn." Miranda smiled at her brother when he winced.

"Great," Caleb replied with a roll of his eyes.

"Do you think he thinks I'm lying about those men not

getting a chance to rape me? That creepy Cord guy touched me everywhere he could reach while on horseback, but we only got to the camp thirty minutes before you all showed up. By the time they tended to the horses, gathered firewood, built a fire, ate dinner, got drunk, sent Roy up the hill, cut me down from the tree, and got serious about violating me, you and Ryan burst on the scene."

"I'm sure he believes you," Caleb replied.

"Maybe the fact that those men had their hands all over me repulses him."

"I'm sure that's not the case," Ash said.

"I'm with Ash. When Tyler tried to force himself on Ash, all I wanted to do was comfort her and kill him. I would have never turned my back on her no matter how much he touched her."

"That brings me to my last theory, that Ryan is having a really difficult time accepting something that happened," Miranda said as she reached over, took Caleb's hand, and looked him in the eye.

"Who slit Cord's throat?"

Ash was curious too but hadn't wanted to ask. She knew Caleb was having some difficulty accepting what he'd done, even though there had been no other option, and Caleb was a lot more mature than Ryan.

"He didn't tell you?" Caleb asked.

"No, you idiot, that's why I'm asking you."

"I don't feel it's my place," Caleb replied.

Miranda yanked her hand away and stood up, tears streaming down her cheeks. "If Ryan did and he's having a difficult time dealing with it, I want to be there for him. If he's pulled away from me because he finds me repulsive now that other men have touched me, I'll punch him so hard in the face it will send him into next week," Miranda fumed.

Caleb got up and turned to face his sister. "Try supporting him first, before resorting to violence. He loves you. He didn't give me the opportunity to finish the job. I think he felt he needed to do it for you," Caleb said as he pulled Miranda into a gentle hug.

She cried for several minutes before she stepped back and wiped her eyes. "Thank you. I needed to know. I hate that he's suffering, but I'm glad it was him. I knew my brother would kill for me, but now I know my husband would too."

Ash's heart went out to Ryan, but she was kind of relieved that Caleb wasn't the only one in Beartooth with blood on his hands.

FIFTY-SEVEN

IN THE DAYS leading up to the celebration of life for Tony, Olivia baked, Ash fussed over her sauerkraut, and Archie and Dennis smoked the sausages they made out of venison and pork.

Shortly before noon on the day of the event, Dillon came over to help Caleb carry the crock of sauerkraut to the community center. Evelyn stayed behind to visit with Ash.

"How's Miranda doing. I haven't seen her in a couple of days," Evelyn asked.

"She's healing physically, but of course, the trauma will take time to get over," Ash said as Caleb and Dillon returned.

Ash gathered up their plates and utensils. Caleb scooped up Sara and led the group out the door. When they reached the community center, it looked like nearly everyone had already arrived. They spotted most of the Fergusons and Adlers and all of the Solomons together and made their way over.

Ash saw Miranda and Ryan standing together. He held her hand, but his face was solemn, and Miranda was on the verge of tears. When Archie announced that the sausages were done, Ryan took two plates and walked away.

"Are things any better?" Ash asked.

"I tried to talk to him about what he's going through. He said he's fine. He made me breakfast like he has every morning since we got back, and then he proceeded to do the dishes, dust and sweep the cabin, and left to go help his folks. He returned home in time to carry our plates and forks, and escort me here," Miranda explained.

"And that's a problem how?" Evelyn asked as she gathered close.

"Because I need him to be a husband, not a caregiver. Physically, I'm still black and blue, but I'm healing. I don't need him to fix me a plate like he's doing now. I need him to hold me and love me and show me everything is going to be alright. I absolutely don't want him sleeping on the couch because he's afraid he might roll over and hurt me. I'm not that fragile. I'm not going to break."

"People have treated me like that my whole life. I've noticed a shift in attitude after what happened. I'm not sure how I feel about it. I'd like people to see me as capable, but not because I shot a man with my bow, but because I'm strong," Evelyn replied.

"Everyone used to think I was strong, but now they're treating me like a helpless victim. I'm not sure everyone, including Ryan, believes that I wasn't raped. I'm tired of pity, and I'm tired of Ryan's distance."

Ash and Caleb listened but said nothing. Ash couldn't relate to what Miranda and Evelyn were going through but was glad they had each other.

"Do you want me to make us each a plate? I'm a little confused if I should or shouldn't at the moment," Caleb whispered to Ash.

"If you don't mind, I'd appreciate it. If we both leave, Sara might throw a fit, and it's hard to go through the food line carrying a toddler and a plate," Ash responded.

Caleb nodded and went to join the line. Sara watched him closely, but when Ash took her from Owen, she was happy.

The afternoon went much like it did when Neal was laid to rest. Dan, Maria, and many others told touching stories about Tony. A lot of tears were shed but it felt healing, not sad.

Everyone enjoyed the food, and Tara contributed the last of her wine for a moving toast to Tony. After the toast, the residents slowly made their way home.

"Ryan, grab the other side of the crock. It's not real heavy, just awkward to carry," Caleb said.

"I should walk Miranda home."

"I'll walk with her. I have to swing by the farm for a bit anyway because Olivia asked me to stop by and pick up something else that she's made for Sara," Ash said.

Ryan looked over at Miranda, doubt in his eyes. "Don't do anything strenuous. I shouldn't be long," he said as he grabbed a handle and walked with Caleb.

They carried the crock and set it on the kitchen table.

"Is everything okay with you and Miranda?" Caleb asked as he walked Ryan out the door.

"I don't know what to do. I've done everything I can think of to make her comfortable and take care of her. I'm terrified I'll accidentally hurt her, so I'm giving her lots of space. I know she's been through a horrible ordeal. I don't know what else I can do for her. Maybe she blames me for not getting there sooner. They almost choked her to death before we got there."

"She doesn't blame you for anything, and she's just as confused as you are on how to move forward. She's worried about you just as much as you're worried about her, so don't shut her out. She doesn't need a cook or a housekeeper, she needs a husband. She needs to feel secure, loved, and beautiful, which I imagine is a little difficult for her with all the cuts and bruises on her face."

"I keep telling her she's still beautiful to me, and the bruises will fade. What do I do? I just want to see her smile again," Ryan asked, frustration lacing his voice.

Caleb paused for a moment and took a deep breath. "I can't believe I'm saying this, but go home, pull Miranda into your arms, kiss her like you never have before, and then take her to bed and make love to her all night long. Don't just tell her she's beautiful and that you love her, show her."

When Ash walked up, the look on Ryan's face was pure shock. He turned beet-red and averted his eyes to avoid looking at her or Caleb.

"Uh, th, th, thanks for the advice," he stuttered as he turned and darted off the porch.

Caleb pulled Ash into a passionate embrace and kissed her until she was breathless. "Where's Sara?"

"With your mom. What did you say to him that had him so flustered?" Ash asked as she tilted her head back and looked up into his handsome face.

"He wanted to know what to do to fix things with Miranda. Against all my brotherly instincts, I told him."

"What did you tell him?"

"When do we need to go get Sara?"

"I told your mom we'd come get her before dinner," Ash replied.

"In that case, let me demonstrate," he said as he scooped her up and kicked the door that stood slightly ajar, open.

Ash threw her head back and laughed. "You are officially the best brother ever."

FIFTY-EIGHT

A WEEK HAD PASSED since Tony's death. A pall of sadness hung over the residents of Beartooth. It served as a constant reminder that they needed to increase security. Fearing the possibility of more of Bennett's men coming to Beartooth, Melora called a meeting for everyone who possessed a weapon or who would be loaned one in an emergency.

Owen walked with Ash and Caleb from the farm to Melora and Tyler's cabin. When they arrived, the group assembled totaled nineteen individuals. Melora stood on the porch facing them.

"The plan today is to update our evacuation plan. If we ever detect trouble, we'll evacuate all residents to our predetermined safe zones as before. With our recent weapons acquisition, we've shuffled a few people around to make the most of our small arsenal. We now have four assault rifles. One will be assigned to each group. That person will be their group's leader. The only change in group leaders is that Ryan will replace Fiona," Melora began.

Ash and Caleb didn't like this change. It would mean that Miranda and Ryan were no longer with the rest of the Solomon family.

"Any person who has more than one weapon will loan the extra weapon to a pre-designated individual. Since I have an assault rifle, Tyler will take my 9mm, and I'll loan my shotgun to Mark. Everyone else with multiple weapons has made their own arrangements. Many of you have never shot a gun before. So, once we go over the basics, we'll practice with as much ammo as we can spare, which isn't as much as I'd like. Any questions?"

No one asked a question, so they began the half-mile trek to the drainage where their safe zones were located.

"The basic premise remains unchanged. If we hear a helicopter, aircraft, gunfire, or the storehouse alarm, or if a wildfire is bearing down on the community, we make our way as quickly as possible to our assigned zone. The group leader will make sure everyone is accounted for. The main thing we're doing today is figuring out where those with weapons will now be staged to ensure we don't shoot each other, and we have the greatest chance of protecting our community," Melora explained.

For the next hour, they hammered out where shooters would be located. Actual weapons training lasted a couple more hours. The first part covered gun safety and a basic orientation to the various weapons the community now possessed. The rest of the time focused on instruction and target practice.

The last item on the agenda was to develop a response plan if the storehouse alarm went off. They didn't want everyone charging into an ambush.

"I wish we could spare the ammo for much more train-ing, but it won't do any good for us to keep practicing and then have nothing to use if we ever have to defend ourselves," Melora said.

"If the number of remaining FAMA militia is accurate, we're still severely outgunned. And, what about predators?" Mark asked.

"Correct me, Dan, if I'm wrong, but the goal is to protect the residents of Beartooth. Whether it's human or animal, if we need to take a shot to save a life or protect a critical food source, we do it," Melora replied.

"That's my feeling on the subject. If anyone else has a different opinion, speak up."

"I'm in agreement, but I'm just sick it's come to this. We settled Beartooth with the goal of building a safe and sustainable community to raise our families and live our lives without all the hate and violence threatening to destroy the country. Now, look at us," Mark said.

Dan slapped Mark on the back. "We gave it a good run as long as we could, but we don't have any other choice but to adapt to our new reality. We owe the next generation that much."

Mark nodded his head and followed the rest of the group back to Beartooth.

After lunch, Ash put Sara down for a nap. When she returned to the kitchen, she found Caleb sitting at the kitchen table, tuning the radio. Soon, scratchy voices came over the airwaves reporting on the President's recent State of the Union address.

"In summary, some progress has been made in reopening food distribution routes. Oil extraction remains at a standstill due to the unavailability of parts to repair infrastructure damaged during the bombing. Climate scientists report that the release of greenhouse gases worldwide has slowed due to the lack of manufacturing and transportation caused by fuel shortages and widespread fighting around the world. And anyone who has stepped outside knows that unity and security are worse than ever. As far as the President's FOCUS initiative, it looks like she hasn't made it past 'F,' which is the grade we'll give her job performance," the newsreader said with a chuckle.

Ash got up, poured a glass of water for them, and sat back down at the table across from Caleb as the newsreader continued.

"When pressed, President Steele admitted that she would not convene a new legislative session after the first of the year as promised due to increased pressure from the multinational forces amassed south of our border. She claimed the military would be unable to provide security for the representatives while needed at the border. Protests immediately erupted around the country."

"I can't imagine anyone really believed she would actually allow the senators and congressional representatives to have any input in the government or hold a presidential election. Many in positions of power don't want to give it up," Caleb said.

"I've become skeptical of any political promise, so I'm not surprised," Ash added.

The newsreader continued with reports on areas where fighting among citizens and clashes with the military were the worst. Eventually, the report landed on the hunt for Jonah Bennett and his Freedom and Morality Alliance followers.

"The Wyoming National Guard recently apprehended two FAMA militia near the former town of Granite Peak, which was destroyed when a landslide-created dam upstream failed, inundating the town. The men claimed Bennett sent them to scout the area to see if there were any structures left standing that could provide their group with shelter. According to the men, they rode with three others who were attacked and killed the night before by what they described as giant greyish-black jaguar-type predators. The Guard doubts their story of enormous, man-eating cats, but stated the men were clearly shaken by something. The men claimed that Jonah Bennett and his militia were holed up at the Littlerock Ranch. When the Guard arrived at the ranch, there was no sign of Bennett's group. Eyewitnesses reported that around thirty-five men vacated the ranch, about half on horseback, heading west. The Guard said they will leave enough troops in Pryor to maintain order and ensure Bennett does not return, but they can't spare the resources to track the group into the mountains and will return to the state capital."

"The Guard may doubt their story about the cats, but I don't. I'm not thrilled to learn that more of those massive predators are hunting not far from here, but what really scares me is not knowing where Bennett and his delusional followers are headed," Caleb said.

Ash didn't know how this would impact the community, but she feared the coming days.

FIFTY-NINE

CALEB LEFT the cabin in a rush to find out if Melora or anyone else had heard the news that Bennett and his goons were heading west from the Littlerock Ranch. He'd only been gone fifteen minutes when Ash heard a knock on the door.

"I came to watch Sara so you can join Caleb and the others at the school," Olivia said as she walked in the door.

Ash hugged her and thanked her, then took off at a run. She wasn't sure what Caleb and the others would do, but she doubted it would be nothing. As she walked into the school, the room was packed. She walked up near the front and stood by Caleb.

"Word travels fast around here," Dan said. "Many of us heard a terrifying report on the radio. A couple of Bennett's men who were apprehended by the Guard claimed they were attacked by giant black cats and three of their comrades were killed. Unfortunately, that wasn't the scary part. They told the Guard where Bennett and his followers were staying. When the Guard got there, they were gone, but eyewitnesses claimed around thirty-five men, half on horses and half on foot, left the area the day before, heading west into the mountains."

There was a lot of mumbling in the crowded room.

"How long do we have before they get here, and what do we do about it? We're a little better armed, but Bennett's followers are ruthless militia, we are peace-loving people who have very little experience with such evil," Henry asked.

Melora stepped up next to Dan. "Since half of the men are reportedly on foot, if they stick together, it should take them a day and a half to reach us, two tops."

"That's not much time. Are we sure they are heading this way?" Heath asked.

"No, but if I was a betting man, I'd gamble everything I had on it," Dan replied.

"We can't just sit here and wait for them. So far, when they show up on our doorstep, it turns out very badly for us. We go on the offensive," Melora said.

"I'm too old to fight, even if I knew how," Henry said.

Several others chimed in with Henry.

"I'm not saying we all go. I suggest a small group. No matter where we meet them, we can't fight them on their terms. We need strategy, surprise, and a heck of a lot of luck," Melora said.

Ash felt sick. She had no doubt who would be included in that small group. Caleb stared straight ahead with his jaw clenched. He didn't look at her, which confirmed her suspicion.

"Volunteers only. I'm going. Caleb, Ryan, and Tyler have volunteered," Melora explained.

"Tyler can't go. What if something happens to him? Who will keep the utilities running?" Heath asked.

"I'm not staying behind while Melora faces down a

dangerous enemy to try and save this community. If she doesn't make it back, I don't want to be here. If none of us survive, electricity and water will be the least of your problems," Tyler replied.

"I'm going too, this time. There is no point in leaving me here with an assault rifle. If Bennett and his FAMA fanatics make it here, one rifle won't be able to defend this place or change the outcome. I'll be more use on the offensive," Dan added.

Ash looked around. Miranda stood next to Ryan, silent. Libby also showed no emotion concerning Dan's declaration. She was glad Olivia was home with Sara but was a little surprised that Owen and Dillon said nothing.

"Where will my rifle be the most effective?" Archie asked.

"Here in Beartooth. We can't forget about the big cats. We're riding out at first light. We've got a lot of prepping and planning to do. I would suggest the rest of you get together, decide if you want to fight or retreat to the safe zones," Melora said.

"If you four have the assault rifles and aren't here, what hope would there be against thirty-five killers?" Heath asked.

"There is always hope. We may not stop them, but I have no doubt we will do serious damage. If they make it here, it won't be all of them," Melora promised.

As typical in Beartooth, everyone accepted the situation with stoic determination. Ash and Miranda walked with Caleb, Ryan, and Dan to Melora and Tyler's cabin. Everyone else stayed behind to talk strategy.

Ash and Miranda stood off to the side and listened as the rest of the group discussed what they would take, when they would leave, which direction they would ride in hopes of intercepting Bennett's group, and strategies to help even the very lopsided odds.

Melora pulled out a map. She showed the group where the ranch was located where Bennett and his men were last seen and the most likely route the group would take if they were heading toward Beartooth.

"With thirty-five men and seventeen or eighteen horses, it should be easy to spot them without getting close. They will be overconfident with their superior numbers and weapons. They will not be expecting anyone to be looking for them. Surprise is a huge equalizer and our best weapon," Melora said.

The more Ash listened, the more she believed that this small group might succeed in stopping Bennett from reaching Beartooth. They were focused, determined, strong, and fighting for so much more than any of Bennett's men. They were fighting for family and survival.

SIXTY

IT WAS STILL DARK out when Ash woke. She felt sick and didn't want to get out of bed. She wasn't sure which of a number of culprits made her feel so nauseous, but she wouldn't burden Caleb with any of them.

He was already up and showered, and she could hear him in the kitchen. She dressed and left the bedroom. He looked up, and she walked into his arms. After several moments, she stepped out of his embrace.

"Do you have time for breakfast?"

"Only if it's something quick. We're riding at sunrise," he replied as he went back to checking his gear.

Ash quickly made scrambled eggs and toast. While he ate, she assembled some food for him to take with him. It wasn't much, but they would be riding light.

She hated to wake Sara, but she had no intention of not seeing him off, so she woke the toddler and dressed her in her warmest clothes. When she came out of Sara's room, Caleb was waiting for them with his arms loaded.

Sara was groggy, so she nuzzled against Ash's chest as they walked out the door and made their way to Bob and

Maggie's ranch. She was surprised to see nearly the entire community there to see them off. Ash found the rest of the Solomon family and stood silently with them.

Fifteen minutes later, Caleb led one of the horses confiscated from the men he killed out of the barn. He walked over to Ash and handed Dillon the reins. He hugged his dad, mom, Miranda, Evelyn, and Dillon. He took Sara from Ash's arms and held her tight. He placed a kiss on the toddler's cheeks and handed her to his mom.

Caleb pulled Ash into his arms and held her tight. "I love you so much," he whispered in her ear.

"I love you more than anything in the world. Please come home," Ash said as tears streamed down her cheeks.

"That's the plan. I have so much to come home to," he replied as he mounted the horse and led the other four riders away from Beartooth.

Ash looked around and saw so many tears from nearly everyone in the community. She hated seeing the sorrow. It made it feel as if everyone had given up on them already. It was an impossible task, but she had to have hope.

"Come, I'll make everyone breakfast. I need my family around me now," Olivia said as she walked away, still holding Sara.

Owen, Dillon, Evelyn, Ash, and Miranda followed Olivia to the Solomon cabin. Once inside, Evelyn entertained Sara until she fell asleep, still groggy from rising so early. Ash and Miranda helped Olivia with breakfast while Owen and Dillon went outside.

By the time breakfast was ready, the men returned. The mood at the table was somber, but not hopeless.

"We ran into Archie and Dennis. They're gathering up everyone without small children. We're going to meet at the school in an hour and talk about what to do if any of those FAMA fanatics slip through," Owen said.

"I think Dillon, Evelyn, Miranda, Ash, and Sara should move in here until we find out if we'll have unwanted visitors," Olivia stated.

"Dad and I talked to a lot of people this morning. The meeting is to discuss what we should do if Bennett's group shows up. There is no guarantee they will. We're not going to roll over, so we will prepare the best we can, but we're going to keep living. Evelyn is planning on class Monday morning. She needs to be in her own home where she's comfortable and can find everything she needs," Dillon replied.

Olivia looked over at Miranda.

Miranda shook her head apologetically. "I'm a nurse. I may be needed before this is over. I can't hide at my parents' cabin. People will expect me to be in the clinic or in my cabin next door."

"But you haven't fully recovered from your ordeal. I should take care of you," Olivia said.

"I'm healed enough to care for others. Ryan rode off on perhaps a suicide mission to protect his family and his community. I'm going to do everything I can as well."

Ash hated seeing the fear in Olivia's eyes, but she had to respect Miranda and Dillon's decision not to cower.

"Ash, will you and Sara stay?"

"I'm sorry. I love you all so much and I appreciate the offer, but I need to carry on as if nothing is wrong for Sara. If Caleb doesn't return, I will have to find the strength to carry on for her, just like my mom did for me. For now, I have to believe they will be successful, and he is coming home. If I don't carry that belief, and I stay here, Sara will know something is wrong and be frightened."

"But Caleb would want you here, especially now," Olivia pleaded.

"Yes, he would. I was only alone one night between when Mom moved out and Caleb moved in. It's time I stand on my own and do what needs to be done. I have responsibilities now."

Ash suddenly felt like her breakfast might come up. She didn't know if it was the tension and emotions running high around the table or if it was morning sickness. She excused herself and ran for the bathroom.

When she returned, all eyes were on her.

"What did mom mean by, *especially now*?" Miranda asked.

Ash hesitated but saw no reason to hide it any longer. "I'm pregnant. Caleb doesn't know. After what happened with the FAMA thugs who showed up and now this, I didn't want to add any more pressure than he's already under. I wanted his head as clear as possible. I know he'll worry about me and Sara, but if he knew we were expecting another baby, it would only add to his burden."

There were no rounds of joyous congratulations like there was when they announced she was pregnant with Sara. The future of Beartooth was far from certain, and the likelihood that Caleb would never come home hung in the air.

After several moments of uncomfortable silence, Owen spoke up. "Well, isn't that a bright spot in all of this gloom and doom."

Ash smiled. "I think so. I know the timing sucks, but this wasn't exactly planned. I'm scared but thrilled. Caleb will be happy, too, when he gets home."

"I'm sure he will, dear," Olivia said as she patted Ash's hand. "I'm sorry, I didn't mean to tell your secret, but I'm glad it's in the open. I'll respect your need to stand on your own but always remember that you've got back-up just a few cabins away."

"Thank you, I will," Ash said as she fought to keep the tears at bay.

"See, this is exactly what I was just talking about. As soon as we clear the dishes, we're heading over to the clinic for an exam. I've got a patient to see," Miranda stated.

"Yes, you do. I couldn't be prouder of all of you than I am right now," Olivia replied with a weak smile.

SIXTY-ONE

CALEB and the others had been riding for nearly five hours with no sign of Bennett and his followers. They stopped for a quick lunch break and to rest the horses.

"I sure hope we're heading in the right direction," Dan stated.

"This route is just my best guess. The radio reporter claimed Bennett was headed west from the ranch. If he thinks Beartooth would be a good place to commandeer and hide out from the Guard, it makes the most sense for his large party to follow these roads and trails," Melora replied.

"I agree. Let's keep moving," Caleb said as he mounted up and waited for the others to follow.

Aside from a few quick breaks to rest the horses, they pushed on. As they rode, Caleb started having doubts. If they couldn't intercept Bennett and his men, they will have left the community unprotected for nothing. But the idea of waiting for them to show up was no better. If thirty-five, well-armed, ruthless fanatics arrived in Beartooth, there would be little chance of a good outcome.

The residents of Beartooth would suffer greatly or could even be completely wiped out.

"It's getting too dark to track anything or keep on this faint trail. Maybe we should find a place to camp for the night," Dan said.

As much as Caleb hated to stop until they found Bennett, he knew Dan was right. The trail was hazardous at night and hard to follow, and they were all exhausted. If they had any hope for success, they needed to be alert, not dead on their feet.

They brought only bedrolls. They didn't want to start a fire in case the militia was in the area since it might alert them to their location. It would be a cold night.

"Let's spread out a little in case someone wanders into camp," Melora suggested.

They each found a flat place to throw their bedroll down where they could still see each other, but not all together in a neat little group for someone to round up.

Caleb jumped when he heard Ryan roll off a string of profanity that he'd never heard before from his brother-in-law.

"What is it?" Caleb asked as he rushed over to where Ryan was standing staring at the ground with his headlamp pointed down.

Melora, Tyler, and Dan quickly joined them and stared at the spot on the ground illuminated by Ryan's light.

"We just can't catch a break," Melora hissed through clenched teeth.

"By the size of those tracks and everyone's reaction, I'm assuming these prints were made by the massive melanistic jaguar-hybrids you found on the big hunt?" Dan asked.

"Yep," Ryan replied, shaking his head.

"What do we do?" Tyler asked.

They all stood there for a moment, staring at the tracks immortalized in dried mud.

"We need to be fresh in the morning. I think we try to sleep and hope for the best. We don't have the numbers to sleep in shifts. The tracks don't look fresh. We've heard and seen no other sign, so maybe they've moved on," Caleb said.

"Easier said than done," Ryan grumbled as he grabbed his bedroll and tossed it down next to Caleb's. "Singles are too easy for a big cat to pick off, so I'm sleeping by you."

"Us too," Melora said as she, Tyler, and Dan approached. "I'd rather take my chances with the militia than one of those damned cats."

SIXTY-TWO

ASH HAD A ROUGH NIGHT. She was scared and wished she had taken Olivia up on her offer to stay with them. But she needed to prove that she could take care of herself and her children even if Caleb didn't come home.

At the informal community meeting the day before, they decided Fiona would fly the drone as far from the community as it would reach each morning, midday, and before dusk. They also developed a patrol schedule. Nearly everyone left in Beartooth who owned a gun would take a shift watching several access points to the community.

Even though she had a sidearm, Ash didn't sign up for a shift since she had no intention of leaving Sara unprotected. She planned to stay close to the cabin and even closer to her daughter.

Other than posting scouts and flying the drone to hopefully provide early warning so they could evacuate, they could think of few other ways to protect themselves. Ash was encouraged though, that everyone seemed willing to shoot if threatened, something she knew few would have been willing to do several months ago. After what happened to Neal, Tony, and Miranda, everyone's resolve had hardened.

Ash was thrilled when Evelyn, Lauren, and Miranda showed up at her door. After her talk of independence the day before, she was a little embarrassed to run over to the Solomon cabin first thing in the morning, but she was anxious and knew being around people would help.

"Where's Sara?" Evelyn asked.

"Still sleeping. I tried to keep things normal and positive yesterday, but I'm sure she sensed my fear when Caleb left."

They sat down around the kitchen table and Ash poured them all a cup of hot tea.

"How's nurse training going?" Ash asked Lauren.

"It's interesting and some of the biology Dad insisted I learn is actually helpful, but don't tell him that," Lauren replied.

"The three of us make a good team. I'm not going to be nearly as nervous when Emily completely steps away, now that Lauren is on board," Miranda added.

"I'm a little surprised that Dad accepted Lauren's decision to move toward medicine as well as he did," Evelyn said.

"Things have changed around here, and we need to change too if we're going to survive. Maybe Dad is finally realizing that," Lauren replied.

Ash took a sip of tea, contemplating what Lauren said. The residents did need to evolve with the changes occurring all around them, especially their generation, if they hoped to hold on to what their parents built.

"We've had some challenges over the past few years, but I think what happened with the FAMA guys has really changed me and Ryan. We can't be naïve about what's happening around us any longer. This may have once been a refuge from the world, but the world has gotten smaller and more dangerous," Miranda said.

"I agree. Everyone keeps acting like I should be traumatized by what I did, but I don't feel bad about it. I'm proud of myself, and I feel empowered. I may be severely sight-challenged, but I'm not helpless. I refuse to be a victim. Caleb said my shot would have eventually killed that man, and I'm okay with it. I hope that doesn't make me a horrible person."

"Not at all. If you hadn't defended yourself, things could have turned out much worse for you, and for those who went after Miranda. The intruders would have had one more man and one more assault rifle for Caleb, Ryan, and Melora to deal with," Ash replied.

"Those men were planning on torturing me until they killed me and taking Evelyn back as a prize for their demented leader. If they make it here, they won't take me so easily again," Miranda said.

"We are better prepared, and I know at least some of us will stand up to any intruder. This is where I want to raise my family, and I'll be damned if I'll let anyone take that away from me without a fight," Ash said.

"Here, here." Evelyn raised her teacup to toast Ash, Miranda, and her sister. "I'm sad that the incident changed us, making us harder and jaded, but it also made us stronger."

"Has Caleb talked about killing all those men?" Lauren asked.

Ash looked at Miranda before answering, not sure if she should divulge that Ryan had killed a man as well. Ash was proud that Caleb had the strength to do what needed done but it made her a little sad that the entire community just assumed Caleb had killed every FAMA militia member involved.

"He's not happy about it. It's never easy to take a life, but when his family and community are threatened, he'll do what's necessary to protect them. I think he can live with it."

"I hope I will be capable of fighting, and others will step up if Jonah Bennett and the rest of his militia make it here," Lauren said.

Ash knew she would be capable of killing if it meant protecting Sara or anyone else in her family or community but said nothing. Clearly, Evelyn was willing, and she suspected Miranda would be now, too. Ash hated that someone as young as Lauren would even have to consider the possibility. She was only five years older than Lauren, but it felt like many more.

"I will do what's necessary, as Ryan did," Miranda spoke quietly as she lifted her cup to her lips.

Evelyn and Lauren looked up, startled.

"It's not common knowledge, but Caleb, Melora, and Ash know the truth."

Ash smiled at Miranda and squeezed her hand, giving her unspoken support.

"Is he okay with it?" Evelyn asked.

Miranda paused. "I believe he's made his peace. He didn't have to do it. He could have left it to Caleb, but he needed to finish it. Things were a little rough when we got back, but I think he was more concerned about me than feeling any remorse. And then all of a sudden, he changed. I don't know why, but things are better between us than ever before. But he had to leave, and I'm terrified he won't come back."

"He will come home, they all will, and I stand by my theory of you two needing a dramatic event or adventure.

I imagine he was so scared of losing you that it lit a fire in him. The incident forced him to mature in a different way in a very short period of time," Evelyn said.

Ash kept quiet. If Miranda didn't know that Caleb urged Ryan into action, it was probably for the best.

"Whatever the reason for his um, recent increased interest and passion, I'm not complaining," Miranda replied with a slight blush.

"At least something positive came out of the ordeal," Evelyn said.

Ash was happy that things were better between Miranda and Ryan, but she was having a hard time following the conversation with her thoughts focused on Caleb, Sara, and their unborn child.

SIXTY-THREE

CALEB WOKE from a fitful sleep to what sounded like distant gunfire. It was still dark out, but he roused the rest of the group.

"What was that?" Ryan asked, rubbing the sleep out of his eyes as the sounds faded.

"Unless I was having a nightmare, I heard a lot of gunfire quite a way from here. It sounded like it was coming from the opposite direction from us as Beartooth, but it's hard to be sure," Caleb stated as he quickly rolled up his bedroll.

"I didn't hear much, but it was real, not a dream. I hope they had a mutiny and decimated their ranks, otherwise, I don't know what to make of it," Melora added.

Within thirty minutes, they were saddled up and back on the trail. It was pitch-black out, so they illuminated their way with their headlamps, making the going slow.

After four hours of slow riding in the dark, they took a break on a high point overlooking a drainage. The sun was just starting to rise over the mountains. The trees were thick, so they were unable to see much below them.

"We got to be getting close to where the shots came from," Melora offered.

"I agree, and I'm wondering what those Turkey Vultures circling down there are so interested in?" Caleb replied.

"Hopefully the remains of Bennett's group, but there's only one way to find out," Dan said as they started down the slope.

When they got closer to where the scavengers gathered, they dismounted, secured their horses, and took out on foot.

"Stay alert. We don't want to walk into an ambush," Melora whispered.

They fanned out and cautiously approached a smoldering fire in a small clearing with guns at the ready. When Caleb caught his first sight of the carnage, he stopped short. Within minutes, the rest of the group converged on him. They stood, frozen, staring at the massacre in front of them.

There was so much blood that the soil was stained dark. Caleb took in the scene, and he cringed. Horses, massive cats, and men littered the ground. What happened here must have been horrific. Visions of what unfolded here brought back memories of their big hunt, but this was far worse.

Melora was the first to break the silence. "Ryan, check the three horses at the edge of the camp. I'll verify the five cats are dead. The rest of you go see if any of the men are still alive. Be careful."

It took Melora only a few minutes to verify the giant beasts were dead. "Cats are dead. There are so many holes in them that it must have been quite the firefight."

"The horses have been eviscerated," Ryan reported.

"Found one man still breathing over here," Caleb shouted.

Melora rushed over to him, and Dan, Ryan, and Tyler joined them after confirming the other eight men were dead.

Blood oozed out of so many wounds that Caleb couldn't tell how many injuries the man had, but he was sure he wouldn't live much longer. The man was barely breathing, but Caleb hoped he had enough strength to speak. "What happened here?" he asked as Melora lifted the man's head, propped it up in her lap, and gave him a sip of water.

"All hell broke loose. God has punished us for our sins," the man gasped barely above a whisper.

"Were you riding with Bennett?" Dan asked.

The man gave a barely perceptible nod.

"Where are they headed?" Caleb demanded.

"Beartooth," the man whispered before he gasped and took his last breath.

SIXTY-FOUR

EVEN THOUGH THE dead men were part of Jonah Bennett's brutal FAMA militia, Caleb hated to leave them on the ground where they died, but time was not on their side. He feared they were now chasing Bennett's group toward Beartooth rather than in a position to intercept them.

They quickly checked the men for weapons and ammunition, but apparently their comrades had stripped them of everything before leaving. One man was left to die alone, and the rest were left on the ground to have their bones picked clean by scavengers. If their leader could spare no time to bury his own men, they couldn't either.

Caleb and the rest of the group left the disturbing scene and returned to their horses.

"I can't imagine there are many more of those beasts out there. Those were all females. Surely if there was even one male in a hundred miles, he would have found this group," Caleb pondered aloud as he checked his horse's cinch.

"If reports of thirty-five in Bennett's party are correct, we're down to twenty-six and three less horses. The odds are getting better all the time," Melora added.

"I wish that made me feel better, but it doesn't," Ryan said.

It took little time to find where the large group of men and horses left the area. As Caleb feared, they hadn't turned back, they were heading in a direction that would lead to Beartooth.

"Wonder how big of a head start they have on us?" Tyler asked.

"From the time we heard the gunshots until we found the scene, and we've been here about thirty minutes already, I'd say we're nearly five hours behind them. They'll be moving slower, but the terrain is rough here, so we won't be going as fast as we'd like," Melora replied.

"They've left a trail nearly anyone could follow, so let's go," Caleb said as he departed the area at a trot, weaving in and out of trees.

They kept up a strong pace, trotting or loping where the terrain allowed, but by early afternoon, they still had seen no sign of Bennett and his men. Caleb knew they were on the right track because their trail was easy to follow, but he had no idea how much ground they had gained on the group.

"Let's take a quick break. The horses could use it and so could I," Dan said.

Caleb reluctantly pulled up and got off. "Ten minutes, no more."

They watered the horses, checked their gear, and were back on the trial in less than Caleb's imposed ten-minute limit. No one spoke as they rode at a fast pace, listening for any indication that they had caught up to Bennett's group.

All Caleb could think about was Ash and Sara. He had been in love with Ash since they were kids. The day they married had been the happiest day of his life, with the birth of their daughter a very close second. All he ever wanted was to be with her and build a life and family together. He would do anything to protect her and Sara. He couldn't survive if anything happened to either one.

He prayed they would catch up to Bennett before they reached Beartooth. Once the dangerous group reached the community, there was little hope for a good outcome.

Caleb wasn't sure what he and the four he rode with could do against so many guns and so much hate, but he'd give his life to protect his family and the community.

"We're less than ten miles from Beartooth, so if we don't catch up to them soon, it may be too late," Melora said as she rode up next to Caleb.

He had thought the same thing but hearing it out loud made his fear for his family intensify.

"As soon as we crest this next hill, it levels out a bit and we can speed up. Once we make it up to the old highway where it's flatter, we'll push these horses as hard as we can," Caleb replied.

Melora nodded and slowed, letting Caleb go ahead and drawing even with Tyler.

Once they crested the hill, Caleb nudged his horse into a lope. He wanted to push it harder, but the ground was still uneven and dotted with holes from burrowing animals. They couldn't afford to cripple a horse at this point.

After several minutes, Ryan loped up alongside him. "What's the plan?"

"First, we have to catch up to them. Then, we kill as many as we can before they reach Beartooth and hope the community is paying attention and can defend against the stragglers," Caleb said.

"Do you think we can catch them in time?" Ryan asked.

"I don't know, but we're sure as heck going to try."

SIXTY-FIVE

ASH HAD JUST PUT Sara down for a nap when she heard frantic pounding on her door. She raced over and yanked it open.

"What's wrong?" she asked as Lauren stood outside gasping for air.

"Fiona spotted at least twenty-five men and fifteen horses a couple of miles from here along the old highway while she was flying the drone. It can only be Bennett and his followers. She was afraid if she sounded the alarm at the storehouse, they might be able to hear it since sound travels so well here. Zane and I are going door-to-door telling everyone to evacuate.

As soon as the words came out, Lauren ran toward the next cabin, and Ash went back inside. She quickly put on her gun belt and stowed the 9mm. She slung Sara's emergency bag with her extra ammunition over one shoulder and then scooped the toddler out of her crib.

Sara stared at her with wide eyes but didn't make a sound as Ash ran out the door. She hadn't gone far when

Owen and Olivia caught up to her. They veered towards Dillon and Evelyn's cabin as the two were just leaving.

"Olivia and Ash, go as fast as you can. We'll be right behind you," Owen ordered.

They ran toward the trees and could see dozens of other residents heading in the same direction. When Ash and Olivia reached their zone, they found the Adlers and Fergusons already there. Once Owen, Dillon, and Evelyn arrived, their group would be accounted for.

"Come on, dear, let's get you and Sara settled in the cavern," Olivia said as she led the way.

"I need you to hold her," Ash said. "I have an assignment and may need to use this if we're found," she replied as she tilted her head toward her gun.

"Of course, I forgot," Olivia replied as she sat down as far back in the shallow cavern as she could and took Sara from Ash's arms.

Ash handed her the bag, which contained a small blanket, snacks, a diaper, and a few toys to hopefully keep Sara occupied. She leaned down and kissed Sara. "You be good for grandma. I'll be close by."

Sara looked at her with some trepidation, but didn't cry, so Ash slipped out of the cavern. Dillon arrived with Evelyn.

"Come with me. I'll get you settled by Olivia, and you can help her keep Sara quiet and entertained," Ash said.

When she emerged from the cavern again, she could see Owen at his perch. Dillon was concealed near the cavern entrance. Ash moved off to the side as they practiced during the last drill, which gave her an additional angle to watch for intruders and guard their zone. The location allowed her to see Dillon, the Adlers, and the Fergusons in hiding. She was relieved to see Lauren and Zane reunited with their parents.

Once settled behind a boulder, she took her gun out and clicked the safety off. She heard Dillon on the radio confirming everyone was accounted for in their group. The others confirmed the same.

Dillon set the radio down and readied an arrow. They were as ready as they could be, and they had a lot to fight for. But would it be enough to survive against such vile men and overwhelming odds?

Ash fought to hold back the tears. They weren't all accounted for. Caleb, Ryan, Dan, Melora, and Tyler were missing. The fact that Bennett and his goons were closing in but with fewer numbers than they had apparently started with made her fear that Caleb and the others had caught up to them and did damage but didn't survive the encounter.

She tried to push the images out of her mind. The thought of losing Caleb was paralyzing, but she had to stay strong for Sara and their unborn child.

They had been sitting for nearly thirty minutes when Ash heard Fiona's voice coming though Dillon's radio. She hadn't realized that Fiona had stayed behind.

"They just arrived. The man in charge, I'm assuming Bennett, has sent a dozen men to check the cabins. I'm pretty well hidden here, so hold tight for updates."

The minutes of silence stretched on before Fiona's voice broke in again. "They're raiding the storehouse. Hopefully that will keep them entertained."

Normally, Ash would worry about losing so much of their food stores, but if they were discovered and didn't survive, it wouldn't matter.

The wait was unbearable. Ash wished she knew what had happened to Caleb. If FAMA had shown up with their full contingent, she would be able to convince herself that

Caleb was still alive, and they had just been unable to intercept Bennett and his men. But the fact that the numbers were down pointed toward a scenario she refused to accept.

"It looks like they are done eating and looking for some indication of where everyone went. I can't imagine it will take long to find evidence of the evacuation of an entire community so be ready."

Ash heard Sara cry. She wanted to go to her but couldn't leave her post. Her group was counting on her. After only a few wails Sara went silent, and Ash exhaled. It probably wouldn't take Bennett long to find them, but if Sara or any of the other babies in the community cried, it would only make their job quicker and easier.

"A half dozen men have stayed behind, which leaves about twenty heading your way. The men who stayed back are spread out, watching all approaches to the community."

Since the invaders didn't know exactly where the residents had gone, it would probably take them longer than the fifteen minutes it usually took to cover the distance between the community and their safe zones. After that, it wouldn't take them long to figure out where they hid.

Soon, twenty well-armed men would descend upon them. Twenty automatic rifles against half that many handguns and hunting rifles. The residents of Beartooth had a strategically advantageous position, but none were fighters, and few had shot more than a few practice rounds in their lives.

These men were fueled by hate and thrived on violence and subduing those they considered weaker. They were accustomed to killing and taking. The residents of Beartooth possessed only a strong will to survive and protect each other. They had thrived by nurturing, giving, and helping provide for a community of peace-loving people.

As the minutes ticked by, Ash prayed that somehow, they could all survive the day.

SIXTY-SIX

WHEN THEY REACHED the old highway, Caleb kicked his horse and the gelding took off, showing no sign of fatigue from the previous hours of riding in rough terrain. As the other four horses came abreast, it spurred more speed out of each animal as if sensing a race.

They covered the last few miles quickly, but he feared it wouldn't be fast enough. As they neared the community, they dismounted, tied the horses in the trees, and proceeded on foot. When they reached the backside of the Adler's cabin, they saw no sign of the residents. Caleb would have been relieved that they had apparently evacuated, but he saw no sign of Bennett's men either, but enough horses to verify they had arrived.

"Psst."

They all spun around with weapons drawn.

"It's me, Fiona," she whispered as she slipped out of the trees.

"Where is everyone?" Caleb demanded.

"They evacuated before Bennett and his goons arrived. I stayed behind with a radio, and I've been communicating with the team leaders. Twenty men including who I assume is Bennett, just left on foot ten minutes ago following the obvious trail through the trees. I've let those in the safe zones know. Bennett left six men behind. I was just trying to figure out if it would be possible to take them out without alerting the others."

"Where are they?" Caleb asked.

Fiona pointed out where the six men were positioned.

"Dan, Tyler, and Fiona, head toward the safe zones and try to flank the men, but stay quiet, and out of sight unless you have to engage. Caleb and Ryan, I hope your knife skills are good," Melora said as she pulled out her blade.

"I don't want to leave you," Tyler said as he took Melora by the arms and looked her in the eyes.

"You have to. I trust no one else with this," she said as she pulled an item out of her pack and handed it to him. "Make sure Bennett and his men are as clustered as possible if you need to lob it."

Tyler kissed her hard on the lips and left with Fiona and Dan without further argument.

Caleb, Ryan, and Melora set down their assault rifles and took out their knives. Melora pointed out which men each was assigned.

"I wish I had my bow, then I wouldn't have to get my hands dirty," Caleb said.

"We have to get this done with what we have right now, no time to get your bow," Melora replied as they split up and slipped silently into the trees.

The FAMA militants were clearly overconfident. All were sprawled out either napping or just letting their recent feast digest. Caleb was able to take out his two targets quickly and easily before either could even stand up or sound an alarm. He looked around for Ryan and

Melora, but didn't see either of them, so made his way back to the Adler's cabin.

He waited only five minutes before he decided to go look for them. Just as he was about to step out into the open, Ryan and Melora jogged up.

Melora was out of breath, and Ryan was covered with blood.

"Are you okay?" Caleb asked.

"Not my blood," Ryan replied, "but thankfully Melora showed up when she did or it might have turned out differently."

"Enough chit-chat. Let's go," Melora said as her breathing slowed.

They picked up their assault rifles and took off at a run. Multiple shots rang out in a steady barrage. Some were clearly from assault rifles, but others were from hunting rifles and handguns. Caleb ran harder, fearing they might be too late.

SIXTY-SEVEN

THE SOUND of Owen's rifle being fired echoed off the walls of the ravine, making Ash flinch. She heard Sara cry, but the sound was drowned out by a return of gunfire. She couldn't see what was going on from her position, but clearly Bennett and his men had found them and engaged.

Gunfire came from all directions. She wanted to join the fight, but her job was to guard the approach to their zone's hiding places.

"What's happening," she shouted to Dillon, no longer worried about keeping quiet.

"I can't see anything. Dad and the others are returning fire, but I have no way to know if any shots have connected. Single-shot rifles are no defense against automatic assault rifles. Dad said they're closing in. We won't be able to hold them off for long."

Ash fought the urge to leave her post. She wanted to go to Sara but knew the best way to protect her daughter was to prevent anyone from entering the cavern, so she stayed alert and in position, ready to engage.

———

When Caleb, Ryan, and Melora caught up to Fiona, Dan, and Tyler, they could see the FAMA militia spread out and advancing on the ravine.

"Which one is Bennett?" Caleb asked.

Fiona pointed him out. He was standing partially concealed behind a large tree as his men advanced. He wasn't as tall as Caleb, but he looked intimidating, decked out in military gear and holding an assault rifle.

Scanning the relatively open area between the trees and the lip of the ravine, Caleb spotted two FAMA men down. He had hoped for more but wasn't surprised. He knew it would be difficult for the four hunting rifle bearers to hit anything at this distance while staying behind cover.

"I got an idea. Hand me your radio," Melora ordered.

Caleb couldn't hear what Melora said, but suddenly all return fire from all zones stopped, except for the one covered by Dennis which put Bennett's men the closest to Caleb and the others hidden in the trees. Bennett's men slowly converged toward the area of fire, clustering up. Caleb smiled as Melora's plan became clearer.

"Hand it over, Babe," Melora said to Tyler.

He reluctantly complied, leaned in, and kissed her. "Be careful."

"Always am. This is probably as good as it gets. Caleb, watch Bennett. The rest of you, cover me," Melora said as she darted out of the trees.

Caleb quickly distanced himself from the others to draw fire away. He noticed Ryan, Dan, Fiona, and Tyler also spreading out. As he fired at Bennett, the others drew gazes away from Melora's sprinting form.

Bennett turned and ran. Caleb dared a look back just

as Melora lobbed the grenade they had taken from the men who had killed Tony. She hit the ground. He prayed it was on purpose, and she hadn't been shot.

As soon as she let go of the grenade, Caleb and the others quit firing and dove to the ground. Caleb put his hands to his ears, but it did little to block the sound of the explosion.

When he stood up, ears ringing, he could see that the few remaining militia were dazed. Melora jumped to her feet and fired. Fiona and Dan joined in.

Caleb glanced back toward where Bennett had been standing. He was gone.

"Come on," he shouted at Ryan, before he took off running after the fleeing man.

By the time they reached Beartooth, Bennett was racing off on horseback. Caleb and Ryan mounted up and rode after Bennett. It didn't take Caleb long to close the gap. He took his sidearm out of its holster and pulled the trigger. The magazine was empty.

He secured the gun and spurred more speed out of the gelding. He saw Ryan was gaining on Bennett as well and was coming up on the opposite side. Bennett reached back and fired in Caleb's direction, but his aim was off, clearly distracted by the second rider.

Before Bennett could shoot again, Caleb was alongside. He shoved Bennett. The man didn't fall off, but he lost his grip on his gun. Caleb reached for Bennett's flailing arm and grabbed his forearm. Bennett pulled back, trying to loosen Caleb's grip, just as the horses split apart. The momentum sent both riders to the ground. They hit hard, rolling down the embankment.

Caleb slammed into a tree. He was dazed but knew he had to finish Bennett off. As long as the man lived, his family would be in danger.

As he struggled to get his feet under him, Bennett slammed into him, sending him back to the ground. The man jumped on top of him and threw a hard fist to Caleb's jaw. Bennett then raised his fist to deliver another blow. Caleb braced for the impact just as Ryan hit Bennett at a run. Bennett rolled off, and Caleb scooted away and watched as Ryan pulled the man to his feet.

"This is for all the women in Pryor that you sick bastards tortured and murdered," Ryan hissed as he threw a right upper-cut, slamming Bennett's head back.

The man staggered back a few steps and lifted his head, glaring at Ryan with pure hatred in his eyes.

Ryan pulled his knife. "And this is for Neal, Tony, and my wife."

"I don't know any of those," Bennett slurred.

"But your men were following your orders and your moral code," Ryan replied as he lunged.

Caleb tried to stand and provide back-up if needed but fell back to his knees. He looked up just as Ryan plunged his knife into Bennett's gut and yanked up hard.

Ryan stepped back and Bennett dropped to the ground. Caleb tried again to stand and winced in pain as he gained his footing. He stood for a moment waiting for the ground to quit spinning.

"Sorry, the horses kept running," Ryan said as he knelt, and cleaned his knife on Bennett's pants.

"As much as I want to see Ash and Sara, I doubt I could get on anyway without passing out. Let's get walking," Caleb replied.

Ryan sheathed his knife and then placed an arm around Caleb to help support him as they started the long walk back to Beartooth.

SIXTY-EIGHT

IT TOOK Ryan and Caleb over half an hour to walk back to Beartooth. When they approached the community, they saw many familiar faces, so they knew the nightmare was over.

Melora, Dan, and Fiona trotted over to them on the three horses they just lost. Caleb was thankful the horses made their way back to Beartooth. He hated the thought of them loose in the wild with saddles on.

"We were heading out after you two. I'm glad you're alive, but you don't look too good," Melora said as they approached.

"The blood's not mine," Ryan replied as they continued to walk.

"I took a tumble off a running horse that really rang my bell, but I'll live," Caleb added.

"I doubt Ash or Miranda will like seeing you this way. Go to the clinic. I'll round them up and give them a little warning," Dan said.

Melora and Fiona got off their horses and walked with

them to the clinic. Melora threw her arms around Caleb, and he nearly passed out.

"Oops, sorry. Did you catch up to Bennett?" Fiona asked.

"Yep. He won't be causing us any more problems," Caleb replied.

"That's a relief. How bad are you hurt?" Melora asked.

"Not as bad as I would have been if Ryan didn't have my back. What's the damage to our community?"

"We didn't lose anyone. The ravine provided the cover we needed to buy us time. If we hadn't gotten that little gift out of Knox's saddlebags, Bennett's men would have eventually breached our defenses, though Dennis did manage to pick off a few," Melora replied.

"Get cleaned up before Miranda and Ash see you," Fiona said. "We're supposed to be rounding up the new horses. Others are moving the six bodies near the community to the safe zone where the rest are."

Melora and Fiona left, and Caleb and Ryan limped into the clinic. Caleb was more scraped and bruised than bloody, but Ryan was covered with blood from his hands to his elbows, and his face and clothes were splattered with red.

Caleb was holding his ribs when Ash and Miranda rushed in the door. Miranda instantly went to Ryan and assessed his injuries, which were minor.

"I'm assuming throwing myself in your arms is out of the question," Ash said as she walked up to Caleb and gently touched the bruise on his cheek.

"Just be gentle," he replied as he wrapped his arms around her.

"I was so scared when we realized Bennett had gotten around us. We knew he was headed this direction and had a huge head start," Caleb whispered in her ear.

"When they arrived a few men short, it was hard not to think the worst," she replied as she looked up and gently kissed his lips.

"Ryan's okay. What can I do to fix this?" Miranda asked as she approached Caleb and waved her hand from his head to toes.

Caleb let go of Ash and gave Miranda a gentle hug. "I'm glad you married Ryan. He's tougher than he looks. He saved my life. All I need now is my little girl. The rest will heal."

"Dan took her to your folks and said he'd tell them you were banged up, but walking. He said he'd stop by Ryan's parents' cabin, too," Ash said.

Caleb closed his eyes for a moment and exhaled. Beartooth had survived. He hoped that eliminating Bennett and his most faithful FAMA followers would bring back the safety and security he wanted for his family. There might be others, but for now, they were out of danger and could return to the life they had built.

"Let's go get our little girl and go home," Caleb said as he draped an arm around Ash's shoulder.

He leaned heavily on her as they walked out the door. Every bone in his body ached, but knowing his family was safe made every pain worth it.

As he looked around as they slowly walked toward the Solomon cabin, he could see bodies being dragged away. He wasn't sure what they would do with them, but that was a worry the others could handle. For now, he needed Ash, Sara, and a good night's sleep.

SIXTY-NINE

ASH HAD BEEN afraid Sara would be frightened when she saw Caleb's face, but she smiled, called out, and reached for him the moment they walked in the door of the Solomon cabin. Olivia's expression wasn't quite as exuberant, but she said nothing and just squeezed Caleb's arm.

Owen walked them home, which Ash appreciated. He propped up Caleb with an arm around his son's waist, and Ash carried Sara.

Once they got home, Ash tended to Sara while Owen helped get Caleb into the bedroom. When she walked into the bedroom carrying Sara, she thought again about how lucky she was to have the Solomons in her life. They had gotten her through some rough times, and she knew they would always be there for her even without Caleb.

"He'll be fine. He probably has a few cracked ribs from a tumble off a running horse, and he took a few punches to his jaw, but he'll mend. He just needs a little time," Owen said as he smiled reassuringly at Ash and kissed Sara on the cheek.

"Thank you," Ash said, fighting to hold back the tears of gratitude and love for this man.

Owen nodded and left.

"Do you want some dinner?" Ash asked.

"No, I just want my girls here with me."

He reached for Sara. Ash wasn't sure it was a good idea, but she handed the toddler to him and sat on the edge of the bed next to him.

Sara nuzzled close to his chest, but didn't say anything, content just to be in his arms. They sat that way in silence until Sara fell asleep.

"Let me put her in her crib, and then I'll help you get into bed," Ash whispered.

When Ash returned, she found Caleb in front of the vanity, looking at his bruised face.

He turned around and leaned against the vanity. He ran a hand down her cheek and tried to smile. "You are so beautiful. I love you so much it hurts sometimes."

"I love you too. Let's get you undressed, showered, and in bed. We can talk when you're more comfortable."

Ash helped him get in the shower and then retrieved her last two pain relievers and a glass of water. When he got out, she dried him off, gave him the pills, and helped him into bed.

Even though it took her only minutes to get ready for bed, it surprised her that he was still awake when she crawled in next to him. She rolled to her side and scooted close to him so she could feel his heat and placed her hand over his heart.

"I wish you would quit scaring the daylights out of me," she said.

"It's not intentional. I hope you know that I do what I do because I want to protect you and Sara. I've been in love with you most of my life, and when I finally admitted it to myself, all I wanted was to be with you forever and build a family with you."

"Do you think we're safe now?"

"As safe as we can be here. I hope the massive jaguars those men killed were the last of them, but there's no way to know for sure. I suppose someone else could come here to check us out, but hopefully they won't be as dangerous as Bennett's delusional bunch of fanatics."

"But you'd feel comfortable growing our family?"

Caleb smiled. "I'd love nothing more, but I'm afraid it may have to wait a few days until I'm a little more healed up."

Ash dropped her gaze, not wanting to look Caleb in the eye. She should have told him weeks ago. Now, she wasn't sure how to say it.

He put his finger under her chin, tilted her head up, and looked into her eyes, brimming with tears. "What's wrong?"

"I'm sorry. I should have told you weeks ago, but the day I planned to, Tony was murdered and Miranda was kidnapped. When you got back, you had a huge burden to work through, and then we learned Bennett and his men were heading our direction. I wanted you focused on what you had to do and not worry about me. We didn't plan this, and the world around us is falling apart, so definitely not ideal timing."

"You're pregnant?"

Ash nodded and tried to smile.

He leaned over and kissed her deeply. "I can't tell you how happy I am. You should have told me, but I understand why you didn't. And, to heck with the rest of the world, we'll make it work and give our kids a great life here."

"You really think we can?"

"Together, we can do anything."

SEVENTY

IT HAD BEEN two weeks since Jonah Bennett and his followers rode into Beartooth. It would take a while before the community got back into a routine. The residents survived the encounter with no loss of life, but they had all seen too much death to emerge unscathed.

Ash held Sara and looked out the cabin window. It was overcast and blustery. Heath said it would probably be the worst winter any of them had ever seen, but it should be the last if the government didn't restart its stratospheric aerosol injection program. Time would tell if his prediction was correct.

Caleb walked out of the third bedroom where they stored their hunting and fishing gear. He set his assault rifle on the table and put on his coat.

"Do you think it's a good idea to go hunting so soon? You're not healed."

"We need to replace some of the food Bennett's men devoured. I can't pull my bowstring yet, so I'm just going to keep the group safe."

Ash hoped there were no more massive cats or

dangerous fanatics out there, but she understood the need to be cautious.

Caleb kissed her and Sara goodbye and left the cabin. After putting Sara down for a nap, Ash returned to the living room and turned the radio on.

"Cross-border conflicts between the U.S. and its northern and southern neighbors have ceased due to fuel and large weapons shortages. All countries involved have agreed to an anti-nuclear agreement while dealing with their respective domestic issues. While fighting and violence rages on in the U.S. capital and most major cities, there have been reports of progress in the rural areas," the newsreader stated. "There has been no sign of Jonah Bennett or his Freedom and Morality Alliance. The citizens of Pryor, Wyoming, with help from the National Guard, have regained control of their city. They have established a new city government and police force, allowing the Guard to pull out and return to the state capital. The success in Pryor has encouraged other resettlement cities to take back their communities."

Ash found the news encouraging and hoped the citizens of Pryor could truly retain control of the city. The beleaguered citizens deserved an opportunity to live without fear and violence. She was also relieved to hear that continental nuclear deployment was not imminent.

"In international news, One World has negotiated a cease fire between ASPA and the EU, though few believe it will hold. As famine continues to spread as a result of unpredictable rainfall and soaring temperatures, the countries most affected are getting more desperate."

Sara called out to her. Ash turned off the radio and retrieved her little girl. After Ash fed Sara lunch, she set her down to play.

Ash stoked the wood stove. She assembled a huge pot

of chili and set it on the stove to simmer. It was a meal that could be ready in a few hours, or it would hold until late in the evening if the hunting party was delayed.

There was a knock on the door, and then Dillon and Evelyn walked in. "We thought we'd wait here until Caleb gets back. Hope you don't mind," Dillon said as he scooped Sara up and nuzzled her.

"Not at all. In fact, I have enough chili to feed an army. Why don't you stay for dinner?"

"If it's no imposition, we'd love to. We haven't even thought about dinner yet," Evelyn replied as she took Sara from Dillon.

The door opened again and Miranda and Lauren walked in.

"I told Ryan we'd wait for him and Zane here," Miranda said.

"Dillon and Evelyn are staying for dinner. I've got plenty for everyone if you want to join us," Ash offered.

"Sure, Zane and Lauren were going to eat with us, but I haven't started anything yet," Miranda replied.

"Need any help?" Lauren asked.

"Someone can set the table, and someone else can put another piece of wood in the stove while I get the corn-bread ready," Ash said.

By the time Caleb, Ryan, and Zane walked in the door, it looked a bit chaotic. Half the group was sprawled on the living room floor playing with Sara. The other half was crowded in the kitchen, filling cups with water, stirring the chili pot, and washing dishes already dirtied during the meal prep.

Dillon stood up and walked over to his brother. "Did you get anything?"

"Yep, two nice bucks. They're already hanging in the storehouse cooler," Caleb replied as he took his and

Ryan's assault rifles and headed toward the room that he used for fletching arrows and storing his hunting and fishing gear.

Ash followed him. After he set his gear down, he turned and pulled her into his arms and kissed her deeply.

"I guess I should think about clearing this room out," he said as he looked around.

"No hurry. Once Sara is done with her crib, we can move it and the rocker into our room. If we have another little girl, they can eventually share a room. I dreamed about sharing a room with a sister."

"What if it's a boy?" Caleb asked with a grin.

"We can lock the weapons up in our room, and everything else in here would probably be just the perfect décor for your son."

Caleb laughed, kissed her again, and they returned to their guests.

Dinner was a lively affair. They talked about the hunt, Lauren's training to be a nurse, and news from the radio.

When Ash looked around the table and thought about all the quiet meals she and her mom shared, a pang of grief struck her chest, but joy filled her heart. She missed her mom so much, but surrounded with such a large extended family, she felt so much love.

Sara sat between her and Caleb in her highchair and the toddler told Caleb all about the newest toy her grandma made for her. Ash smiled at Caleb as he reached over, took her hand, and brought it to his lips.

"We should help clean up and get out of your hair. I'm sure it's been a long day for everyone," Evelyn said.

"I can take care of the dishes tomorrow. It's the first time we've had this group around the table for a shared meal, and it feels good. Every one of you are so special to me. When I see us together, it gives me a great deal of hope for the future."

Miranda was sitting on the other side of Ash. She took Ash's hand and gave it a squeeze. "Don't make me cry. I've vowed to be tougher, like you and Evelyn."

Evelyn laughed. "Growing up, I'm certain no one would have categorized me as tough. Most people liked to pat my blonde curls and talk about how little I was or how cute my dimples were."

"You are pretty cute," Dillon added.

Evelyn gave him a mock punch, and he leaned over and placed a kiss on her cheek.

"You've always been tough. I got plenty of bruises and scratches from fighting with you when we were younger. No one should let your size or limited sight fool them," Lauren said.

"And, you've grown into an amazing young woman. I'm proud you're my sister," Evelyn replied back.

Ash couldn't help but notice that the only two not speaking were the Ferguson brothers. Ryan had always been quiet, and it seemed that Zane was more like Ryan than she realized. She wasn't sure that was a bad thing. Ryan had proved himself multiple times, and Zane was maturing rapidly.

For the next half an hour, they sat around the table laughing and joking. Sara was the first to break up the party. Ash got up and took her to her room. By the time she got back, the table had been cleaned off, and everyone was gone. Ash heard voices outside. She grabbed her coat and went out to see what the commotion was about.

"Can you believe it's actually snowing?" Lauren said.

Ash was mesmerized. She had never seen it snow before. Caleb remembered it snowing once in Beartooth, but she was too young to remember.

"It won't stick, but it is pretty amazing to see," Caleb added as he draped his arm around Ash's shoulders.

The big, wet flakes tapered off nearly as quickly as they started, leaving no evidence that snow had fallen in Beartooth for the first time in over two decades. The entire group left together, animatedly discussing the sight of snow.

Ash and Caleb went inside, and the cabin was now silent. Caleb pulled Ash into his arms and held her. For several moments, neither spoke.

"The group around our table tonight represents the future of Beartooth. They are the strength we need to overcome whatever comes our way. I hope we're up for the challenge," Ash said as she looked up into his eyes.

"Me too. Others will play a role, but ultimately, we will determine the fate of this community. I have faith we will not only survive but thrive."

THANK YOU FOR READING

———

Did you enjoy this book?

We invite you to leave a review at your favorite book site, such as Goodreads, Amazon, Barnes & Noble, etc.

DID YOU KNOW THAT LEAVING A REVIEW...

- Helps other readers find books they may enjoy.
- Gives you a chance to let your voice be heard.
- Gives authors recognition for their hard work.
- Doesn't have to be long. A sentence or two about why you liked the book will do.

ABOUT THE AUTHOR

Kim McMahill started out writing nonfiction, but her passion for adventure, stories of survival against the odds, and speculating about the future of humanity and our planet, soon turned her attention towards fiction. Along with her novels, she has published over eighty travel and human-interest articles, and contributed to a travel story anthology. Growing up in a small community surrounded by mountains, traveling the world, and enjoying a rewarding career with the National Park Service, has given her the opportunity to live in amazing places, experience incredible adventures, and witness many changes in our world, all of which have helped shape her stories.

To learn more about Kim and her writing, visit:

KimMcMahill.blogspot.com

facebook.com/KimMcMahillAuthor
instagram.com/kimmcmahill
threads.com/kimmcmahill

ALSO BY KIM MCMAHILL

WITH FIRE AND ICE YOUNG ADULT BOOKS

The Beartooth Chronicles

Refuge from the World

Above the Abyss

Isolated from Anarchy

Evil Under the Mountain

Winter Resurgence

www.ingramcontent.com/pod-product-compliance
Lightning Source LLC
Chambersburg PA
CBHW020508020726
47493CB00001B/242